PENDANT OF DRAGONS BOOK TWO

CUSTODIANS OF THE PAST

K. ISABELLA FROST

Printed in Australia
First Printing, 2019
ISBN: 978-0-6485929-1-4

White Light Publishing
Melton, VIC, Australia 3337
whitelightpublishing.com.au

For my Mum, Lynne, who started my love of literature and encouraged me to write my stories down... partly because I was driving her insane and she needed to get dinner started. Thank you, Mum.

Acknowledgements

Before I finished writing "The Aldrich Legacy" I knew that it would end with a cliffhanger. So there had to be a sequel, and as soon as I began toying with the ideas for the second book it became very clear that "Pendant of Dragons" was going to be a bigger series than I had originally planned. Getting to that final confrontation is so much further away than I had ever thought, but it also means that there is so much more life in the series than I ever thought there would be, when I was a little kid first drawing pictures and telling my mother stories of a young princess and her dragon. And while trying to follow my career as an actress, I wanted to create a short film based on these characters which led to a script about Leander and Mithras in the dungeons of Aneuran. That script became the basis of this book, and once again, there were a lot of people involved in inspiring and helping me as I began this new journey through High-Realm with my characters.

Once again, I want to thank my parents, Lynne and Kevin, for introducing me to literature at a young age, as well as my godparents, Sandy and Charlie Ponchard, and my grandparents, Betty and Fred Webster. To my brothers David and Rick and my sister Jess, who have always inspired me in their ways; thank you for your support.

To Kade for being an inspiration to me during our years together and for still being a source of support even though he isn't with me now. I miss you.

A special big thank you to Charles R Slucki, my acting mentor and friend who stood beside me during some pretty intense times and has always believed in me as an actress and writer. I still laugh when I think of Leander's final monologue in this book and how when I performed it for you, you nearly fell out of your chair.

To all of my wonderful mentors and teachers at Mystical Dragon, especially Jennifer Valente, Amanda Godfrey, Brooke Kelly, Harmony Carbone, and Ray and Nolene Horner. Without your knowledge and guidance, I don't think I would have made it to publishing this book or writing further than this.

And to Lauren, Christie and everyone at White Light Publishing, staff and authors alike, who have supported me through the process of bringing this book to life. Without you and your efforts I would still be struggling on my own.

Lastly, to the readers, both new and returning. Thank you for reading these books and I hope you enjoy each new adventure Leander and her friends embark on.

- Isabella Frost

CONTENTS

Preface

Falling in love had never truly been something I had given much thought to any more than the thought of having to lose that love once I had it. Love had seemed so foreign to me, something I had only ever dreamed of; a beautiful concept within the pages of the books I adored reading. And now that I had come to know its touch, I never wanted to feel its absence again.

Where I had only felt pain and emptiness, he had shown me what it meant to truly be loved, and to love in return. I would do anything for him, because I knew in my heart – now and forever – that he was the One. He was truly my soul mate.

So, despite his protests, and my own dark, unrelenting fears of what the monster before us was proposing, I could make only one choice. After all, how could I possibly make any other? Especially if it meant losing him forever.

So, I chose the only alternative that I had left to me...

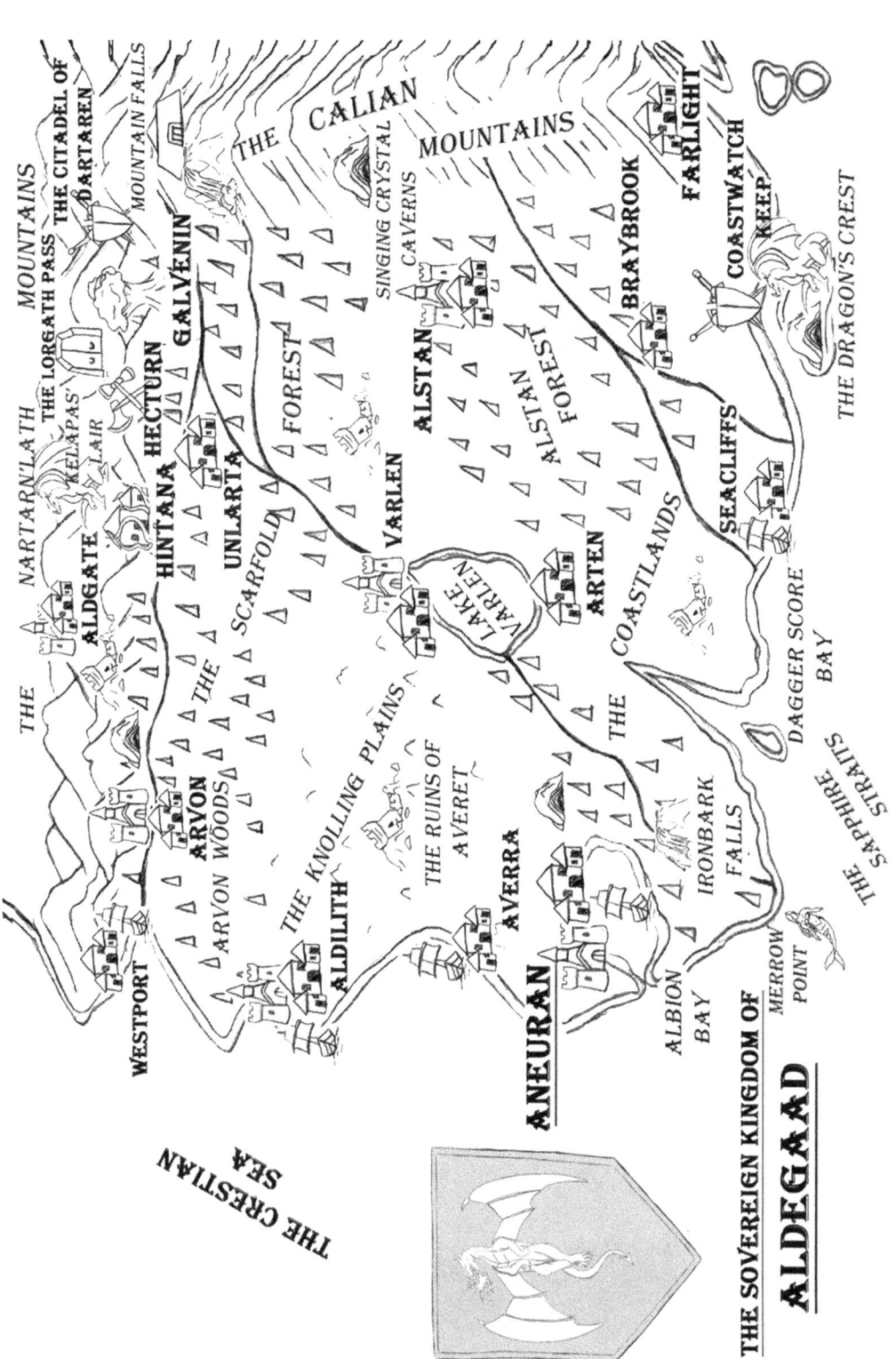

THE SOVEREIGN KINGDOM OF
ALDEGAAD

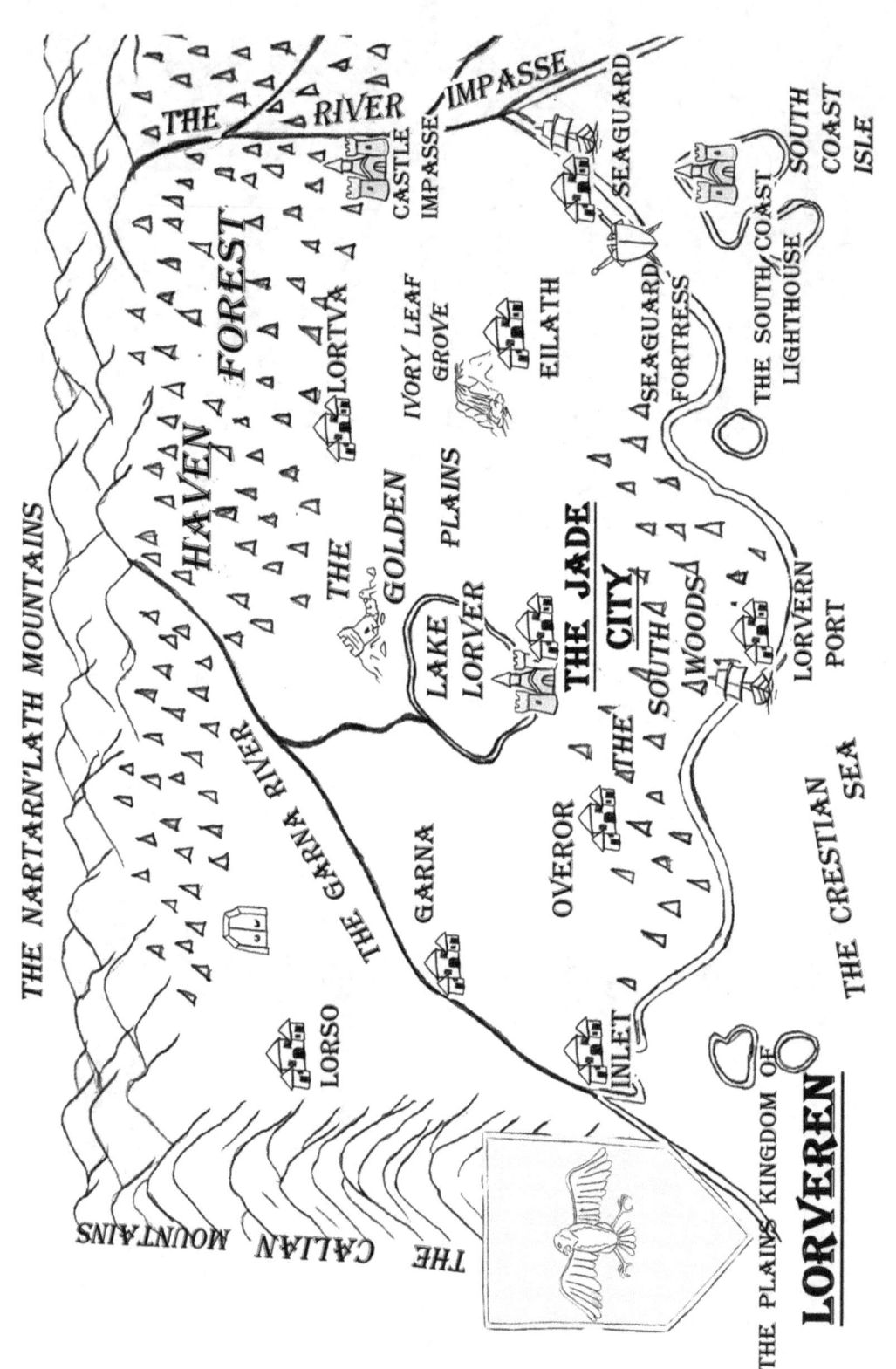

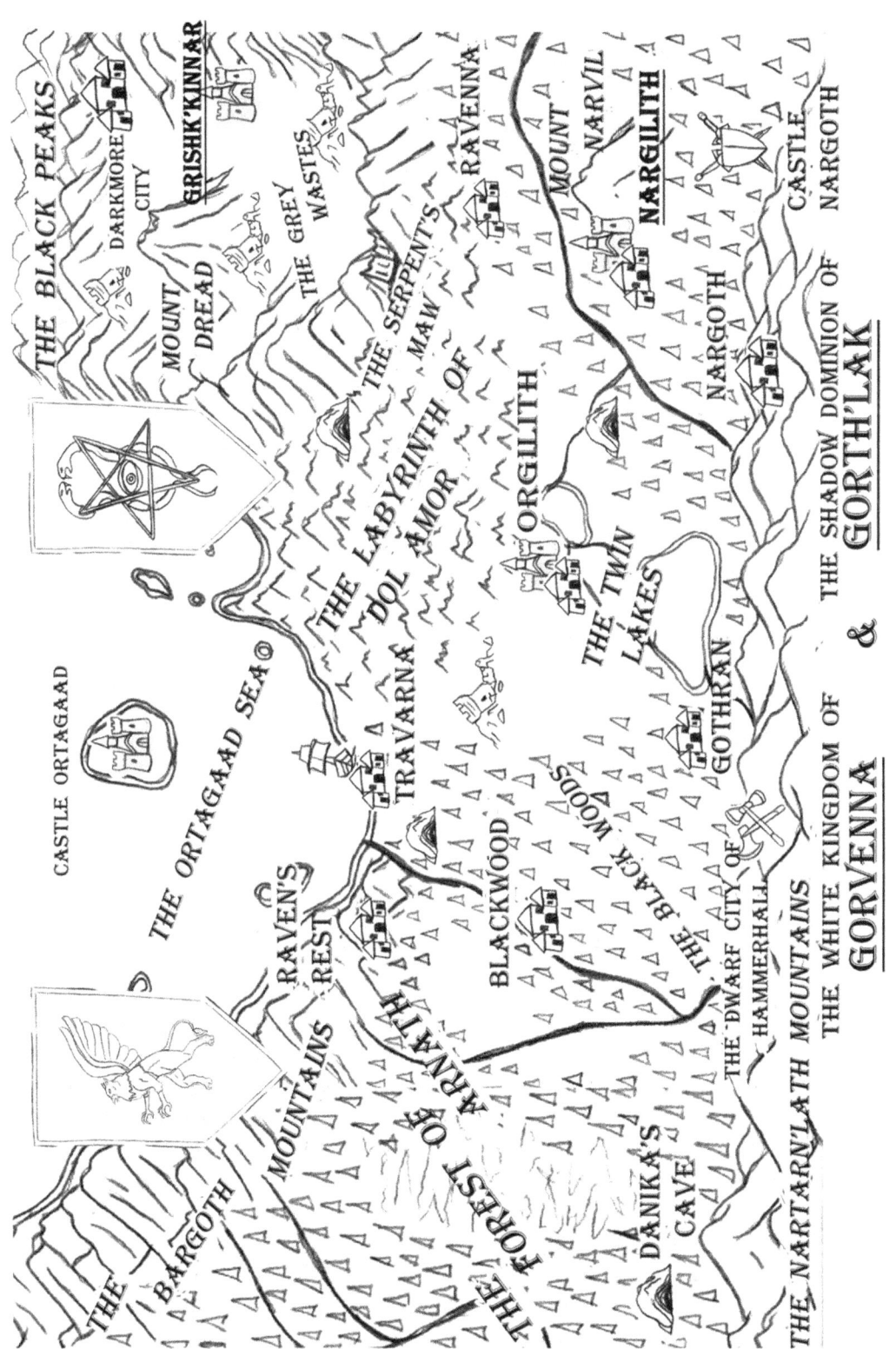

THE BLACK PEAKS

DARKMORE CITY

GRISHK'KINNAR

THE GREY WASTES

MOUNT DREAD

THE SERPENT'S MAW

RAVENNA

MOUNT NARVIL

NARGILITH

NARGOTH

CASTLE NARGOTH

THE LABYRINTH OF DOL AMOR

ORGILITH

THE ORTAGAAD SEA

CASTLE ORTAGAAD

TRAVARNA

THE TWIN LAKES

GOTHRAN

THE SHADOW DOMINION OF GORTH'LAK

&

RAVEN'S REST

BLACKWOOD

THE BLACK WOODS

THE DWARF CITY OF HAMMERHALL

THE WHITE KINGDOM OF GORVENNA

THE BARGOTH MOUNTAINS

THE FOREST OF ARNATH

DANIKA'S CAVE

THE NARTARN'LATH MOUNTAINS

Chapter One
The Dungeons of Aneuran

S creams echoed through the depths of the palace dungeons; horrible cries of anguish reaching up to its highest points. So many prisoners wept in the darkness with only the fewest of torches illuminating the shadows. Soldiers patrolled the dark stoned corridors, the lesser criminals silent, unconscious or crying, while the worst of them were delivering outright threats to the passing jailors. They would have once been executed in centuries past; a sentence never carried out in our time, for which I was glad.

I sat there silently on the stone floor, my hands resting in front of me, cold iron manacles locked around my slender wrists. I was dressed only in a green sackcloth tunic slip that was almost too short to cover the top of my legs, my arms left completely bare. My own clothes had been stripped from me when I was brought to the dungeons, this scant humiliation all that was left to cover my modesty.

I struggled against the freezing cold of the dank cell, trembling as I hugged my knees to my chest. My face was hidden behind the curtains of my dark hair, shielding me from sight and allowing me to hide, even if it was just a little. I'd had enough of being stared at repeatedly by angry guards and rapacious prisoners, longing to be invisible. The blue and gold surcoats and the emblem of the proud dragon that had once brought me comfort now only served to cause me fear. The men and women who had been my protectors had now become my captors.

I sighed glumly, staring back down at my hands. I just wanted to be safe back in Castle Arvon, to be with my parents, to have them alive again. I wanted to be away from the terrible things that had been happening.

I felt cold tears wet my cheeks. *I don't want to be here. Please, Gods, don't let this be real. Let it be a nightmare that I'm going to wake up from. Please... Please...*

Out of the corner of my eye I could see the cell opposite mine, two dishevelled men watching me through the bars, their eyes like dark coals still burning faintly. They looked almost hungry as they stared at me, most likely having not seen a woman in some time who was not a guard. And certainly not a young girl like me.

As the two dirty men grinned – one gripping the bars with grimy hands and shackled wrists – I shied away and glanced towards the barred wall to my right. Mithras was lying face down on the floor of that cell, his arms sprawled over his head, a nasty bruise on his forehead just below his greying hairline. He had laid there for so long, unmoving and silent, that I worried that he wasn't alive anymore.

It upset me to see him like this. He had been stripped of his armour and weapons, left now in a larger sackcloth tunic like the one I wore, except he wore pants. I wasn't granted such a kindness.

I sucked in a shaking breath and closed my eyes, trying to find the calm I needed. I was exhausted, the time now far beyond midnight. I didn't know where I was in the dungeons as I had been blindfolded before being brought into this cell. All I knew was that I still had to be in the palace, our road never having led outside into the cold, wintry air.

I started thinking about Carden and Tallinn, my heart heavy with worry for my two friends. I thought back to the battle on the palace's mezzanine; the image of the blonde haired, tan skinned Tallinn and of the tall, handsome, green eyed Carden at her side strong in my mind.

I had gazed into Carden's eyes almost pleadingly as he had stared back at me in helpless horror, left to do the only thing he could. As abruptly as a winter storm in the Nartarn'lath Mountains, the two Guardians had turned and leaped from the mezzanine into the bay below, vanishing from the guards' grasps and my sight.

I kept playing that over and over in mind, my heart lurching and my stomach churning hard. I was so afraid that they hadn't survived, that they had met a gruesome fate on the rocks below.

The thought of losing Carden was like a knife tearing through my chest, making me feel sick.

He's not dead, I told myself silently. *He and Tallinn survived. They're getting the others, making a plan and coming for us. Carden will save me... I know he will...* It felt like I was trying to convince myself of this instead of believing it, and that didn't help me at all.

I felt an overwhelming grief set in and began to cry softly, burying my face into my arms. I had done this on and off for the past few hours since being chained in this cell, no end to the pain that I felt. I had sat there listening to the jeering comments of the guards and hoped that Mithras would soon wake, wanting him to protect me like when I was a child. In that dark place all I desired was to be accompanied, to not be left alone with the murderers and rapists. So, thinking of Carden was all that kept me from truly breaking.

There came a groan from my right that suddenly drew my attention. I looked up, a flicker of relief flaring in my heart as I saw Mithras rising to a kneeling position.

The Knight sat back on his haunches, rubbing his forehead groggily and wobbling unsteadily. He blinked his dark eyes, squinting as he looked around at the cell he came to find himself in. The clang of the chains on his wrists drew his gaze to the iron links but elicited no real reaction from him.

"Well," he mused grimly, "this is a fine predicament to wake up in."

"Mithras?" I stared through the bars at him, relief clear in my voice.

He turned at the sound of my voice, his eyes widening and his jaw dropping as he came to see me. For a moment he was speechless as he stared at me in the dark, then he came to the bars at a sideways slide, reaching one hand through to me.

"Leander?" he pressed a hand to my cheek, staring at the streaks of tears that had passed down my face. "Are you alright? Are you hurt?"

I shook my head, speaking softly and meekly: "No. Are you?"

"Merely a bump on the head, it seems," Mithras smiled weakly, though it seemed worse than that. "How long have we been in these cells?"

I shrugged uncertainly. "I'm not sure. Six hours. Six days. I honestly don't know."

He nodded, turning his eyes around the cells again before casting them over himself.

"They've stripped me of my armour," he noted, turning back to me. "And you? They left you naught but such a scant garment?"

"I'm lucky they granted me that kindness," I murmured coldly. "They might have left me naked."

"Yes," Mithras eyed the other prisoners across the way callously. "A foul idea to place on a young girl. Especially considering the company we seem to have in our new... *accommodations*."

I was silent, staring at Mithras sadly. He was gazing through the bars, my eyes following his as he studied the other cells where the worst criminals of Aldegaad were pacing. All of their cold, malicious eyes were still set on me, not one of them focused on him. I knew that he could see their thoughts, could tell what foul desires passed through their depraved minds for me. I could see it myself, after all.

"Do you not remember anything before waking?" I asked, drawing his gaze back to me.

"The King's death," Mithras responded with simple graveness. "Attempting to escape the palace via the mezzanine level... Soldiers.... Your screams. Then... nothing. Just pain and darkness."

I nodded grimly, looking down at my hands again as Mithras reclaimed his seat and rested with his back to the stone wall.

"Carden and Tallinn," he realised with a gentle, sedate tone in his gruff voice. "What has become of them?"

"They escaped," I looked up at him through the bars, wishing we sat in the same cell at least. "They dived into the bay. I'm not sure what has become of them."

"Then perhaps we may have a chance," Mithras found hope where I had begun to feel none.

I just shrugged, feeling hopeless, despair crushing down on me.

I so desperately wish that we were anywhere but here. Anywhere. Gods, I should have stayed at Mountain Falls as Ser Callenhad desired. Maybe... if we hadn't come here... Uncle Aric might...

My tears flowed as my thoughts plagued me, poisoning my heart with their bitter words. Fresh sobs began to slip free softly as I pulled my knees tighter to my chest.

"We never should have come here," I murmured sadly, staring at my hands. "It's all my fault."

"What is?" the Knight asked gently.

"Everything," I confessed through heartbroken, guilt ridden sobs. "My Mother... my Father... Aunt Evangeline, Uncle Aric... They're all dead... because of..." I sniffed hard, "...because of me."

"That's not true, Leander," he insisted gently, sympathetically. "You did *not* kill them. You held neither blade, nor poison, nor ill will against them. You defended your father against demons and rushed here to save the King from an assassination. You did *not* harm them."

"It's still because of me," I half whispered.

He shook his head. "No. It is not..."

"All of this was designed to hurt me," I sobbed into my arms. "If I had just been taken at Averet, if the Guardians had not rescued me, they'd all still be alive, and we wouldn't be here now..."

"Leander!" Mithras snapped firmly, drawing my tear-filled eyes as he grasped the bars with both hands. "I want you to listen to me, child. *None* of this is *your* fault. Lay the fault with those who *are* responsible."

I looked up at him slowly, tears still rolling down my cheeks. "But..."

"It is *not* your fault," Mithras emphasised. "Understand that, child."

I nodded softly, wiping my nose against my palm.

He's right. Of course he is. My family isn't dead because of anything I have done. It's all because of Fane and these other traitors to Aldegaad. I can't blame myself for what they have done here.

"What are they going to do with us?" I asked softly, my heart thudding hard in my chest, my eyes flicking worriedly to his face.

"I do not know, but listen to me, girl," he said to me firmly, "I swear that I will never allow them to hurt you. We *will* find a way out of this. I promise you."

I reached out my hand to him, his coarse, larger fingers squeezing my smaller, softer ones so very gently. His hand's warmth made me feel less afraid.

"It is going to be alright, Leander," he cooed softly, holding my hand gently. "Do not fear."

"I hope you're right, Mithras," I whispered, closing my eyes and resting my head against the wall. "I really do..."

I jumped then as the heavy thuds and clicks of locks opening reached my ears. I looked up towards the corridor leading away to my right, a high set of spiralling stairs visible through the stone archway. The sound of armoured footsteps grew louder, a number of guards approaching. Panic filled me and I tensed, trembling as my mind raced with all the terrible thoughts of what they were intending to do to us.

"Leander, look at me!" Mithras made me turn back to him, urgency firmly in his gaze as his hand cupped my cheek. "No matter what happens, I need you to be strong! Alright?! I know you're frightened, but you *must* be strong! Promise me, girl!"

I nodded quickly, utterly terrified. I found it impossible to speak, my throat tight as fear choked me, but it was enough to satisfy Mithras, the Knight returning my nod gently.

"It *will* be alright," he insisted softly.

I looked past him again, pulling myself into the corner closest to his cell. I grasped the horizontal section of the bars, staring up past my arms in fear as the soldiers appeared from the stairwell, Mithras withdrawing his hand from me and turning to them stoically.

Knight-Commander Tavish entered with at least another four soldiers behind him in addition to the four who had preceded him, his eyes surveying the dungeons before him with cruel iciness as his lips twisted in a scowl. Tavish was a hard man, aged somewhere in his early middle years. He had neatly cropped short white hair, his eyes pale blue and his face beardless. He stood at about six foot five, his brash attitude aiding his arrogance as he gained domination over his prisoners. He wore the same silver plate armour, blue and gold surcoat, and cloak that Mithras had always worn, his sword across his back with his shield.

As they approached our cells, Mithras stood slowly, hands before him, his dark blue eyes locked on the arrogant younger knight's face.

"How the mighty have fallen," Tavish mused with a smug grin. "Ser Mithras, loyal defender of the township of Arvon and the ancestral home of the Aldrich Royal Bloodline, now reduced... to *this*."

"What's this, Tavish?" Mithras demanded of the smarmy man. "Your version of the student surpassing the master? Could you not have found a more inventive and original way of doing such?"

Tavish smirked. "Still on that high horse I see. Just like when you were the knight who took me as a squire. Tell me, why did you refuse the position of Aneuran's Knight-Commander? I'm curious."

"Because I had a greater purpose; to serve my King by protecting his brother and his nieces, not to head up the garrison in this city," was his answer, given slowly and deliberately.

"That just shows weakness," Tavish scoffed, eyeing me off for a moment before looking back to Mithras. "Abandoning advancement for a pair of little girls? Pathetic."

Tavish's arrogant words caused my blood to boil in my chilled skin. *He has no right to claim the title of knight, let alone knight-commander. Gods, if I were strong enough and able, I would slap that smarmy mouth as hard as I could and teach him to be humble. But he'd probably just hurt me if I tried anything. He's as bad as my wretched uncle and the others responsible for putting us here.*

"Was there a reason you came to bother me in my nice cold cell?" Mithras commented snidely, his voice breaking me from my silent musings. "Or did you just want to trade insults?"

Tavish glared at him, straightening up from the cell. He looked as if he were straining not to strike out at my protector.

"The Regent has summoned you," he said curtly.

"And why would *your* lord want to see me?" Mithras demanded icily.

Tavish eyed him harshly, folding his arms and narrowing his eyes. The two men were staring each other down, the fire in their eyes capable of melting steel if it were a tangible flame.

"The Regent's reasons are his own," Tavish replied. "I do not question them, I merely obey."

"What a good little lapdog you are, Tavish," Mithras shot back venomously. "Does he like it when you get down on all fours and lick his boots too? Maybe sniff his arse?"

I wanted to laugh, but I couldn't, my fear of this cruel man who was holding us far too great to allow me even to smile a little.

Tavish's bright blue eyes were filled with violent rage, his hands clenching as he dropped them to his sides. Then, he lashed out and I heard a sickening impact, gasping in shock. Mithras fell to the floor, landing on his knees as new tears of concern burned my eyes.

"Mithras!" I screamed, then threw my panicked gaze to Tavish. "Stop it! Just stop! Please!"

I heard the scraping of feet on stone and a low chuckle as Mithras stood up again, smirking through a line of blood that had been torn from the corner of his mouth with Tavish's strike.

"What's the matter, Tavish?" Mithras chuckled softly, a little too brazenly. "Touch a nerve, did I?"

Tavish snapped his fingers and two guards moved forward. "Take him," he commanded.

The cell door was opened, and Mithras was dragged out, the guards awkwardly controlling him with the manacles on his wrists. He remained as calm and defiant as ever, standing still as the door was closed again.

"Mithras?" my voice was small and frightened.

He looked to me gently through the bars, trying to be reassuring: "Be brave, child," and he was led from the room, the four guards keeping him under heavy escort.

I was left there staring at the stairs as he disappeared, my heart heavy in my chest and my hands tight on the bars of my cell.

Tavish stepped into my line of sight, the arrogant knight smirking down at me as I met his gaze.

"Where are you taking him?" I demanded with less than enough strength to be commanding.

"To confess his crimes," Tavish responded evenly. "He killed the King and Queen."

"No he didn't! They're not *his* crimes!" I protested angrily. "They're *yours*!"

Tavish chuckled, suddenly reaching through the bars and grasping my hair firmly, pulling me closer to him as I let out a terrified yelp of panic. I braced my hands against the door as hard as I could, staring up at the arrogant knight, pain twisting through me with my awkward angle. I whimpered, trying to pull away, but there was no escaping his grasp as my bare knees crushed against the stone floor uncomfortably.

"Again with your baseless accusations, Princess?" he sneered down at me. "Will you never stop lying to yourself?"

I shuddered in disgust, closing my eyes against the tears threatening to flood my face. I took in a heavy, shaking breath, my throat aching with a large lump forming, feeling utterly helpless against him.

"Now then," he glared into my frightened eyes as I opened them, "I want you to tell me how many accomplices Ser Mithras has."

I refused to answer. I just stared at Tavish in silence, fighting to keep my calm, stubbornly clamping my teeth shut behind my lips.

The Knight-Commander raised one dark, greying eyebrow at me curiously. "Do you not want justice for your uncle, your aunt and your parents? Do you not want justice for the destruction of Arvon, your home?"

I swallowed back hard, closing my eyes against my tears, twisting my wrists in another attempt to slip free of my restraints.

He pressed on: "Tell me, girl, how horrified were you to watch someone you trusted as much as Ser Mithras *murdering* your mother and father? How frightened were you when he forced you to witness his slaying of the King and Queen?"

I glared up at him, sick of this farce: "I want to speak to my uncle," my voice was soft, little more than a murmur.

Tavish ignored my request, continuing with his questioning, a cold smile on his face: "What did you have to do to ensure that Mithras and that *boy* we chased from the palace did not take your life as well?"

I felt rage choking me, fighting harder to keep my composure as I heard his foul words tumbling from his vile, villainous mouth. I clenched my fists and slowly tensed against my cold, iron restraints, wishing to break them and make my move.

Tavish eyed me daringly, smirking as he leaned more closely towards me. "Did the boy do things to you? Did he force himself on you?"

I took in a shaking breath, my eyes locked on his arrogant face with silent, savage rage. "I want to see my uncle. *Now*."

"Is that why you do not answer, your Highness?" he prodded cruelly. "Did he say he would hurt you if you didn't go along with their murderous plot? Did he threaten to violate you?"

"Stop this!" I yelled, feeling my chest hurt with each breath I took. "Just stop! Now!"

Just hearing him even suggest that Carden would do such a vile thing to me was like being stabbed through my heart with sharp ice.

Carden could never hurt me. He wouldn't...

"Just tell me where they are," Tavish urged me, feigning sympathy. "Please, Princess, will you not give up your abductors so that they may answer for their crimes?"

I looked up at him, realisation hitting me. "You haven't found them yet. Have you?"

For a moment Tavish looked frustrated. I didn't need him to answer me, feeling a new hope growing inside of me, already knowing what his answer would be.

"We have soldiers searching the bay and the surrounding shores," he responded in an attempt to appear in control, his eyes stern, but betraying him. "We will find their bodies, I assure you."

I felt a sudden surge in me, gathering my strength and sitting up straighter. The pressure of his hand tugging on my hair and the angle that my neck was bent into hurt, but I fought to keep calm against the pain now that I had regained my determination.

"Why are you continuing with this farce, Knight-Commander?" I questioned him calmly, though my voice did wobble as I managed to dam up my tears again with a few deep breaths. "You know I won't give you what you want."

"You aren't such a fool," he said smugly, but he didn't smile. "Are you, girl?

I eyed him coldly: "I know that you're a part of the conspiracy against my family. I know that you helped my uncle orchestrate all of this, that you aided him in murdering my father and Uncle Aric."

Now he demanded the answer outright: "Where are your other allies?"

"I'll never tell you!" I replied firmly, finding my courage. "You're a traitor to your King, your country and your friend! Mithras trusted you and you betrayed him! You betrayed all of us!"

I cried out in shock and momentary pain, the slap of his palm to my cheek so hard and sudden that I was temporarily blinded and deafened by the impact.

"There is no disloyalty when your King is a feeble old man who cares nothing for the security of the nation," he hissed lowly into my ear, pulling hard on my hair, squeezing my throat with his other hand tightly. "And when the heir to the throne is a pathetic adolescent girl lucky enough to have the title of Princess. You have a duty to preserve said security; even if drastic actions *must* be taken to secure the throne anew."

"Are you going to kill me now?" I asked, fearful, but managing to sound strong.

"Kill you?" he frowned down at me.

Painfully, I nodded: "As you've said, I *am* the heir to the throne, and now that Uncle Aric and my Father are dead, I *am* the Queen of Aldegaad. Uncle Fane is only Regent and will stay as such until my death or my abdication. While I live, he can *never* rule."

"You're a girl of eighteen winters," Tavish smirked. "Until your twenty-first year you will remain Princess and the Regent will rule in your stead."

I glared at him hard: "Either way, I'm the last threat to my uncle's rule."

He nodded slowly. "Indeed, you are."

I sucked in a shaky breath, tears welling up in my eyes heavily as I thought of what that would mean for me. I didn't want to die, but I knew that there was a high chance that in order to gain the throne my uncle and his co-conspirators would murder me as they had the rest of my family. That thought alone terrified me for so many reasons that I didn't want to confess even to myself.

"Do not fear, Princess," Tavish regarded me coldly. "You are too valuable a prisoner in the Regent's mind for us to murder you."

I stared at him uneasily, shaking as he twisted my hair again. Then, he threw me back from the bars, my body hitting the floor hard as I grunted in pain. I looked up at him as he turned away from me, his blue cloak flowing behind him as he walked out and up the stairs again, the remaining soldiers following swiftly. Moments later there came a heavy bang and the locks to the chamber were set with several bold, resounding clicks.

I couldn't think straight, nothing really passing through my mind as I sat there shaking with fear and cold, the cruel semi-violent encounter leaving me shaken and desperate to escape the fear that plagued me. I soon found myself searching my cell with my eyes aimlessly, nothing distracting me, not even the other prisoners' words or movements in their cells. I felt so alone again.

Carden... Gods, Carden, I wish you were here. I wish you were breaking through that door to free me from this terrible nightmare.

I let my head sink and I started to cry openly, my tears the only warmth I had now in the chill of that dark, stone place. I closed my eyes, trying to hold back the tears as they fled my eyelids.

I was exhausted and all I wanted to do was sleep, yet I couldn't bring myself to move to the bed and its sparse covers in the corner of the room. I ended up settling back against the wall and pulled my knees up to hug them again. This was all I could do now, trembling from the cold of that awful cell.

I couldn't believe that this was really happening, that after everything we had gone through since Arvon was attacked, I was being held prisoner by my own uncle.

Maybe he won't kill a girl. Maybe that's why I'm still alive, I thought coldly. *Or maybe he has another use for me... a darker one...*

Huddling in the corner of my cell, I thought of my friends and hoped that they were alright.

Carden will be thinking of something by now, I know he will, and at least he has my pendant. It's safe with him and away from Fane's evil grasp. I can't imagine what he would do if he got his hands on it. Or on Amethyst. Gods, I'm glad I didn't bring her with me. She's still just a baby, after all, even though she is as big as a wolf hound now. A sigh escaped my lips as my memories showed the young Guardian to me again in my mind's eye, a smile imagined on his handsome face. *How I wish I was safe in his arms right now, away from all of this and with him in the warmth of a simple inn or a Guardian stronghold. Anywhere. It wouldn't matter, as long as we're together... I just wish he was here with me...*

I began imagining that he *was* with me in that cell. I could see his handsome green eyes and that lopsided smile that made me feel so safe. His sharp, gorgeous features and his tall frame were as clear to me as if he were standing there in front of me in the flesh.

I wanted him to wrap his arms around me and hold me close, to stroke my hair and let me lay my head against his broad chest where I could just take in the perfect scent that was his. This thought allowed me to relax as I rested my head against the wall, my heavy eyelids starting to droop.

Slowly, I slipped into the safety of sleep, forgetting this nightmare for a while at least and dreaming of better things.

Chapter Two
The Regent's Treachery

I opened my eyes to brilliantly bright sunlight, breathing in the warm spring air and savouring it. I stretched out my hands above me, yawning and shielding my eyes from the dazzling sun with my fingers' shadows, my whole body feeling soothed and relieved by the sensations surrounding me.

I was dressed in a white long-sleeved dress and a dark cobalt velvet gown with golden trims like the ones I was used to. All around me were tall pine trees and great oaks; the Nartarn'lath Mountains above my head where I lay in the soft, green grass and amidst vibrant flowers of purple, white, gold and blue. There was a purplish haze over the mountains, and I could just see the white of snow through the thick grey clouds that always hung over them.

A figure moved over me to my right and I looked up at him with bleary, tired eyes. My heart fluttered as I stared at those handsome, sharp features, his young face so beautiful to me. His cheekbones were well defined, his jaw ending in a squared chin. His jade green eyes were dazzling and full of care, his lips parting to show his perfect white teeth, his upper canines a little longer than the others and reminding me of fangs. His lips curved into that familiar lopsided grin as he looked down at me, the wind catching at his collar length black hair lightly.

Carden lay beside me, resting on his left side and propping himself up on his elbow so that he was leaning over me. He was dressed in a dark blue shirt, his brown boots pulled on over his dark coloured pants while my feet were left bare in the grass.

I let my eyes trace the shape of his beautifully handsome face and travel down his strong neck to where it plunged beneath his shirt's open collar. I could see the slight definition of his chest beneath the fabric, my heart fluttering. I had never known anyone to be so handsome in my life, not one of the suitors my mother had always sent towards me ever matching his attractiveness and his heart. And that was why I refused them: none of them had his heart.

I smiled, lowering my hands into the grass beside my shoulders. "How long have I been asleep?"

"A little while," Carden replied softly, staring at me with a gaze that was so deeply caring. "I couldn't bear to wake you. You just looked so beautiful."

Slowly, I propped myself up on my elbows and looked around at the grove surrounding us, my long dark hair catching in the breeze and flowing around my shoulders.

"I remember this place," I said softly, feeling so at peace. "I used to come here with Aislinn when I was a child. It's my most favourite place in the world."

He nodded softly, gazing around admiringly: "I can see why you like coming here. It truly is a beautiful place," he looked back to me, a deep care in those jade pools, "but only half as beautiful as you."

I sat up a little more as he did the same, our eyes meeting. I felt myself blushing, cursing my cheeks for betraying me with the heat rising in them. Still, I couldn't deny that I was flattered by his affections.

"How is it that I never noticed how handsome you are?" I asked him softly, my heart racing in a good way.

He smiled faintly; his face so close to mine: "I think you've always noticed me the way that I have you."

I sighed, nodding slowly. "But this can never be, Carden."

"Why not?" he asked me gently as he leaned a little closer to me again.

I shrugged gently as I felt tears threatening to purge from my eyes. I looked down at my knees, drawing them to my chest to hug them, taking in a shaking breath as I longed to be with him always; to never be away from his loving touch.

"Because this isn't real; this is *only* a dream," I said sadly, my heart aching.

I sighed softly and closed my eyes against the tears I felt, longing for this truth to not be so. Then I felt two coarse, warm fingers touch me under my chin and tilt my head up. I opened my eyes to meet his green gaze, his handsome, smooth, perfect face so gentle, his skin slightly more tanned than mine. There was an understanding in his eyes mixed with the care he expressed there, and I felt suddenly more at ease.

"Is it such a bad thing that this is a dream?" he asked me with all seriousness.

"I should *really* be with you," I admitted with a sigh, his hand slowly coiling around mine. "That's what my heart wants."

"Then follow your heart," he smiled at me. "I will follow you no matter the path you take. I swear this to you, my beautiful girl."

I felt him laying me back down into the grass and flowers, his touch so kind and careful, his eyes locked with mine. There was a fear in my heart, but it was a good fear.

"Please, Carden," I whispered, staring up into his eyes and through to his soul, "stay with me."

"I'm not going anywhere," he promised, laying back beside me and pulling me into his arms, stroking my hair and shoulders lovingly.

I closed my eyes as he held me, savouring every touch and every moment that we were together. I never wanted to leave this place. I would gladly live here with him forever, knowing in my heart there could never be another for me...

* * * * *

A loud bang woke me and for a moment I felt too disoriented to know where I was. The cold was what drew me back to the waking world and I opened my eyes to my grievous situation. I was still sitting in the corner of that terrible cell with my back to the stone wall and the shackles tight around my wrists. I was still trapped in Aneuran, still imprisoned in this darkened purgatory. My dream had been nothing more than exactly that: a beautiful dream.

Despair filled my heart anew as I stared out into the torch lit chamber of the dungeons, the cells outside mine not quite as darkened now that morning had come. I immediately wanted to cry but held myself together. I had to be strong.

I was wrapped in one of the blankets from the bed, obviously having crawled over and taken it to keep myself warm. It did little to guard me against the chill as the early morning light filtered into my cell, the opening in the wall allowing the cold ocean air to fill the room.

I could barely keep myself from trembling under the blanket. My bare legs and arms weren't helping with my battle against the cold and I began to worry that I could get sick sitting there so exposed.

I turned to the bars to my right, hoping that Mithras would be there. But he wasn't. Dismay filled my heart and I curled up, burying my face into my arms.

Suddenly, there came the sound of the chamber door unlocking and I looked up in alarm, wondering what horror would come today. Two guards entered carrying trays, a third standing outside with the keys to the cell block. The two guards started to move to the cells as the third called out: "Mealtime, prisoners."

One of the guards came to my cell as the other went to the one opposite, his pale eyes locking on my trembling shape where I sat wrapped in the tattered blanket. He set the tray on a nearby table and took a small bowl from it, crouching down beside the bars.

Crawling to the bars, I took what he offered carefully and settled back into my corner, cradling the wooden bowl in my palms and staring down at the contents uncertainly. It was a pale mush that was cold and lumpy, looking very unappetising.

"And here's your water allowance for today," he set a pitcher of water, a metal cup and a metal spoon through the bars and onto the floor at my feet.

I nodded to him from beneath my dishevelled hair and said: "Thank you."

The guard nodded to me, then took another bowl and pitcher before heading to the next cell.

I took the spoon and dipped it into the oatmeal uncertainly, studying the spoonful cautiously. I tasted it experimentally, finding that it wasn't completely awful, but it wasn't tasty either. It was the most horribly bland thing I had ever tasted, but I slowly began to eat, my hunger urging me on.

Keeping myself occupied was impossible after that. I explored the cell for a while, analysing every corner of it. There wasn't much to see, and I ended up sitting on the small bed, counting the bricks in the walls. I lost count at somewhere between two hundred and three hundred before I was given a second meal sometime after what I could only guess was midday, this time only brown bread with nothing else. I huddled under the blankets in the far corner of my cell, eating it ravenously, finding that my hunger was only increasing.

My eyes kept finding their way to the door into the cell block, desperation filling me as I hoped Mithras would be brought back soon. But he wasn't.

Night came and with it a cold stew that made me feel sick. I had only been here a short time and I was already feeling like I could break from the hunger, the cold, the boredom and the crushing loneliness.

I waited as long as I could manage for Mithras, my eyes getting heavier as the hours passed. Soon, I found my way to the worn old bed and curled up, starting to cry as everything overwhelmed me until I finally fell asleep.

For what felt like days I waited for Mithras to be brought back, and when he finally was, I nearly broke down, collapsing to my knees in horror. They had done so much to him; burns, bruises and cuts all over what skin he had exposed, his clothes now tattered and dirtied. He wasn't really aware of where he was as the guards dumped him in his cell like an unwanted sack of garbage, leaving him lying there weak and broken. I just wanted to reach him and take care of him, to help him recover, but the bars between us made that impossible. All I could do was sit and wait, hoping he would eventually open his eyes.

I lost track of how long we had been there now, the dungeons playing tricks with my mind. I felt like I had spent months trapped in that single room, though to be honest I wasn't sure it had been more than a week.

What I could only guess had been maybe two days later; a sound drew my gaze from where I sat, and I looked to the edge of my cell.

"Mithras?" I called out hoarsely, my hair feeling greasy as it hung in unclean clumps around my now grimy face. "Mithras?"

A low growl came from his cell: "Argh... Well, this is an ever-cheery place to wake up."

"Mithras," I felt so relieved. "Are you alright?"

"Leander?" he sounded a little disoriented. "How long have I been out?"

I shrugged, shivering: "I don't really know. I can't tell how long we've been here."

"About a week," he responded and groaned as he sat up.

"How can you tell?"

"I'm estimating," was his answer. "I see we have oatmeal for breakfast, if you can call it that."

I shuddered, remembering the taste that I had desperately tried to wash out of my mouth with the water I had been given.

"I think it's getting worse," I muttered.

"Yes, well, your Uncle Fane has never thought much about prisoners."

I just nodded, very aware of my least favourite uncle's stance on the subject.

"Have you eaten?" he asked me, taking up the bowl distastefully.

I cringed, trying not to be sick. "What little I could manage."

He sighed. "Well, we need to keep up our strength. They'll be back for me eventually."

"Why are they doing this to us?" I felt like I could have screamed the question, my voice shaking as if it couldn't reach that tone. "They're our own people. This doesn't make sense."

"The Regent is playing a cruel political game," Mithras explained gravely between mouthfuls of food. "He wants a scapegoat for the people to blame for the King's murder. And you're the next in line for the throne, so he's keeping you out of the way."

I sighed and slumped onto the bed, laying my head on my folded arms, my chains rattling. "Then why doesn't he just kill me? It just doesn't make sense."

"You're right," he agreed thoughtfully, "it doesn't make sense. Someone else is involved, I can feel that, yet I'm not sure who."

"The Shadow Lord?" I suggested, realising that this was the first time in days that I had even thought of my mysterious pursuer.

"It could be him," he agreed. "but I doubt that he would come after you just to aid in Aldegaad's power changing hands. Shadow Lords aren't so provincial in their designs."

I shook my head glumly. "Maybe Fane is trying to use me somehow. Tavish seemed to suggest that they're playing this as if I'm a victim, not an accomplice."

"A ploy for the people's sympathies then," Mithras surmised. "If the Regent is seen as the rescuer of the King's chosen heir and is now caring for her in her so-called vulnerable state, then he could garner great support to take the throne for himself."

"So, how is the Shadow Lord involved, then?" I wondered, turning my steel blue eyes up from my feet to him, resting my chin on my forearms.

"I'm not certain he is. I believe the Gymphs that attacked Arvon were sent because the Shadow Lord was taking advantage of an opportunity to reach you," he theorised. "I doubt any other connection."

I felt that familiar bite of pain in my heart at the mention of that night. Father's death returned to me and I felt an old sorrow fill me. But I couldn't wallow in my resurging grief, even if I had wanted to. The sounds of doors being unlocked from somewhere outside the cell block reached my ears and my heart sank farther into my chest.

"They come for me anew," Mithras sighed and I heard the springs of his bed groan as he stood.

I curled up under the blankets, trying to be as small and unnoticeable as possible. Even though it wasn't me they were coming for I still didn't want the guards to lock their gazes in my direction.

Tavish entered with the same pomposity that he usually carried, his hand resting on his sword. He said nothing, merely gesturing to two of the six guards that came with him. Mithras' cell was opened, and he was brought out by his chains once again.

"Am I to spend another day in your company, Tavish?" Mithras said with great confidence, trying to irritate the man. "I hope you're offering me a candle lit meal along with your charms."

Tavish snorted a laugh so small it almost wasn't anything but a grimace. He let loose with a single backhanded strike to Mithras' face, making me cringe in sympathetic pain. But Mithras only stared back with stony eyes and relentlessly calm defiance.

"Your resistance is most irritating, Mithras," Tavish told him harshly. "That's why we'll be having someone accompany you."

I gulped. *Oh... no... Gods, no... Please...*

"Bring the girl," Tavish ordered, two of the guards immediately moving to my cell.

"No!" Mithras roared, struggling against the men holding him. "This is between us, Tavish! Leave the girl out of this!"

The cell was opened, and the two guards stalked inside, towering over me where I lay. I cringed back in fear, trying to hide, but they grabbed me and dragged me up from the bed. One guard held the chains on my wrists, forcing my hands in front of me despite my struggles.

"Let me go!" I yelled, trying to fight them off me. "Let me go! Get off me!"

They forced me through the door and into the main chamber, bringing me to a halt before the cruel Knight-Commander. Tavish stared down at me, reaching out one slightly chilled hand to touch my chin, my attempts to struggle away useless.

"I hope you'll show a little more decorum in front of the Regent, girl," Tavish smirked at me.

"Get your filthy hands off her!" Mithras snarled loudly. "I swear by my oath as a knight that I will kill you if you harm this girl!"

"Your oath means nothing now, Mithras," Tavish nodded to the guards. "Bring them."

The Knight-Commander turned on his heel and strode out of the room with a swirl of his cloak, the six guards flanking us and following, forcing us forward roughly.

"It's going to be alright, Leander," Mithras tried to reassure me as I struggled to look back at him.

"Mithras?" I whimpered.

"It *will* be alright," he repeated in a firmer tone. "I promise you, child. But whatever happens, stay strong."

I sucked in a deep breath and nodded.

I lost track of our path so quickly, the darkened corridors all looking the same, our pace too fast for me to really take in any subtle changes. I felt so small amongst the men surrounding me, my tall stature meaningless compared to their greater ones. Just as Aldegaadian women are some of the tallest of my sex in Therras, so too are our men equally taller than us.

The guards took us down a long corridor past a heavy iron and wood reinforced door, only a few torches lighting the way. There were guards watching our approach from the far end where a set of doubled doors waited, also reinforced with iron.

I threw a worried glance to Mithras, but he was staring ahead with a deep calm I barely knew and had no hope of mustering. *How can he be so calm?* I wondered silently.

The doors were opened, and we were brought into a horrible, dark room. I instantly stared around at the vast space inside, noticing its finer details immediately. My eyes were now well adjusted to the darkness of the prisons and I could see perfectly, though I wish I couldn't, given the layout of the room before me.

There was a large fireplace set into the far corner of the room on my left, almost directly in front of the doors, its light illuminating the stone floors and walls. Chains hung from mounts in the ceiling, steel shackles forged perfectly into the lowest links as they swung in the mild, chilly breeze that came from somewhere in the chamber. There were even shackles on the walls, meant clearly to hold a person against the hard stone and stretch them out painfully. Throughout the room were a few table-like devices, all with restraints attached, an iron maiden set in the far-right corner. There were three diagonally standing racks set around the room's right side as well as various other sinister devices.

My heart sank and I felt as if I would vomit as I took it all in, trembling helplessly.

The doors were shut, and the guards took up positions around the room, two flanking Mithras, one holding me. Tavish stood back beside the door, hands clasped in front of him as he watched on with calm amusement.

I tried to struggle free in the hands of the guard who held my shoulders tightly, but my efforts were in vain, my eyes then settling on the other three figures in the room. Two tall men in black hoods stood before us, dressed in simple shirts, trousers, boots and aprons, only their eyes visible through the cloth of their hoods. They were staring at us coldly, almost with anticipation, their hands twitching at their sides. But as terrifying as they were, my gaze turned instead to the one figure that made my blood run cold.

Fane was staring into the fireplace, his hands clasped behind his back, his blue eyes gleaming coldly. He was dressed in blue, grey and gold finery, his black boots polished and a princely circlet of gold set on his dark brown-haired head. I felt sick just seeing him after all that he had done.

"I never agreed with my grandfather's desire to discontinue the use of this chamber," he was musing to himself, putting on a show for us. "He believed that it was a barbaric practice to torture prisoners, just as he believed that execution was uncalled for. And of course, my father and brothers all too eagerly followed his thoughts on the matter."

He turned his thin, bearded face towards Mithras and I, his expression cold and distant, as if he were thinking of better days. He smiled faintly as he crossed towards one of the racks and waved a vague hand.

"I, on the other hand, believe that only torture brings out the truth. You only see what people truly are when they are forced to confront themselves through pain; a universal truth, I think," he smirked coldly.

I was horrified by what he was suggesting, looking to Mithras in fear as Fane approached him.

Mithras was stalwart, keeping his eyes forward, refusing to let his emotions register, even as Fane stood to his left, taller than him and glaring with extreme arrogance.

"You've spent a considerable amount of time in this chamber of late, Ser Mithras," my uncle said in a nasty tone, standing right up to Mithras' face. "I wonder how much you fear setting foot within these walls?"

"Why would I fear a room?" Mithras responded sternly, showing no signs of capitulating to Fane's will.

"You have fallen," Fane said, pacing slowly around behind him, watching him closely as he did. "Fallen from the honour of a knight to the petty failure that you have become."

"If I have fallen," Mithras turned his gaze to his right, meeting Fane there, "then it is not due to my own actions, but the actions of treasonous dogs like you."

Again, Tavish moved forward and backhanded him for his insolence, the older knight still showing no reaction, my own cringe enough for both of us.

"Do not forget, Mithras," Fane hissed at him as he turned away, "with my brothers dead, *I* am your Regent and will soon be your King."

"You are no King," Mithras retorted calmly. "In Aldegaad the King does not come to power by assassinating the previous King and all those who would otherwise inherit the throne."

Fane nodded with a faint smile: "Ah. But the people of Aldegaad do not need to know *that* particular version of history. Not when we have the *true* murderer of our King in custody."

"A vicious lie concocted to claim the throne for yourself and a means to dispose of the rightful heir," Mithras' eyes were hard, and his jaw set firmly.

Fane turned his attention to me, moving to stand over me, imposing and cruel. I cringed back into the guard that was holding me, my eyes staying locked on my uncle's harsh face.

"You refer to a girl as being the true heir," he scoffed arrogantly. "A girl with no real power or strength, barely on the cusp of womanhood; which is why the people will believe that she was forced to be exploited as part of *your* crimes."

Mithras rolled his eyes and snorted: "Again you attempt to coerce a false confession from me? I would have thought that had gotten a little tired by now."

Fane sneered at him: "I prefer to think of it as a convenient truth."

"How do you plan to get away with this?" I murmured, drawing his gaze as I tensed against the guard's hold on my arms. "The people won't follow you and you know that. But that's why you're keeping me alive. Isn't it?"

Fane smiled: "Clever girl. You always were the smart one, Leander."

"You're a monster," I shook my head, my voice cold and quiet. "We were your family. We trusted you."

"Which is why I would never be suspected," Fane faced Mithras again. "Not when the deranged and fallen Knight-Commander of Arvon publicly confesses his guilt in a few days."

Mithras snorted, eyeing Fane with contempt. "And how do you propose I do that when I am innocent of such heinous crimes, Fane?"

"You *will* confess," Fane promised him, gesturing then to the devices littering the room. "If not by will, then we will force it from you."

"You can torture me all you want," Mithras responded evenly, showing no fear. "I will never confess to crimes I did not commit."

"I had anticipated that this would be your answer," Fane looked to me cruelly. "Which is why *she* is here."

I stared at him in horror, shaking my head in disbelief. *He can't mean... He couldn't... He wouldn't!*

"No!" Mithras shouted, trying to get to me, but he was beaten back by the guards as I was dragged forward.

I struggled against the guard holding me, but I wasn't strong enough. Another guard freed me from my restraints and forced my arms up over my head. I felt the pinching cold steel of shackles snapping shut around my vulnerable wrists, the chain stretching my body so that I had to stand on my toes.

Desperate and panicking, I tried to wriggle loose, staring up at the shackles helplessly. I felt tears beginning to burn my eyes just as the guards stepped away from me, my chest heaving under the sack cloth tunic that was all but riding up towards my hips now.

A hand touched my face, one of the hooded torturers drawing my gaze as he hooked his fingers through my long dark locks. I whimpered, the man pulling hard on my hair so I would stop squirming.

He made me face Mithras, who was now staring at me with a pale white face that made him look as if he had become suddenly sick.

"Perhaps you do not fear pain for yourself," Fane regarded Mithras with an icy smirk, "but what of the girl? Could your conscience bear the weight of her suffering because of your defiance? Could you live out your imprisoned days knowing that *she* suffered for *your* honour?"

Mithras stared at me in horror. I knew that he would rather save me, but I wouldn't accept the cost. It would just be too great.

"Mithras!" I shouted, calling his attention, my arms already aching and my feet cramping with the cold. "Don't do it!" I pleaded fervently. "Please! Don't listen to him! Don't do what he wants!"

"Leander..." he stared at me with haunted eyes.

"Please, Mithras," I said more softly, "Don't."

"What do you say?" Fane demanded quietly, glaring at him and ignoring me.

Mithras studied me for a moment, his eyes changing and his strength returning. He looked to Fane icily: "Can you bear the consequences of torturing your own niece, Regent?"

Fane didn't look happy. He turned from Mithras, the guards chaining the Knight to the wall as my cruel uncle moved to stand over me, his eyes harsh as he met my gaze. I just stared straight back, clamping my teeth shut behind my lips and letting all of my anger bubble up to overtake my fear.

"Leander," he sounded like he was trying to appeal to me, but his effort was lacking. "Why are you doing this to yourself? Just let Mithras confess."

"I won't let you frame an innocent man," I replied coldly, my voice and body trembling.

Fane smirked darkly, nodding as he stroked his knuckles against my right cheek, my eyes fluttering shut and my nerves shuddering against his touch.

"Brave girl; I suppose I never fully appreciated your virtues until now," he nodded to the torturers. "I think a mild beating followed by some flagellation would be appropriate," then he sneered at me and added: "As a start."

I cringed as my uncle stepped away from me, closing my eyes as the torturer let go of my hair. I didn't want to see the first hits, one of them slugging me in the left cheek and causing my face to swing hard to my right. I couldn't help crying out at first, this kind of pain completely unknown to me. Somehow, though, I forced myself to look up as I took the next blow to the ribs. A heavy cough escaped my lips and I struggled to keep myself together. I was worried that my ribs had just been broken, but I had to focus on getting through this.

An open palm slapped me in the face, and I was punched in the diaphragm again, coughing heavily as I cried out softly. My hair was pulled, and I was slapped and punched, but I managed to squeeze my eyes and my lips shut, only grimacing with the pain breaking through me as my fingers clawed uselessly at the air, shaking against the shackles above me.

This went on for a while, the two men relentlessly beating me, drawing tears from my eyes, blood from my lip and cries from my breath. Still, despite my desire for relief, I held strong, determined not to give in.

"Enough!" Fane snapped and the two men stepped away from me. He tilted my chin, forcing me to look at him: "Well, Leander, have you had enough?"

Despite the agonising aches in my beaten and trembling body, I hissed at him: "Go to the Void you evil bastard!"

His eyes narrowed and he growled: "You stupid little girl!"

As my uncle stepped away one of the torturers came forward carrying a whip. I stared at it in horror, the man moving up behind me as my uncle made sure that I was facing him. I could hear the whip's lashes licking the floor, my heart pounding in my throat. In seconds I knew I would feel the worst pain I had ever felt in my life so far, that I would likely scream. But what was really scary was the fact that they could do so much worse to me still.

"Be strong," I murmured to myself, my eyes shutting tightly. "Just be strong."

There came the cracking of the whip and a pain so great across my back that my entire body wrenched up and forward, my gag reflex reacting too. Sharp, shuddering breaths were pulling into my lungs, my body shaking as I fought to keep myself standing. If it wasn't for the chains holding me up, I would have been on the floor screaming.

I sobbed out a tiny squeak instead of a scream, squeezing my eyes against the agony shredding through my flesh as I tried to resist. Pain ripped through my back just as my flesh tore beneath my clothing with the next strike that came. I managed to stifle another scream as my skin burned with the next lash which seemed to follow quicker than the one before it. Another blow hit me, my eyes squeezing tighter and my teeth clenching. Then another blow and another, and another.

I hung there, stubborn against my desire to scream as the cracking of the leather flail echoed through the chamber, punctuated by excruciating pain that screamed through every nerve ending in my adolescent body. Only whimpering sobs escaped my lips amidst the snapping of the whip, its harsh cracking deafening to my vulnerable ears.

I thought that if I could make this pain stop, I would plead, I would cry, I would do anything that condemned myself. But I wouldn't scream. I wouldn't. And I definitely wouldn't let him condemn Mithras.

I won't give him the satisfaction...

Chapter Three
Whispers in the Dark

For a while I felt like I was floating, dreamily lost in a deep, dark ocean, sinking into its cold depths. It was strange that the water could be so soothing, but also so damning at the same time. Its coolness was gentle on my skin, easing my pain for a few moments. It would have been so easy to fall asleep like that, but I wasn't going to.

I opened my eyes, my dark auburn locks swirling in a ghostly wave in front of me, taking on a slightly reddish tint in the water. It was beautiful in a way, the shimmer of the light shining through the strands dancing across the stone ground that I found myself staring at.

Then, suddenly, like a wave crushing down on me, reality came flooding back.

My nostrils flared and my lungs ached as the fiery lack of air consumed me. I was lightheaded, the world feeling like it was swirling and spinning around me. I was suddenly aware of the hard hands pushing me down, one clamped on the back of my neck, the other firmly gripping my left arm.

Panic overtook my peacefulness and I struggled fervently, thrashing around as hard as I could against the pain in my chest. Blood was tainting the water a faint red and I suddenly realised that it was mine, panicking a little more.

Suddenly, I was pulled backwards, the audible bubbling of water rushing loudly through my ears as I was brought to an upright position, breaking free of the water's surface. I gasped loudly, groaning and struggling to recover. My laboured breaths were loud and frantic, my body shaking as I braced my bound hands against the edge of the trough in frantic anticipation of the next assault.

I looked up through my drenched hair, my eyes blurry and choked by strange colours as I coughed heavily, my body retching violently.

The torturer's hands were still on me, the one on my neck now grasping a fistful of my dark hair and keeping my head up. I cried in panicky desperation, wanting this to stop, but knowing too well what it would mean if I begged for its end.

Movement caught my attention and I looked up towards it. For a moment I imagined the sinister skull-like face of the Shadow Lord staring out from beneath his cowl at me. I was afraid, but I knew it wasn't him.

My vision cleared and I came face-to-face with my uncle, the hatred in my heart revitalising me.

"You're quite a stubborn girl, aren't you?" he observed with a cold harshness in his voice.

I managed to glare up at him for a moment, trying to blink the water from my eyes as my chest heaved with my desperately drawn in breaths.

We were daring each other silently; him urging me to react while I challenged him to do worse. I would never give my traitorous uncle what he wanted. I still hadn't screamed as loudly or as desperately as I could have, even though my back was now a red raw mess, my tattered tunic stained with my blood.

"Well, Mithras?" Fane turned his gaze over his shoulder after a few moments. "Do you have anything to say now?"

I followed his gaze towards the wall where Mithras was shackled. He looked so weak and tired as he stared at me, his eyes full of concern and guilt.

"Well?" Fane raised an expectant eyebrow at him. "Will you capitulate? Or shall we continue?"

Mithras was breaking, I could tell. His eyes were heavy with tears that were threatening to fall, his care and devotion for me actually starting to hurt him. All I could do was silently hope that he wouldn't give in, the thought of that a worse torment to me than anything I could imagine.

He suddenly blinked, glared at Fane and shook his head as Tavish grasped him harder around the throat, forcing him to watch.

"Again," Fane scowled violently.

As quickly as I could I drew in a deep breath and closed my eyes. I was shoved forward, my head and shoulders plunging back into the cold water, the shock of it enough to wake me up from the daze I had unknowingly found myself in.

I struggled again, fighting for air, my heart thundering in my ears and seeming to echo off the walls of the trough. I pushed and thrashed, the pressure of the torturer's hands holding me down causing me to panic even more.

I'm going to drown! Oh Gods! I'm going to drown! No! Don't let me die!

The torturer hauled me up out of the water again, the spray coming off my hair in heavy waves flooding down my face, neck, cleavage and shoulders. I choked in a grateful, desperate lungful of air, panicky whimpers and gasps escaping me. I slumped back against the torturer, my bent knees giving out and making me nearly sit. If he hadn't been there, I would have fallen to the stone floor, my body too weak to hold me up now.

I blinked back the water from my eyes again, trying to focus on my uncle as he glared at me.

"Well, Mithras?" Fane turned to the Knight again. "Will you confess?"

"D-don't," I managed hoarsely, coughing up more water. "Mithras... don't... That's... unh... that's an order."

Mithras smirked and eyed Fane coldly: "I do as my *Queen* commands."

"*Again*," Fane snarled loudly and I was slammed face down into the water once more.

I was desperately frantic this time as I felt the water rushing into my throat and trying to find its way to my lungs. I could feel my hands slipping against the wet edge of the trough, my fingers flexing awkwardly to find something to hold onto. Conscious thought was escaping me, and I was sure that this would be it.

Suddenly, I was yanked up, the water breaking around me as I gasped loudly, thirstily gulping in the air as if I were drinking it. I opened my eyes against the flood that was pouring down my face to see my uncle eyeing me, his hand up to the torturer, who released me without hesitation.

I slumped onto my side, shivering with the cold my wet clothing was adding to my skin. I managed to look up at him as he crouched in front of me, his eyes softening, but I could still see the cruelty in them.

"You really are a brave girl, Leander," he observed coldly, staring into my teary eyes, my chest heaving with my breathlessness. "You seem determined to keep him from admitting his guilt."

I wanted to throw some smart mouthed comment at Fane, but my vocal cords had become paralysed with fear and exhaustion. I just stared at him, breathing heavily and swiftly as I tried to recover. I was so dizzy that I felt like I was spinning, grateful to be lying down.

"Humph," Fane grunted, glaring at me. "So like your father. Ewan was just as stubborn as you are. Like father like daughter I suppose."

I felt a new tear trickle down my cheek at the mention of my father and I flinched again, the pain overwhelming me both physically and emotionally.

"Oh, poor girl," he said with mocking sympathy, stroking my soaked hair as he held one hand under my jaw. "Do you want the pain to stop?"

Slowly, feeling horrible guilt gripping my heart tightly, I nodded, tears flowing silently.

"*I* am *not* the man who can save you from this fate," Fane told me.

He grasped me in his arms and pulled me to my feet, my whimpers of pain ignored. He held me close, my back to his chest, grabbing a fistful of my long hair and pulling my head up roughly. I winced as he turned me towards Mithras, making us face one another.

"*He* can save you," he whispered in my ear. "He need only confess, and you need only let him."

I stared through my tears at Mithras, meeting his dark eyed gaze. I could see the pain that this was causing him, my heart aching for him, but I had to stay my course.

"What do you say?" Fane asked me, looking down at me from my right. "Let him confess and your pain ends."

I looked to him past my shoulder, my pain feeling like a dull throb for a moment. "No," I answered simply, shivering. "I won't."

Fane growled and pushed me to the floor, the cold, hard stone meeting me heavily as I landed. I lay there on my stomach, turning my face onto its right side and staring up as Fane stood over me. I was afraid that he would continue hurting me, but I kept reminding myself to be strong. *That is how a queen should be, after all. Strong in the face of adversity.*

I felt his kick in my ribs before I saw him move, crying out in pain as I felt a horrible, sickening crack in my side. Another, harder kick and I gagged violently, nearly throwing up. He threw a third and final one, leaving me doubled over and close to sobbing.

Fane crouched beside me again, this time just behind me, staring down at me as I coughed violently into my arms against the pain in my abdomen.

"Are you really so willing to suffer for him, my dear niece?" he questioned me softly, but coldly. "Can you really give up your life just to protect Mithras' honour?"

I remained silent and defiant, glaring forward at the ground, bracing myself on my elbows. It was a struggle just to breathe.

"There are much crueller, more painful tortures I can impose on you, Leander," he warned me, hinting at his desire to enact such intentions. "You see, the men torturing you, they don't really have the opportunity to apply their trade to the fairer sex. Imagine how their lust must be mounting seeing a beautiful young woman before them and at their mercy."

I couldn't help reacting, my body immediately shaking at the prospect of *that* torture.

I heard the smirk in his voice as he went on: "I can't begin to imagine how painful it will be to have them carry out such an act. The first time is rather... *messy...*"

I swallowed hard, trembling in fear, closing my eyes as I felt worried tears trying to fight their way free. *No... Not that! Please, not that!* I wanted to scream, but I couldn't even utter a croak.

"That is something I would seriously consider having them do to you, girl," he said cruelly. "I can only imagine how much you will scream."

I started to cry softly, closing my eyes tight. If they decided to do that, I would have no way of stopping them, my body too weak to fight back after all the torture I had endured. And even if I could manage to summon enough strength to attempt to defend myself the two men would easily overpower me, both of them twice my size. In the end all I would do is scream and beg until it ended, but for the moment I had to hope that he was just bluffing.

"That's enough, Fane!" Mithras shouted angrily. "Leave her alone! She's a child, for gods' sakes!"

"*You* can save her from that fate, *Knight!*" Fane spun around and snapped at him.

"Does your cruelty know no bounds?!" Mithras snarled lowly but was ignored. "You would let these men violate your own niece just to gain my false confession?! You cannot allow this!"

"That is where you are wrong, Mithras," Fane turned back to me, tilting my chin so I had to look at him where I lay. "I will allow them that pleasure, Leander. And I promise that you will die weeping."

"N-no... please... don't," I said in a tiny voice, shaking from cold and fear.

"Don't worry, my dear girl," my uncle smiled at me with false kindness, stroking my hair. "I won't have you go through that just yet. Not while you can see."

I frowned at him in confusion as he stood. He turned to the torturers and I became suddenly aware of where they were in the room. One was near the fireplace stoking the fiery coals with a long iron poker, the other standing behind me.

Fane commanded evenly, sneering down at me: "Set a fire in her eyes."

"What?! No!" I screamed, the torturer behind me grabbing me by both arms and hauling me to my feet.

I kicked and struggled, trying to get loose as the second torturer turned towards me, lifting the poker up in one hand. I stared in horror at the white-hot glowing point of the poker, my body trembling as I imagined what he was about to do with it.

"It really is a shame," Fane commented, staring at me with a mockingly thoughtful look. "She has such beautiful steel blue eyes; *true* Aldegaadian eyes. Oh well."

I struggled as hard as I could, the torturer holding me firmly as the other came towards me with the poker. I squirmed frantically, my bare feet slipping on the wet stone floor.

"No! Don't do this to me, uncle! Please! Don't do this to me!" I screamed hysterically. "PLEASE! PLEASE! DON'T! DON'T!"

The first torturer tilted my head back as the second stood over me, bringing the poker to my face. I could feel the heat coming off the metal, knowing that the pain I was about to experience would be horrific and leave me in permanent darkness for as long as I lived.

"NO! DON'T!" I screamed, tears flooding my face. "PLEASE! NO! NO!"

Staring right at the point of the burning iron all I could think was how much this was going to hurt. The pain of the other tortures hadn't really been much to me because I knew I would heal. But losing my eyes...

"ALRIGHT!" a voice cried out through my panicked screams and sobs "I'LL DO IT! I'LL CONFESS!"

The poker was drawn back from my face, my eyes safe as I blinked against the heat.

I turned my saved sight to my left as the torturers paused. My uncle had ordered them to stop, his hand outstretched towards us, palm down. He wasn't looking at me, his eyes set firmly on Mithras.

Looking up through my tears, I stared at Mithras in horror. He was trembling, tears in his eyes as well, his face like that of a father who had just seen his daughter horribly murdered. It was haunting.

Mithras looked to Fane, his voice shaking as he spoke: "I will do whatever you ask, Prince Fane! I'll confess to the crimes you desire! Just, please, leave the girl alone! Do not hurt her anymore!"

I closed my eyes, slumping down onto the floor in the torturer's arms, crying now out of fear, relief and guilt. *He gave in... to save my sight. No... no...*

I opened my eyes and watched my uncle move towards Mithras as the guards freed him from his shackles and forced him to his knees. Mithras slumped down, defeated, his eyes turning to me, red with his own tears.

"Please forgive me, Leander," he said sorrowfully. "I could not bear to see you suffer anymore."

"Mithras... no..." I sobbed, feeling too weak to keep myself upright.

Fane smirked, looking back at me for a moment as exhaustion overwhelmed me. I felt sick, the pain from my wounds and fear draining me. I sagged in the torturer's arms, feeling like I couldn't stay awake anymore. In only a few moments I slipped into the welcoming darkness of unconsciousness and the peace it brought...

* * * * *

The cold stone floor was the first thing I felt, hard beneath me and sending heavy shivers up my spine. I weakly opened my eyes, groaning as I came back to consciousness as they took a few moments to adjust to the darkness that surrounded me; the only light in the room came from the torch outside my cell. I tried to turn onto my back, crying out in pain suddenly. The slashes through my skin from the whip were intense, my flesh feeling torn and too sensitive to lay on.

Clenching my teeth, I turned onto my stomach and side, resting my head on my arms to cushion it against the stone. I was in so much pain now that I couldn't bring myself to sleep again. But on the plus, I wasn't manacled at least, though that brought me little comfort.

Gingerly, I turned my head towards the cell's bars, trying to see the room beyond. A pitcher of water had been left there for me, just out of my reach where I lay. I tried to crawl closer to the bars, managing to pull myself onto my knees, my entire body burning with pain from the small effort. Awkwardly, I reached for the metal cup that sat beside the water pitcher, grasping it carefully. My hand was shaking, and lifting the pitcher hurt my shoulder, the slashes in my skin feeling as if they were opening up.

There was another wince of pain as I put the pitcher down, my fingers curling around the cold metal of the cup and bringing it to my cracked lips. I was so grateful to have freshwater cascading down my dry, raw throat, feeling refreshed quickly, though not really much better in truth. I downed the entire contents of the cup before setting it on the stone floor and taking a long breath that I hadn't thought I needed.

A sad sigh slipped free as my mind turned Mithras: *How could he do that? How could he just give up like that? Oh, Gods, what's going to happen to him? And what about me? How long will it be now until my uncle decides I'm a liability? How long do I have to live, trapped here in the dark?*

I looked up towards Mithras' cell, a tiny spark of hope inside of me. "M-Mithras," I stuttered from cold, "a-are you there?"

There was nothing but silence.

I tried again, my voice weak and hoarse: "Mithras? Mithras?"

Still nothing.

I closed my eyes, slumping into my arms again, terrifying thoughts running through my head as I lay there, tears wetting my cheeks: *Is he dead? Have they killed him after his coerced confession? Have I just lost someone else I care for?*

Sobs were trying to push their way past my lips, my chest heaving fiercely now. I could feel myself breaking down, the loneliness like a heavy boot crushing me into the dirt with its large heel.

Suddenly, I felt that eerie, familiar presence. The room felt colder, like a ghost had just passed by, the air becoming icy. Unease became dread and I felt cold eyes watching me through the darkness of my prison.

"This must be so distressing for you," he said softly, his voice like terrible, haunting music.

I froze as that coldly even voice spoke, the tone so much like he was a close friend, but darker. I didn't have to look up to know that it was him. I was so scared of him, but I tried to hide it, not wanting to let him see my weakness.

He continued, analysing me: "You are the most beautiful woman in all of Aldegaad, considered a treasure by all those around you; descendant of the Great Heroine of High-Realm – Leander Idona Aldrich the First – your namesake."

I slowly glanced over my shoulder as I heard him stand from the bed, trembling in fear at his gaze. I saw him move, a black shape in my vision, haunting and truly evil.

"Now look at you," he said, standing only a few feet from me, "imprisoned by your own uncle, stripped of your rights and abandoned in the dark," he smirked icily. "With me."

I still didn't answer, trying not to pass out from pain again as I felt him moving closer.

"A pity," he remarked, almost to himself, "you held such promise as Aldegaad's next ruler. Yet, now you cannot even gain the respect of your jailors; jailors who intend such dark depravities as they look upon your young, vulnerable shape."

I managed to push myself onto my knees, turning gingerly to him. He was standing there before the bed, his hands hidden in his sleeves, arms crossed firmly before his chest. I couldn't really see his face through the shadows of his cowl, my memory of him and my imagination filling in the gaps.

I sucked in a shaky breath as I stared at him, my heart feeling as if it were in a vice, my chest hurting like it was breaking from within. I couldn't begin to imagine how I must have looked to him, beaten and broken as I was. I wondered if it amused him, or if he was just beyond such things.

"You," I croaked softly, feeling my eyes widening as I met his gaze. "You were at the Citadel when the Scourge attacked us."

I saw the ghostly flicker of movement beneath the cowl that indicated a smile: "I was, yes."

"And you were there when we escaped from Arvon."

"Was I?" he sounded like he was smirking.

I gulped back: "And at Averet. You were the one Fawkner and the mercenaries kidnapped me for. It was you... It's *always* been you..."

"Poor girl," he chuckled. "Did the guards hit you too hard? Has your memory been affected by their abuse?"

I cringed back as I stared up at him: "Who are you?"

"I could say that I am your Guardian Angel," the Shadow Lord walked slowly to my right, pausing there and meeting my gaze again, "however, I doubt that you would believe that I am either of those things."

"You're right," I agreed. "I wouldn't believe that."

"*What* I am is a Shadow Lord," the cloaked and hooded figure told me in a way that gave me no more information than I already knew. "A sorcerer of great and unimaginable dark power."

"From the Shadow Age," I nodded slowly.

The Shadow Lord cracked a small smile and nodded, mildly impressed. "You know your history."

"Yes," I confirmed quietly. "How could I not?"

The Shadow Lord agreed: "Of course. Eighteen years of being told how much like your ancestor you are would ensure that," he considered that for a moment then turned to me evenly, studying my face: "Did you know that you look *exactly* like my old enemy?"

I frowned: "Your old enemy?"

He nodded slowly, moving to stand before me again, his green eyes gleaming in what little light there was. "You know her by so many names," he regarded me coldly, speaking plainly. "I called her Princess, just as I do you."

"L-Leander?" I stuttered. "You *knew* Leander the First?"

He nodded. "I must say that the resemblance is remarkable. Uncanny in fact."

I felt even more uncomfortable, not liking the way this sinister man was staring at me. I struggled to my feet, swaying unsteadily and wincing with the tearing pain in my hips, back and shoulders; just waiting for my body to give out and collapse beneath me.

He moved towards me, his facial features a little clearer to me now that I could see beneath his cowl. I cringed at his nearness to me, feeling even more trapped.

"I had almost forgotten her beauty in all the centuries it has taken me to return to High-Realm," he considered as he mimicked running a hand over me as if to stroke my hair and face.

"I'm... I'm not... I'm not her," I stuttered uneasily, feeling so unnerved by this.

The Shadow Lord moved around me, studying me as he did so. "Only in appearance and legacy are you and she alike," he stated, then observed: "I can't help but notice the absence of your pendant."

I felt a sudden flicker of panic rush through me, forcing myself to swiftly try to hide it.

"I... uh... I don't know what you're talking about," I lied.

The Shadow Lord smiled coldly, recognising the lie instantly: "Yes, you do. You possess one of the thirteen Dragon Pendants, which were forged several millennia ago. When you are in danger it protects you with powerful warding magic and calls a dragon to your aid; a dragon that hatched only a few months ago."

I glanced over my shoulder at him. "How do you...?"

"I know everything," he spoke with power, not arrogance, evil to his core. "I can watch you whenever and however I choose. Just as I did the night my order murdered your parents."

Violent rage burst out of me and I swung around. I threw a punch right at his grey skinned, skull-like face, his form evaporating into black mist as I nearly connected, making me stagger forward and fall towards the wall. I quickly flung my hands out in front of me to stop myself from hitting the stone, pressing my palms there and looking over my shoulder as a laugh sounded.

The Shadow Lord stood behind me, seeming as solid as the wall, the last of the shadowy wisps coming together to finish forming his visage.

"Do you really think you can harm me, girl?" he asked evenly. "I am no creature of flesh and blood like you. I am like unto a god."

"You're no god," I turned around and faced him, forcing myself to be strong, bracing myself against the wall. "A god doesn't need others to do his dirty work for him."

The Shadow Lord studied me again, considering me as if I were some great oddity: "Hm, you are a brave one, despite your meekness. Your strength lies in your will and heart, not your limbs. But believe me, if I could, I might snap them like twigs for no greater purpose..." he flashed me a dark smile, "...than to hear you scream."

I felt a new rush of fear at the wishful threat that had just been delivered to me. I stared at him nervously, a few heavy breaths slipping from my lips as I pressed my back against the wall in some vain effort to evade him.

He smiled cruelly: "Then again, that may come soon enough after tomorrow's festivities."

I raised a worried eyebrow at him. "What do you mean by *"festivities"*?"

He stood over me, smirking: "The Regent plans to execute the Knight tomorrow at noon. He will be tried for treason and the death penalty will be reinstituted in Aldegaad after so many centuries."

"No... They... they can't..." I gasped, shaking head, my voice nearly a whisper.

"They will behead him," the Shadow Lord said as I slumped to the floor. "They will murder him right in front of you, and you will scream as yet another of your loved ones is taken into the Beyond."

I chewed on my bottom lip, desperately trying to think of what to do.

"You may try to save him," the monster said, whispering in the dark at me, "but I promise you this: no matter what is done, Mithras *will* die. It is unavoidable."

"No," I shook my head, fighting back tears. "No, I... I can't let them kill him. He's innocent."

"Guilty men will always condemn innocent ones for their own crimes," he remarked as though he were a philosopher. "It is in their nature."

I sighed, closing my eyes. He was a monster and a creature of great and terrible evil, but that didn't make him any less right. I knew what Fane was like and that a man's life was less precious to him than gold. Murdering Mithras by claiming him to have committed high treason was not beyond his devious and deceptive mind.

"You are no safer than the Knight," he said softly, causing me to slowly turn my gaze back to him.

"They're going to kill me too?" I stared at him in fear, guessing his meaning.

He nodded, moving slowly towards me, his black robes flowing with him. He stood over me, some six or seven inches extra height compared to my stature if I were standing, an impressive shade in the dark.

"Yes," the Shadow Lord nodded slowly. "Against my wishes and our agreement, your treacherous uncle plans your demise."

I was almost afraid to ask: "H-how?"

"Secretly," was his chilling reply. "The Knight-Commander plans to violate you first, to take your maidenhood and allow his most loyal men to have their fill of your unwilling touch."

I cringed, feeling sick.

"Then," he said, moving to stand behind me, my body frozen in place as I listened fearfully, "when you can take no more, when your body lies broken and your spirit spent, and when only tears remain to you, Tavish will wrap his fingers around your throat. Then, he need only squeeze for a few short moments and... you are no more."

I trembled, whimpering as he moved past me with the sweeping rustle of his robes.

"The Knight will be executed in public to gain the nation's favour, while you are secretly murdered, leaving your uncle to say you died from an illness or your wounds," he turned to me, our eyes meeting. "And so, your uncle – the next in line to the throne – becomes King of Aldegaad and realises his plans to destroy Ivansten."

"Why are you telling me this?" I asked in a tiny whisper, glancing up at him from the floor.

"Because," he said evenly, "I have no desire to see you die in these cells. You are of far greater use to me alive."

"Then, what do I do?" I begged softly, fearful and confused by his willingness to help me.

"Call to the guards," he instructed me. "Have them take you to your uncle where he now eats with his co-conspirators. Bargain for your lives. It is the only way to save yourself and the Knight from certain death."

"Bargaining for our lives could mean giving him everything," I pointed out uneasily. "He could still kill us no matter what. Besides, I don't have anything he wants."

"He does not realise your true value," the Shadow Lord advised me. "The young princess rescued from those who destroyed Arvon and murdered most of the royal family, rises to become Queen of Aldegaad. He would still command everything as Regent and you would be but a puppet, merely a figurehead. Yet, at least you could save your friend... and yourself."

I drew in a shaky, sharp breath: "It's wrong..."

"What choice do you have? At least if you do this there is a chance to contact your companions and escape the city."

I hadn't even thought of that. He was right. *I never thought I would ever agree with a Shadow Lord...*

"Alright," I nodded my agreement. "If you think this will work, then I'll do it."

I saw a smile form on his thin, pale, grey lips and I felt a sickening surge rush through me.

"Go," he gestured with one long, bony finger towards the bars. "Call to them."

Feeling strangely compelled to listen, I got to my feet, turned and grasped the bars, bracing myself against them as the pain from my wounds screamed at me again.

"Guards!" I shouted, waking the other prisoners, their grumbling softly echoing from their cells. "Guards!"

In only a few moments the door was opened, and two armoured guards walked in, their hands ready at their swords as if they were expecting trouble.

"What do you want, prisoner?" one demanded icily, glaring at me as if I had committed some truly horrific crime.

"I want to see the Regent," I answered, trying to be as strong in my voice as I could. "I want... I want to make a deal with him."

I am going to regret this...

Chapter Four
Deal with a Devil

The guards dragged me by my arms at a hurried pace through the corridors, my hands bound behind my back. I tried not to struggle as they forced me forward through the dark underbelly of the palace, but it was hard not to while knowing all that I did and still feeling such strong pain. My eyesight had been restricted by a coarse blindfold to stop me from seeing the way out just in case I was sent back in. It seemed like such a stupid practice to me, but I didn't dare protest.

I couldn't tell if the Shadow Lord was with me now, wondering if he had the power of invisibility so the guards didn't see him, but it seemed like it was possible. My feelings on him were mixed suddenly. Was he an ally in this, or – more likely – just trying to manipulate the situation for his own gain? Either way, I had no choice but to do as he had said. Especially if I wanted to stay alive.

The cold stone floor suddenly changed and I felt steps under my bare feet, the guards' armour clanking around me as they forced me upwards into the unknown. I heard a door open ahead of me with a resounding creak, and the coarse stone became smooth marble, the air smelling and feeling cleaner.

We were in the palace now; I could only imagine the white and gold marble grandeur around me, my temporary blindness leaving me with only my memories of the place I had visited so often as a child.

They led me along a short corridor, then out into a much larger one. We turned left and I felt carpet under my feet, knowing immediately that this was the main hall as we began heading upward. There were more stairs, much larger and wider this time, my legs struggling to keep up with the guards' broader strides. I counted thirty steps before we were at the top, walking swiftly through a vast space towards the sounds of laughing voices.

We passed through large doors that creaked deeply as they were opened, the guards turning me left as I had expected and passing through the columns that I knew - even while I was blinded - surrounded the throne room, the thrones set on the dais at its far end. I felt the closeness of another archway above me, the guards bringing me into the comforting warmth of the banquet hall.

We came to a stop here, the voices ceasing immediately, and all was silence. I froze in place, unable to see anything, my eyes so effectively pinned shut by the blindfold. I swallowed hard.

"Guard?" my uncle's voice echoed lowly through the room from ahead of me. "Why have you brought this prisoner here?"

"With all due respect, Regent," the guard said earnestly, "she says she wishes to make a deal with you."

I felt a hard lump forming in the back of my throat. I couldn't tell what my uncle was thinking in the silence that followed the guard's words, wondering if this quietness was just to torment me or if it truly denoted tangible thought, something I never took him to possess.

"You can go, gentlemen," Fane authorised them evenly. "I will attend to her."

"As you command, my Lord," the guard said and I felt him and the other man turn away, the doors shutting behind me a few moments later.

I stood still, shaking from cold, humiliation and worry. No one moved towards me, no one spoke, all of them leaving me afraid. I felt like I had been put on display by the guards like a slave at an auction in the Blackfelds and left there in what little clothing I had, completely helpless against the people who now stared me down, gawking at me as if I were some strange oddity.

"Well now," I heard Fane state in a mocking tone, "it seems that our *guest* has finally decided that the cells are too much for her to endure after all."

Laughter ripped through the air and I cringed at it, feeling it like the whip wounds in my skin. I couldn't tell how many people were there, only that they had to be on Fane's side to act this way.

"So, Leander, my dear niece," Fane mewed, "what can I do for you?"

I hesitated, too afraid to speak, the blindfold making me very anxious and the restraints making me more so as I twisted my wrists behind me.

"Knight-Commander," Fane called out evenly across the room, "would you be so kind as to remove the girl's blindfold? I would see her eyes while we speak."

I heard movement, freezing in place for a moment as the sound of heavy boots reached my ears. I flinched violently as hands grabbed at me, pulling me closer to their owner, my heart pounding like a rabbit's foot. The hands were at my head in moments and I felt the pressure of the blindfold release as it fell away, finally freeing my sight as I squinted against the sudden light that filled my gaze.

Slowly, my vision cleared, and I could see again, taking in the details of the room at a glance. Like most of the palace, the banquet hall was dressed in the blue tapestries and banners so common in Aldegaadian houses of nobility; the walls made of white marble and trimmed in gold. Before me was a long table with two shorter tables set in parallel at its ends, forming a squared off U shape, every seat there occupied by a traitor.

I gazed around at the faces of the nobles sitting there, all of them familiar to me. I knew them from the countless balls and galas I had attended here in Aneuran as well as in Arvon and seeing them made me sick.

I cringed as soon as I saw Baron Henry Emerton, his flabby jowls covered in the ruins of meat he had been stuffing into his face, his fat belly bunching out from beneath the table. His eyes were roving my body, taking in my scant appearance with an air of depraved lust so horrid it almost made a stench.

On my right I recognised Renton and Angora Seward, both white haired and dressed in blue and gold finery, their snobbery like stale air. Their son, Tibain, sat with them, a smarmy grin locked on his young, admittedly handsome face, his eyes unflinchingly focused on my scantily clad shape more ardently than the Baron's. I even more visibly cringed.

In the centre of the gathering of nobles were my own family; Patrice wearing her hair back and long across her shoulders, and Fane sitting beside her, a gold chain around his neck, his clothing of fine blue, gold and black velvet. My cousin, Farah, sat at his father's left side. His clean-shaven face was less condemning than the others that surrounded me, but that didn't mean anything.

By my count there were five of the noble houses of major influence in Aldegaad here as well as three of the lesser ones – meaning Emerton and two others. It was staggering to really understand the true treachery of our nation's nobility and it disgusted me.

Is this what my family stood for? Is this our legacy? How pathetic.

"Now then, Leander," Fane regarded me evenly, trying to appear kind, "what is it that you have come to ask of me?"

I decided to be a little stubborn at first.

"Where's Mithras?" I demanded in a small, but defiant voice.

"What concern is that of yours?" my uncle asked.

"Just tell me where he is. I want to know that he's safe," I murmured.

"He's in a cell in the deepest section of the dungeons," was his response. "He's awaiting his public execution tomorrow."

"No! You can't!" I cried out before I could stop myself. "He's innocent!"

"This means nothing to them, girl," that cold voice that had whispered to me in the dark spoke evenly.

I turned slowly to my right to see the deep shadows of one of the room's corners pulling together and forming a figure. *He* stepped forward, his shape solidifying as if it were water becoming ice, his robes flowing as he moved with unnatural grace. His cold, glowing green eyes stared at me as he passed to stand behind my uncle, his hands knitted together against his stomach.

"Innocence means little to the truly guilty," he stated, rewording what he had said earlier, "Especially if they can foist their guilt on another, in this case, your protector and yourself."

"I'm surprised to see you, my Lord," Fane regarded the figure respectfully, but with mild contempt that he tried to hide.

"Do not be, Regent," the Shadow Lord spoke purposefully, his eyes locked on me, "I promised you my aid in your endeavours, and so I continue to gift it to you."

"You're working with the Shadow Lord?!" I exclaimed, staring in horror at my uncle as Tavish held my shoulders firmly. "Uncle Fane, how could you?!"

"It is an alliance of necessity, Leander!" Fane snapped, standing up from his seat and glaring at me. "I am doing what I *must* to defend our people!"

"You only defend yourself!" I retorted angrily, trying to break free of Tavish's hold. "How can you be so willing to give into the demands of a monster like him?!"

"I will do whatever is necessary to gain the throne and safeguard our great nation."

"But Uncle Aric..."

"Aric!" Fane roared, rounding the table and closing in on me bitterly. "Let me tell you something about Aric and Ewan! They were weak men determined to give our sovereignty to the Ivanstenian dogs! They conspired to place a pathetic child on the throne! How did they ever plan to ensure the best interests of Aldegaad if their heir was a mewling little adolescent girl?!"

"They chose me because I'm not a power-hungry traitor like you!"

I cried out in pain as I heard the hard slap of skin hitting skin, my ears vibrating from the impact. I turned my gaze to the floor swiftly and involuntarily, my left cheek hurting even more than it already had been.

Tavish seized me by my hair and pulled my head back, forcing me to face my uncle now. Our eyes met and my chest heaved beneath my tattered clothes, my wrists twisting behind my back as the ropes cut into them with burning tightness.

"You test me, girl," Fane hissed down at me, his eyes full of silent rage. "Do not speak poorly of your betters. *I* am the ruler of Aldegaad now. Not you."

"You think locking me up makes you a king?" I scoffed at him, astounded. "You really *are* an idiot."

Another growl of rage and I was slapped again, my cheek feeling like it could tear open and bleed if he hit me any harder.

He smirked at me cruelly, yet knowingly: "It does after you die from the wounds you received while being held by Mithras and his accomplices."

I couldn't hold back the fear anymore, trembling as my uncle confirmed the Shadow Lord's deductions. Images of that terrible fate swept through my thoughts, trapping me in their swell like the tides would by the rocks of the shore, my stomach churning near to vomiting in response.

"My Lord Fane," the Shadow Lord growled lowly from the shadows in which he stood, "you promised that you would give me the girl for my own ends. *That* was the deal you made with me to gain the necessary powers to overthrow your brothers, and take command of Aldegaad."

Fane turned to him with a snide expression: "You have no real power here, daemon. You are naught but a ghost in our world, an inconsequential and immaterial being; for all rights *impotent*."

I worried that my uncle was about to be slain with that same supernatural fire the Shadow Lord had used at Averet, but nothing happened. The hooded figure just glared from beneath his cowl, his green eyes blazing with energy, his mouth set into a hard line.

"She is worth more alive than dead, Fane," the Shadow Lord hissed warningly. "Can you not see past your petty power play for one moment and recognise that?"

Is he actually pleading for my life? I wondered.

"Well, I suppose that's what she's come to discuss with me," Fane turned his eyes to me slowly, staring at me coldly. "You don't want to die. Do you, girl?"

I shook my head, holding back tears. "N-no. No, I don't."

"But what could you offer me?" Fane considered, raising a hand to stroke his beard in thought. "You have nothing I desire."

"W-what about me?" I suggested, hating myself for even saying it. "I... I can offer... myself."

He raised a curious eyebrow. "Yourself?"

I tried to speak evenly: "You want the people to side with you, right?"

He nodded but didn't speak.

"They already think you've saved me," I reasoned, "and they're probably expecting me to take the throne now anyway."

"I suppose," he wasn't happy hearing that.

I shrugged, the ropes really hurting my wrists and my shoulders aching from their unnatural position: "Use me to win them over to you. Make me a public figure for them to see," the words tasted bitter in my mouth despite my reluctance. "Make... make me Queen."

He frowned, but he was curious: "Place *you* on the throne? Why would I do that?"

"Think of what she's saying," the Shadow Lord spoke up, now at my right shoulder. "Your people are looking for a leader and you have the heir to the throne before you. Making her Queen doesn't mean giving *her* control of the kingdom."

"Yes," Fane smiled to himself. "Yes, she's Queen only in appearance and name, but *I* am the ruler."

"Leander cannot be Queen until her twenty-first year," Patrice spoke up from where she sat, her eyes locked on me coldly. "That means that even if she were to take the throne a Regent is still required, my love."

"It does indeed," Fane agreed, turning to me sternly. "But how do I ensure your loyalty, Leander? How do I know that you will do as I tell you?"

I shrugged again, my voice shaking as I spoke: "Because you'll kill me otherwise."

Fane nodded slowly. "True. But what more do you want?"

I looked down at my toes reluctantly: "I want you to spare Mithras. I want you to let him live. If you do, then I will serve as Queen under your command, uncle."

He was musing carefully over this: "Still, I'm not certain that this is enough," he stated with a frown. "After all, I don't trust you, my girl. We need a way to control you..."

"A marriage," Patrice suggested, her eyes alight with a plan. "We have her marry someone to stand as Duke of Aneuran, someone who can keep her in line and under our control."

I cringed, feeling hot tears fighting my resolve. What they were suggesting was against everything in me, this deal with a devil getting worse and worse than I had thought it would with each passing moment.

"Yes," Fane smiled victoriously down at me. "A marriage would be just the right thing. But who to gift you to...?"

I didn't need to guess what was coming next.

"My son," Angora Seward stated, standing and setting her hands on Tibain's broad shoulders. "He would make an excellent choice, my Lord Regent. And he has held a long attraction for the Princess."

"What say you, Tibain?" Fane turned to the young man. "Would you do this?"

"Of course," Tibain smirked at me, undressing me with his eyes. "I have long desired to place her into the marriage bed. I could desire no finer wife, nor higher a calling, my Lord Regent."

I cringed, fighting the bile rising in my throat and the tears choking my eyes.

"And what say you, Leander?" Fane rounded on me again, his eyes burning through me. "Will you marry Tibain and be Queen of Aldegaad under *my* regency?"

I stared at him, bewildered by what he was saying. No matter what I did I was going to be tortured and punished, even if I agreed.

"I'll remind you," Fane said, placing one hand under my chin and making me face him, "that if you refuse, then Mithras *will* be executed, and you *will* die *screaming*. Marriage or death; it is your choice, Leander."

I knew what Tibain would put me through once we were wed, and that scared me more than the other option. No matter my decision either way it would be the same fate; only one meant my death would come sooner.

Unable to hold back anymore, I let my head drop as tears found their way to freedom. *At least if I agree I might be able to do something to protect the people from this treachery. Even if it costs me my life.*

"I'll... I'll do it," I whispered sadly. "I'll marry Tibain and be your Queen. As long as you spare Mithras."

"Consider him spared," Fane pledged, then gestured for the guards at the doors. "Take the Princess and have her cleaned up and given clothing more befitting a woman of her standing. Then, take her to quarters and set up a day and night guard just to be safe," he turned back to me, tilting my face up again to stare into my eyes: "We can't risk our future Queen becoming the target of assassins. Now can we?"

* * * * *

Once I was attended to by servants and a physician, then dressed in a teal, long sleeved dress and a dark blue velvet over dress identical to my usual style, I was brought to the far end of the west wing. Tavish forced me through into a beautiful gold trimmed, blue walled room. The floor was made of the same perfect white marble, blue and gold carpets covering the central area where the large oaken four poster bed sat.

Tavish shoved me forward, letting go of my arm so that I staggered and fell to the floor. I crumpled there, turning around and looking up at him, breathing heavily.

"Just because the Regent has decided to give you some basic rights, do not believe for one moment that you deserve much, girl," he told me harshly, smirking down at me. "You're still just a prisoner to me."

We stared at each other for a few more moments, then the Knight-Commander turned and made for the door. I didn't take my eyes from him, feeling my body tremble as rage and fear bubbled up inside me.

"I will have some food sent for you, Princess," he said with the mocking ghost of respect. "Do not try to escape these rooms. If you do, Ser Mithras' life is forfeit and you will receive the treatment that you have so desperately wished to avoid."

He paused, letting his eyes run over the length of my shaking body. I sucked in a worried breath, staring at him where I lay, trembling at the thought of what he was suggesting while building strength from my anger.

"Touch me," I hissed at him threateningly, trying to regain some power here, "and you'll wish you had never joined with my treacherous uncle."

"Watch your pretty little tongue," he delivered his own threat in kind to me, "lest you learn the true pain of which men are capable of gifting you."

I let out a tiny whimper that I immediately wished I could have hidden.

Tavish sneered cruelly at me, his eyes victorious as he saw that he had succeeded in scaring me. He turned on his heel and strode out of the room, his blue cloak flowing majestically behind him. He nodded to the two guards that were standing outside, then continued down the hall as they shut the doors, sealing me in. I heard the locks click heavily and I was suddenly all alone in the lamp light of my new palatial prison.

I couldn't move at first, stunned into paralysis. The threats had been so much that my heart and mind had nearly fled from me into oblivion. But, slowly, I got to my feet, the long velvet folds of my gowns straightening to hang around me as I looked at the room, trying to decide what I was to do next. I could only take stock of everything there, studying the details of my surroundings and memorising them in some sort of hope that I could find a way out of this.

The windows were behind me, opposite the door and facing out over the ocean below. All that I could see was a dark expanse below another lesser one that was the sky. The vastness of it all was bewildering and nothing like the view of the Nartarn'lath Mountains that I'd had out of my own window back in Castle Arvon.

Set before the windows nearer the bed was an oaken desk and a cushioned chair; parchment paper piled up in one corner along with ink and quill pens for writing. Along the wall opposite the bed was the door leading into the bathroom, a tall, gold trimmed, oak wardrobe set beside it. Next to the four-poster bed were two night tables, identical to the desk and the wardrobe, a lamp lit with its flame on the one nearest the window.

The bed was clothed in deep blue covers with a fur blanket folded up at the foot, everything on it made of the finest silks available in Aldegaad. Deep blue velvet curtains hung around it, pulled together with golden velvet ropes to allow me easy access to the bed.

As if under some sort of spell, I moved to the bed and slumped down onto it. I lay my head in the pillows, drawing my knees up and burying my face into my elbows. I started to cry, my heart hurting in my chest as I began to truly comprehend what I had agreed to.

"What have I done?" I sobbed to myself, closing my eyes as tears rolled down my cheeks.

I couldn't breathe, my lungs were filling and emptying so quickly. My chest was hurting, and my head was swimming as I became dizzy, the bed all that kept me from collapsing to the floor. I started wishing to pass out, but I wasn't granted such a small hope as that.

The unlocking of the doors startled me, drawing me to look up just as they opened. I cringed in despair as Tibain walked in, the door shutting behind him as his grey eyes locked onto me. A harsh smile formed on his face, his hands clasped behind his back, his blue tunic tied around the waist with his belt.

Oh my gods. What does he want with me now?

"Leander," he smirked, striding towards me casually, his eyes locked on my face, "I can't tell you how pleased I am with your decision tonight."

He reached the bed and I threw myself off it, standing up swiftly, my bare feet smashing against the carpeted floor as I moved. I stared at him through my dark waves, my heart pounding and my breath rushing. I wouldn't let him touch me if I could help it.

Tibain gave me a curious expression, still smirking as he moved around the bed towards me.

"Come now, my love," he said in a vain attempt to appear romantic, "you shouldn't be acting so childish."

"Childish?!" I exclaimed in disbelief. "You wanted to rape me! You were going to!"

"That's all in the past," he said, getting closer to me, his eyes darting to my chest momentarily. "Besides, we're betrothed now, my love..."

"Don't call me that," I grumbled, trying to back away from him.

"Don't call you what?" he asked me, knowing full well what I meant.

For a moment I could only stare at the sword at his belt. I started wondering if I could snatch it from him and put the blade to his throat. I would do whatever I could to force him away from me, but I knew that I couldn't manage to reach it before he would have me pinned.

I looked up at him, realising that he was moving me slowly backwards towards the bed: "I'm not your love. It's offensive hearing you call me that."

He scowled a little, but kept smiling: "Really? And are you going to refuse me your touch?"

I tried to pull away, but he quickly seized me by both wrists and forced me down onto the bed. I struggled violently underneath him, desperately trying to squirm free. He twisted my arms above my head, causing me to cry out in pain as he brought his face close to mine.

"You're going to show me some respect, Leander," he hissed as he stared down at me, pinning my legs beneath his.

"I won't show or give you anything!" I cried out, turning my fear into an angry snarl.

"As if you have a choice anymore, you stupid little bitch," he hissed cruelly, dropping his act. "You're mine in three days, and while I have promised my parents that I will now wait to consummate our marriage with you until our wedding night, I am all too happy..."

I gasped and sobbed, struggling as he reached to my skirts and started lifting them as he pinned my wrists together with one large hand. I felt the roughness of his skin on my soft inner thigh, whimpering fearfully.

He smirked cruelly at me, lust burning in his pale eyes: "... to find other things I can do."

"No," I whimpered, tears running down my cheeks as he edged his fingers up my leg slowly, tauntingly. "Please... please don't..."

Suddenly, the door opened again and we both looked up. I had never been so relieved to see my cousin in my life, Farah's dark blue eyes taking in the scene before him with a heavy frown of disapproval.

"Tibain," Farah scolded lowly. "What are you doing in here?"

Tibain – looking like a guilty child trying to steal a cookie – straightened up, withdrew his hand from my leg and faced my cousin. I breathed a heavy sigh, relieved as he released my wrists.

"I am enjoying a tender moment with the woman I am to marry, my Liege," came the arrogant noble's response.

"A tender moment?" Farah queried dubiously. "Is that what you call it? Because, to me, it seems that you are violating and frightening her."

"I –"

"Regardless of what my father has decreed and of the agreement that has been entered upon in regard to Leander's betrothal," Farah said warningly, "I am *still* her cousin and she *is* under *my* protection. If you think that you can take her virtue from her before you are wed, then I will see to it that you do not reach your wedding day. Do I make myself clear, Tibain?"

I glanced between the two men uneasily, lying still on the bed. Tibain was looking at Farah worriedly, his eyes flicking between the two of us, his face paling two shades of grey. It was obvious that he was afraid of Farah, my cousin stern and refusing to back down, three times the warrior Tibain was.

At last, Tibain stood from the bed and nodded to Farah. "My apologies, your Highness," he bowed his head to the man respectfully. "I... uh... I will take my leave."

Farah just nodded, his arms crossed as I sat up and drew my knees to my chest, both of us watching Tibain leave. A servant stood in the doorway with a tray of food, stepping aside as my disgusting excuse for an intended stormed out in frustration.

"Put the tray on the sideboard," Farah directed the woman, "then go attend to your other duties. I would speak with my cousin in private."

The woman obeyed without hesitation, then hurried from the room, the doors shutting behind her.

Farah turned to me, his expression softer, though he still frowned. "Are you alright, Leander?"

I stared at him in shock, then nodded meekly.

"He didn't hurt you, did he?" he asked.

I shrugged, rubbing my wrists in turn: "Not really."

"Good," he nodded, turning his gaze towards the windows quietly. "I'm glad."

I studied him for a few moments, grateful for his timely intervention, but confused by his willingness to keep me prisoner.

"I brought you some food," he said, gesturing to the tray, then meeting my gaze. "Tavish was planning on giving you the same as if you were in the prisons, but I said you should be fed better. After all, you must be hungry."

Hesitantly, I nodded, slipping from the bed and crossing to where he stood. I lifted the lid off the plate, studying the food beneath: an assortment of vegetables with roasted lamb and a crust of bread. There was a cup and some water in a wooden pitcher as well as metal cutlery with it.

"I will let you eat in peace," he said, meaning to go, though he was hesitant.

I ran a hand through my hair, brushing it past my left ear and over my shoulder as I turned to Farah.

"How can you let your father do this to me?" I looked up at him, feeling tears threatening me again. "Does our cousinly relationship mean nothing to you?"

"I stand by my father, Leander," he replied, turning back to me with a hint of sadness behind that mask of conviction he wore. "Blood is blood, and my loyalty is to my family."

"How can you say that? You've watched your father destroy most of our family and you've done nothing to stop him."

"It isn't my place."

I gasped angrily. "Where's your voice in this, Farah? You can get him to stop this, to let Mithras and I go..."

"I can't," he said, clearly upset, staring out the windows. "Do not ask me for this, cousin."

"He's your father," I tried. "He'll listen to you."

"Do you think I haven't tried already?" he spun around, anger and hurt in his eyes. "Do you think I'm alright with knowing that my father has killed both of my aunts and uncles; that he plans to rule Aldegaad and now threatens you, my little cousin?"

He came right up to me so fast that I staggered back, bracing my hands against the edge of the desk as I looked up at him. For a moment I worried that he was going to hurt me, but he pulled back, staring at me with saddened eyes.

"When first I heard my father's plans, I did everything I could to prevent them," he confessed sadly. "I overheard him talking in his study a year ago with that man in the black cowl."

"The Shadow Lord," I said softly.

"Yes. He gave father the means to murder Uncle Ewan and Aunt Caralyn, and to take the throne from Uncle Aric; for a price."

"Me," I said with a solemn nod. "The Shadow Lord wants me."

Farah nodded gravely: "I don't know why, but yes. He never even told father, saying only that you were vital to his plans. And now that father has betrayed him, I dread to think what he will do to us."

"Because Uncle Fane won't give me up," I murmured. "He doesn't give up what he sees as his."

"Exactly. I know what he planned to do to you, and I spoke up against it," he explained. "Father beat me back into my place and made it clear that if I spoke against him again that he would make me watch them kill you. I couldn't bear to see that."

I was shocked into silence. My cousin had tried to stop this already and failed. He had stepped back from helping me only to protect me. Suddenly I felt less alone.

"I really am sorry, Leander," he said to me honestly. "I wish I could help you, but I can't if it costs you your life. I'm so, so sorry."

I just nodded, feeling tears coming again and cursing them silently.

Farah walked to the door and opened it, pausing as he turned back to me. "I'll check in on you as often as I can, little cousin," he said softly. "Please, get as much rest as you can. Now that the wedding has been set for three days' time you really need to have as much strength for it as you can muster."

"Farah," I called as he turned to leave, drawing his gaze back to me. "Thank you."

He nodded then left me alone, the door being sealed and locked again.

I turned back to my food, not really feeling very hungry anymore.

Why would I be now that I know my fate? I wondered grimly, turning my gaze to look out of the windows at the cold, dark night.

I decided to try to sleep, but I found it impossible. Sleep escaped me the same way that freedom did, the thought of what was to happen to me starting to crush down harder than it had a few hours ago. I hadn't bothered to change, lying on the bed in my dress, my legs buried beneath the bedcovers as I tried unsuccessfully to escape waking awareness.

A vast onslaught of thoughts were rushing through my head, choking my mind as I lay there, only one lamp lit now as I found myself needing the light. It was an attempt to find comfort that really wasn't working for me, yet I persisted.

My thoughts turned to Mithras, and I wondered if he was alright, if he had been treated well now that I had agreed to this. But somehow, I doubted that my uncle would have been so kind to him.

He only spared his life to get me to obey him, and my continued obedience is all that keeps my friend alive. I sighed, thinking again of my friends, hoping that they were still out there. *The Guardians will be trying to come up with a plan, but I'm not so sure they will be able to rescue us now. How can they?*

A sound broke me out of my sadness, bringing me to look around the room for its source. I frowned, curiosity touching me as I heard a tapping sound. It was coming from my right and I turned my eyes towards the windows.

The windows? How could someone be at the windows?

I pulled back the covers and set my feet to the floor gingerly. Padding to the windows I tried to trace the sound, moving to the centre most one. I quickly found the latch and pulled the window open, darkness and thick sea air reaching me as I did, my hair blowing around my shoulders. There was nothing out there, only the sheer drop to the roiling black ocean at the base of the cliffs below. I frowned again, wondering if I was hearing things.

Suddenly, there came the rushing of wings and I jumped as a bird flapped up into the room. I staggered backwards as it came to sit on the top of the desk, settling there and bringing its wings down. It was a falcon, its feathers brown and greyish-white, its golden eyes locking onto me as if it knew me. It let out a loud caw, flapping its wings and disturbing the papers that rested there on the desk.

It can't be. I edged towards the bird cautiously, staring at it as I came to recognise its markings.

"Farsight," I asked her softly, "is that you?"

As if to answer me, the falcon called again and raised her wings.

Relief filled me, a tear of joy forming and slipping down my cheek coldly.

"I'm so glad to see you, Farsight," I told her happily, dropping into the chair and reaching out to stroke her head gently. "Is Fawkner out there? Can he see me now?"

She crowed again and I took that as a yes.

"They're trying to rescue me, aren't they?"

Another cry.

I knew that there would be no way that my friends would know of my cruel fate, so I had to work fast before my captors came to check on me. I took a piece of paper from the desk and chose a quill, dipping the pen into the ink and quickly scrawling a message across the page to Fawkner, knowing that it would be he who received the note from his faithful bird.

I picked my words carefully, chewing on my bottom lip as I scrawled the quill, only dipping the pen into the ink a few times before completing my message.

Fawkner,

I hope you get this note and not some guard in the city. I'm being held hostage in the palace's west wing by my uncle and his allies. They were going to execute Mithras for killing the King and Queen, and they plan to murder us both if I don't do what they want.

I've been forced to agree to marry Tibain Seward so that my uncle can take control of the throne. He plans to make me Queen and use me to start a war with Ivansten.

The wedding has been set for three days from tonight.

I hope this reaches you in time. Please, Fawkner! Help me! They have us both under constant guard and I know Tibain is planning on hurting me! Worse still, the Shadow Lord is here! He has made an alliance with my uncle and the other conspirators. He planned all of this.

I don't know if Carden and Tallinn are alright, but I hope they are. I'm so worried about them both.

Please, Fawkner. Help us!

Leander.

I set the quill back in place and rolled up the note, tying it with a ribbon that was in one of the drawers of the desk. I turned to Farsight, holding the scrolled note to her as a new desperation started running through me.

"Farsight, take this to Fawkner," I told her, taking her on my arm and moving to the window. "Make sure he gets it right away. Alright?"

She cawed in response, grasping the note tightly in one of her taloned feet.

I thrust my arm out the window, the falcon launching herself into the air and screeching as she flew up into the sky. She circled once, calling to me as if to tell me not to worry, then flew north, heading towards the cliffs where I knew my friends had been waiting for us to come back.

As I watched the bird fly away gracefully, I hoped that she would succeed and that Fawkner and the others could do something, anything, to help us.

I hope this works. I really do, I thought uneasily.

Chapter Five
Commitment Coerced

I couldn't breathe, my heart thundering hard in my throat and making me want to choke.

I'm doing this to save Mithras. To save both of us. I... I have no choice... Gods, why am I doing this? It's... it's wrong. All I could do as I called up these thoughts was meet my own gaze in the large mirror that stood before me, tensing as I took in the saddened stare of my reflection.

My steel blue eyes were soft and clear, filled with tears beginning their slow rise from my grief and fear. My rounded, oval shaped face was smooth and pale, my skin as imperfect as perfect, my flaws filling me with the only pride I had left. My eyes were encircled with black, my eyelashes darkened and standing out more obviously than before, and my eyelids were dusted in a silvery colouring. My lips were painted a dark crimson, my cheeks blushed in a gentle pink that accented my cheekbones and made my face seem narrower.

The gown was beautiful, there was no doubt. It fit closely around my slender, curvy shape, its neckline plunging to show my throat, collarbones and cleavage. Silvery embroidery coiled around my hips to rest in a slight curl on either side of the part in the middle of the silk dress, flanking it like two serpentine sentinels. Silken white sleeves fit closely around my wrists and reached up the entire length of my arms, the white over dress very much like what I was used to wearing, only more ornate. Long billowing sleeves fell from my elbows over the dress' closer fitted sleeves, reaching to my shins; the shoulders of the gown parted in a slip, but otherwise close fitting to the elbow.

Silver embroidery ran around the scooped collar of the dress, lacing of the same colour holding the front closed over the soft under gown. The two gowns flowed behind me into a long, pooling train of white silk and silvery embroidered designs; graceful and delicate, truly beautiful in their combined outline. Still, regardless of the dress' beauty, I could hardly feel appreciation for it.

I closed my eyes, drew in a shaking breath, then glanced back at the mirror as the women attending me continued fussing with my gowns to ensure perfection. One of the women began settling my hair into place, letting the long strands fall across my back and shoulders while also pulling it away from my face with a silvery clasp. She stepped away and I studied the way my dark auburn locks hung around my shoulders.

She turned to the other woman who was carrying a small oaken box in her hands. The older woman opened the box, revealing a slender, elegant silver circlet; the crown of a princess. She took the small crown delicately in her gnarled hands and turned to me. Carefully, she placed it around my head, the most striking of its designs set over my brow. She turned to a second girl who stood with us, this one carrying a sheer fabric cloth of white colouring.

I couldn't help a tiny whimper escaping as the old handmaiden turned back to me and carefully set the comb attached to the fabric into my hair. With tears in my eyes I watched as she straightened out the veil and let it fall to hang down my back, pooling over the gown's train behind me. The only mercy was that she didn't cover my face beneath the veil, my heart filling with wild and silent panic as she finished her work.

This can't be. I can't be this reflection the mirror shows me. Please, Gods, I don't want this. Not like this... I took in another shaking, scared breath, fighting back my tears as I stared at the frightened young bride that gazed back at me from the mirror.

"Such beauty," the harsh, hard voice spoke from behind me, his black visage moving past the handmaidens to stand at my side. "You make a wonderful bride, Princess."

I glanced up to stare into the mirror, seeing him standing there with me, those inhuman green eyes seeming almost to glow as they burned through me. His gaunt, monstrous, grey face was concealed beneath his crimson rimmed black cowl, but I could see him clearly in the late morning daylight shining through the golden windows of this marble room.

"This... this isn't me," I whispered, fighting back tears, my heart feeling shattered within me. "I'm not ready for such a commitment."

"Of course not," the Shadow Lord agreed, watching my reflection over my left shoulder. "You are barely a woman, a child by so many standards. You have never known love or affection of the kind required for such an act. *How* could you possibly be ready for this?"

I sucked in a shaking breath, trying to find my resolve, twisting my fingers together in front of me nervously.

"Are you trying to plant doubt in my mind?" I asked him softly, my attempt to sound strong a vain one.

"Merely making an observation, your Highness," the Shadow Lord paced slowly to stand on my right, leaning over my shoulder without touching me. "Besides, I do not need to spread doubt when it already lingers within your young heart."

I shook my head, pressing my lips together: "I won't let Mithras die, or my people suffer. If my uncle demands this sacrifice from me... then... how can I refuse?"

"Marrying a man you hate?" he questioned me calmly. "Condemning yourself to the horrors he will inflict upon you for the sake of another? Why?"

"Because it is the right thing to do," I replied with silent, grief filled conviction. "I can't allow my uncle to murder an innocent man whose only crime was protecting me from those who desire my family's kingdom. My life means nothing if I let him die. And even less if I don't try to protect my people."

"So young. So beautiful. So selfless," the Shadow Lord said softly, running one hand over my hair, veil and shoulder as if he meant to touch me.

I shuddered at his incorporeal caress.

"Yet, your heart belongs to another," he murmured, his stare locked squarely on my face, not my reflection. "Can you truly betray the feelings you have for *him*? Can you justify *that* sacrifice?"

I closed my eyes, feeling a tear trickle down my cheek. *Carden…*

He was the one who meant more to me than any other person I had left. He was my friend, my confidant and the one I would give all of my heart to. I had come to know this, but it wasn't until the daemon standing beside me had spoken those words that I truly understood or even acknowledged this. It wouldn't only be a betrayal of my beloved, but of my own heart.

"Your tears speak in greater volumes than your voice ever could," the Shadow Lord told me, smiling cruelly as I opened my eyes again. "You do not wish to go through with this battle any more than you wish to lose your friend. Yet, one *must* occur for the other to be avoided. Either the Knight dies, or you have your freedom and virtue taken by force, and thusly shall never know True Love's embrace."

I felt him moving around me slowly, his arms still folded, his green glowing eyes securely focused on my trembling shape.

"If you go through with this you will be made to endure the greatest travesties of your young life," he expressed in a slow, calm tone as he paced around me purposefully, waving to the handmaidens to leave us. "You cannot allow these deeds to be inflicted upon you."

"I have no choice," I said sadly, my voice shaking as hard as my body was.

"The ceremony is mere minutes away, Princess," he mewed in a coldly sinister tone. "And this will hold only the first and lesser indignity that you will endure. The Kiss will be the proclamation of your body being forfeited to this mewling retch that has the undeserved fortune of being referred to as a lord. Do you imagine that he will be gentle with you, even before such a grand audience?"

I fought back the urge to scream, knowing that this monster was right. Again.

The Shadow Lord continued, pausing to my right after fully circling me, his eyes now set on my face, his visage clear in my peripheral as I stared onwards at my haunted reflection: "And what of tonight?" he asked me darkly. "You will be condemned to his keeping and imprisoned in his chambers alone with him. Do you not imagine what he will force you to do? Does that thought not linger in your unprepared little mind?"

I cringed, squeezing my eyes shut at the thought of his cruel words. I knew *exactly* what he meant; the horror he spoke of already having haunted my sleep for the last three days.

"It is truly *detestable* that your uncle would condemn you to such a fate," he went on softly in my ear, towering above me. "Does he know nothing of familial care and obligations? How can he doom his adolescent niece to such violation?"

"Tibain won't touch me," I retorted, the hard lump in my throat choking me. "I won't let him."

"You do not have your pendant," he reminded me coldly, shedding a horrified chill down my spine. "Your friends are not able to reach you under such heavy guard, and the old knight who you now try to save with this farce can do nothing but sit in his cell and know your fate. You are alone, Princess."

I shuddered as he simulated stroking my face with the back of one grey hand, an unnatural chill seeming to caress me instead of his skin.

"This day you will be robbed of your freedom, your will and your identity," he whispered to me. "This night your virtue and innocence will be destroyed, and you will be reduced to a quivering mess on the marble floor of this palace. Your pain will be unspeakable, your grief and pleas ignored. You will scream against his assaults and he will discard your sobs of agony with a crushing blow to your cheek to silence your voice. You will be broken tonight, Princess Leander. I promise you that much."

I was unable to hold back my tears at the thought of this horrible fate any longer. I couldn't deny that the Shadow Lord was right.

Tibain won't be kind, and he won't be tolerant. He'll force me to do what he wants, beat me down... rape me... And I can't escape him once I'm bound to him through marriage. Even though I will cry against his touch it will be legal for him to force me. Oh gods...

"Be honest with me, girl," he drew my mind back to him with his gentle tone, "are you not afraid?"

I couldn't stop my tears' terrible march, my heart breaking inside me: "I... I am."

I turned my head to him, staring into those supernatural green eyes and the shadows of that sinister cowl, my heart racing and my chest hurting.

"I don't want this," I sobbed softly. "I don't want to go through this, to marry him, to be used by him, to endure my uncle's desires for a needless war... I can't."

He hushed me with false kindness, but it was welcome to me now regardless: "It does not have to be this way, dear, sweet girl."

"It doesn't?" I felt hope fill me.

He nodded: "*I* can give you the choice your uncle has not. *I* can save you from this fate, just as I can save your mentor. All you need do is *surrender* to me, to *willingly* come with me to Gorth'lak, and you shall never be violated in such a detestable way. This I vow."

I stared up at him in horror, trying to comprehend what he was saying to me. If I said yes then this monster got what he wanted, but if I said no then two other monsters got what they wanted. Regardless, I couldn't deny that I was tempted to give in to him if only to spare myself the pain and humiliation yet to come, but it was only for a moment as my own values held firmly again.

"I... I can't," I shook my head fearfully.

His expression turned hard as he stared down at me: "This is your *only* chance to escape the carnal tortures that wretched boy will force upon you this dread night."

"I know that, but I won't give in to you either," I tried to sound strong against him, gathering what anger and strength I could manage, but all I heard in my voice was fear.

"You test my patience, girl," he seethed calmly, folding his arms more firmly this time.

"If you offer damnation for damnation, then I refuse," I replied as powerfully as I could.

"Foolish girl!" the monster roared, the shadows in the room seeming to grow around me as I dropped backwards, half crouching in terror. "I offer you freedom from the greatest torture a woman can face, and you deny me? Does your virtue and innocence mean nothing to you?"

"I guess my honour and the safety of the people I love means more," I responded in a small, but convicted voice. "If I go with you then I can't guarantee any of that. If I stay, it's assured. Besides, my ancestor never gave in to a Shadow Lord. So I won't either."

His eyes narrowed and I was even more terrified of him. I cringed back into the floor, trembling, breathing hard and fast. If I didn't know he was incorporeal I would have feared his fist breaking me, but as it was it was his dark magic that I dreaded and shied away from.

"You have made a terrible mistake," the Shadow Lord hissed icily. "Regardless of your decision you *will* find yourself in Gorth'lak as *my* prisoner. You have only condemned yourself to far *greater* pain and torment than if you had taken my offer."

I nodded slowly, getting to my feet again as I heard the double doors to the room open. I faced the monster, meeting his gaze and literally standing up to him, forcing myself to glare at him with all the strength I had.

"I will *never* surrender to you," I said to him so only we could hear, very aware of the figures striding towards us. "You will have to take me the same way Tibain will tonight: by force."

The Shadow Lord stared back at me with a conviction rivalling my own, a cold, angry sneer curling his thin lips: "If that is your wish, Princess."

"Ah," Fane's voice echoed around the palatial room as the group came towards us, "my Lord."

"Regent," the Shadow Lord turned to him and nodded his head. "I was keeping the bride company."

"Yes," my uncle smiled, his blue eyes taking in my visage as he came to a stop before us. "And what a bride she makes."

"I only look like a bride," I hissed at him. "No matter how you dress me up I am still a prisoner."

Fane moved to stand over me with a cold glare in his icy eyes. He wore his very best clothes along with his ceremonial armour chest and shoulder plates. At his hip was his sword, a royal blue sash crossing from his right shoulder to his left hip, his long hair clasped back to keep his neatly bearded face clear. His blue and gold cloak hung down his back, adding grace to his appearance.

Behind him were Aunt Patrice and my cousin, both regal and well dressed as they stood with Knight-Commander Tavish at their backs. My aunt's sharp eyebrows were raised as she stared at me, her lips pressed together as a cruel smile tugged at the corner of her mouth. But Farah was nothing like his parents. In the blue eyes that were set on my helpless expression I could see the knowledge that what he was witnessing was wrong. I desperately wanted to scream for him to help me, though I knew he couldn't.

"*This* was the choice *you* made, my dear niece," Fane reminded me severely. "I agreed to spare Mithras' life and your own *if* you surrendered yourself to Lord Seward's son and became Queen on your twenty-first year."

I glanced at the Shadow Lord, finding him - in a strangely eerie way - to be my only powerful ally in this room. He stared at me with those haunting eyes as if telling me to speak my mind. And I listened.

I returned my gaze to Fane's harsh face with a new conviction. "And what of tonight?" I asked, fighting the hard lump in my throat. "I won't be permitted the right to consent. Tibain will take me against my will and you know it."

"This is the price with which you have bought your lives," Fane smiled nastily, caressing my cheek and making me shudder in revulsion. "You cannot pick and choose what parts of this you endure, Leander. You will fulfil your duties as Tibain's newly wedded wife, and it does not matter if you scream against him or not. After all, the law is clear that a woman cannot refuse the touch of her husband, even if she wants to. Or, at least it will once I change it to mean such."

"You would do this, Father?" Farah demanded, clearly unable to keep his silence any longer. "You would condemn her to be used by that *bastard* nightly, if not hourly, just to achieve your own ends?"

"Remember your place, Farah!" Fane snapped at his son coldly.

"I will *not* allow this!" Farah retorted and I felt hope rekindle within me. "She's just a girl!"

"Out!" Fane roared. "Get out now! I will hear nothing more of this, Farah! Your cousin has made her choice, now abide by it!"

Farah looked scared, clearly under his father's thumb. He threw me a worried and apologetic gaze, then bowed his head in shame and left the room.

"Now then," Fane turned to me, ignoring the tears streaking my face and tilting my chin so that I had to look at him. "It is nearly time for the wedding. Only one thing remains, Leander."

I looked between the four figures standing over me as the old handmaiden returned, carrying a bouquet of blue, white and purple flowers.

"Knight-Commander," Fane nodded to Tavish, "if you please."

"Of course, my Liege," Tavish bowed his head and turned to me.

As he passed by Patrice and strode towards me, I saw what was in his hand. I recoiled at the rope he carried with him, knowing exactly what he intended.

"No!" I pleaded, turning to my uncle desperately. "Please! You don't have to do this!"

"Guards," Fane called to the two soldiers that had stopped at the door when they entered. "Hold her."

Without question, the two armoured soldiers came to me and reached out for my arms. I fought against them, struggling desperately to pull from their grasps, but my efforts were for nothing. My forearms were seized, my upper arms held firmly, and I was secured between the two men helplessly.

I fought as hard as I could as Tavish approached me, reaching out one hand towards my arms as he unfurled the rope. I struggled in vain, feeling my hands being forced together and the rope begin to twirl around my slender wrists. I closed my eyes and tried to relax, my body still tensing against the horror of this situation.

What bride is bound like this on her wedding day? Why are they being so cruel to me? I opened my eyes, jerking my shoulders against the soldiers, both men keeping me steady as I glared at my uncle.

"Why are you doing this to me?" I demanded quietly, glaring at him. "Why must my wrists be bound?"

"Quite simply, my darling niece, I do not trust you," Fane responded, his hands clasped at the small of his back. "If I leave you unbound you will most likely cause a scene and I cannot allow that in front of the citizenry. It would hurt our position."

"And if the citizenry should learn you have me bound?" I asked in a harsh snarl. "What then, *uncle*?" I spat venom into the last word.

"We have a way to conceal it," he responded, then said lowly and threateningly: "But I am certain that you would not *dare* to reveal such information to the people, my girl. Not when it will risk Mithras' life..." he sneered cruelly, "...*and* your own."

I sighed disconsolately, yanking my hands to my chest as Tavish stepped back with a cold smirk. I studied the ropes with hopelessness, the knots tight and the coiling strands firm. The bouquet was set into my hands and I felt tears burning my eyes, knowing that there was no escape now.

"It is time, Leander," Fane spoke, drawing my teary gaze.

I took in a slow breath to compose myself, bowing my head sadly and nodding. This was it.

Fane led the way with Patrice, Farah following on behind them and in front of me. He kept throwing me worried looks that I acknowledged with sad eyes. We both seemed to be prisoners to our family, only he wasn't the one restrained and bound for doom.

It was strange that I was grateful for the Shadow Lord's presence as he walked beside my right shoulder, his black robes flowing behind him with his gentle pace. His imposing form was the eeriest comfort I had ever known, especially in a place I had once found so familiar and safe, but now no longer.

I threw him a sideways glance, gaining his unnaturally kind gaze. The monster allowed himself a small smile and nodded gently to me as if to reassure me.

We came to the main doors of the palace and I heard them open, looking up through my tears as sunlight flooded the white and gold marble halls. Beyond was an honour guard set waiting for us, some ten knights in their blue cloaks with their silvery armour shining in the morning light.

The knights took up their positions around us and we began the slow walk through the palace courtyard, and across the sea bridge linking the two cliffs of the bay. I threw my gaze left, staring out west at the Crestian Sea and feeling the cold air touching my face, the smell of the sea giving me a moment's comfort.

I couldn't stop myself crying, closing my eyes as I walked, my head down to hide my sorrow filled face. I started thinking of Carden, missing him so deeply and wishing he was here with me. *I would do anything just to see him one last time, to tell him how I really feel. That I love him...*

"My Lord," I heard the Shadow Lord speak, glancing up at him worriedly. "I shall take my leave before the populace sees your group."

"Yes," Fane nodded, stopping at the walkway that led down the hillside. "We cannot allow the people to see us in congress. Will you attend the ceremony?"

"I will be awaiting your arrival," the Shadow Lord responded with a soft nod, then turned to me. "*Enjoy* your wedding day, Princess."

I shuddered against that comment, feeling the bile rising in my throat. The Shadow Lord smiled cruelly at me, then he was nothing more than a deep cloud bank of wispy black shadowy smoke that faded into the wind.

"Come, Leander," Fane's eyes were locked on me sternly as he spoke. "The ceremony begins soon."

Reluctantly, I nodded, feeling Tavish's gauntleted hand close around my right upper arm. He smirked down at me from beneath his greying hair and started leading me after my family.

Soon a heavy shadow fell over me and I opened my eyes to see the mammoth shape of the Aneuran Basilica towering above me, its main doors open and the sound of bells ringing clear in the air. My heart sank and I couldn't hold back my fear or my sobs, struggling a little against Tavish's hard grasp.

The Knight-Commander forced me through the doors, and I was led into the main foyer outside the basilica itself. We stopped here and my uncle turned to my aunt and cousin, the honour guard now standing ready outside.

"Patrice, my beloved," Fane smiled at her, "why don't you and Farah take your seats inside? I shall prepare Leander for her grand entrance."

"Of course, my darling," Patrice responded, kissing him lightly and turning to Farah. "Come, Farah."

The two of them turned towards the doors, Farah pausing and facing me with sadness in his blue eyes.

He leaned close to me and whispered in my ear: "I am so sorry, cousin. Truly, I am."

"I know, Farah," I responded as my tears kept slipping down my cheeks. "I don't blame you."

Farah nodded softly, a tear trickling from his eye as regret plastered his face. He leaned closer to me and kissed me on the cheek, then, hesitantly, pulled back and walked with his mother into the basilica, leaving me alone with Fane and his knights.

I was facing the doors now, my wrists aching from the ropes binding them together. The silken sleeves of my gown were all I had to protect my skin from their bite, but even that wasn't enough to ease my panicking heart.

"Why do you cry, my beautiful niece?" Fane asked me in a mockingly gentle tone as he came up beside me. "You should be happy to be following your sister's path so soon after her own nuptials."

"Aislinn wasn't tied up and forced to marry Sten as I am with Tibain," I responded through my sobs, my chest hurting heavily and making me feel as if my lungs were burning. "I'm no more a true bride than I am free to choose my own fate."

My uncle turned to me, standing over me and staring at my face. I put my eyes down, nearly closing them in an attempt to avoid his gaze. He pressed two fingers under my chin and tilted my face so I had no choice but to meet his stare.

"This," he said to me, "is the fate *you* chose."

"Please, Uncle, don't," I wept, looking up at him, trembling with desperation and fear. "Don't make me go through with this. Please. I'm... I'm so scared."

"That is normal for a young bride," Fane smiled coldly at me, brushing tears roughly from my cheeks with his thumb. "You're apprehensive, I know. But do not fear, child. I will be with you to the altar."

I took in a heavily shaking breath as fresh tears found their way to my eyes: "My father should have been the one to escort me to my betrothed, but you and the Shadow Lord arranged his and Mother's murder. You are a coward..."

His hand suddenly crushed around the back of my neck and I gasped in pain. I fought the urge to scream, knowing that it would only draw attention to me from the people inside the basilica beyond those hard wood doors.

"Watch your tongue, you insolent little brat," Fane hissed at me, tilting my head and shoulders back so that I was struggling to keep my balance. "I am *very* close to silencing your wretched little mouth once and for all. So, do *not* push me."

"You can't hurt me," I reminded him, feeling a new strength from that knowledge. "The people would revolt against you immediately," a small laugh escaped my lips. "I guess you shouldn't have played up my innocence."

"You're right," Fane agreed, releasing my neck and eyeing me for a moment before nodding to Tavish. "I can't hurt *you*, Leander."

Tavish bowed his head and walked to one set of doors to my right. He opened them and two knights dragged a dishevelled figure into the foyer with manacles rattling around his wrists and ankles. He was thrown to his knees, his dark eyes staring up at me in surprise.

"Mithras!" I exclaimed, turning to him.

"Leander?" Mithras stared at me with stunned, wide eyes, his fists resting on his thighs where he knelt.

"What is this?!" I demanded, staring at Fane savagely.

"I thought he would like to see the ceremony," Fane responded, smirking with malicious intent. "You only get married once, after all."

"Married?" Mithras looked up at me with an expression of great shock and horror. "Is that why you are dressed as a bride, child?"

"It was the only way to save you, Mithras," I whispered, sobbing softly.

"Save me?" he frowned.

I took in a grievous breath, struggling against my sobs: "I had to do this, or you would have been executed for treason."

"Who are you marrying?" he asked darkly.

I looked at him through my tears shamefully: "Tibain Seward."

"No, girl, no," Mithras shook his head grievously at me. "You would never allow that filth to touch you in all the years he sought your hand."

"I don't have a choice," I sobbed. "I had to, Mithras. For both our sakes. I'm so, so sorry."

"No!" he roared, the knights holding his shoulders to keep him on his knees. "I swore to your father and uncle that I would protect you to my dying breath, and that is exactly what I will do! Refuse this, Leander! Rescind your pledge now, before it is too late!"

"Knight-Commander," Fane ordered, and with one fluid movement and the scraping of steel on steel, Tavish had his sword in hand, the blade at Mithras' throat.

"No!" I cried out huskily in panic, a knight grabbing my arms and pulling me back firmly when I tried to reach Mithras, dropping the bouquet. "No, don't! Please!"

"This is what your refusal will bear, Leander," Fane turned savagely to me, one hand on the sword at his hip. "Can you live with this?"

I heard Mithras gag, the tears burning my eyes making it hard for me to see him. Still, my gaze was locked on the sword's blade hovering just above his throat, pressing faintly into his bearded jaw.

No! Please, not this! Please! Gods, please, don't let this happen! Please!

"No, Leander!" Mithras gagged, struggling to keep his calm intact as he glanced briefly at the blade threatening him. "Do not give in to this monster! My life is expendable! Yours is not!"

"Walk through those doors, girl, and take your place at your betrothed's side," Fane commanded me cruelly, glaring down at me. "Do this or Mithras dies."

"Kill me you traitorous dog!" Mithras snapped violently at Fane. "I would rather lose my head on the block than endure the vicious crime you are forcing on this child!"

Fane ignored him, eyes locked on my teary face: "Do this or watch him die, Leander."

I trembled, unable to stop myself from showing my fear.

"Please, Uncle," I sobbed, staring up at him pleadingly. "Don't do this. Please."

"As you wish," Fane nodded and turned to Tavish. "Kill him."

"NO!" I screamed, halting their movements as I began begging frantically. "I'll do it! I'll marry Tibain! Please, just don't hurt Mithras! Please!"

"Leander, no," Mithras pleaded with me softly. "Do not let them win, child. Do not."

I looked up through my tears as Fane crouched to pick up the bouquet, turning his eyes back to me. I couldn't keep myself from crying heavily now, breathing hard, my chest heaving rapidly beneath the scooped necks of my gowns.

"I promise you, my sweet niece," Fane cooed as I cried with my eyes closed, "that this truly is for the best. Your mother and father would be *so* proud."

"No, they wouldn't!" Mithras hissed at him. "They would condemn you for doing this to their youngest daughter! You truly are a monster, Fane!"

"Make sure Mithras can see the ceremony," Fane commanded of Tavish. "He won't want to miss seeing his princess make her vows."

"No!" Mithras cried out, being hauled to his feet and dragged back through the doors he had been brought from. "Be strong, Leander! Refuse them! REFUSE!"

I stood with my eyes shut until the moment his voice faded away into silence, unable to even face the man who stood as my teacher and protector. It hurt too much.

"Now then, my girl," Fane spoke gently, a cold smile in his voice. "Are you ready?"

I opened my eyes and looked up at him through my tears, shaking hard. My chest felt as if it were filled with sand, breathing nearly impossible without it heaving hard. I pressed my lips into a grim line in an attempt to control my sobs, facing him with all the courage that I could muster.

"Do I have a choice?" I asked softly as he made me hold the bouquet again, shielding my bound hands from sight.

Fane smirked at me as he took his place at my right side, linking his arm through mine and holding on tightly as he turned us towards the doors.

"Not if you want both to live," he hissed back at me, making me cringe again.

I closed my eyes and took in several deep breaths, trying to compose myself before entering the basilica and facing my cruel fate.

I thought of Carden again, softly whispering to myself *and* to him, wherever he was: "I love you, Carden."

Chapter Six
Objections

The sound of the door to the basilica groaning drew my attention and I opened my eyes again as the scent of incense assaulted my senses. I stared through the doors at the grand archways that towered high above the pews, the stained-glass windows spreading coloured light over the floors as the midday sun shone across the eastern side of the basilica.

The knights stood ready as Tavish returned to join us in the foyer, his armour clinking loudly. He looked to the knights surrounding us and nodded, turning with them towards the doors. The ten knights were in two lines of five, all of them carrying the flag of Aldegaad on large poles. They began marching ceremoniously down the aisle in perfectly practiced formation.

Tavish reached the end of the long aisle, stopped there at the edge of the altar then turned to face the doors. He smiled falsely as voices echoed throughout the room, the nobility, and the high and middle-class citizens in the crowd standing up. The knights stopped in positions along the aisle, spaced perfectly even, the two lines mirrors of each other.

To my left I saw movement, immediately looking to see several gold and orange robed figures stepping through the double doors there. I recognised the hooded priests and priestesses as the Holy Ones of the Divine Seven, all of them having a circle with seven stars surrounding it on the chests of their robes. They were moving with their heads hidden beneath their cowls, their faces visible with golden circlets over their foreheads.

Behind them came the Archbishop of Aneuran, his robes blood red with white, his head covered with a tall hat rather than a hood.

"Archbishop," Fane bowed his head to the kindly old man who stood tall above me.

"My Lord Regent," the Archbishop bowed in return. "It is an honour to receive you this day," he then turned his eyes to me, smiling softly: "And your Highness, you are a vision of loveliness. It truly is a privilege to preside over your wedding. I am honoured."

I went to speak, but my uncle slipped in first to keep me silent, likely fearing that I would give him and his conspirators away.

"She is indeed, your Grace," Fane smiled forcefully at the Archbishop. "Now, let us not keep the happy couple waiting."

"Of course. Forgive me, Princess," the Archbishop bowed his head to me, then turned and started down the aisle.

I wanted to call out to him, to make him realise the truth behind this so-called happy day. If the Archbishop knew that I was being coerced into this marriage he might have seen things differently.

I could ask for sanctuary if I could just escape my uncle's grasp, and there would be no guard, knight or lustful noble that could touch me ever again, I thought wishfully.

I turned my gaze to the altar as the old man moved towards it, tensing all of my muscles. I really had to force back the urge to vomit as I saw my disgusting excuse for a husband-to-be standing there with his father, both of them in their very best clothes and armoured chest and shoulder plates.

I gasped in sudden pain, biting my bottom lip and squeezing my eyes shut to prevent myself from screaming out. My right arm was hurting at the elbow and I turned my gaze up at my uncle as he squeezed it harder.

Fane said coldly and clearly, threatening me: "Do *nothing* to arouse suspicion, girl. I warn you, if you try to signal anyone that you are being forced into this, I *will* have Mithras beheaded tomorrow in the city centre," he brought his face closer and lifted my arm up so that I was on my toes facing him. "And I will make you watch him die before sending you to join him. Do you understand?"

"Y-yes, Uncle," I nodded softly, feeling so helpless as I met his severe gaze.

"Good," Fane smirked coldly, squeezing my arm a little harder and making me wince in pain. "Now, best foot forward, Leander."

I nodded meekly as he settled me back down and turned his gaze to the way ahead of us. I glanced quickly between him and the basilica, dreading the disaster to come.

There's no escaping it then. I have no choice but to obey.

He led me forward, both of us stepping down on our right feet, his cloak and my gown trailing behind us. I gulped hard and tried to stay strong, staring at my feet so that I wouldn't trip and fall. With my heart racing and my breathing slow, deep and painful, I began my measured, arduous walk down the aisle, hating every step I took.

I looked up from beneath my long, black eyelashes at the audience watching me. They all smiled at me as if this was the most beautiful sight they had ever seen, as if this was some great honour. If only they knew the truth.

My breathing wavered heavily, and I felt certain that I would start crying again. With all the strength I had left I barely managed to calm myself down, Fane's firm, rough hand squeezing my arm again warningly as I did.

"Don't you start crying," he hissed under his breath at me.

I made no move to indicate that I had heard him, remaining as silent and as calm as I could manage.

At that moment a strange sense came over me and I looked up, scanning the crowd again, my steps never faltering at my sinister uncle's side. I was searching for some sign of whatever it was that I had felt, soon finding it.

Off to one side in one of the antechambers I could see Mithras standing with two knights holding his arms, an old cloth wedged in his mouth to keep him silent. His eyes were set fully on me, sorrow clear on his aging face.

I'm so sorry, Mithras, I thought sadly. *I really am.*

Then, I glanced above him to one of the walkways over the main hall of the basilica. Standing behind the marble barrier were two figures in dark robes. One was an eerily beautiful woman in her late middle years, her jet-black hair in a kind of strange up style as well as having two long, thick braids hanging down her shoulders and chest. She was dressed in a purple and black gown with broad sleeves and gold detailing, a black cloak and hood hanging from her slender shoulders. She was clearly not Aldegaadian, her pale skin corrupted with blackish green veins, her eyes like two solid pieces of coal. Her purple lips were pressed together grimly, and her thin hands rested at her sides. But as striking as she was, my eyes didn't linger on her for long, instead turning to her companion.

I recognised the Shadow Lord immediately, his black cowled face shrouded in near perfect darkness, his arms folded firmly in front of his broad chest. His robes were so dark that he seemed almost to blend into the shadows of the basilica like some kind of sinister shade. There was a momentary flash of eerie green beneath his cowl and I knew he had seen me, imagining the sinister smile that would be on his gaunt, skull-like face clearly in my mind.

I'm not getting away from this. There really is no escape. Oh Gods! Why is this happening to me?! I looked up at the altar, only a few feet from it now, the faces of those waiting for us perfectly clear in my vision.

The Archbishop stood behind the altar prominently as the gold and orange clad priests and priestesses formed a half circle behind him. He was smiling brightly, his cleanly shaven face so full of pride and kindness.

To my right was Tavish, looking very noble in his strong silvery armour and his gold rimmed cobalt cloak. He was smirking to himself, his head held high as if he were posing for a portrait. Farah and Patrice stood behind him in front of the seats that had been set beside the altar for them. Patrice was smiling broadly, looking periodically towards the gathered audience as if she were seeking their attention. She always was one for the people's gaze. Farah, however, looked as crestfallen as I felt, concern burning behind his eyes.

To my left Lord and Lady Seward stood before a mirroring set of seats. Renton held himself tall and proud, his short white hair neat, his beard well groomed. At his side Angora looked just as self-absorbed and attention seeking as my horrid aunt, her hands clasped gently together in front of her hips, her grey hair tied back into two braided coils behind her head and neck.

My sight then landed on their son's arrogant face, his eyes bright and possessive as he saw me. He had his dark hair tied back, his own blue cloak trailing behind him, his hand set firmly on his sword.

I can think of a few words for a man like him who tends to let his hand touch his "sword" a lot, I thought scathingly.

I met his gaze with a savage one of my own, fighting back the urge to mouth off as I had so many times before. I didn't think that he would slap my face in front of the two or three hundred people there, but I couldn't risk the off chance that he would.

Fane smiled to him: "Tibain, much joy to you on this momentous day."

"Thank you, Regent," Tibain bowed his head, holding out his right hand.

Fane let Tibain hook his arm through my left elbow, my wrists pulling painfully against my hidden restraints as I was stretched between them briefly. I tried not to groan, biting the inside of my cheek to distract myself from the pain.

Fane unhooked his arm from mine and nodded to us: "May your new life together be filled with much joy."

I clamped my teeth together in an attempt to hold my tongue, closing my eyes briefly as I reviled Tibain's unwavering touch. I threw my uncle a tear battling, angry sideways glance, his smile merely broadening at my expression as he joined Patrice and Farah.

"You look so beautiful, Leander," Tibain said in a whisper to me as we climbed the steps to the altar. "I am a truly lucky man."

"*Shut up*," I hissed at him quietly, my tone extremely venomous and my eyes fiery. "I *hate* you with *all* of my heart, you *loathsome* bastard."

"Come now, my darling," Tibain smirked, amused by my hushed insults, "let us not fight on our wedding day."

I glared at him violently: "If my hands weren't tied, I would be strangling you where you stand."

He squeezed my arm tightly, making me seethe in pain. "No more, my darling," he commanded in a harsh whisper, though he never stopped smiling. "I would hate to have to hurt you tonight."

"You're going to hurt me anyway," I responded, facing my eyes forward. "I won't let you touch me willingly."

"Who said I wanted you to be willing?" he threw me a malicious gaze and smirked. "In an hour you're mine, and after that it is your duty to do as I command as my wife. Now, shut your stupid little mouth or I'll shut it for you. Do you understand, *my love*?"

I guess that means that he will definitely hit me in front of the crowd. All I did was nod my understanding, hating him with every fibre of my being.

We came to a stop at the altar, the Archbishop still smiling brightly. Clearly he hadn't heard our venomous exchange.

With Tibain taking his hand from my arm, I thought for a moment to try and make a run for it, but a glance at him told me to rethink that. I had an hour to figure out an escape plan for myself and Mithras.

*How can a girl of eighteen years with her hands tied and facing a forced wedding rescue herself and a knight, **and** escape a city full of soldiers?* I wondered worriedly. *It just doesn't seem possible.* I looked up at the seven stained glass windows behind the altar that showed the depictions of the seven gods and goddesses, silently praying that one of them would step in and stop this. *Thringar is the god of justice. Where is he in all of this?*

"Dearly beloved," the Archbishop spoke clearly, his voice loud and echoing around the basilica, "we are gathered here today to join this man, Lord Tibain Evan Seward, and this woman, Princess Leander Idona Aldrich the Second, in the unbreakable bonds of holy matrimony, as ordained by the Goddess of Love, Isnari."

As he began talking about the wonder of marriage, I let my mind wander, falling into a different line of thought about my situation. *I could always escape after the marriage is completed today; try to flee before the banquet and make my way from the palace. They can't keep my hands bound during the banquet. It would raise too many questions. So, that will be my chance...*

I would be legally bound to Tibain, but as long as I escaped before nightfall brought the destruction of my maidenhood, I would be alright. The very thought of seeing him laying over me in that vile act of defilement made my skin crawl.

*No. He may marry me and steal my chance for a true wedding wrought from love, but I will **not** let him violate me with that torture he plans for me. I am not his! Not **ever**!* I sighed. *On the bright side, being heir to the throne means I keep my own last name instead of taking his. I suppose that's something. At least I'll still be an Aldrich...*

I felt a hand crush my upper arm just above my elbow and I snapped back to reality, grunting quietly through my gritted teeth. I glanced up to my left, seeing Tibain watching me gravely as the Archbishop was currently doing a blessing over us. I recognised this from Aislinn's wedding, panic filling me suddenly. We were coming to the vows soon and I wouldn't have any longer than a few minutes to escape this.

"Now we come to the pledging of the vows," the Archbishop smiled at us, gesturing with his hands. "If you would kindly face each other, and if you would hold your bride's hands, Lord Tibain."

Tibain nodded, turning towards me, his hand still on my arm and squeezing lightly. I turned around to face him, fighting the urge to cry, my eyes meeting his a moment later. His rough hands held my soft ones tightly as we both held the bouquet shielding my wrists. I cringed at the feeling of his skin on mine, suppressing a dry wretch in my throat.

The Archbishop continued, turning to Tibain first as he spoke: "Lord Tibain, please repeat after me: I, Tibain, do take you, Leander, to be my lawfully wedded wife."

"I, Tibain, do take you, Leander, to be my lawfully wedded wife," Tibain repeated, staring down at me.

The Archbishop urged: "I will be your guiding light that illuminates your world. I will be your sword arm and stand in your defence. I will honour and love you for all my life, until Azmerath takes me into death."

"I will be your guiding light that illuminates your world," Tibain was smiling at me, feigning love, his hands tightening around mine possessively. "I will be your sword arm and stand in your defence. I will honour and love you for all my life, until Azmerath takes me into death."

The Archbishop smiled and turned to me. "Your Highness, please repeat after me: I, Leander, do take you, Tibain, to be my lawfully wedded husband."

I froze, trembling as terror overwhelmed me. I couldn't speak, realising that this was it and that I couldn't escape now.

My next words will either condemn both Mithras and I, or just condemn myself. That thought made me shiver as I felt tears welling up in my eyes again.

"Ahem," Tibain cleared his throat, squeezing my hands until they were hurting.

I sucked in a sharp breath quickly, trying so very hard not to cry out at his crushing grip as I stared up at him, tears threatening to slide down my face. With my stomach churning and my heart breaking, I forced myself to do what I hated most.

"I-I, Leander, d-do take you, Tibain, to be my lawfully wedded h- ," I closed my eyes, my tears finally breaking my defences and running down my face, "my lawfully wedded husband," I choked the words out.

The Archbishop urged me on, oblivious to my grief and reluctance: "I will be your greatest strength and the one who holds you in highest honour."

"I will be your greatest strength... and the one who holds you in highest honour," I could barely keep myself from crying now.

"I will honour and love you for all my life, until Azmerath takes me into death," the Archbishop recited, watching me with a strange frown now.

I grievously completed my unwilling pledge: "I will honour and," the word made me feel sick, "l-love... you... for all my life, until Azmerath takes me into death."

Oh, please, Azmerath, just take me now! Please!

The Archbishop nodded and held out a cushion with two white rings set on its red surface, one large and thick, the other small and delicate.

"These rings are a symbol of your union," he expressed, holding them up above him as if to the heavens. "They are blessed by the Creator, Ankorect, and the Goddess of Love, Isnari, for only they may ordain this union between these two young people," he set the rings back on the altar and turned to Tibain, gesturing to him. "Lord Tibain, take the ring for your bride, make your pledge and place it upon her finger."

Tibain took the smaller of the two rings and turned back to me, never releasing my hands.

Oh no! What will I do when it comes to my turn to place the ring on his finger?! I can't do this part of the ceremony without revealing that my hands are bound! I silently began to panic.

The Archbishop spoke, smiling: "Do you, Tibain, take this woman to be your lawfully wedded wife; to have her and to hold her, in sickness and in health, through richer and poorer? Will you stand by her through all of life's trials as her husband and companion, forevermore?"

"I do," Tibain smiled at me and slid the ring onto my left ring finger, my hands otherwise crushing around the bouquet's stems in utter terror.

He reached out and took the ring for himself, placing it in my palm beneath the bouquet. The expression on the Archbishop's face told me that he was surprised by this, yet he *still* went on with this farce. I couldn't believe it!

"Do you, Leander, take this man to be your lawfully wedded husband; to have him and to hold him, in sickness and in health, through richer and poorer? Will you stand by him through all of life's trials as his wife and companion, forevermore?"

I was sobbing now, feeling Tibain put the ring on himself. My tears were blurring my vision and I felt weak at the knees, certain that I would drop to the floor at any time. The only good thing about that would be that I wouldn't have to answer.

I couldn't make my lips move, my throat feeling blocked for a moment as the lump of fear crushed down on it just as Tibain's fingers squeezed around my slender hands again in order to urge me to make my vow.

"I... I do," I whispered sadly, my voice shuddering obviously as my sobs continued.

Tibain smirked menacingly, victory clear in his eyes. He had beaten me and finally gotten what he wanted. I felt violated already, my hopes to plan an escape gone now, defeat imminent.

"If there are any here who can claim reason why these two should not be wed," the Archbishop declared to the congregation, "then speak now, or forever hold your peace."

I closed my eyes and silently prayed. *Please, someone has to speak up against this! I can't stand the thought of his foul lips touching me in the kiss that will seal my fate! Please, someone! Don't let this be how I have my first kiss!*

Silence. No one spoke up and my heart shattered.

No! No, please! Ankorect, Isnari, Thringar, Azmerath, Kelos, Sungar, Maveria! Please, one of you do something! I silently screamed in my head to the Divines.

I opened my eyes as Tibain smirked down at me, trembling hard and crying more obviously now as I knew there was no escape. This wasn't how I wanted this to happen. This wasn't how my wedding day should have been.

"In the name of Isnari," the Archbishop said proudly, though puzzled by my grief, "I now pronounce you husband and..."

A loud bang echoed around the basilica and I turned my head towards the main entrance quickly. Three figures were walking through the doors, the sunlight shining through to silhouette them as if they were sent by the gods themselves in answer to my desperate prayers.

"I OBJECT!" a strong voice called out powerfully, echoing around us.

That's Carden's voice! Oh, Carden, I knew you'd come for me! I knew it! My heart soared.

Aldwyn strode forward with his mage's staff in hand, his leather over-tunic flapping around him and his cloak swirling behind him. His dark eyes were hard and set on Tibain and I, his long hair billowing across his shoulders and his bearded jaw was set severely.

To his right walked Fawkner, the Lorveren man's fur topped cloak moving around him swiftly as the wind caught behind them. His scarred face was stern, concern spreading over it as he saw my teary visage, the look in his eyes like that of an alarmed parent.

To Aldwyn's left was Carden, his collar length hair catching in the wind, his cloak billowing behind him heroically, his left hand hovering near the sword at his hip. His jade green eyes were haunted as he saw me, his jaw setting and his teeth clearly gritting. My heart fluttered faster than ever as I saw him.

The people gasped in shock as the three Guardians began striding in perfect step with each other along the aisle towards us.

"Carden!" I cried out, turning towards the Guardians with desperation.

"No you don't!" Tibain hissed, grabbing me by my shoulders and pulling me back against his chest, his pale eyes burning through me viciously.

"Let her go!" Carden shouted, his right hand moving to the hilt of his sword, ready to draw it at a moment's notice while straining not to rush to me.

"What right do you have to interrupt this wedding?!" Fane roared with rage, glaring at the three men as he moved down the altar steps to block them.

"You know very well who we are, Regent," Aldwyn declared, the three men coming to a stop about ten or twelve feet from us. "We are Guardians, called upon by Prince Ewan Aldrich and his wife Duchess Caralyn, and by your late King, Aric, ruler of Aldegaad, to protect Princess Leander, the *true* heir to the throne. We have come to aid her against this unlawful abuse of her rights."

"How *dare* you!" Fane seethed furiously. "You accuse us of forcing her into this union?"

"You are!" I yelled, throwing down the bouquet, not caring anymore if my bound wrists were seen. "I take back my vow! I *hate* this man! I *won't* marry him! I *won't!*"

Carden smiled at my rejection of the vows, but suddenly looked horrified as Tibain squeezed me around my waist, holding me tight enough to make me feel as if I would vomit. I felt lightheaded, fearing that I would lose consciousness with his grip.

"Let go of me!" I screamed at him. "I hate you! Let me go!"

"Shut your mouth!" Tibain roared, throwing me to the floor and kicking me in the ribs.

I coughed hard and heard a sword being drawn amidst the crowd's horrified gasps. Opening my eyes, I saw Carden standing ready to defend me, his stare furious as he glared at Tibain.

"Don't you *ever* touch her like that again!" the young Guardian snarled loudly, his deep tenor voice sounding so powerful in the basilica's echo.

"This is wrong!" the Archbishop exclaimed frantically. "Why is that girl bound?! Why do you bring so much violence into the House of the Divines?!"

"Shut your mouth, old man!" Tibain snapped at the Archbishop, standing over me menacingly. "And you, you lying little bitch!"

I cried out in pain as I took another kick to the ribs, Fane staring at Tibain in mocked shock. He would play this to the end, ensuring that he appeared innocent.

"Enough!" Fane ordered Tibain. "I had no idea of the violence of which you were capable, Tibain!"

"Nor did I," Renton Seward said with false anger, deciding to maintain his own standing with the horrified audience. "We didn't raise you to be so abusive to women, Tibain!"

"You shame our family!" Angora Seward pretended to cry.

Tibain looked around, his face paling and horror filling his eyes as he realised they were offering him up as a sacrifice to save themselves. He reached down with rage and grabbed me by the back of my neck, hauling me to my feet painfully. I cringed and struggled, but he was too strong, holding me firmly in place.

"Stay back!" he hissed, glaring at everyone around him before focusing on me. "Now, Leander," he whispered into my ear as I watched four new figures approaching through the doors at the far end of the massive room, "Mithras will die for your betrayal."

I smirked knowingly: "I don't think so."

"TRAITORS!" Mithras' voice boomed, causing all eyes to turn to the doors. "CRIMINALS!"

Mithras strode into sight, still beaten and bruised, but now he was free of those awful prisoner clothes and restored to his Aldegaadian knight's armour, his blue cloak swirling behind him in the winds. On either side of him came the Axton brothers; Dolin's face severe and Holger's eager for violence, their weapons at the ready. Behind them was Joran's towering eight-foot form, the burly greyish mauve skinned giant storming forward with his hands by his sides and his violet eyes locked on us.

There were gasps and I looked around as three figures hurriedly moved into view. To my right Tallinn came with her hood cast back, her blonde hair in a neat plait, bow in hand with an arrow aimed at Tibain. To my left Ellora appeared, the Elven Huntress calmly lacing an arrow to her bow and aiming it at Fane and Tavish, her turquoise eyes piercingly fierce. Behind her came a hooded and scarfed man who stood over six feet tall, his dark brown eyes stern, his bow unwavering as he locked his own arrow on Tavish. I didn't know him, but I didn't care for now.

"Let the girl go, Tibain!" Mithras commanded, bringing Joran and the Dwarves close to the centre of the aisle, just short of the knights that stood there. "She will *never* be yours!"

"I should have known!" Fane was furious, but I could see the hint of a smile on his lips. "The King's assassin has escaped the prisons and now stands here with his accomplices to once again abduct the Princess!"

"They *aren't* abducting me!" I screamed at him, struggling in Tibain's grasp. "They're rescuing me from you!"

"Do you hear this?!" Fane asked with a gesture to me, playing to the crowd. "Our treasured Princess has been corrupted against her own people by these monsters! By their malcontent and black magic!"

"There is no black magic in our hands, Regent," Aldwyn declared with a stern gaze, "only the pledge of the Guardians to protect the innocent. Release the Princess or face us, by the codes of our Order and the law of the Divines themselves, I command you."

"You are outnumbered," Fane smirked at the Mage, the knights, soldiers and Tavish drawing their blades readily. "You can do nothing to save yourselves. Surrender and confess to your crimes, and I will show you mercy."

"You think we have no reinforcement?" Fawkner smirked, looking so amused.

"You're very wrong," Tallinn remarked from where she stood.

"Leander, catch!" Carden lunged forward, readying his sword.

I elbowed both arms back into Tibain's rib cage, the arrogant young lord grunting in pain. I threw myself forward, reaching out both hands as a silvery glimmer flew through the air from Carden's outstretched left hand. My fingers closed around it and I felt the warmed metal in my palms, relief filling me. I stopped myself steadily at the edge of the altar, holding my prize between my hands and feeling the links of its chain gratefully.

"No you don't!" Tibain roared; metal scraping loudly and violently, a sword suddenly at my throat.

He pulled me back into his chest and I let out a frightened yelp of surprise as he held me firmly, my eyes glancing up at him over my right shoulder and wayward strands of dark hair.

"I am *really* going to hurt you now, girl," he hissed viciously into my ear, causing me to tremble in fear. "You're afraid of being violated? Well, I promise you that when I'm done that you will need a new word for the kind of assault I will force on you."

I gulped hard, the terror I felt overwhelming me. I thought of what he was going to do to me, of the pain that his assault on my virginal body would cause me and I couldn't help crying.

Please, I vividly thought, pleading desperately, *save me from him now! Please!*

Almost as if in answer, I felt that familiar heat spreading from my hands, purple light beginning to shine through the gaps between my fingers. I opened my palms and stared down at my pendant, the purple stone at its heart glowing with bright violet light.

"The Pendant," I heard my uncle gasp, fear in his voice. "*She* has it..."

Suddenly, there came a mighty roar from outside the basilica as if from some great and large beast, the sound rocking the marble and stone walls around us. The roar echoed its bellowing howl again, staggering us all where we stood, the citizens and nobility in the room crying out in panic.

"What is that?!" Tibain turned with me towards the great arched stained-glass window depicting the Dragon, Ankorect, fear plastering his face.

A shadow moved over the coloured glass, coming nearer and nearer as shouts outside broke the momentary silence. The shape of a large winged creature became more obvious in the shadow, the sunlight spreading strong beams around the shape. There was a tremendous shattering of glass, metal and stone as the massive creature plunged through the window with its four clawed feet leading it. A gigantic tail swept at the air, a spear-like feathered barb slashing at its tip as great magenta wings flapped powerfully, the purple, blue and silvery scaled beast now revealed. A long snout parted its jaws to allow another bellowing roar to reach out, shattering every window in the basilica.

"DRAGON!" a guard shouted in panic. "IT'S A REAL DRAGON!"

While my captors and the audience panicked, I could only stare in wonder at the molten orange eyes that locked on me and softened with familiarity.

"Amethyst," I smiled up at her, so happy and awed to see my beloved friend.

Amethyst settled down onto her feet, smashing into one side of the room and crushing the pews that had now been vacated. She was enormous, especially considering that only a week ago she had been the size of a hunting dog. Now she was a little more than three times the size of a large horse on her four legs, the two horns on her head twice the length of my arm and the webbed frills behind her jaw fully developed.

The sunlight gleamed over the Dragon's scales as she turned to us, outstretching her powerful wings and letting out another snapping roar that was so loud it felt as if I would be deafened.

"The... the legends are true," Fane gasped in bewilderment, staring at Amethyst. "It *is* one of the Dragon Pendants."

"You see, Fane," Mithras decreed, drawing his sword and shield, "in fact it is *you* who is outnumbered."

"THE MAGE HAS SUMMONED A DRAGON TO KILL US ALL!" Patrice screamed, trying to terrorise the congregation.

I tried to pull away as panic began to ensue, Tibain grasping me tightly and preventing my escape.

"The only place you're going is to our bedchambers, Leander!" he shouted, spinning us around and glaring at the Archbishop. "Finish it! Marry us, now!"

Amethyst roared angrily and lashed out with her large tail, smashing the altar to shards of rubble. I was thrown from my feet with the shockwave of her strike, hitting the marble floor hard; Tibain cast some twenty feet to my right and the Archbishop falling backwards in bewilderment. I groaned and rolled onto my back, the veil tugging painfully at my hair. I opened my eyes to see Amethyst snapping at the soldiers as the frightened citizens began running for the exits. They were trying to attack her with their spears and swords but were too fearful of the Dragon to get very close.

Suddenly, I felt a hand grab me and I let out a panicked scream, two jade eyes meeting my blue gaze a moment later and calming me immediately.

"Carden," I felt so relieved.

"Are you alright?" he asked me quickly.

I nodded: "Yes. Just untie me. Please."

"Hold still," he directed, slipping the blade of his sword between my wrists.

I felt a heavy tug and the pressure binding my wrists was gone, Carden quickly helping me to my feet. We turned together to the scene before us, our gazes set on the chaos. The soldiers were fighting Mithras, Aldwyn, Fawkner, Joran and the Dwarves as Ellora, Tallinn and the masked man rushed to surround the two of us defensively.

Carden pulled me into his embrace, encircling me in his left arm and slightly under his black and silver cloak, his sword ready to defend me.

Then, I heard a shrilled scream and eerie green flames erupted from the darkness of the room. A soldier was howling the most horrific sound I had ever heard, terrifying supernatural emerald flames tearing through his eyes. His body dissolved and he became dust, his blackened skeleton crumpling to the floor uselessly to reveal his killer.

The Shadow Lord stared from beneath his black cowl with furious glowing eyes, his evil so potent that it was choking the air in the room. Silence fell and the fighting stopped; the soldiers, knights and my companions staring at him in bewilderment. Beside him stood the woman, her black eyes shining viciously, her fingers seeming to crackle with magenta energy. She *had* to be a witch.

The Shadow Lord stared at me as I clung to Carden, glaring with those horrid glowing green eyes, his left hand still held up in a loosely closed fist as green flames lapped at his flesh.

The flames receded and he simply lowered his arm to his side, watching me with an unblinking determination as all eyes in the room now fell on him...

Chapter Seven
A Rock and a Hard Place

Fane did as I knew he would, stepping forward and speaking with a loud voice to show the people that *he* was their salvation. "How dare you invade my kingdom, daemon!" my uncle staged, the Shadow Lord turning towards him. "I am the Regent of Aldegaad until my niece is Queen, and I stand ready to defend my people."

"Your people are nothing but mice, Regent of Aldegaad," the Shadow Lord spoke as naturally as he ever did, clearly much better at this than my uncle was. "They are pathetic, mewling retches that need to be... *exterminated*," he held up both hands, his fingers coiled viciously, green flames gracefully curling to life above his skin as he smirked evilly. "Let us attend to such a matter. Shall we?"

He turned and lashed out with his right arm, the flame erupting larger and exploding in a tremendous fireball. It lanced from his palm as the flames seemed to swirl from around his black robed arm to his hand, striking out at the people hatefully. The ball of fire exploded against one of the stone walls, shattering it and destroying two columns. He spun quickly to his left and lashed out with another fireball, casting it into the pews and sending burning wood and stone rubble into the air.

The people were screaming and running as his assault continued, his witch companion watching on with her black eyes full of malicious pleasure.

"Stop him!" Fane shouted to the soldiers.

Three of them rushed forward only to face the Shadow Lord's raised right hand. I screamed and shielded my face in Carden's chest as the same flames erupted from the men's eye sockets, their agonised screams ending moments later with burnt piles of blackened ashes on the floor.

The room was emptying quickly as the Shadow Lord held out his left hand, muttering something in a harsh, guttural language I didn't recognise. Almost instantly the shadows in the room began to come to life. The sweeping black robed forms of Shade Seekers slowly emerged from the darkness, their glowing blue eyes bright, their haunting ghoulish mouths hidden beneath their shroud wrappings. They began looking around viciously, swooping in and attacking victims, carrying them up into the darkened rafters above the basilica floor where they ended them.

The seven creatures swooped and dived as Aldwyn immediately tried to cast a defensive shield of magic to safeguard the civilians from their attacks. Carden,

Tallinn, Ellora and the Stranger kept me between them as Amethyst roared angrily, snapping at any that came near her. Even the Shade Seekers, it seemed, weren't foolish enough to take on a dragon.

Strange shadowy portals were opening all around us, black armoured Shadow Knights emerging with their swords in hand and their shields at the ready, their cloaks swirling behind them as men in black armour followed. There were only four of them, but with the undead soldiers that followed they were more than enough to kill everyone in that room.

The citizens scattered as the demonic creatures began killing the knights and guards, whose focus was now the defence of the people, not my continued imprisonment.

Fane watched on behind me as Tibain was helped to his feet by his mother and father, the Archbishop the only member of the clergy left there with us.

The room cleared and soon we were the only ones who still stood inside the ruined basilica.

The Shadow Lord cast one final glance to the exit, then turned to us as the Shade Seekers, Undead Legions, Shadow Legion and the Shadow Knights began surrounding us, the soldiers of my people looking around nervously.

"Now," the Shadow Lord smirked at me, "Princess."

He slowly started towards me; his glowing eyes set on my face intently.

I turned my front towards Carden, cringing into his chest in fear and looking over my left shoulder at the monster. Carden's left arm pulled around me, holding me tightly and I heard him growl in his throat as he kept his sword ready and aimed at the Shadow Lord's approaching shape.

"Don't worry, Leander," he grumbled to me. "I won't let him touch you. I promise."

I felt a little comfort as I heard this, glad to have him protecting me. My blue eyes then turned back to the Shadow Lord, my nerves hurting with the intensity of my body's shaking, my fingers tightening around my pendant.

"It is time for this to end," the Shadow Lord remarked coldly, his eyes moving from me for a moment to settle on my uncle. "I have played your little game for long enough, Fane. Now the time has come for you to honour our deal."

"Honour our deal?!" Fane stared at him in disgusted disbelief. "I do not have what was promised me! You have terrorised and maimed my people and destroyed one of our greatest landmarks!"

"I have only aided your cause," the Shadow Lord responded evenly, one hand clasping the other wrist.

"*Aided* my cause?!" Fane scoffed.

"Indeed," the hooded figure nodded. "In front of your people you have appeared the stronger ruler over the girl: you who stood against a Shadow Lord *and* survived."

My uncle was staring at him with a heavy frown, his arms crossed sternly. He looked like he was going to explode, his face turning scarlet and his shoulders shuddering against his rage.

"I have given you control of Aldegaad, Regent," the monster continued evenly, his eyes hard. "All of your people present have seen how you stood up to face me while your niece cowered in the arms of a Guardian. She now looks weak and you now rule over the entirety of this nation. And I can ensure that it remains this way."

He glanced at me, his gaze making me cringe harder into Carden's protective embrace, my fingers curling into the Guardian's shirt.

"All I ask is that you do as we previously agreed upon when we first forged this alliance," the sorcerer said coldly, "and *give* me the girl."

I froze in place, my jaw tightening, fear filling me as my eyes watered, my gaze locked on him. *This was his plan all along!* I realised, my previous feelings of the Shadow Lord now dissolving. *He wasn't trying to help me escape their murder plot! He was setting the stage for this encounter! To give Fane what he wanted! To take me as his own!* I cringed at that knowledge as Carden gripped around my shoulders with his left hand, holding me tighter, his muscles tensing hard. *I knew he couldn't be trusted!*

All around me my friends closed ranks, worry on their faces and their weapons at the ready. There was no way that they would let him, or any of the monsters or men that surrounded us near me if they could. But our only advantage was my dragon, and I hoped that she was enough to save us all.

The Shadow Lord narrowed his eyes dangerously at my uncle's silence, his jaw clenching. "You promised me your niece, Regent. She is worth far more to me than she is to you. Give her to me."

"Regent?!" the Archbishop stepped in front of me, throwing me a worried expression and gesturing fervently towards the Shadow Lord. "You struck a bargain with this... this... this daemon?! The Princess for the throne?! Are you truly such a cruel man?! She is your niece!"

Fane and the Shadow Lord both regarded the old man coldly, both bearing cruel, sinister gazes towards him. But he went on, indignant and enraged.

"I cannot believe that you would do such a vile thing, Regent," the Archbishop exclaimed, "to your own niece, your brother's daughter!"

"The Princess," the cowled monster hissed, "is *mine*."

"No," the Archbishop shook his head, holding up his hand towards the monster defensively. "I *will not* allow this young woman to come to any harm! The Divines, all mighty, will defend us! And you, daemon, will linger, lost in the Void along with this traitorous murderer who calls himself the Regent!" he then turned to Mithras and said: "Do not fear, Ser Mithras. I now see your innocence in these crimes of which you have been accused, and I *will* testify against the Regent and his demonic accomplice."

"Your Grace," Mithras warned, "please, stop..."

But the Archbishop didn't listen. He just moved towards the Shadow Lord, pointing at him angrily, determined to banish him.

"In the names of Ankorect, Azmerath, Isnari, Sungar, Kelos, Maveria and Thringar," he bellowed, "I cast you into the eternal darkness! This girl is now under the protection of this church! Leave this hallowed place, unholy Void spawn! Be gone!"

The Shadow Lord rolled his eyes and held up his hand with a vague wave. I screamed and hid my face with my eyes shut as the old Archbishop's body erupted in an explosion of eerie green flames. All I saw was the flickering of light through my eyelids; the screeching howls, the crackling of the flames and the smell hitting me as hard as any of the beatings I had taken.

The heat faded after a few moments and I sobbed in panic, feeling Carden's frantic heartbeat as he staggered backwards with me. He was scared too.

"I grow tired of these distractions," the Shadow Lord scowled, drawing my teary gaze again as he turned his eyes to my uncle coldly: "You will *not* keep me from my prize, Fane. Give me the girl *now*."

Fane scowled icily and gestured towards me. "Be my guest, your Lordship. I suppose I have no real use for her now, anyway."

The Shadow Lord turned to me, smirking as his eyes flashed with a brighter glow.

"Stay back, monster!" Carden growled, brandishing his blade forward. "I won't let you touch her!"

"Foolish boy," the Shadow Lord glowered. "I will simply kill you and take the girl to Gorth'lak, kicking and screaming. You cannot stand in my way."

"Be gone, Hessiik!" Joran snarled, stomping between us and him, his violet eyes hard. "You shall not lay one hand upon my Sarissi! I will defend her unto my dying breath!"

"If that is your wish," the Shadow Lord shrugged.

Suddenly, a bright sapphire orb of light exploded against the Shadow Lord, throwing him across the room and sprawling him on the marble floors. He snarled, crawling to his feet and glaring up at the figure that had attacked him.

Aldwyn stood ready, his staff in both hands, the crystal in its tip glowing with the same blue energy. He narrowed his dark eyes at the monster, keeping himself between us and him.

"The Princess is under Guardian protection, Shadow Lord," he said, commanding and confident. "Leave or be destroyed."

The Shadow Lord laughed: "You can do nothing to destroy me, Guardian. Only *one* has that power, and it is not you."

There came the sudden grinding rush of swords being drawn and I looked around in shock. A number of the Aldegaadian soldiers and knights had their blades pointed at the Shadow Lord, moving to defend me against him. I was stunned, certain that they would fight for Fane instead.

"Guards," Fane commanded. "Stand down. Give her over, now."

"We can't do that, Regent," one female knight – the Knight-Captain – said sternly. "You have proven yourself a traitor and the usurper to the throne, the one who murdered our true king and queen. We will *not* surrender our princess and future queen to this monster, nor will we follow you."

"Captain Loren," Tavish snarled, stepping in front of Fane angrily. "You are disobeying your Regent's orders."

"I am upholding my oath and sworn duty, Knight-Commander," she stated strongly. "The Princess is our rightful ruler and we will defend her from this monster... *and* from you."

"You'll die for this," Fane hissed angrily, drawing his own sword as Patrice rushed to hide behind him.

Tibain, his father and the soldiers allied with them drew their own weapons, glaring at us viciously.

"If I can't make you my wife," Tibain glared at me with cruel rage, "then I will be too happy to hand you to this monster; *after* I have my fun, of course."

"Will someone please shut this moron up?" Tallinn rolled her eyes.

"Enough!" Fane bellowed. "Kill the traitors! Secure the Princess, now!"

"Bring her to me!" the Shadow Lord commanded.

"No!" Fane howled. "Destroy him too! The girl belongs to us!"

"Kill them all!" the Shadow Lord roared, his voice echoing around the walls.

Then everything became chaos. The Regent's soldiers and the Shadow Lord's monsters all attacked at once, the few soldiers that stood with us pressing back towards us defensively as Patrice, Farah and the Sewards took cover. Swords clanged in a heavy cacophony of metal meeting metal, the Shade Seekers shrieking and beginning their runs against us anew.

Holger smashed his hammer into the chest of an undead soldier, casting it down as Dolin's axe met the face of another. "Now this is a fight, brother!" he bellowed happily.

"Aye! That it is!" Dolin agreed, blocking another soldier as Fawkner pushed back our attackers with Joran's support.

An undead soldier reached for me but Carden pulled me backwards just in time, the two of us dropping down behind the destroyed altar as Mithras smashed his shield into its rotting skull and threw it backwards.

"Defend the Princess!" Knight-Captain Loren shouted, her knights and guards fighting off the two attacking sides.

I looked over the ruined dais at the erupting battle, stunned by its sudden outbreak. We were fighting two sides; my own nation's forces and the supernatural minions of the Shadow Lord. It definitely seemed to resemble being stuck between a rock and a hard place to me.

Aldwyn had his sword drawn and was swinging both it and his staff expertly, casting down enemies with ease. Tallinn and Ellora were slinging arrows from their bows, not hesitating against any that were attacking us, human or monster.

Amethyst launched an attack of her own, the Dragon snapping with her jaws and managing to snatch a few enemies into the air. She caught a Shade Seeker in the blasting gusts of her wings and threw it into the sunlight, its body erupting in bright orange and red flames before exploding.

The Shadow Lord scowled at her. He turned his hand towards her, and a blast of green lightning shot from his fingers, hitting her in the face.

"Amethyst!" I screamed in panic, Carden pinning me down and swinging his sword to kill an undead that attempted to attack us a moment later.

Amethyst roared, staggering backwards and flapping her wings. She launched into the air, howling in pain as she flew away into the rafters, then turned back towards the fight. She landed again, saving Fawkner and the Dwarves by crushing two Shadow Knights under foot.

"Leander!" Carden turned to me as we crouched low behind the altar. "Stay down, alright! Just stay down!"

"Wait! Carden!" I cried out in panic.

Carden jumped up and ran into the battle, swinging his sword to help Ellora, who was under attack. They were only a few feet from me, but it felt like miles.

I scurried into the protection of the main shrine, trying to find cover from the storm of steel, clutching the Pendant in my hand. I didn't even think to put it around my neck despite my painful awareness of it.

Mithras and Ser Loren rushed towards me with two soldiers, battling down more of our own men as they went. They were trying not to kill them, I noticed, aiming instead to neutralise them.

"Mithras!" I shouted, fear gripping me.

"Leander!" he rushed to me, pulling me up his free hand and shoving me behind him. "Stay behind us!"

Carden and Ellora joined us a moment later, Carden pushing back another undead soldier and severing its head with one sweep of his sword. He came right up to me, standing on my right and in front of me as Ellora came to my left, her bow firing swiftly at the monsters.

"We need a path for escape!" Ellora declared, slaying two more undead creatures.

"There's a secret passage in the chapel behind us to our left," Ser Loren responded, stabbing her sword through an undead and smashing her shield into its face. "We need to clear the way!"

"Wait! What about the others?!" I cried out.

"Our priority is you, your Highness!" the Knight-Captain responded.

"Then you two get her out of here!" Mithras commanded Ellora and Carden.

"No! Mithras!" I shouted defiantly. "Not without you!"

"I swore to protect you to my dying breath!" he retorted fiercely, beating down one of Fane's men. "I will uphold my oath, Leander! Now, go!"

Ellora grabbed my shoulder. "Come, Princess, there's no time!"

I nodded, turning and running with her and Carden, ripping the veil and circlet away from my head and throwing them down as I did, then casting the wedding ring away with them. I grabbed the folds of my white dress to make it easier to run, cursing the slippers I was wearing instead of my more practical boots.

As we ran for the chapel, my uncle charged with two soldiers and Tavish. He rushed at me, the soldiers snapping into a fight with my two protectors as I tried to duck away.

I cried out in panic at my uncle's hard grasp as he snagged my wrist, screaming and struggling to free myself.

"You're not going anywhere, Leander!" Fane shouted at me, fighting against my struggles.

"Get off me!" I screamed, punching him in the face and staggering us both.

He dropped his sword, growling with rage and snatching at my free wrist, pulling my arms together tightly. I fought and kicked at him, trying to throw him off me angrily, but he was too strong.

A body slammed into us, tackling us to the floor in a heap. Carden was on Fane, forcing him away from me and striking him in the face with the pommel of his sword. I heard a sickening crack and my uncle's howl of pain as blood poured from his broken nose.

Before I could fully register what had happened, Carden pulled me backwards, trying to defend me now as Tavish swung with his own sword at us. He fought and struggled, but Tavish was stronger, the Knight throwing us to the floor hard. He punched Carden and dazed him, then turned to me with fury in his eyes.

Lying on my back, I propped myself up on my elbows, staring up at him in fear. He raised his sword, aiming its point at me, the cold steel gleaming with the red of blood. I pulled myself down against the floor, whimpering and taking in a sharp breath. I heard a cracking sound abruptly fill my ears, but it wasn't the sword going through my rib cage as I had expected.

Tavish's eyes were wide as he lost his grip on his sword. It clattered to the floor, his gaze dropping to the blade that had broken through his armour and his heart. He gagged, blood spurting from his mouth as he staggered against the figure behind him.

Carden clambered to my side, pulling me into his arms and startling me out of my shocked stare. I gave him a brief glance before turning back to my rescuer.

"I swore if you harmed this girl that I would kill you, Tavish," Mithras told him, pressing his sword further through the man's chest. "And I *always* uphold *my* vows."

With a groan of exhaustion, Tavish's eyes rolled back in his head and he collapsed forward to the floor as Mithras withdrew his sword. The cruel Knight-Commander lay dead in a pool of his own blood, his life ended by my protector.

Mithras smiled at me. "It's alright, Leander. You're s-," he was cut off with a yelp: "Argh!"

I heard the cracking of steel and bone, and the tearing of flesh as he threw his head back in pain. A silvery blade was poking through his shoulder and chest on the right side, dropping him to one knee as blood spewed from the wound.

"MITHRAS!" I shrieked, my heart sinking inside me. "NO!"

Fane looked up from the floor, his face bloody, his hands around his sword's hilt, driving it through Mithras' side. Mithras turned on him and struck him hard with his gauntlet, throwing the man down and tearing the sword from his shoulder in the process.

Ellora jumped up, rushing to his aid swiftly. Mithras staggered against her, switching his sword to his left hand, his right now too injured. He turned his hard eyes to Carden as he fought to stay standing.

"Carden, get her out of here!" he commanded.

"But -" I tried, but Carden pulled me back as Mithras and Ellora started covering us.

I didn't like leaving Mithras, but I had to obey his commands.

We ran into the chapel, but as we went a figure suddenly materialised in front of us, green eyes glowing as a blast of green energy exploding the marble floor in before us. We were thrown away from each other, Carden slamming his head against a pillar, stunned and dizzy as I crumpled to the floor several feet away.

I turned from lying on my stomach, pushing myself up on my palms as the Shadow Lord turned his gaze down towards me.

He said nothing, narrowing his eyes at me, a gleam in his collar catching my attention. I stared at the necklace he wore; a five-pointed star shaped pendant with a midnight black stone at its centre. I looked back to him, his scowl cold, the eerily beautiful witch moving to stand behind him at his left shoulder, her black eyes set intently on me.

I heard the heavy clanking of armoured boots, turning over my shoulder to see a Shadow Knight and two Shade Seekers coming towards me. There was no way I could fight them all on my own, even if I had a sword. I could easily be defeated.

Don't let them take me... I thought desperately.

At that moment heat filled my hand and I glanced down at the Pendant in my fingers. Its stone was glowing and there came a bellowing roar that echoed off the walls. Amethyst smashed down on the Shadow Knight and crushed it, then threw the two Shade Seekers into the sunlight with a powerful blast of her wings, their bodies burning to ash. She roared and turned on the Shadow Lord and the Witch, my eyes locking on the sorcerer just in time to see his pendant glow with dark energy.

What? It... it can't be...

Another roar ripped through the air and the ceiling was destroyed. A huge purplish black dragon soared through the debris, its powerful wings a blood red colour, its head crowed with four pointed black horns. It snapped at Amethyst, its eyes glowing brightly as she drew back defensively.

I watched on helplessly as the Dragons launched themselves through the already ruined giant window of the basilica, smashing that entire back wall to pieces. They were fighting and crashing back into the marble structure, snapping at each other fiercely.

Bewildered, I let out a shocked gasp as a hand grabbed me. Two dark brown eyes met my blue ones, the masked and hooded stranger crouching beside me. I glanced past him and saw Tallinn rushing to help Carden as a column fell, blocking the two of us from them.

"Princess, we must go!" the Stranger shouted over the fighting of the Dragons.

"Wait... I..." I looked up at Carden, his eyes open and on me as our friends were running with the knights defending our escape, the Shadow Lord staggering backwards as a section of ceiling fell between us and him.

"Go with him, Princess!" Tallinn shouted to me as more rubble came down. "Run!"

"Come on, girl!" the man snagged me by the arm and hauled me up.

I didn't even have a chance to think, this man – who I knew nothing about – suddenly hurrying me away from the fight and towards the only escape route we had left. Trust wasn't even something that I could consider right now, desperation and fear all that fuelled me.

He dragged me by the crook of my arm towards the back wall of the chapel, shoving open a passage behind a tapestry just as I glimpsed the Shadow Lord scowling at us through the debris. The Stranger hurled me into a darkened tunnel, sealing the door behind us and towing me blindly on through the cold blackness in a desperate attempt to escape...

Chapter Eight
The Wanderer

Darkness clouded my vision, my feet carrying me as fast as they could while my heart pounded in my ears. I couldn't think, I couldn't see, my breathing echoing around me with our desperate, rushing footfalls.

Running was hard with the Stranger's hand grasping tightly around my forearm, his legs so much longer than mine. I was staggering, blind and relying on this man I didn't even know, but I had no choice now. I just had to run. The man didn't speak; he just dragged me forward, constantly pushing me to keep moving.

Fear filled me and I began wondering if the Shadow Lord was watching us, waiting in the darkness somewhere. But no orbs of energy or evil green flames attacked us, the dark all that there was.

It felt like we had been running forever, the stone walls ringing out with our frantic footsteps. I was struggling to breathe, the air stale, like it was thick with decay. Then, the smell of fresh air hit us, and I felt relief fill me for a moment, but only a moment. A crack of light shone through up ahead, daylight reaching out to us through the darkness. It was a way out, excitement filling me as we raced towards it, the dark stone brightening around us. I could even see the shape of my cloaked and hooded rescuer in front of me as we reached what looked like a dead end.

The Stranger smashed his body into the hard surface with a grunt of effort, releasing my wrist to use both hands. He braced his palms against the wall, pushing it open with some strain and allowing the sunlight to flood into the tunnel. I squinted against it, blinded for a few seconds, but he didn't wait for me to recover, dragging me forward roughly with my wrist in his coarse hand again.

We rushed down a set of steps and into a cave, the entrance only a few feet from us. We were moving through the sloped opening, finally breaking out into the sea air of the southern Coastlands. I paused, taking in a deep breath of the cool air, relief flooding through me. For the first time in more than a week I felt free, savouring the feeling of the wind on my skin.

Suddenly, a hand closed around my upper arm, startling me back into reality. I looked up into the Stranger's brown eyes, staring at him with confusion and fear.

"Come on, girl!" he urged me. "We don't have time to stand around smelling the sea air!"

Before I could speak, a horn sounded from the city in the distance behind me. It was a deep, hollow sound that rang out several times, signalling the city's garrison to rally. It almost felt like a perfectly timed response to the Stranger's warning.

I stared up at the white city walls, trembling at the thought of the soldiers that would be swarming the hills right now. *Oh gods!*

Not needing him to say anything else, I spun around, grabbing the hems of my skirts and running as fast as I could. He ran beside me, drawing his sword now as he threw a glance over his shoulder.

The Coastlands weren't that well stocked with places to hide, but there was a thin clustering of trees that would serve well enough. It stretched for a while surrounding Aneuran, then it spread south a little with the river, thickening at it got closer to the water.

"If we can reach the river," the Stranger called back to me as we ran, "then we can hide in the thicker woods! Just stay close to me, girl! Try to keep up!"

Regardless of whether I wanted to or not, I didn't dignify him with a response, my lungs burning too much to allow me to speak.

I silently cursed my wedding gown as I ran, wishing I was in my old clothes instead. Though running in my usual dress was not easy, the train on this one made it so much harder for me to navigate the shrubs and the woods. It turned out that the white dress had another downfall. It was easily spotted.

I heard shouts from my left, looking up the hill to see a group of five soldiers standing there, their blue cloaks swirling around them in the winds. They had seen the white of my clothing and one was pointing straight at me, sword in hand.

"Damn!" the Stranger cried out, grabbing me and thrusting me forward. "Run, girl!"

I didn't hesitate, following his command immediately, gripping my dress hems firmly. I started sprinting beside him through the woods, the soldiers shouting after us, their footfalls thundering through the thick underbrush violently.

Again, I silently cursed my clothing: *Formal slippers aren't worth anything when you're running for your life!*

The crunching of boots drew my attention and I let out a startled shriek, ducking away as a soldier reached out to snag my hair. I managed to avoid him, the Stranger lashing out and stabbing him in the shoulder with his sword, drawing a scream from his lips.

The Stranger threw me forward, kicking the soldier to the ground, still alive, but screaming in pain. I realised that this mysterious man helping me escape wasn't like my friends. He was willing to kill without care, which scared me.

Angry shouts rang out from behind me, but this time I was too scared to look back. The soldiers were chasing us now more for what the Stranger had done to their man, not just because of having an escaping prisoner to recapture.

We ran through the woods for what felt like ages, the sounds of the soldiers closing in around us. It seemed like they were everywhere, like escape was going to be impossible. I was so certain that they had surrounded us.

I threw my gaze over my shoulder as I ran, my long hair catching around my face as it streamed behind me. I could see the glimmer of silvery chainmail through the trees along with the flapping of blue fabric. The soldiers were slower, but they were still catching up with us despite this dense woodland terrain.

I saw the Stranger ahead of me, his movements slowing a little as he turned back to me. I could see the brown eyes that lingered beneath the hood and mask, their gaze focused and driven. He still had his sword in hand, ready to fight if he needed to.

"Hurry!" he shouted to me, rushing on through the shrubs and trees.

I ran harder than before, pushing myself to keep moving even though my legs were burning with exhaustion. I knew I had to keep going. I had to escape the soldiers closing in on me, no matter what. I couldn't go back to my uncle or the Shadow Lord. I just couldn't.

The Stranger began to fall back, covering me as he watched the soldiers. Their shouts were getting closer now as we continued to struggle through the woods, the cracking of swords breaking tree limbs echoing all around us.

Suddenly, I felt my right foot hook into something, and I fell. I hit the ground hard, stunned for a few moments as I lay there in the dirt. Turning over, I looked to my foot, seeing a vine wrapped around my ankle. Panic filled me again as I fought to pull myself free, but I was unable to get my foot loose.

The Stranger came up beside me, not needing to ask me anything as his brown eyes locked immediately on the vines. He took his sword and slashed them away, then grabbed me by the arm and heaved me to my feet.

We ran together, the soldiers getting closer, their heavy trudging sounding all around us.

They're getting so close! How can we ever escape them?! I don't know if we even can... I can barely breathe... They're catching up... Oh no... We can't...

The Stranger pressed his hand to my shoulder, signalling me to stop. I paused, breathing heavily as I watched him. He seemed to be listening to the sounds around us while he surveyed the woods.

My heart racing, I stared at him worriedly, not really sure what he was doing. I could hear the soldiers getting closer, fear spreading through me like an infection with every trampling footstep they made.

Then, the Stranger jabbed a finger towards a random direction and shoved me forward.

I turned and started running again, throwing my gaze back at him worriedly. I couldn't understand what he was doing, but I was glad that I had someone to tell me what to do right now. I needed that.

Turning my eyes ahead of me, I ran as hard as I could, the sounds of the soldiers gaining on me making my heart scream inside my chest. Anxiety became full blown fear and I was scared that I could start screaming if I didn't hide soon.

I slipped again, stumbling and rolling down a small incline before slamming into the ground hard. I lay there for a moment, then propped myself up on my stomach, my right ankle hurting. A hiss of seething pain escaped my lips as I realised I had twisted it, my ankle most likely sprained. I tried to ignore it, dragging myself to my feet and moving at a limping run, gathering my dress hems in my palms again.

Suddenly, I was very aware of my pendant in my right hand, realising I probably should put it on. I slowed my pace behind a massive tree and pressed my back to it, looking over my shoulder and around the trunk apprehensively. There was no one there, but I knew the soldiers wouldn't be far.

I quickly unlatched the chain of the Pendant and slipped it around my neck, refastening it a few moments later. A strange relief filled me at having it back, the purple stone in the silver pendant's heart seeming to gleam as if it had gained a new life with me wearing it.

I heard twigs snap... and I froze.

Slowly, cautiously, I looked around the edge of the tree again, watching over my right shoulder. I couldn't see anything, but I knew I had heard something. Trembling with unease, I turned back around and tried to scream as a hard hand clamped over my mouth. I fought and struggled, grabbing at the wrist as I was forced to the ground, fighting as hard as I could.

I froze immediately as I was held back into the ground, angled so that it would be easy for me to fall if I tried to pull away. A sword was at my throat, my eyes full of frantic tears as the gleaming metal stared back at me.

The Stranger was glaring down at me over his mask, his brown eyes stern and his grasp on me tight.

I cried out in desperate fear, feeling the cold of his blade touching my skin, trying to wriggle loose. But he just held me tighter, stifling my screams to nothing more than frantic, muffled whimpers.

"Calm yourself, girl," he murmured to me sternly. "I am *not* going to hurt you, but you must be quiet."

I didn't listen, screaming as hard as I could manage with my mouth and jaw pinned like this. He pulled me closer, my hands scrambling against him as I tried to fight him off me.

"Calm down!" he barked quietly. "I swear that I won't hurt you. You need to be quiet or the soldiers will hear you. Understand?"

I froze as I heard footsteps, instantly submitting to the Stranger's commands. I was shaking hard now as he pulled me back into his chest, his sword in front of me, his hand still over my mouth. I gripped his wrist with both hands, trying to stay silent as he dragged me into the cover of the tree's roots.

We hid there under the tree's base where the earth had been eaten away by the weather, the two of us silent and watchful. He pulled his dark brown cloak around our bodies, trying to hide my white clothing from sight.

Footsteps thudded closer and closer, the soldiers' armour clinking loudly as they approached. I was breathing so hard now, struggling to calm my frantic heart and failing.

"Shh," he whispered into my ear. "Just stay calm and do as I've said. It's going to be alright; I promise."

How do I know that?! I wondered, trembling in his arms. *How do I know I'm going to be alright when you're holding a sword at my throat?! I don't even know you! Gods, I wish I could say something right now!*

I stayed as still as I could, looking up uneasily at the roots of the tree above us. The falling dirt told me that the soldiers were up there. I swallowed against a hard lump in my throat, my heart thudding so loudly that I worried they would hear it.

"Looks like we lost them," one of the soldiers was saying gravely. "Gods damn it!"

"The Regent won't be happy if we don't retrieve the girl," another soldier warned. "None of the others matter like she does. *She's* the one he wants."

"How did they vanish so fast?" a third asked. "One second I saw her white dress, then... nothing."

"They couldn't have gotten far," the second soldier agreed. "Maybe we just need to scour the area. They have to be close."

I worried that they would look down where we were hiding and find us. There was no way the Stranger could fight so many off on his own, not with me in the middle.

We just need a distraction. I thought. *Anything...*

A roar broke the silence and the soldiers ducked away frantically. The sound of massive wings shook the ground and I looked up to see a purple, silver, blue and magenta shape whip up through the thin tree canopy.

"There's one of those dragons that attacked the basilica!" the first soldier shouted.

"Look out!" the third soldier cried out and something hard smashed heavily into the ground, shaking everything.

A shrilled roar ripped through the air, making my ears hurt as a tail snapped into view for a moment before vanishing again.

"Hm, that's convenient," the Stranger commented, then gazed down at me. "Come on. Let's move."

I nodded up at him as his hand slithered back from my mouth.

We got to our feet and carefully slipped away from our hiding place, both of us trying to catch a glimpse of what was happening. The purple dragon was lashing out at the soldiers, six of them standing there trying very hard not to get hit.

The Stranger grabbed me by the arm, and we took our chance, running headlong into the thickening woods and away from the fight. *How did Amethyst find us? She just appeared out of nowhere the moment I thought about a distraction. That's... I don't know what that is...*

* * * * *

I don't know how long we ran, only that my body was aching all over and I was so exhausted. I wasn't really sure that I could keep going much longer, at least not if we were running.

At last we began to slow down, the two of us breathing hard now, neither of us speaking, mostly because we just couldn't. I leaned against a tree, trying to catch my breath, my arms crossed above me, my forehead resting on them. I tried to fill my lungs with as much air as I could, my chest heaving and hurting.

The sounds of the Dragon's roars and the soldiers' shouts had faded away ages ago now as day was becoming dusk. The air had become quiet and a cold wind had begun to pick up, the smell and sound of a river wafting through the thick woods towards us. It was so soothing, yet the chill was bitter.

"Come, girl," the Stranger said after a few minutes, drawing my eyes to him. "We have to move."

"Please, just give me a minute," I begged breathlessly, closing my eyes against my arms and the pain in my heaving chest.

"We don't have a minute right now," he responded, grabbing my arm and spinning me around to face him. "You and I need to keep moving before the soldiers find us."

"Why should I go with you?" I demanded icily. "I don't even know you, let alone trust you."

"Because I'm all that's keeping you out of the Regent's clutches right now," he responded with a vague shrug, sheathing his sword. "Besides, what choice do you really have?"

I couldn't really say anything to that. He made a really good point; I just didn't have a choice, no matter what I thought or felt right now. I *had* to go with him.

I just nodded in response, the man turning and striding away through the underbrush. I followed on in silence, clinging to the hems of my skirts and trying to keep myself from falling again. It was easier to do now that we were walking, my balance steadier and my head no longer swimming after easing off my breathlessness.

We found our way to the edge of a small southward flowing river, the scent so clean and refreshing. I instantly wanted to drink from the clear waters, but my companion just kept walking along the banks. So, I followed, trying to suppress my growing thirst.

We kept walking as night fell, finding ourselves making our way down the slopes of a craggy hill beside a rushing waterfall. The Stranger began traversing a small rock passage behind the falls, leading me through carefully. I found myself staring up in wonder at the cascading curtains of water, the gleam of the dying light shedding beams of golden orange through the streams. Tiny rainbows seemed to form in the dense air, shimmering with the ending of the day.

"Here," the Stranger called to me, standing in a shallow cavern at the waterfalls' heart. "We can rest here tonight."

I just nodded as I stepped off the narrow ledge and came to stand with him, my arms wrapped around my shivering body. It was cold there.

A pack was nestled there amongst some rocks along with firewood and other provisions. Clearly, it had been left there on purpose, hidden away from view.

I frowned as he moved to the bag and started rustling through it: "Why have you got supplies here?"

"I always stash supplies around the unbeaten trails in case the need arises for me to hide somewhere," he replied without looking up.

I tightened my arms around me and raised an eyebrow: "So, you do this a lot, huh?"

"Travelling, yes," he responded with a shrug as he worked, "running from the city guardsmen, not really."

"Neither do I," I murmured, staring out at the waterfalls, shivering fiercely.

He took a pile of clothes from his bag and turned towards me, offering them to me. "Here. You should put these on. I doubt you'll want to stay in that damned wedding dress. And, you'll be a lot warmer."

I frowned, taking the clothes sceptically. "You just happened to have women's clothes with you?"

He shrugged: "I got them out of the prisoner effects lockup once I agreed to help your friends. It was always my intent to come and pick them up from here after our escape," he chuckled. "Didn't think I'd be dragging you along with me when I did, lass."

I stared at the clothes and unfurled them. There was a pair of dark leggings, a white under dress with thin shoulder straps, a pale blue dress with long sleeves and a smoothed squared neck, and a silk lined, velvet main dress with wide sleeves.

"These are my clothes," I realised.

"Get changed over there," he directed me. "That outcropping will give you a little privacy."

"Um... thank you," I murmured, taking the clothes and moving where he had directed me.

It took me quite a few minutes to exchange my wedding gown for my own clothes, but I was soon wearing them and feeling much warmer thanks to the velvet. I fastened the cord of the bodice, managed to lace up the long pale blue sleeves and adjusted everything, then I stepped out of my changing space with the white gown wrapped up in my hands.

The Stranger was sitting on a flat rock with a fire burning, his elbows resting on his knees, his hood and scarf now removed to show his face. He was a very handsome man, golden red haired, brown eyed and with a beard covering his chin, lip and jaw. He looked like he was in the middle of his third decade, his red hair hanging down past his collar, grazing his very broad shoulders and his back. His skin was a deeper cream colour than mine, almost olive and tanned by the sun's rays.

He turned his gaze to me, smiling faintly, his thin lips pressed together. "Is that more comfortable, lass?" he asked.

I nodded as I crossed to him. "Yes. It's much better, thank you."

"Take a seat," he indicated a section of the rocky floor beside him. "We might as well settle in for the night."

I obeyed, moving and lowering myself gingerly to the ground, pushing my back up against the wall. At least it was warmer by the fire.

"I'm afraid I don't have a lot I can offer you to eat," he said softly, taking a small bowl from the stone he sat on. "But you're welcome to it."

"Thank you," I murmured, taking the bowl and studying its contents.

It was boar meat, heavily salted to keep it from spoiling. I didn't exactly trust the look of it, but food was food and I was hungry.

"Here," he tossed me a red apple, which looked more appealing than the meat. "Take that too."

I just nodded my thanks and took a bite of the apple. It was very juicy, soothing my aching throat and making me feel more at ease. I hadn't really realised how hungry I was, especially considering that I hadn't been allowed to eat much before the ceremony earlier.

As I ate the apple, I glanced up at him, chewing slowly and studying him. This man was such a mystery to me, so much about him and his actions today not making any sense. I couldn't figure out why he had helped me or why he was being so kind to me. I also couldn't figure out if I was really safe with him or not.

"So," I spoke up after a few silent minutes, "you said that you always keep supplies hidden away like this?"

He nodded, sitting back and peeling an apple with a small knife. "Aye, lass, that I do."

I shrugged curiously. "Why?"

"As I said, I like to travel and as I go, I like to make sure I've got food and clothing stashed away in case I have a need of it."

"And this is something you've done for a long time?"

He smiled curiously at me: "You're a very inquisitive young lass, now aren't you? Why is that?"

I swallowed a mouthful before I answered honestly: "I'm trying to figure you out, I guess."

"Figure me out?" he asked, popping a wedge of apple into his mouth.

I nodded. "I mean, I don't really know anything about you. I'm just wondering... if I... if I can really trust you."

He chuckled, shaking his head.

I frowned: "What?"

"Just you," he wiped a tear from his eye, amused with me. "Are you really so suspicious?"

I shrugged uneasily. "I don't know anything about you and, well, I haven't really got a lot of reasons to trust people nowadays."

He leaned forward, elbows on his knees, knife and apple in his hands as he locked his gaze with mine. "You think I'm going to hurt you or that I'm kidnapping you, is that it?" he guessed.

I shrugged again, more nervously, my eyes darting around automatically for an escape route: "Um... maybe."

"Well, don't worry your pretty little head, girl," he assured me, peeling more of his apple as he spoke. "I've got no intention of doing anything like that to you."

I let us sit in silence for a few moments, absorbing his words and trying to discern any meanings behind them. I turned my blue eyes back to him, brushing a hand through my dark hair subconsciously.

"Then, what *are* you intending?" I asked softly and – admittedly – suspiciously.

"Join up with your Guardian friends and get you to the safety of that keep they've been talking about," he replied, chewing on another piece of apple. "A pretty young girl like you needs all the help she can get in this kind of situation, I'll wager."

"And you're fine with this?" I met his gaze, having worked out a lot about him already. "Helping someone like me, I mean?"

He frowned, his chewing stopping midstream as he stared at me. "And... what do you mean by that, lass?"

"Helping an Aldegaadian can't be something you're all that comfortable with," I said evenly, "especially considering *who* I am."

His frown deepened, suspicion in his eyes now as he was silently placing the pieces together from what I was saying.

"You think I wouldn't help you because you're Aldegaadian?" he leaned forward again with a curious and stunned expression.

I shrugged: "Historically, our peoples haven't exactly gotten along."

"Our peoples?"

"You're an Ivanstenian, aren't you?"

His eyes brightened with realisation and he began to nod, sitting back slowly and crossing his arms.

"And what makes you say that I'm from Ivansten, lass?" he questioned me curiously, smiling with amusement.

"A lot of things," I answered, pulling my knees up and resting my elbows together on them. "Your accent gives you away, for one thing. I've only ever heard Dwarves and Ivanstenians use the word 'lass' and, well, you're clearly not a Dwarf."

He nodded in agreement. "What else?"

I went on: "You're over six feet tall. You have that sort of gingery red hair, brown eyes and warm tan skin that Ivanstenians are known for. And your sword's hilt has the insignia of the stag on it, which is only found in Ivansten and only carried by Ivanstenians. Specifically, soldiers."

He was impressed: "And you figured all that out by... what... observing me?"

I nodded softly. "Living in Arvon was so quiet that I had to find ways to keep myself occupied. Observing people and learning all I could about them was one of the best distractions I had. Also, I've always been curious about people," I frowned and indicated towards him with my left shoulder. "Is your nationality the reason why you wear the mask?"

He set his back to the wall and crossed his ankles, one knee to the ground, the other to the air. I suddenly worried that I had offended this strange man, but he was so at ease that I couldn't have.

"It's not easy being an Ivanstenian in Aldegaad," he agreed with a nod. "In some small towns I can get away with showing my face because they mistake me for someone from Lorveren or Vorhalaas."

"I can see how people could make that mistake," I nodded with a thin thoughtfulness.

"Most of the time I keep my face covered in these lands for my own piece of mind," he confessed. "The soldiers leave me well enough alone, but townsfolk – especially in the northern cities – can be a little less... accommodating."

"I can't imagine what that must be like," I sighed, shaking my head and staring at my knees.

"And what about you, girl?" he asked, drawing my gaze again. "Do you hate Ivanstenians like so many of your countrymen do?"

"No," I replied honestly. "I don't hate Ivanstenians at all. I mean, I know there's bad blood between our countries, but I would never hate anyone from Ivansten just because that's where they come from."

He seemed surprised: "You wouldn't, huh?"

"I judge people on their actions and intentions," I told him in earnest, "not the place from which they hail. In the last three months I've been in the company of a Dorvan Ranger, a man from Gorvenna, a mage from Safferan, a mercenary from Lorveren, two Hecturn Dwarves, a Galvenin Wood Elf and a Storvari warrior. And even if I hadn't, my father taught me not to discriminate on race, creed, status or any other defining factors other than actions."

"It sounds like your father's a very wise man," the Stranger nodded, smiling and stoking the fire with a stick. "So, how come he doesn't worry that you're out here in such danger then? Surely his daughter's safety would mean a great deal to him."

A pang of pain struck my heart and I sighed, staring at my knees again so I was not meeting his expectant gaze. If I did, I would just start to cry, and I didn't want to do that.

"My... my father's dead," I murmured sadly, not looking up. "So is my mother... and my uncle and aunt... They're all dead."

I felt the air change as he stared at me, slowly looking up to see sympathy in his eyes.

"Oh, I'm so sorry, lass," he offered me honestly. "I know it's hard to lose the ones you love. Believe me, it's a pain I know all too well."

I shook my head, pressing my lips firmly together and staring at my feet aimlessly. "There was nothing I could do to save any of them," I confessed, feeling new, cold tears fighting my defences. "And I've spent the last two months crying because of it. I just wish I could stop."

"Who were your parents?" he asked softly.

I looked up at him gravely. "You know who I am, do you not?"

"I do, Princess," he confirmed with a small, vague nod. "But I do not know enough about Aldegaadian nobles to know whose daughter you are."

"Ewan and Caralyn's," I responded a little too harshly, my parents' names hurting my heart. "They were the Duke and Duchess of Arvon, but that town's been burned to the ground."

There was silence between us again, my appetite having disappeared during our conversation.

The Stranger stood and moved towards me, taking up an old blanket from the floor as he went. He stooped beside me into a crouch, tilting my chin up to look at him as I felt tears slip down my cheeks again, a shiver hitting me hard and fast.

"You look cold, lass," he said, throwing the blanket across my shoulders and drawing it around me firmly.

I frowned curiously at the old blanket, smelled the musty scent coming off it, then looked up at him.

"Good thing I always keep a spare lying around, eh?" he smiled faintly, trying to be comforting. "Can't have you catching your death of cold, now can we?"

I nodded slowly, taking in a small breath as I thought of something to ask him. I needed to find anything I could use to distract myself from our previous line of discussion.

"Why do you do it?" I asked softly, wiping away the few tears that had escaped me. "Why do you travel like this, I mean?"

He shrugged, settling down to sit beside me, one forearm slung over his raised knee. "The road just calls to me, I suppose. And I don't have anyone to go back to in Ivansten, so I wander the rest of High-Realm."

"You're a Wanderer?"

"I am," he studied my face as he spoke. "Do you know much about men and women like me?"

I shook my head. "Not a lot. I've never really met one before. Not living in Castle Arvon, anyway."

"Wanderers," he explained, "are wayward folk who travel for one reason or another. We're not so much poorly behaved as we are uncertain where we belong. The open roads and wilds are often a better home to us than any village in our homelands. Some seek adventure and fortune, others solitude and a kind of oneness with nature. But whatever the reason, most aren't dangerous unless attacked, and most are as kind and obliging as any villager or guardsmen that walks the town streets."

"So, why do *you* do it?" I asked quietly. "Do you just like to travel?"

He nodded: "I guess I do. I was never really suited for any other life and I do enjoy seeing all the other parts of High-Realm, which is why I started off as a soldier; not that I stayed one for very long. It really is a beautiful land."

"I used to want to see the world," I said wistfully, thinking of home again. "Now all I want is to be back in my own bed with my mother and father still alive."

"We can only look to the road ahead," he told me, putting an arm around my shoulders. "And there's a path laid out for us tomorrow, Princess."

"Please, don't call me 'Princess'," I looked up at him uncomfortably. "I've heard it enough in the last week."

He shrugged: "I just don't know what else to call you, lass."

"My name is Leander," I introduced myself quietly, meeting his eyes. "What should I call you?"

"Tristan," he answered with a smile. "That's all I go by these days."

"Tristan the Wanderer?" I raised a curious eyebrow.

"Just Tristan," he reiterated. "And I suppose you go by Princess Leander?"

"Sometimes," I shrugged. "I just let people close to me refer to me however they want, but I prefer that they just use my name."

"Well, lass, it may be a little too presumptuous for me to call you by name only just yet," Tristan said evenly, "so I'll just refer to you as 'Princess' or 'lass', if that's alright."

"I think I'd prefer 'lass'," I responded.

"You've got it, lass," he smiled, pulling his arm back and sitting against the wall, taking a thick fur from the bag to use as a blanket.

Because I was so uneasy and because it was so cold under the thundering waterfalls, I found myself crawling closer to him. I curled up beside him, letting my head rest on his chest as I snuggled under the heavy blanket he had given me.

Tristan stared down at me, surprised by my sudden closeness. He pulled the fur over us to shield us from the cold, drawing me closer with his left arm around my shoulders, his hand stroking my hair gently as he shared his body's warmth with me.

"Are we safe here?" I asked in a hushed, small voice, snuggling closer to him.

"Safe enough," he responded, still stroking my hair kindly. "It's only for the night. Tomorrow we'll head out and meet up with your friends."

I sighed uncertainly, watching the cascading waters fall at the mouth of the small cave.

"Don't worry, lass," he said to me in a whisper, his lips close to my forehead. "You're safe with me."

"Tristan," I looked up at him tiredly. "Thank you."

He nodded to me then let me lie my head against him. I allowed my eyes to close and took in a deep, restful breath, settling down for the first time in more than a week. At last, I finally felt like I could really sleep.

Chapter Nine
The Black Asp

Morning broke with a chilled wind that gust through the waterfalls to reach us where we lay. The sun was beginning its slow rise, a gentle orange haze lining the distant horizon of thick trees.

I awoke slowly, thinking it was strange how I found peace lying on the hard, cold stone floor of a cavern behind thundering waterfalls. I was on my side, wrapped in the heavy fur blanket Tristan had placed on me the night before, allowing myself a few moments to just enjoy the feeling of ease that I woke up to.

At first, I could only take glimpses of the world around me, my eyelids still heavy with sleep. I took in the rushing grey of the water cascading down the rocks in front of the cavern's mouth, the sky beyond murky and black. Movement caught my attention and I leaned up on my elbows, my dark hair falling in a curtain past my right shoulder.

Tristan was crouched beside his pack, stowing items into it that he had used during the night. I caught a glimpse of white silk and knew he had packed my so-called wedding dress as well, though I did not care what became of it. Beautiful, though it was, it remained a cold reminder of what had nearly been forced on me only several hours ago.

The Wanderer turned back to the smouldering remains of the fire, the heat from it fading as he checked what he had put there. It was a small pot with what smelled like porridge inside.

My stomach growled, the apple I had partially eaten last night all that I'd had in more than a day. Slowly, a little blearily, I pulled myself to sit amongst the makeshift bed that had been crafted for me, stretching my arms and letting out a yawn behind my hand.

"Nice to see you're awake, lass," Tristan greeted me, drawing my gaze as he served up the food into two wooden bowls. "I trust you're hungry now?"

"I am," I confessed, curling my knees up under me as he approached with the bowls.

"Here you go," he said as he offered me one. "I'm afraid you're going to have to make do with your hands. I don't really carry utensils."

"It's fine," I replied, taking the food and immediately dipping my fingers into its warmth.

I forgot myself for a few moments, too hungry to really care how I looked. Besides, I was sitting in a cave with a man who expected no manners beyond my gratitude, so eating with my hands eagerly was of no real concern here.

"Well now, you are hungry, aren't you, lass?" he chuckled, settling down opposite me and eating his own food.

"They weren't exactly generous when it came to feeding me," I replied between mouthfuls.

"Traitorous bastards are like that," he agreed.

He reached towards the bag and took a pair of dark brown boots and a long, brown, hooded coat from beside it. He tossed them down in front of me, drawing my attention again. I just frowned for a few moments, then looked up at him.

"You'll need these," he explained. "And while those lovely little slippers you're wearing are pretty, they're not practical."

"I couldn't agree more," I said, taking the new clothing items gratefully.

"Well, eat up, girl," he instructed me. "We have to start out in the next few minutes if we hope to avoid the patrols."

I could not and did not want to argue with that.

We ate our meal in silence, washed up with water he had gathered from the falls, then set about preparing to leave. I traded the formal slippers for my recovered boots, pulling them on and finding a welcome sense of comfort and security from their shapes clinging up to my ankles. I pulled on the coat he had given me, hiding my soft velvet dress beneath its coarser fabric, leaving it open at the front. It reached to my knees and fit around me perfectly, as if it were designed for a woman's use while being a size larger on me than I was used to.

We set out as the sun was reaching past the horizon, thunder growling from the dark grey clouds that choked the sky. It would certainly rain today, but I didn't really worry, the rain the least of the things on my mind. I simply drew the hood and hid beneath it, my long hair streaming out from under its rims to hang to my chest.

Tristan led me through the woods, our path moving alongside the small river at the base of the falls. The ground here was flatter and more even, which only made for a much easier journey.

As rain started to fall on us, I began to wonder about the others, especially Mithras. The image of that sword going through his body was branded across my thoughts; staying put stubbornly and refusing to shift itself. I also kept wondering about Tristan, his motives for helping me still a mystery. There could be any number of reasons why he was doing this, but I couldn't come to a solid conclusion as to what that reason was.

I suppose there are many reasons why a man like this would help a girl like me, I mused silently. *I just hope his intentions are more noble and less like those of so many I have met in this nightmare.*

The mystery that was Tristan kept me occupied for a long time as we traversed the slowly thinning woods and the beginning of the seaside grasslands that were the main body of the Coastlands. I was lost in my thoughts for hours, not thinking about anything else with the exception of where I placed my feet.

"You've been quiet," he observed as we walked side-by-side through the thigh high grass. "You alright?"

"I've just been thinking, that's all," I answered, my eyes on the ground ahead of me.

He nodded, eyes up on the horizon: "I imagine you would have a lot on your mind, lass. I can't even begin to understand what you've gone through."

I just nodded, staying silent and keeping my eyes forward.

He turned his face to me, his hood back and his jaw bared, his brown hide coat and his old cloak flowing around him in the heavy sea breeze.

"How old are you then?" he asked.

"Excuse me?" I turned my eyes to meet his, stunned by his abruptness.

"I was wondering how old you are," he repeated. "To look at you I would have to say you're... what? Sixteen?"

"I'm eighteen," I replied.

He chuckled: "Well, then you look young for your age."

"It's a family trait," I explained. "At least it is for the women on my mother's side. We all keep our youth for decades after reaching adulthood."

"And you've not yet come of age, am I right?"

"No, I haven't," I answered, turning my eyes ahead of me again. "I won't for three more years."

"Twenty-one isn't such a great age," he confessed offhandedly. "There's the drinking, and trust me, while it seems fun at first the aftereffects are terrible."

"That comes down to choice, I suppose."

"Aye, that it does," he nodded.

"How old are you?" I asked, directing his question back to him. "It just seems to me that if we're to travel together that you should tell me as much about you as I am about me."

"Fair enough," he consented. "I'm thirty-two winters."

"You don't look a day over twenty-eight," I observed.

He smiled lightly at me. "Well, isn't that sweet of you?"

I shrugged, not really trying to be sweet towards him. I kept my eyes forward, walking as carefully as I could, my fingers tight on my skirts.

"Can I ask you something else?" I turned back to him, managing to steady myself on the slightly rougher ground.

"Aye, girl, that you can," he replied.

"Where are you taking me?"

"Still don't trust me?"

"I'm just wondering where we're headed."

He nodded to himself, eyes ahead towards the blue haze that was clearly recognisable as the sea. "There's a place a few more hours walk ahead of us called Dagger Score Bay," he explained evenly. "It's named that because it's a long carving into the cliffs that looks like a dagger wound."

"I've heard of it," I said with a nod.

"Well, we're meeting the Guardians there," he continued, staring down at me for a moment. "That Aldwyn fellow has arranged transport to the keep he wants to take you to, and we were all told that if we got separated to make camp for the night, then meet at the bay," he smiled at me with amusement. "Who would ever have guessed that you and I would be paired up for this journey, eh, lass?"

I just nodded, grimacing a little and keeping my eyes ahead of me. I couldn't be sure from where his amusement was born; his comprehension of our situation compared to Aldwyn's plans, or some other intentions of his own that were not yet apparent to me. I decided to stay quiet and be watchful.

* * * * *

As the sun began to sink towards setting, we reached the coast and began walking along the paved highway that ran through there. We passed by some merchants on the way, Tristan drawing his cowl and scarf to shield his face while I huddled beneath my coat's hood. Neither of us wanted anyone looking at our faces, especially mine. I was just too easily recognisable everywhere in Aldegaad.

This fear worsened as a patrol of blue cloaked and silver armoured soldiers came marching towards us. We were heading east along the road at this point as they were marching west.

They stopped us beside another merchant caravan that was heading west, the merchants a mixture of Dwarves and a couple of the large, green skinned, burly Orcs, who were obviously their escorts. I shuddered at the sight of the Orcs, knowing that their race had connections to the Shadow Lord and the Scourge, though I knew not all of them were that monster's servants.

The soldiers questioned us, Tristan easily stepping in to answer everything. I was just grateful that I didn't have to speak up, too uneasy to face the soldiers. I had no idea where their loyalties lay, and while Uncle Aric's men would have protected me, I could not take the risk that they were Fane's loyalists.

Tristan convinced them that we were just a pair of Wanderers passing through, my silence attributed to an illness that had inflamed my throat, preventing me from speaking. The soldiers seemed to accept that explanation and allowed us to continue unhindered.

It was the beginning edge of sunset when we finally came to the place Tristan had told me about. As he had said, the bay was a long, narrow split in the land that truly did resemble a dagger's scoring on the earth. The sea reached deep into this wound; the shore set only a few meters back from the water's edge.

I narrowed my eyes to see the dark shape that was nestled just inside the mouth of the bay, realising what it was after a few moments. The ship had two masts standing tall on the deck, the sails bundled away neatly. Its hull was made of dark timber unlike anything that was found in Aldegaad, meaning the ship was *not* of Aldegaadian make. I felt strangely sceptical about the vessel as we began to descend the break in the cliffs to the beach below.

This is part of Aldwyn's plans? Then why am I feeling so uneasy at the sight of this ship?

Tristan led me to the beach, our boots leaving deep treads in the wet sand behind us. I lifted my skirt hems so they didn't drag on the ground, making my way cautiously behind him. That's when I saw them.

A longboat was set on the shore at the water's edge, five large, dark skinned men standing there dressed in clothing that I knew was not of any Aldegaadian tailor's design. They each carried a sword at their hips as well as daggers, two of them armed with crossbows.

"Tristan," I murmured, grasping his wrist and staggering my pace. "I'm not sure about this."

"Relax, girl," he assured me. "You've got nothing to worry about. Alright?"

Against my better judgement, I nodded, following on and staying very close behind him.

Tristan greeted the men with a raised hand: "Greetings, friends. I'm looking for the Guardian named Aldwyn Draken. I was told to meet him here."

"And who are you and your... ahem... friend?" the obvious leader of the five men asked, looking at me with lustful eyes. "She's a pretty one."

I cringed in repulsion.

"We're part of the Guardians' party seeking passage to their keep," Tristan answered the man. "Have the others arrived yet?"

The strange, dark skinned man was staring at me, his bearded jaw clenching as he smirked at me. He was running his eyes up and down my body, almost as though he were trying to decide whether to act on his revolting desires or not.

He took a step forward, reaching out his sea salt-soaked hand towards my hood: "Let's just take a look at that pretty little face, sweet girl."

Tristan snapped his hand up and secured the man's wrist, pulling it away from me. His eyes were hard and his jaw set as he stared him down.

"The girl's *not* to be touched," he warned severely. "She's under the Guardians' protection and my own. Are we clear, friend?"

The dark-skinned man scowled and withdrew his hand, nodding. "The Mage is aboard the ship with the rest of his party. We'll take you and the girl to them now."

"Much obliged," Tristan smiled at him, then put his arm around my back. "Just stay close to me, girl," he urged me quietly while the men escorted us to the boat. "Men like this can be rather unpredictable."

Swallowing back my unease, I just nodded, stepping into the boat with his help. We settled in together, the sailors – if they could be called that – dragging the boat into the surf before climbing in themselves. There was a lot of chop in the waves with the stormy winds and thunder high above us, the small boat being thrown around quite violently. I just huddled into Tristan's shoulder and chest as he held me close, trying to stay hidden under my hood.

The dark-skinned men were silent, focused on their task as they ferried us towards their black hulled ship with expert navigation. I recognised their accents and their race as one that was not considered to be a part of High-Realm. They were from the land known to us as Harredi, a country south of Vorhalaas in High-Realm's farthest south-east regions. The Harredi were known for their black hair, gold eyes and dark skin as much for their red and brown garments.

The ship was soon upon us, a monstrous black thing. It was a brig, not the largest of vessels, but large enough to accommodate cargo and passengers if the need arose. The plaque on the hull read: *Black Asp*. That in itself was ominous sounding to me.

The lead man climbed up the ladder rungs that were secured to the hull with ease, another of his men following. Tristan went next, climbing confidently to the top as I began my more unsteady ascent.

One of the men in the boat helped me onto the rungs, then pushed me up as I tried to climb. Tristan reached out his hand to me, grasping firmly around my wrist and helping me onto the ship's deck. The sailor came right up behind me, he and Tristan helping me to reach safety from the churning seas below.

"There now," Tristan smiled at me, holding me by both upper arms to steady me, "that wasn't so bad, now was it, lass?"

I shook my head, trembling from the anxiety that still coursed through my body.

I turned my attention to the ship's deck, taking in the dozens of men that surrounded us. They were all Harredi, dressed in dirty, ragged clothes, the stench disgusting, but that came from being at sea for so long with so little. They were hardened looking men, all of them seeming like they had known a full life of harsh conditions. The way they stared at me made my heart pound frantically in my chest to the point of hurting. They observed me the same way many men who did not see women often would, and that left me once again fearing for my immediate safety.

"So then," the lead sailor who had brought us to the ship turned to me, smiling roughly, "why don't you tell us your name, pretty girl?"

"Back off," Tristan snarled, holding me tightly as I cringed into his chest. "We've already had this discussion."

"You're on my ship now, so it is my rules in play here, not yours, Wanderer," the sailor retorted, grabbing my wrist and trying to pull me away. "Now, come here, girl!"

I fought against him, Tristan holding onto me and trying to push him away.

"I said, back off!" he shouted.

Before any of us could move there was the sound of a sword being drawn and a blade was suddenly at the sailor's throat. He froze, staring at it uneasily, but still holding onto me tightly.

I recognised the messily brushed, off-black coloured hair, the hard-set jaw, handsome young features and green eyes of the sword's owner. Carden snarled at the sailor, his brow furrowed deeply, his teeth clenched hard.

"Let. Her. Go," he snarled lowly at the sailor.

The sailors had been gathering around us but were now backing off as familiar faces rushed forward with weapons ready. Fawkner, Ellora and the Dwarves sped into view, the four of them surrounding us in defence.

"As you say, young Guardian," the sailor responded, letting go of my arm and stepping back from me, his eyes still on Carden. "As you say."

"Leander," Fawkner smirked, looking over his shoulder at me as he levelled his sword at one of the sailors. "Fancy meeting you here."

"It truly is good to see you, Fawkner," I managed a small smile as Tristan pulled me away from the lustful sailor Carden was threatening.

"As it is to see you, Princess," Dolin nodded to me from behind his thick beard, keeping his axe aimed at his target.

"Yeah, so glad you could join us," Holger added gruffly, winking at me, then snarling at his targets and brandishing his war hammer.

"Kal Vashor!" a thunderous voice lashed out in what I immediately recognised as Storvari. "What is the meaning of this gravmanook? This transgression?"

At first, I thought the voice belonged to Joran, but the Storvari that appeared was not him. He was as muscular and large as Joran and had the same gold markings on the left side of his face, but he looked very different. His head was bald, his pointed ears suddenly more obvious because of this, as were the ridges in his greyish mauve skinned forehead. A deep scar crossed over his right eye from his forehead and down to his cheek, the eye a milky white indicating blindness. The other eye was the typical violet of his species and filled with potent rage.

Unlike Joran – who carried dual swords – this man carried a massive battle axe of Storvari make, his clothing designed to match the men's surrounding us. He also had a black beard which only covered his jaw, his lip left hairless as two braids hung from his chin.

The men around us shrunk back at the sight of him, and further still as Joran came up behind him. It made sense, two large, angry Storvari more than enough to avoid upsetting.

"Sarissi," Joran stared down at me.

"Joran!" I pulled away from Tristan, running straight into the giant's waiting arms, my hood falling back as he crouched down to meet my eyes.

"Are you injured, Sarissi?" Joran asked me, his massive hand pressing to my shoulder.

"No. I'm alright, Joran," I assured him, feeling like a child beside him.

"What have you been doing here, veshtrans?!" the other Storvari barked viciously at the sailors. "You would defy your calnovarkin's commands?! These women are not to be touched! *Any* of them!"

"Calm yourself, Kororsh," a female voice spoke up evenly.

The angry Storvari turned to gaze down at a woman of Harredi heritage as she moved out from a doorway leading below deck. She was shorter than me by a few inches and slighter of build, her black hair tied back neatly beneath a red bandana, gold earrings hanging from her ears. Her dark gold eyes surveyed the scene as she moved forward, dressed in a black leather coat, crimson tunic shirt and dark brown pants, her hand on the sword at her hip.

"I am certain my men were not disobeying my orders," the woman was staring around at the sailors with calmly severe eyes. "They know very well that I do *not* tolerate such behaviours against my guests."

The lead sailor who had started this was staring back at her as she walked right up to him, his trembling less from fear of the giant and more of her. I could only guess that she must have had a reputation that would attract such a strong response.

"This girl – like the Elf and the Guardian – is not to be touched by any man here without her expressed permission," she warned him coldly. "If you make a move to do so again, I will ensure that it is the last thing you do. Am I understood, Vamdrim?"

"Aye, Captain," the crewman, Vamdrim, responded more submissively. "It won't happen again."

"See that it doesn't," the Captain growled, nodding to Carden, who withdrew his sword from the sailor's throat.

As the Captain turned back to Joran and me several more figures appeared in the doorway.

"Are there problems, Captain Karrer?" Aldwyn asked as he, Mithras and Tallinn came into sight.

The Harredi woman turned to him and shook her head as she moved towards us. "A few of my men took it into their heads to try their luck with your young ward. Kororsh and I have settled it, I assure you," then she turned her attention to the large Storvari named Kororsh. "Set sail and follow the heading Master Draken has provided us. I will see to it that our new arrivals are given accommodations."

Kororsh snapped his forearm to his burly chest and bowed his head. "As you command, Sarissi," he turned and roared out: "Make sail! Bring the ship about!"

Immediately, the Harredi crew started rushing to follow his commands, their work to get the ship ready clearing the deck for us.

Captain Karrer turned her eyes to me and smiled lightly. "You must be Princess Leander. Aldwyn has told me so much about you."

"Thank you for stepping in like that, Captain," I thanked her. "I'm not sure what I would have done if you and my companions had not acted as you did."

"You must pardon my men, Princess," Karrer said respectfully, folding her arms. "They do not often see women of your natural beauty and are mostly at sea with no female face to behold besides my own. It is just in the nature of our line of work, unfortunately."

"Yes, well, pirates aren't always known for their manners," Mithras commented gruffly, cradling his right arm in a sling.

"Pirates?!" I exclaimed in disbelief, turning towards Aldwyn furiously. "You made a deal with pirates?!"

"Harredi pirates are the best people for navigating the coastal regions without drawing attention, Princess," Aldwyn told me simply. "And given our current situation with the Aldegaadian military I would advise against charting an Aldegaadian vessel."

"You have nothing to fear from us, Princess," Karrer said gently and honestly. "Though we are pirates, you will come to no harm here aboard my ship. And we will get you where you are going."

"I'm sorry," I said, shaking my head. "It's just that the last few weeks have been a lot to deal with. I don't mean to appear ungrateful for your help, Captain."

"Think nothing of it," Karrer responded with a smile. "You are understandably sceptical, as are many of your party here."

"You'll excuse us if we don't jump for joy at being with a bunch of brigands like yourselves," Dolin scowled as he and Holger came up to stand at my side with Carden close behind.

"Of course," Karrer nodded, then gestured to Kororsh. "In the meantime, we should get you and your companion settled in, Princess. This is my first mate, Kororsh of Hordreg Jaaktar. If you have any need, please, do not hesitate to ask for either him or myself to assist you."

"We are set on course, Sarissi," Kororsh told Karrer gruffly. "It will take several days to round the coast and reach our passengers' destination."

"Excuse me," I said, looking between them and Aldwyn, " but, where are we going? Tristan only mentioned a keep."

Aldwyn explained: "We are making for the Guardian stronghold of Coastwatch Keep along the southern coasts of Aldegaad."

"It is the closest safe haven we can reach from here, Princess," Tallinn added, crossing her arms, her blonde hair catching in the cold wind. "Once we arrive there no one who means you harm will ever be able to reach you. You'll be safe."

"Alright," I nodded, understanding completely for a change. "That sounds like a good plan."

"Then, let us get you and Tristan settled," Karrer indicated for us to follow her. "You are our honoured guests during your stay with us. Welcome aboard the *Black Asp*."

I just smiled and nodded.

Tristan and I were then led to quarters below deck by the Captain while her Storvari first officer saw to the activities of the ship's crew. Tristan was paired into a room with Carden, which I have to admit Carden did not seem to appreciate. I saw a clear lack of trust towards the Wanderer from the Guardian, dismissing it as simply being watchful regarding my protection.

Joran followed us to the room that was set aside for me. It was a small single cabin with no windows to show me the sea. I was relieved by that point, not feeling so confident about my ability to handle sea travel.

"It isn't much," Captain Karrer said, looking around at the space, "but it should serve you well enough during the duration of your stay with us."

"It's fine," I assured her. "Believe me, I've stayed in worse places than this."

"As you say, Princess," she nodded to me, passing through the doorway and stopping beside Joran. "Dinner is in two hours. You and your companions are dining with me tonight. Will that suit?"

"Yes," I responded with a nod. "Thank you, Captain."

"I will leave you to settle in," she smiled and nodded, then turned down the rocking hall, Joran closing the door to my cabin behind her, obviously intending to remain outside.

I stood there staring at the room around me for a few moments, trying to get used to the idea that I was no longer my uncle's prisoner. I was back with people I trusted, even if we *were* on a ship full of people I did not know and whose morals were questionable at best.

Slowly, I sat down on the edge of the bed and let out a soft sigh. I couldn't even begin to comprehend what I was facing now, but at least I was safe enough.

There came a knock at the door and before I could move it was opening. Mithras stepped into the room and smiled warmly at me. My heart leaped with joy in my chest at seeing him and a smile spread over my face instantly.

"Mithras!" I cried out, running up to him and throwing my arms around him. "I'm so glad to see you!"

"As I am glad to see you, Leander," Mithras responded evenly.

He winced in pain and I stepped back quickly, staring up at him in concern.

"Are you badly hurt?" I asked him softly.

He shook his head, trying to give me a reassuring smile. "I believe I've had worse than this, my girl."

"I was so worried about you," I confessed as he led me to sit on the bed with him. "I was certain my uncle had wounded you mortally."

"Not yet, it seems," he assured me.

"Then, you're alright?" my voice sounded unconvinced, even to me.

He took in a painful breath and shook his head gravely. "I wouldn't say that I am alright, Leander. I definitely have suffered a great injury that will take time to heal."

I just nodded, resting my hands on the edge of the bed on either side of me.

There was another knock at the door and Aldwyn stepped in, carrying his blue stone topped staff with him.

"Forgive my intrusion, your Highness," he bowed his head respectfully. "Mithras, if you don't mind, I must treat the Princess for the injuries she sustained while she was imprisoned."

Mithras nodded, standing up gingerly. "Yes. That would be a good idea given the torture they forced upon her."

"Mithras," I grabbed his left wrist and he looked down at me. "Don't leave me."

"Do not fear," he smiled back at me. "I will see you at dinner. Now, let Aldwyn heal you. You certainly need it."

"Alright," I nodded softly, agreeing with him.

"I am glad you're safe, Leander," Mithras smiled, then left the room.

Aldwyn shut the door and turned back to me with gentle eyes. "Just lay back, your Highness, and we'll begin."

I did as I was told, slipping out of the brown coat then laying on my stomach and resting my head on the pillows, my arms folded beneath them.

Aldwyn sat on the side of the bed and began casting healing spells over me. I felt my injuries closing up immediately, the pain lingering for a little while and making me wince, but it started fading away soon enough.

"Your injuries are indeed severe, Princess," Aldwyn stated, observing my damaged skin as he healed it. "However, I assure you that you will soon be free of any scars, cuts or wounds. It will be as if the events in Aneuran had never even happened to you."

"That's good to know," I murmured, wincing as I felt the whip wounds in my back closing up.

As I lay there I thought: *I wish my memories of such terrible things could be erased as easily...*

Chapter Ten
The Dragon's Crest Passage

Dinner was certainly an interesting and somewhat comforting event. I was able to sit with my friends anew, free to be as I had become so accustomed to being while in their company. Set between Mithras and Carden I felt so relaxed, enjoying a meal of Northern Crestian Salmon from the ship's stores.

We didn't speak on what had transpired in Aneuran, none of us eager to recount those dire events yet. I was content to listen to the Dwarves singing tavern songs and to involve myself in the joking my friends chose to create. The Captain was as courteous a host as any noble I had ever dined with, her status as a pirate not excluding her from the social niceties I had been raised to show others myself.

When dinner came to its end - very late into the evening - I was both glad and disappointed. I didn't want to leave my companions after having been separated from them for so long, but I needed to rest and recover from the tortures inflicted on me.

I returned to my cabin, finding that I was exhausted after all that the last few months had put me through. The bed was inviting, calling me into it with a gentle yearning that lingered within me. Aldwyn's magic and the potion he had made me drink were still working on my body's healing and had made me drowsy. I was able to fall asleep with ease, the gentle rocking of the ship around me only helping me to slip away.

I don't know how long I slept before it began. All I know is what I saw was terrifying.

I woke to find myself lying on a cold stone floor, the walls, floors and ceilings all black. The air was chilled, clawing at me like the icy fingers of the dead. There was very little light, and what there was did not resemble real flames. The sinister sconces on the walls were like black steel hands with razor barbed claws on each of their five fingers. In their centre burned cold blue flames that were as frigid as the air surrounding them. Their glow barely illuminated anything at all, but it was enough to let me take in my surroundings.

I was in a long corridor that seemed to go on forever on either side of me. It was built of black stone and steel; the archways reaching so high above me that they were nearly unseen in the shadows. There were sinister hooded statues set evenly in pairs along the walls, each with a sword in its hands, point to the floor.

Where am I? What is this place?

I slowly brought myself to stand from where I had sat on the chilled floor, moving with caution, fearing what lingered in the dark. A sound caught my attention, drawing my gaze towards my right. It had sounded like a low growl, almost like that of a very large, very dangerous animal.

My curiosity urged me to move and I found myself edging along the corridor nervously. My heart was pounding in my chest, my pulse throbbing in my ears. I tried not to breathe too loudly as I brought myself to the section of the corridor where light began to appear. The light had a distinctive aqua-green hue, eerie and almost seeming alive.

I pulled myself slowly into the shadows, fearing that someone or something – whatever lingered in this dark place – would find me. I froze, my blue eyes searching the darkened space beyond, seeing the glow of the eerie light that flickered within. Gathering my courage, I slowly straightened up and stepped through the mammoth archway.

I was faced with an echoing chamber of stone and steel, a great chasm falling into deep shadow below. I was standing at the top of a giant stone staircase that led down to a long bridge reaching towards the centre of the cavernous space. That was where the light was coming from, the source eerie aqua coloured flames burning in bowls atop pedestals encircling the central floor.

Cautiously, I started down the stairs, afraid that I would fall. The chasm staring up at me made me feel lightheaded, my fear of heights beginning to affect me. There were no banisters, no railings at all to hold onto, this an easy way to meet my death if I wasn't careful. I tried to forget the immeasurably deep fall all around me, walking in the centre of the huge staircase, my eyes forward. I was focused on the bridge ahead of me and the rounded platform of stone it led to.

My eyes locked on a shape before me as I stepped off the bridge and onto the large circular platform as I passed by towering, haunting statues with sinister, deathly faces. They stared down at me as if they were about to spring to life and try to hurt me, but they weren't what scared me the most.

The black throne was a monstrous looking thing, razor sharp spines curving up from its frame, its main body made of black marble that gleamed coldly in the aqua light. A hideous skull face stared down from the head of the throne; great, sweeping black wings like a bat's held up and coiled around it imposingly. It was a true terror on its own, but it seated an even greater one.

I froze, staring in unadulterated terror at the figure sitting on the throne, my heart in my throat and my fingertips hurting so much they were numb. I couldn't breathe, my chest heaving so fast that I was feeling dizzy.

He sat there, long, grey fingers hooked over the front of each of the chair's arms, his robes making him appear as a deep living blackness. His hooded head was gently bowed, his face shrouded in the shadows that lived beneath it.

Suddenly, a low growl echoed around me and I looked up at the hulking shape that was rising behind the throne. A gigantic black horned head rose from the shadows of the chasm on a long armour scaled neck. Orange glowing eyes stared down at me as teeth as long as short swords gleamed from beneath the blackish lips. A shimmer of eerie green energy flashed through the beast's eyes as it stood up from the abyss, its claws crashing to the stone floor thunderously.

I staggered backwards, staring at the dragon in paralysing fear.

Movement caught my attention and I turned my eyes towards the figure on the throne, trembling as he began to move. He lifted his head with slow purpose, his green eyes seeming to glow beneath his crimson rimmed, black cowl's shadows. His monstrous face was stern at first, then it twisted into a sinister smile. I caught a glimpse of that black star pendant around his neck, the dark stone at its centre shimmering and surging with power. My eyes darted from it to its wearer's face, meeting that sinister gaze again.

"Princess," he hissed maliciously, smiling with evil glee. "I see you."

I staggered and fell backwards as he stood, hitting the ground hard, then propping myself up on my elbows and looking back at him again in fear. I tried to drag myself backwards, but he was moving towards me, on me in only a few moments and I felt a cold hand close around my throat, but it didn't choke me. He lifted me, hanging me helplessly as I grasped his wrist in desperation. He brought his face close to mine, smirking at me with vicious pleasure as I stared wide eyed back at him.

"You cannot hide from me, girl," he said evenly, his eyes very obviously glowing brighter now. "You can *never* hide from *me*."

I felt that comforting warmth enwrap me, and a purple light drew my gaze to the Pendant around my neck. Its stone glowed brightly and began to spread energy over everything.

The monster's eyes widened, and he snarled in rage, but he could do nothing. The Pendant shed a blast of energy through him, casting him away from me.

I fell towards the floor as he slammed back into his throne, shouting out in rage...

I woke suddenly, my chest heaving, my breaths short and quick. I was sweating through fear, my heart cracking hard against my ribcage, threatening to explode from my chest.

I sat up and looked around, my legs tangled up in the sheets. Anxiously, I took in the dully lit room that surrounded me, the boards groaning against the swell of the sea battering the hull. That was when I remembered that I was on a ship, that this was the cabin I had been given aboard the *Black Asp*.

A sigh of relief and frustration escaped my lips as I buried my face in my hands. I took in deep, frantic breaths, my chest shuddering hard, my shoulders shaking, hidden beneath my dark auburn locks.

After a few moments, I managed to calm myself, looking up at the room around me as I ran my hands through my hair, brushing it past my ears and shoulders.

That dream... It was too real. That evil place, the monster dragon... the Shadow Lord. It was all far too real. He couldn't have really seen me... Right? No. No, if he had he would already be here attacking me. It was just a dream. Yet, it must have meant something, but what?

Too uneasy to go back to sleep, I got up and threw my purple cloak on over my nightgown, then headed up to the deck. As soon as I stepped through the deck doors, I felt relief wash over me with the fresh, cool, salty air.

I looked around at the few people that were there, noting that Joran was speaking with Kororsh at the helm, Ellora standing at his side. I didn't need to approach them, not seeking comfort or company just yet. If anything, it was solitude I needed.

I wandered across the deck, paying no attention to the pirates that were on the night watch. I felt their eyes on me, but I chose not to react, knowing how they would respond. There was just no need to trudge through that mess right now.

I came to the ship's bow and rested my arms there on the forward wood railing. Hidden beneath my hood I felt more secure than if I had been without it. The flimsy fabric was a comfort to me in that moment and it shielded me from the cold westerly winds that came up from behind us as well as any unwelcome stares.

The shore was a shadowy blue-black to my left, the *Black Asp* not sailing close enough to allow me a detailed view. It seemed so distant, yet I knew we were not but a short way from it, still close enough to see the settlements and details of the natural shores by the light of day.

I started replaying my nightmare in my head, trying to uncover what its meaning was.

This could likely just be my fears playing on my mind. The Shadow Lord is after me and has planned my abduction for a reason that is still a mystery to me. It makes perfect sense that I should be afraid of him. What sane person wouldn't be?

Footsteps broke me from my thoughts, and I gritted my teeth in annoyance. The last thing I wanted was to be disturbed by one of those disgusting pirates for their perverted pleasures. I didn't need that.

"Leander?" *that* voice was comforting and welcomed by my heart, which fluttered in my chest upon hearing it.

I looked up as Carden came to my right side, his silver edged black cloak wrapped around him, his neatly cut hair flicking up in the wind. His eyes were full of care, but also concern. For a moment I thought to throw my arms around his neck and make my feelings known, but my uncertainty took hold and refused to release me.

"Carden," I said, surprised, but glad.

He leaned his folded arms on the railing with mine, his jade eyes never leaving my face. The torches of the ship were all that illuminated us to one another with the dark clouds high above.

"What are you doing out here all alone?" he asked me kindly.

I turned my eyes to the sea and shrugged. "I couldn't sleep."

"Nightmares?" he was so perceptive.

I nodded softly. "Yes."

"What about?"

I drew in a deep, shaky breath: "The Shadow Lord."

Carden just nodded, not seeming even the slightest bit surprised. "He frightens you," it wasn't a question; he just knew.

I nodded, fighting back the fear in my throat. "He really does."

"It's alright," he tried to be reassuring, his hand pressed to my back gently. "He can't hurt you here. You're safe."

I shook my head, turning my back to lean against the wooden railing. "I don't know if I feel safe anywhere."

"I can understand that," Carden said gently, following my gesture, his arms crossed. "You haven't exactly had much success when it comes to finding safe places since this all began."

"Even Aneuran wasn't safe," I sighed, more to myself than to him. "I... I grew up visiting my uncle in the palace. Nowhere outside of Arvon was safer to me than Aneuran... but now Fane has destroyed that."

There was silence between us for a few moments, neither of us knowing what to say. So many things were rushing through my mind, but I wasn't sure that I could speak them aloud. Not yet anyway.

I wanted to tell Carden how I felt about him. I wanted him to know the truth about what lay within my heart. I just wasn't ready for him to know it all yet. I also wasn't ready to tell him that it was thanks to our enemy that I had finally understood why I was so drawn to him. Four months of such close proximity and trust had led me to this, and I wanted to know what else was to come from it. Then again, I also had obligations, and a princess could not pledge herself to a man of orphaned heritage, as would be the case here. But I loved him. And these two things were waging a silent war inside me now, fighting with me, trying to make me confess as though they were my captors and interrogators.

"I'm sorry I left you behind," he spoke with guilt in his voice, his eyes on his boots now. "I should never have run from the battle as I did. Not when you needed me."

"Carden," I drew his gaze to me, looking him in the eyes, "you *didn't* abandon me. You came for me and protected me, as I knew you would."

He smiled sheepishly. "Well, were it not for the note you sent to Fawkner we would never have found our avenue to rescue you."

"I didn't really do anything," I said, feeling a heat rush my cheeks as I fought the urge to blush.

He grasped my hand, making my heart flutter again as I nervously met his gaze. "You stayed strong," he told me, pride in his handsomely velvet voice. "You stalled the Regent against killing you and Mithras and gave us an opportunity to mount a rescue. You risked everything for a chance to escape that nightmare, and so you have."

I smiled meekly, running a hand through my hair bashfully. "I... I had my reasons for staying strong. And it wasn't just to keep myself alive."

He frowned curiously. "What kept you so strong, Leander?"

I met his gaze, my chest feeling heavy as a shuddering breath filled my lungs. I had to really fight not to blush now, forcing myself to be as even toned as I could be.

"I wanted... to see you again," I admitted a little too girlishly.

"Me?" he was genuinely surprised.

I nodded, leaning my left hand on the rail, looking at the deck beneath us absentmindedly. "Thinking of you was what kept me going," I told him, carefully picking my words.

"Really?" he was half smiling, half stunned.

I met his gaze and gave him a tiny nod. "Yes. I couldn't bear it if I didn't get to see you one more time. You... you mean a lot to me, Carden."

He came closer, his hand on my shoulder, his face closing on mine very slowly: "You mean a lot to me too."

I felt myself shaking at his touch.

We were slowly coming together, and I wondered if I was truly ready for this. I hadn't known Carden anywhere near as long as my sister had known her husband before they had first embraced. But I *ached* for this. Every part of my being was screaming at me to accept this, to allow myself to feel what lived in my heart. And I wanted to. More than anything in the world I wanted to, yearning deeply for his touch.

"Leander," he said softly, his voice slightly breathy as our eyes locked.

"Yes?" I whispered, feeling like this would be it.

"I-"

"There you are, lad," a voice called out and we slowly drew back from each other.

Disappointed, I turned my gaze in time with Carden's to see Dolin and Holger walking up to us, Dolin having been the one to call out. I silently cursed the two Dwarves for interfering in our moment, but it was gone.

"Yes, Dolin?" Carden addressed the Dwarf, hiding his own frustration so well, if he was frustrated at all.

"My apologies for the intrusion, your Highness," Dolin bowed his head to me respectfully, then looked back to Carden, "but Aldwyn has asked that all Guardians meet in his cabin."

Carden groaned and nodded. "Alright. I'm coming."

He went to leave, then paused and turned back to me, his eyes falling to my pendant.

"I'm just glad I could return your pendant to you, Princess," he said softly, his tone one of professionalism now.

Feeling a little taken aback, I placed a hand to my pendant on my collarbones, meeting his gaze. "Thank you for caring for it. And for Amethyst as well," I said a little too softly.

"I was happy to do it," he nodded to me. "I hope you can sleep better now after taking in the air. Goodnight, your Highness."

"Goodnight," I murmured as he walked away, the two Dwarves pausing for a moment.

"Goodnight, Princess," Dolin nodded to me and I gave him a silent nod in return.

"Princess," Holger regarded me with gruff respect, then turned and followed his brother.

I stood for a few seconds, a little lost by what had just happened. I was annoyed that the moment had been ruined by the Dwarves' untimely interjection, no matter how respectful they were. But I also felt a certain sadness in my heart.

Maybe it's better this way. Maybe I should just accept that a girl like me could never be with a man like him, I thought grimly.

I sighed, looking down at my hands as I twisted my fingers together gently.

"Well, that was awkward," a voice observed, making me jump.

I looked to my right to see Tristan standing there in the shadows of the forward mast, his brown eyes locked on me. I hated to think that he had seen all of that, that he had watched my failure to admit my feelings to Carden. It felt like in his silence that he had invaded our moment worse than the Dwarves had.

"How much of that did you see?" I asked with more harshness in my tone than I liked.

"Enough," he replied with a shrug. "Care for some advice?"

"No," I snapped softly. "And keep what you saw to yourself. It's none of your concern."

"As you say, Princess," he nodded. "Goodnight."

"Right," I muttered. "Goodnight."

I strode away as calmly, but as quickly as I could, not interested in dealing with this any further. Now I only longed for the solitude of my temporary bed and the quiet of my own company. I immediately missed Amethyst and started to wonder where my dragon was at that moment.

* * * * *

Carden and I didn't speak of our conversation on the first night for the rest of the short trip. It seemed like it was better left alone for now, and I was too unsure to bring it up again. I was only glad that he still chose to spend time with me, though this was mostly with the others in sight.

I also didn't see Mithras at all after the first night. He had secluded himself in his cabin to rest from his injuries, which I could only agree with his reasoning. A sword through the shoulder wasn't something he could just get over. For the most part I did the same, staying in my cabin and sleeping away the tiredness the dungeons and my narrowly avoided wedding had caused. I could only thank the Divines that I had escaped that horror.

It was late morning when the *Black Asp* came into sight of the seaside town of Seacliff, the passage to the keep only another half an hour from our position. I joined the others on deck as they gathered, the pirates moving quickly to hide the ship's colours and make it less attractive to the city's soldiers.

"How do you fare, Sarissi?" Joran asked, coming up to stand beside me.

"I'm alright, Joran," I responded, noting Kororsh moving to stand with the Captain at the helm. "What about you?"

"I have travelled the sea quite often," Joran responded evenly. "I enjoy the rocking of the waves."

"I meant about the other Storvari," I said. "How is it seeing one of your own kind here?"

The stare he gave me could have curdled milk and made crows leave crops: "It is as it would be in my homeland; respectful and brief."

"What do you mean?" I frowned.

"Kororsh and I have conversed," he explained in that never altering even tone, "and we have shown each other the respect necessary of our people. But there is nothing else to be gained through continued conversing."

That surprised me: "Really? I would think you'd want to spend some time with one of your own people with so many humans around you."

"Storvari do not carry the same importance on verbal bonding as you humans do," he expressed a little coldly. "We say all we need to in as few words as possible so that we do not waste our words. It is the way of our people and I have no need to deviate from that path."

"Alright," was all I could say.

Joran just nodded and moved away as Fawkner and Mithras came over to me. I was too afraid to say anything else to Joran, his tone and gaze freezing my blood.

"Trying to get a Storvari to socialise more than he does with his own people is never a good idea," Mithras commented, smiling at me. "Not even for the holder of his life debt."

"I was only curious," I confessed, crossing my arms beneath my cloak.

"Do not fear, girl," Fawkner said evenly. "It is an easy mistake to make. Storvari aren't the most talkative amongst our kind, and that goes the same for their own."

"I understand that now," I said, shaking my head, then frowned as I noticed the purplish swelling around his left eye and cheek. "Gods! Fawkner, what happened to your face?!"

"I had a little... ahem... *disagreement*," he confessed guardedly, but sheepishly.

"With who?" I stared at him sternly, for a moment thinking I sounded like my mother.

"Carden and I... had words," was his response.

"Carden hit you? Why?" I was shocked.

"It's best left between me and him," Fawkner answered evasively.

I nodded dubiously at him, then looked to Mithras: "Well, speaking of injuries, how are you, Mithras?"

"Well enough," he said.

I frowned again. "You're looking paler than you were when last I saw you."

"Just tiredness, Leander," he assured me. "Do not worry."

One of the pirates shouted out something in the Harredi language and the crew began moving frantically. I looked around in confusion as they rushed about, Carden coming to my side swiftly and pulling me away from their activities.

"What's happening?" I asked, confused.

"The lookout has seen a ship in the Seacliff port," Fawkner explained, obviously knowing the language well enough since one of his men who'd abducted me in the past had been Harredi. "An Aldegaadian frigate flying the military standard."

"Which could cause us some trouble," Captain Karrer agreed, standing at the helm with Aldwyn, Tallinn and Ellora only a few feet away from us. "From the way they're situated it looks like they could be on look out."

"Are we likely to be boarded?" Aldwyn asked her, hidden under his cloak and hood from the cold.

Captain Karrer shook her head, hands on the helm wheel. "No. We're already entering the Dragon's Crest Passage. They won't follow. The waters get violent here. Brace yourselves."

"Hold onto me," Carden instructed me, pulling me into his arms and placing my hands on the railing.

My back was pressed into his chest, his larger frame keeping me secured, his hands holding mine firmly, but gently. My heart skipped a beat at his closeness and my pulse accelerated. This felt right.

Tristan, Joran and the Dwarves were on the deck below where we stood, bracing themselves as Mithras, Fawkner, Aldwyn, Tallinn and Ellora did the same around us. The pirates were rushing to secure themselves now, the sails having been brought to half-mast. A knot formed in my stomach and I became suddenly worried over what was about to happen next.

The ship seemed to lurch and shake, the cliffs closing in around us on both sides, but closer on the ship's port side. A large island cliff was off to starboard but was far enough away that it didn't affect us all that much, though I certainly tensed up at the thought of colliding with it.

Captain Karrer was bracing herself against the helm, forcing it to hold firm, Kororsh taking over a moment later and allowing her to press herself against the aft railing instead. The ship was bucking all over the place, the rapid movements making me feel like I would be sick at any time.

"Hold on!" Captain Karrer shouted from where she braced herself beside Aldwyn and Tallinn. "This part gets a little tricky!"

The water was rushing over the ship's lower exposed deck now, the sound of the waves thunderous in my ears. The rocky cliffs were jutting out in all directions and the ship had to be navigated carefully. Just seeing the jagged rocks made me worry that we would hit them and sink. But we didn't. We made it through the passage unscathed.

After a few minutes, Captain Karrer shouted out to her crew: "Way anchor! Drop canvas! All hands!"

The ship began to settle as the crew did as they were instructed. The others in our party began to move and Carden released his grasp on me, allowing me to turn around.

"Are you alright, Leander?" he asked softly.

I nodded. "I'm just feeling a little sick from the waves. Otherwise I'm fine."

Captain Karrer turned to Aldwyn: "This is as far as we can take the *Black Asp*. Any farther and we risk significant damage to the hull and rudder."

"It's alright, Captain," Aldwyn assured her gently, staff in hand, Tallinn looking ill beside him. "We are close enough to the keep that we can walk from the shore."

"As you wish, Guardian," Captain Karrer nodded, arms crossed over her ample chest. "I will have some of my men take you ashore, then we'll be heading on our way. Contact me through the usual way if you have any further need of us."

"Here's your payment, as agreed upon," Aldwyn took a pouch of gold from his belt and handed it to her. "You have our thanks."

Captain Karrer turned to me then: "Princess, I wish you luck and hope you find the safety you seek."

I nodded to her, feeling too sick to say anything, but I tried. "Th-thank you, Captain Karrer..."

We gathered what few belongings we still had – including my own bag – and loaded into three boats. The pirates took us to the shore within sight of the bow, dropping us off here before heading back to the ship.

We began walking along the sandy and rocky beach, Aldwyn and Tallinn leading the way towards a cliff path that led up and out of the narrow channel we had found ourselves in.

Carden and Tristan stayed close to me, the three of us walking together in silence, the Dwarves and Joran at our heels. That old familiar feeling of being overprotected returned to me and I silently cursed it, though I was also somewhat glad of it too.

It took us about an hour to traverse the cliffs, finally coming within sight of the keep. It was a large stone castle very similar to the way Castle Arvon had been before the attack that destroyed it. There was a single large tower at the heart of the fortress, four smaller towers forming the corners with a bridge and tower set across into another section that was formed over a breach in the cliffs.

"Am I really going to be safe here?" I asked Carden uncertainly.

He nodded. "Coastwatch Keep is one of the oldest Guardian strongholds. It's been around since the original Order was founded four thousand years ago. You couldn't be safer."

"I'm glad," I nodded, my eyes forward as I walked beside him. "I don't want to deal with any more of what I've had to lately. It's too much as it is."

He was looking at me, his stare drawing my gaze instinctually. My heart fluttered and again I longed to express my truest emotions to him.

"I promise you, Leander, that I will never allow you to come to any harm," Carden vowed, honesty and deepest care in his eyes.

"I know you won't," I smiled and kissed him on the cheek.

He smiled back, blushing a little at my touch.

I tried to hide my own blushing cheeks beneath my hood and my hair, succeeding somewhat.

It took us a few minutes longer, but we came at last to the main gates of the keep. They stood before us, intimidating and impressive. And also... open.

I frowned as I saw this, Carden stepping in front of me as Tristan came up behind me, both men wearing severe expressions. I threw a glance to Aldwyn, the Mage's brow furrowed as he slowed his pace, the rest of us doing the same.

Tallinn had her bow in hand and an arrow laced to the string in anticipation, her hazel eyes severe, her blonde hair catching lightly in the wind. She followed close to Aldwyn, the two cautious as we approached the gates.

Fawkner and Ellora stayed on either side of Mithras, both drawing their swords and moving carefully, the old knight uncharacteristically leaving his own weapon sheathed. He was surely in great pain.

A loud dual grinding of metal told me that Joran had his swords ready, the giant close behind me. Dolin and Holger drew their axes and hammer, both of them suspicious as they came up on our left carefully.

I pushed my hood back, looking up at the grey walls before us, nothing seeming damaged as far as I could tell. But something was definitely wrong.

There came a rush of wind and a massive shape swooped in and landed to my left. We all started as a large, but sleek purple and blue scaled dragon settled to the sandy, grassy ground, her orange eyes locking on me immediately.

"Amethyst," I moved to her, staring up at her in awe and relief. "I'm so happy to see you," I reached out to pat her nose, but withdrew my hand at her agitation.

Amethyst growled lowly, almost warningly, her eyes turning towards the keep's open gates, her wings raised agitatedly.

"What is it?" I asked, looking to the others.

"Something's not right here," Aldwyn noted grimly, his dark eyes surveying our surroundings carefully. "The gates should not be open as they are."

"There should also be guards," Tallinn added, her worry clear, though she tried to control it. "Gods, where is everyone?"

"What do we do?" Tristan asked, his own bow in hand, his other poised to snatch an arrow from his back at any second.

After a few moments, Aldwyn said: "We go in carefully and see if we can find someone. This is our last bastion of safety for the Princess and we must ensure its security."

With that decided, we began our way in, though Amethyst gave me a low growl that made me feel we shouldn't enter the keep. All I could do was try to swallow back my fear and keep close to my protectors. But there was no shaking the feeling that something here was terribly wrong.

Chapter Eleven
Coastwatch Keep

Entering the courtyard felt more and more like a bad idea with every step we took. Yet, we continued on, our party slowly edging farther into the seemingly deserted confines of the fortress' battlements and stone walls. I clung close to Carden and Tristan, both men offering some sense of safety to me as a deep feeling of dread forced its way into my chest. Even the knowledge that I wore my pendant around my neck did nothing to ease my newfound fear.

"Strange," Ellora remarked, having moved to the head of the group, stepping foot over foot in a graceful movement as her turquoise eyes scanned our surroundings, "a stronghold such as this one should not be so... empty."

Tallinn had moved up in a parallel position with her bow ready, her eyes roving the sun-drenched courtyard nervously.

"There are no signs of battle here," she observed gravely. "Nothing to suggest an attack," she paused near the central well and glanced down as Fawkner slowed near her. She frowned as she turned her gaze around at the walls. "Everyone's just..."

"Gone," Fawkner agreed, carrying his falcon on his arm, his other hand resting on the pommel of his sword.

The Dwarves had moved to the smithy and were staring at the worktables and forge beneath the thatched roof and wooden framed walls. I was close enough to see the fire burning in the forge and smell the heat of the coals.

"The forge is still hot," Dolin observed, closing one gloved hand around the hilt of a sword that remained in it. He drew the weapon out to reveal that its blade had been melted beyond recognition. "This sword was left to the mercy of the fire and coals. No smith would do such a thing."

"Aye," Holger agreed, twitchy and ready with his hammer in both hands. "Some dread thing must have befallen the denizens of this castle."

Could this be the Shadow Lord's work? I wondered uneasily, twisting my hands together nervously beneath my cloak, my mind drifting back to that night at the Citadel of Dartaren. *Has he countered us again?*

"Look," Tristan kicked over a basket that lay on the ground, fruit and vegetables scattered across the stone paving around it. "This food's at least a few hours old."

"Whatever happened here happened swiftly," Ellora deduced as she moved to study the basket and fruits. "And likely within the day."

"It may still be happening," Tallinn stated gravely, worry hidden in her hazel eyes. "What should we do Aldwyn?"

Aldwyn glanced to me where I stayed between Carden and Joran, Amethyst's large form ducking through the gates and slowly moving up behind us. I looked to her, seeing the strange expression in her orange eyes and knew that she was worried.

I glanced to Mithras, his eyes set on the castle keep that lay before us, his left hand on his sword, his right slung tightly to his chest. He wore his silver armour, but he didn't look so strong in it, if anything seeming more like he was straining under its weight. A new concern for him flooded my heart and mind, and I moved to his side as Aldwyn decided our next course of action.

"We'll make our way into the main keep," Aldwyn decreed in a low, quiet tone, both hands gripping his staff. "But we must be on our guard and have our weapons at the ready. We cannot be certain of what has happened here."

"Something dire, perhaps?" Fawkner grumbled.

"We must not assume anything," Aldwyn advised him wisely. "Set your falcon to the skies, Fawkner. Let us know if she sees anything from above."

With that, Fawkner whispered to Farsight, his lips close to her head. He turned and launched her into the air, the falcon calling out as she began her ascent towards the grey cloudy sky, the sun peeking through meekly with golden rays that silhouetted her graceful winged form.

I reached Mithras, studying his pallid skin and the cold sweat that was dampening his hair and beading his brow. His eyes had grown darker and he was trembling as if shivering with cold.

"Mithras?" I placed a hand on his steel plated arm, drawing his almost distracted gaze. "Are you alright?"

"Sorry?" he turned his eyes to me, blinking as if sleep clung to his eyelids.

"I said, are you alright?" I repeated softly, frowning at him.

"Yes, yes, Leander, I'm fine," he forced a smile at me. "I'm just tired. I suppose I need more rest from my injuries than that which the journey on the *Black Asp* has afforded me."

"You're sure?" I asked doubtfully.

He nodded fervently. "I assure you, my girl, that I am fine. Are you?"

"I'm worried about you," I admitted. "You don't look well."

"As I've said, I am in need of rest," he said evenly, wobbling on his feet a little.

"She's right, Ser Mithras," Carden joined us with a grave expression, his black and silver cloak swaying behind him. "Truly, you look ill."

"Do not chide me the way you would an enfeebled old man!" Mithras snapped at both of us. "I need not the wasted pity of children thrown so carelessly my way!"

"Mithras!" Ellora called to him, everyone staring at us. "Carden and the Princess are only concerned for you. As are we all."

Mithras blinked as if coming out of a trance, staring at me with bewildered eyes.

He let his left hand drift to my cheek and touched my skin softly: "Forgive me, Leander. I meant nothing by my outburst. I grow tired and irritable with my injuries."

"It's alright, Mithras," I tried to reassure him, though I couldn't reassure my nagging heart.

Aldwyn had moved to us now and was right at our sides with a deep frown on his tanned face. "Are you able to continue with us, my friend?" he asked of Mithras.

Mithras nodded: "I will be fine. Though, to be sure that I am I think Leander should stay by my side to keep me company, and for her own safety."

"I agree," Aldwyn looked to Carden. "Stay at their backs as we enter the keep. Have your sword ready."

"Of course, Aldwyn," Carden responded, drawing his sword in his right hand.

"Alright," Aldwyn called to our group clearly and concisely. "We'll take this slow as we enter the keep. Fawkner, Tallinn and I will take the lead, Tristan and Ellora next, the Dwarves and Joran to cover the rear."

He turned with a swish of his black and silver mage's over-robe, drawing his sword as he started up the steps to the keep's doors.

We started to follow, Amethyst moving to block mine, Mithras' and Carden's path. She growled warningly; the sound mournful like she thought she wouldn't see us again.

"It's alright, Amethyst," I tried to reassure her, suddenly feeling that this was my part in this new situation. "Just stay here and if we need you, come. Alright?"

She snorted and growled again, bringing her head close to my face.

"I'll be safe with the others," I said, somehow understanding her. "I promise. Trust me."

Reluctantly, the Dragon pulled her head up on her long neck and began to walk around behind us, letting us pass by her towards the keep. I glanced over my shoulder at her, then continued forward, both hands on Mithras' left arm.

Leaving Amethyst to guard the courtyard, we made our way up the main stairs and through the keep's enormous steel reinforced wooden doors. Beyond them was a large entry hall with many stone pillars, light shining through a stained-glass window above the door depicting the Guardian crest of the shield and two swords crossed behind it. Black and silver drapes hung from the walls with the same emblem sewn onto them, the windows along one wall letting the sunlight in. The floors were bare stone aside from the large running carpet of black with silver trims that went from the entrance to another large door at the far end of the hall. Except for a few stone carvings of what could be assumed to be depicting Guardians, and four long wooden benches mirroring each other on opposing sides of the room, there was very little furnishing.

"The main stairway is behind these doors," Aldwyn directed as we traversed the space and reached the far end of the hall. "This will lead up to the Great Hall. Perhaps the rest of our brethren are there."

"Are you sure, Aldwyn?" Tallinn looked doubtful.

Aldwyn gave her a half-hearted look, then pushed open the doors without a word.

Tallinn threw Carden, Mithras and I a worried expression, then followed behind Fawkner as I felt that familiar hard lump in my throat and the claw of dread around my heart again.

Mithras, Carden and I followed behind Ellora and Tristan, passing through the doors into a large circular chamber, a stone spiral staircase going up the tower in front of us. There was one torch lit in a sconce, but the rest were dark, the only other light coming through the sparsely spaced windows that allowed the daylight in. I kept my arm around Mithras' waist as we started up the stairs, his left arm squeezing across my shoulders.

I lost count of the number of times that we had circled around the stairway, feeling suddenly disoriented. At first, I just assumed it was the darkness, but something else started to stir inside me. I began to hallucinate, strange flashes forming in front of my eyes, but not frequent enough, long enough or clear enough to discern. My heart grew heavy and I felt an awful, oozing heat rise over me as if I had sunk slowly into some terrible, gooey, thick liquid.

Ellora slowed near us behind Tristan, her turquoise eyes so prominent in the poor light. Her arms were at her sides, her bow in her left hand, her legs tensing their muscles beneath her brown and green Elvish light armour. She turned her head slowly as she studied the way above us, her long red locks sweeping across the middle of her back gently. Her pointed ears twitched as she took in slow, laboured breaths, almost as if she had developed an affliction of the chest.

"Do you smell that?" she asked of us gravely. "The air is stale, old, as if none have passed through these passages in centuries."

"What do you mean?" Carden looked up curiously from behind Mithras and me.

"The only places I have smelled such a scent is in the crypts and burial chambers of High-Realm," she confessed, turning her turquoise gaze towards us. "Such places are ancient and long undisturbed. This scent does not belong in a place such as this."

"These halls reek of death," Joran declared in a low, ominous voice further behind us. "This place is calmenok vanar."

"What does that mean?" I asked, looking up at Mithras for the answers.

"That's Storvari," he explained grimly, "for 'damned by evil death'."

"Not very comforting," Dolin grumbled as he lumbered up behind us.

"We must keep moving," Aldwyn called from ahead, glancing past Tallinn, Fawkner and Tristan at the rest of us. "Carefully and quietly lest we draw any unwanted attention to ourselves."

"Like the attention of ghosts," Tristan murmured, maybe thinking none of us could hear him.

I gulped nervously and continued forward with Mithras a little awkwardly.

As we climbed the stairs the smell became stronger, choking my nostrils and making me feel worse. I suddenly felt lightheaded, breathing seeming impossible as I tried to take in a sharp, loud, desperate gust of air. Dizziness overwhelmed me and I fell against the wall, only just hearing Mithras call out my name and Carden swearing as they both reached for me.

I slumped against my left shoulder and back, my knees buckling, Carden catching me before I could fall. I grasped desperately at my throat, green and black spots blurring my vision as heat and dizziness threw me into a deep nausea. More cries echoed around me, but I wasn't able to break through the suffocating haze to register them.

Swift flashes entered my mind as I saw what I could only describe as a nightmarish retelling of what had happened in the fortress. In the early hours of the morning a sinister, towering figure stalked towards the front gates of the castle; clad in blood crimson robes and an ebony cloak, black steel armour covering his entire body with clawed gauntlets clenching at his sides. Terrifying red glowing eyes shone through the blackness behind a masked helm and hood, a sinister darkness living within the armour.

The Guardians were fighting what I could only see as their own forces; Guardians battling Guardians. Then I noticed that many of the aggressors were living dead dressed as Guardians.

I saw the crimson clad knight - lacking a better word to describe his armoured form - striding ominously through the halls, grasping a Guardian man by the throat who tried to stop him. He drained the life from the man, seeming to make him another living, shambling corpse.

As the battle continued the monstrous figure let loose a horrifying, ear splitting shriek, making the living cower in terror. He turned to a door somewhere in the fortress and strode towards it...

"Leander!" Mithras' worried voice pulled me back to the real world just as I vomited on the steps, feeling horribly sick.

"Eck! Charming!" Holger growled, jumping away from me. "The lass can't keep her food down!"

"Shut up, Holger!" Dolin snapped at him. "Leave the wee girl be."

I was sitting on the wide step with my knees up and my back to the wall, breathing hard and sweating coldly. Mithras' cool hand was brushing across my forehead as he looked to me worriedly.

"Thank the Gods," Carden breathed a sigh of relief, crouching at my side. "We thought we'd lost you."

"What... what happened?" I croaked, my throat burning, my hands useless at my sides.

"You collapsed," Mithras explained as calmly as he could manage. "The three of you nearly lost consciousness."

"The three of us?" I raised an eyebrow at him. "Who else fell?"

"Aldwyn and Tristan," Carden explained.

"Are they hurt?" my voice sounded a lot more frantic than I had meant it to.

"No," Mithras replied. "But you've hit your head, Leander. Sit still for a moment."

"Aldwyn?" Tallinn's voice drew my weak gaze up the stairs to where the others were.

From where I rested, I saw Tristan sitting facing us with his head in his hands while Ellora gently rubbed his back. Aldwyn was behind him with Tallinn and Fawkner standing over him. He was still on his feet, though up against the wall and leaning forward into his staff, breathing heavily.

"Aldwyn, are you alright?" Tallinn sounded so much like a frantic daughter worrying for her father.

"I'm alright," Aldwyn coughed, clearing his throat and straightening up as she held his arm to steady him. He turned his gaze down the stairs and said: "Who else has fallen?"

"Tristan and Leander," Carden called back to him. "Leander's very sick and has hit her head."

"Tristan's quite wobbly and dazed, but otherwise fine," Ellora responded calmly as she continued to tend to him.

"Aldwyn?" Tallinn urged her mentor gently, her hazel eyes locked softly on his face as her brow furrowed with concern. "What happened?"

"I felt suddenly sick and disoriented," he explained gravely, still a little nauseous, blinking against his own sick sweat dampening his skin. "It was like being hurled into the air and continuously cast in different directions without any discernible order."

"What did this?" Fawkner wondered aloud, glancing at the three of us who had collapsed. "And why you three?"

"There is only one thing that I know of to be capable of causing such an affliction on people," Aldwyn deduced direfully. "Tristan, the Princess and I have just encountered an intrusion from the powers of an immensely potent necromancer."

"A necromancer?" Carden asked incredulously and fearfully.

"A sorcerer whose main discipline is directed towards raising and dominating the dead," Aldwyn replied. "Which explains the visions I saw. Did either of you see visions?"

"That I did," Tristan coughed, covering his mouth as if to vomit.

I just nodded, finding that I had no strength to speak.

"As did Leander," Mithras answered for me.

"Then why didn't the necromancer's powers affect the rest of us?" Dolin asked. "I felt nothing."

"Me neither," Holger added.

Ellora explained, more knowledgeable than even Aldwyn, who was looking very confused and unwell: "Aldwyn is a mage and, I am assuming, so is Tristan."

"Untrained," Tristan responded hoarsely. "My Mam was one and so am I."

"Which is why they've both been affected," she continued.

"I'm... I'm not a mage," I croaked, trying awkwardly to sit up straighter, Mithras holding my shoulder to support me. "That makes... no sense..."

"Though you are no mage you are still affected because of *what* you are, Princess," Ellora answered evenly.

"What does that mean?" Carden was frowning as he stayed at my side, glancing between Ellora and I.

Mithras answered gravely: "Necromancers can only cause this effect on two types of people: Mages and Pendant holders. Because she carries one of the thirteen Dragon Pendants Leander can be afflicted by the illness powerful necromancers cause as she too carries magic within her, though a different sort to that which mages command."

"Great," I groaned. "Just what I need. Something else that can hurt me."

"Does... does that mean the n-n-necromancer is still here?" Tallinn was trembling in the fiercest fear I had ever seen come over her.

"Perhaps," Aldwyn admitted grimly. "The affliction we've felt could be his sudden departure, however it could also mean that he has unleashed his power up in the higher levels of the keep."

"What now?" Tristan asked, trying to recover as best he could.

"Our best chance to... to recover would be to reach a safe location inside the keep," Aldwyn staggered, looking like he had nearly blacked out. "We'll have to go on but be careful; the necromancer has been casting. There could be reanimated dead all over the tower. Be on your... your guard."

"Come on, Leander," Carden helped me to my feet, he and Mithras steadying me enough that I could walk.

"It's alright, child, I've got you," Mithras assured me, holding me around my waist as I held onto him.

Unsteadily, I staggered beside him, letting Mithras lead me carefully, Carden now in front of us. I was still struggling to see without dizziness and spots in my vision, but I was less weakened than I had been before.

We reached the top of the stairs, Ellora and Fawkner now leading as our vanguard, both with a sword at the ready. Aldwyn followed with Tallinn, who was very uneasy as she tightly gripped her sword. I had never seen the blonde-haired girl look so worried in all my time knowing her, every shadow and spider's web seeming to frighten her all of a sudden.

There's something about necromancers that scares Tallinn more than anything else, I thought curiously, barely putting the words together in my aching head. *I wonder why they frighten her so much.*

Ellora and Fawkner led us into another hallway similar to the one that had led us to the stairs. The difference here was that this one was in ruins and there were bodies everywhere, the battle suddenly very obvious. Among them were Guardians that looked as if they had just died as well as others who looked much more decayed.

I vomited again, heaving at my feet as the smell hit me, Mithras pausing and trying to soothe me.

"Careful," Ellora had taken the lead now that Aldwyn was too ill to continue. "If a necromancer is here, any of these corpses could become an enemy."

"Watch your step," Fawkner directed us, edging forward with Ellora, his sword at the ready, but low at his side.

"Don't look, Leander," Mithras urged me as I felt sure I would faint from the sight of the bodies, as well as the smell of the desiccated flesh and spilled blood. "Close your eyes. I've got you."

I just nodded and clung to Mithras, letting him lead me blindly through the slaughter, though there hadn't been more than ten or twelve bodies. Still, to me that was far too many.

We traversed the room hazardously, each of us waiting for any kind of an attack to come, but nothing did. All remained silent and it was just us and the slumbering dead.

I opened my eyes and found my courage as we reached the doors at the far end. We passed through and into a hall which contained another set of doors before us, two others to our right and left. The doors before us were closed, the others open wide, devastation lingering within and more bodies sprawling on the stone floors.

Ellora and Fawkner moved to the closed doors and pushed against them, but they didn't budge, groaning and clanking loudly against whatever blocked them.

"The way is barred," Fawkner stated grimly. "Whatever lies behind here must be of great importance."

"It's the Great Hall," Aldwyn said, looking a little stronger as he stood with Tallinn, the colour returning to his cheeks. "We must enter these doors."

"Joran," Fawkner gestured for the giant.

"Sarissi?" Joran looked down at me with his violet eyes for my approval.

I just nodded, still feeling too ill to really say or do much.

Without any further orders, the Storvari lumbered forward and braced his enormous palms to each door. He gritted his teeth behind closed lips and strained only very slightly as he pushed the doors, his bare arms flexing, their muscles even more obvious with the mild exertion.

There came the tumbling crash of whatever lay behind as he walked forward slowly, opening the doors. I got only a short glance at the room beyond before being thrown into the cover of the nearest column as arrows and crossbow bolts hurtled towards us.

"Kill it!" someone shouted from inside the hall. "The necromancer has called up some kind of brute!"

Joran had moved surprisingly fast to my side with Mithras and Carden, the four of us hiding there as the others took cover around us.

"Must we come under attack everywhere we go?!" Fawkner shouted as he shied away from the shots with Ellora, holding her to his chest and away from being hit.

"Stop!" Aldwyn called loudly into the room beyond the doors. "We are not your enemies! I am a Guardian!"

"Identify yourself!" someone shouted.

"I am Aldwyn Draken, Mage of Safferan and Master Guardian of the Isle's Peak Tower contingent," Aldwyn declared loudly. "I sent word ahead to the Coastwatch Warden announcing my party's intention to come here."

"Lower your weapons!" another voice was ordering, but not of us. "They are not with the enemy who attacked us."

There were a few moments of awkward tension as we heard the sounds of weapons being lowered and movement inside the hall. I glanced up at Carden as he held me close in his arms, Mithras pressing his good hand to my back as we stayed in the cover of the column.

"May we enter?" Aldwyn requested.

"Come forth, friend," the second voice granted. "The way is clear."

"Slowly," Aldwyn directed the rest of us, he and Tallinn bravely stepping into view of the doors and going first.

The rest of us followed cautiously, moving into the Great Hall behind the two Guardians. The room was a round space with a domed ceiling of stonework, the columns supporting it each holding a sconce with a lit torch. Light streamed in from the high, narrow slats in the walls, the chilled sea air frosting the atmosphere inside the room. There were black and silver banners hanging from the walls with the Guardian emblem on them just like in the rooms we had passed through before, the largest of these hanging from the wall opposite the doors we were entering. There was a great brazier burning in the centre of the room, its heat spreading the only warmth the centuries old fortress chamber seemed to possess.

There were around thirty people assembled there, some injured, some tending to them, the rest armed and ready. They were a gathering of many races from all over High-Realm; humans of the seven nations - though mostly Aldegaad - Elves, Dwarves, and even a few Orcs. Behind the Orcs I noted a golden eyed, pale skinned woman with an eerie pallor and a haunting beauty. I gained a frightening chill from her unlike with all the other Guardians, then noticed Carden's long stare at her before he tore his gaze away. It was strange, but I didn't think anything of it.

Regardless of their race or creed, each individual wore varying styles of clothing, all wearing at least one article in black with silver trims, and all with the black and silver Guardian cloaks.

I felt a rush of relief to see that the Guardians of Coastwatch still lived. At least some of them.

One stood out amongst the rest; a tall Aldegaadian man with long dark hair that had silver around the temples and a neat beard darkening his fair skinned jaw. His cloak was more ornate than the other Guardians and he wore silver shoulder plates with it, the cloak attached to them. He sheathed his long elegant sword at his hip as he strode forward from behind the barricade of furniture that he and his fellow Guardians hid behind. He smiled and reached out, he and Aldwyn grasping each other's forearms with their right hands in welcome.

"It is so good to see you, my friend," the Guardian said to Aldwyn in tired joy.

"And you, Riordan," Aldwyn replied, smiling, then introducing the others in our company. "You know my Junior, Tallinn Landrace, and my Apprentice, Carden Highever."

"Of course," Riordan nodded to them both as they stowed their swords again. "Though it has been a few years since last we met."

"Allow me to introduce Riordan Drostan," Aldwyn said, placing a hand on the man's shoulder and turning to the rest of us, "a son of Aldegaad and Guardian Warden of Coastwatch Keep."

"A pleasure," Riordan nodded to us, then said: "Forgive me but I must secure the keep," he turned and gestured with one hand to several Guardians, saying clearly and with strength: "Search the stronghold. Seek out the intruder and ensure that the dead no longer walk."

"Yes, Warden," twelve Guardians responded together and hurried from the room with their weapons ready, passing us by.

"I received your message from Aneuran," Riordan turned back to us, facing Aldwyn again, "but as you can see, we've had some... *difficulties*."

"What happened here, Riordan?" Aldwyn asked gravely.

Riordan sighed, clasping his hands at the small of his back. "At dawn a traveller came to the gates and stood there, unmoving and silent, showing no signs of life for more than an hour," he explained. "Suddenly, there were shouts from the halls and we found ourselves under attack," his face and voice grew darker: "From our own dead."

"Then it *was* a necromancer who lay siege to the keep," Ellora nodded in grave thought.

"He had the walking dead open the gates to allow him passage," Riordan explained coldly. "We barely had a chance to bring the civilian members of the keep inside to safety."

It was then that I noticed that there were Aldegaadian peasants cowering at the edges of the room, several women moving around to help the injured along with the Guardian healers. There were children huddling there, trembling in fear. My heart began to ache for them.

I moved towards a pair of dark-haired children sitting with their frightened mother, Joran following at my back slowly.

"The risen dead were killing without thought or care," Riordan continued behind me. "And worse still those that fell were resurrected by that sorcerer to swell his dire rank. Imagine it! Our own being turned to fight against us!"

I crouched before the children and their mother, pushing back the folds of my purple cloak to free my hands. I ran a hand through my hair, brushing it over my ear and out of my face, trying to show them sympathetic and caring eyes.

"Hello," I said softly. "Are you alright?"

The two children nodded as they hugged their knees tightly, their mother holding them in one arm each, turning her gaze to me as I spoke.

"What are your names?" I asked of them kindly.

"I'm Duane," the boy murmured up at me, his eyes transfixed on my face. He pointed to his younger sister: "That's Ciara."

I smiled softly at them. "It's nice to meet you."

Behind me the Guardians were still talking.

"Where is this necromancer now?" Fawkner was asking, his hand on the pommel of his sword at his hip.

"If you have not encountered the dead walking beyond these doors," Riordan said coldly, "then he must have departed the keep."

"That would have been the strange sense that made you and the other two ill," Ellora surmised, turning her turquoise gaze to Aldwyn.

"What's your name?" the little girl asked me, her mother's eyes wide as she stared at me, drawing my attention back from the Guardians.

Hesitantly, I answered: "My name's Leander."

"You're the Princess, aren't you?" the mother stared at me in shock and awe.

"You're a princess?!" the little girl cried out too loudly, drawing all eyes to me.

I cringed, then nodded. "Yes. I am."

"She's *our* princess, Ciara, darling," the mother whispered to her child. "One day to be our Queen."

I felt the urge to cry at her words and suppressed it harshly behind my throat and eyes.

"Are we going to be alright?" the little girl asked me with fearful hope in her big blue eyes. "Are the monsters going to come back and get us?"

I forced a tiny smile and stroked hers and her brother's heads softly. "No, they won't come back. We're safe now."

"How do you know?" Duane muttered in an icy demand too adult for a child.

"Because I'm your princess," I replied kindly, "and I won't let them hurt you."

"Sarissi," Joran pressed a large hand to my shoulder and I glanced up at him.

Knowing he meant for me to come back to the others, I offered the children and their mother a reassuring smile then stood up, moving with the Storvari.

"Forgive me, Princess Leander," Riordan bowed his head to me as I re-joined the group. "I should have introduced myself to you first."

"It's alright, Warden," I responded with a nod, twisting my hands together at my waist. "But I want to know if we're safe here."

"If the Necromancer has departed, then yes," he nodded, but I felt like he wasn't so sure.

"Do you have any idea as to his identity?" Aldwyn enquired, crossing his arms, his staff pinned to his chest.

Riordan's face fell and he became suddenly very cold and pale. He shuddered and looked like he had seen a ghost as he considered the answer.

"The Revenant of Arnath," was his uneasy reply.

"Oh gods!" Tallinn clamped both hands over her mouth, tears flooding her cheeks as she slumped to the floor, her knees giving out.

"Tallinn!" Carden was at her side as the rest of us turned to her with concern that she had fainted.

"Please, Ankorect, not him!" she nearly screamed, sobbing heavily into Carden's chest as he held her. "Please, don't let it be him!"

"What's wrong?" I asked, worry strong in my voice. "Is she alright?"

"Tallinn's from Dorvana," Carden explained to me softly. "The Forests of Arnath spread through a good portion of Dorvana's landscape and mountains, and that's where the Necromancer resides."

"He can't be here!" Tallinn wailed mournfully. "Please, he can't be!"

Aldwyn moved to me as Mithras came to my side to place his hand on my shoulder.

"Tallinn was once part of a clan of Dorvan Rangers wandering the hills and wilds," the Mage explained softly, drawing my gaze. "The Revenant killed most of her clan, including her father and brother, and used them in his castings."

"Oh gods... I... I had no idea," I murmured, feeling numb as I heard this.

Gods, Tallinn knows tragedy like I do, but so much worse. How could she ever have endured such an abomination? I wondered silently.

"Carden, Fawkner, take Tallinn to another room so that she may lie down," Aldwyn directed the two men.

"The guest wing is down that corridor," Riordan pointed to an archway off to his right as the two men took the sobbing, hysterical girl from the room.

"What possible reason could the Revenant have had for coming all the way from Dorvana to Aldegaad just to attack *this* stronghold?" Aldwyn was wondering as he faced Riordan again. "That is no short journey."

"I do not know," Riordan folded his arms, stroking his jaw thoughtfully. "But he made straight for the library."

"Why the library?" Ellora asked, her arms crossed before her armoured chest.

Riordan shrugged and shook his head. "I have no idea. But when we faced him there, he slew five of my brothers and sisters without effort. From the destruction he was causing it was as if he was searching for something."

"Do you have any idea what?" Aldwyn frowned, analysing Riordan's account.

"None. We'll have a better understanding once we've restored order to the keep," Riordan turned to me respectfully. "In the meantime, Princess, we need to arrange quarters for you and your company."

Suddenly, there came a loud clattering of metal, all of us spinning around to the source. Mithras had staggered and fallen against a table, knocking the silver jug, platter and goblets to the floor. He looked horribly pale and he was shaking. He gave me a weak glance, then he dropped from his feet, knocking the table across the room and hitting the floor hard.

"Mithras!" I cried out, running to him without a second thought and dropping to my knees.

Joran was at my side in moments and helping me to turn Mithras onto his back to save his injured arm from further harm. Aldwyn, Tristan, Ellora, Riordan and the Dwarves were around us so fast that I barely saw them move.

My eyes were set on the right side of his chest and shoulder. Blood stained his tunic, turning the fabric an ever-darkening shade of blackish red beneath his armour. He coughed loudly but remained unconscious.

"Mithras!" I cried out again, placing my hands to his chest plate. "Mithras, can you hear me?! Mithras!"

"Mithras," Ellora crouched beside me at his head, speaking in a calmer voice than my panicked one. "Mithras, it is Ellora. Can you hear me?"

"What's wrong with him?!" I looked to her, my vision blurred by hot, panicky tears, my heart cracking against my breastbone.

"His wound," the Elven Huntress murmured. "We need healers! Now!"

"Come on, lass," Tristan grabbed me around my arms, grasping my wrists and pulling me away from Mithras.

"No! Let me stay with him!" I yelled, struggling in vain against the Wanderer's coarse hands.

"It'll be alright," he whispered to me, holding me tightly, my back against his chest. "He's going to be just fine, lass."

I watched helplessly as the two Guardian healers ran over to help, my eyes set on Mithras' pallid and unconscious face. Ellora turned her gaze past the red strands of hair that had flicked over her face, concern clear there in her turquoise eyes. She tried to look reassuringly to me, then returned to the scene unfolding before us.

"Mithras," I whispered fearfully, slumping tiredly into Tristan's arms as tears threatened to spill from my eyes once again.

The Shadow Lord's words stuck in my head suddenly, taunting me as I remembered the moment where he had stood over me in the darkness of the dungeons, whispering his threats. *You may try to save him, but I promise you this: no matter what is done, Mithras will die. It is unavoidable.* I felt my chest heave faster and my tears fall as those words were spoken in my mind as if by the Shadow Lord's own voice once again.

Please... just let him be okay. Please... I pleaded desperately, hoping that the monster was wrong.

Chapter Twelve
The Tests of a Guardian

S tanding there was hard. Too hard. I had to stay back near the door into the room to let them work, Tristan and Ellora remaining at my side to comfort me. I felt as helpless now as I had the nights my parents, aunt and uncle had died, and my fearful heart ached at the thought that I could be about to relive that terror again in that room's gently lit chill.

Aldwyn stood over the bed with one of the Guardian healers as they attended to Mithras. They did not look hopeful. The healer was pulling back the opening of his shirt and trying to tend to the wound, which looked so horrible now. It had turned an awful purplish black around the deep red cut, blood still oozing forth on its own accord.

I closed my eyes and turned my face to the floor beneath my long dark hair, clasping my hands together and holding them to my breast tightly.

Please, Azmerath, don't take him, I pleaded to the God of Death. *Please, just let him be alright. Please.*

Seeing my distress, Ellora put her arm around me, hugging me close and letting me sob into her shoulder. She stroked my hair and back, and I began thinking of my mother. I remembered her cradling me as a child, singing sweet songs to ease my grief and fear, and the warmth of her loving touch. Oh, how I missed her.

"That's it," the healer said softly, drawing my eyes to the bed, the silver haired woman looking to Aldwyn gravely from her seat at the bedside: "I can do no more for him."

"Will he survive?" Tristan asked in a coarse, croaking voice.

The woman shook her head, looking at Mithras: "I cannot say. If he does, then it is because Ankorect wishes it. Otherwise, we can only pray that he has been just and true enough to gain safe passage through Azmerath's realm."

She stood and came over to me as I turned to the bed, folding my arms palm to elbow, my chest heaving fiercely and tears wetting my cheeks.

"I'm sorry I can do more, Princess," the healer said and quietly left the room.

The five of us stood in silence for a few moments, Joran ever watchful at the door, bending to poke his head through at us. All I could do was stare at Mithras' face. It was so haggard, all the light and strength he had once had now depleted, making him look like a frail old man.

After a while, Aldwyn cleared his throat, taking his staff from where he had leaned it against the wall. "I'd best go and confer with the Warden and other remaining masters," he paused and looked to me sadly. "I am sorry we have no better news, your Highness. Truly, I am."

I just nodded numbly as he left.

Slowly, my eyes on Mithras' silent face, I moved towards the bed, hesitant to approach him. I felt afraid that any movement could end his breathing and bring my worst fears on anew. So, I carefully took the seat near Mithras, facing him from his left side.

"Do you want us to leave?" Tristan asked softly.

I shook my head, my voice trembling. "You don't have to."

"We'll stay as long as you want us," Ellora pledged gently, moving to stand behind me.

I felt her slender hand smoothly glide onto my shoulder, my right hand automatically reaching up and holding it there.

I don't know how long I must have sat there by that bed; waiting, hoping, praying. It felt like an eternity, going on endlessly, all thoughts other than my mentor and protector's health slipping from my waking mind. Eventually, I ended up alone, only Joran remaining outside the door as my ever-vigilant sentinel.

There were no words to be spoken, no thoughts to tell, no pleas left for me to make. All I could do was sit there cradling Mithras' large, coarse hand between my smaller, slender ones. With each second, though, I could feel the heat in his skin fading despite his chest still rising steadily with his breaths.

Suddenly, a hand was on my back between my shoulder blades, gently shaking me awake. I sat up with a start, not even remembering falling asleep. Dolin stood beside me dressed in his most basic clothes, his hair neatly pulled back and his beard cleaner. He stared at me with kind brown eyes, his own concern too clear.

"You need to get some sleep, lassie," he urged me gently. "You've been sitting here near a day and a half."

"I don't want to leave him," I whispered tiredly.

"You've not eaten, and you've barely drank anything," he reminded me.

"I *have* to be here for him," I snapped at the Dwarf, turning my teary gaze back to Mithras, my voice softer again. "He's always been there for me."

"It's alright, lassie," Dolin assured me softly, placing his other hand to my wrist, drawing my gaze again, "I'll stay with him. Go, rest, get some fresh air, just get out of this dark room for a while. You can't waste away waiting for him to wake."

Though I disagreed, he was right.

I nodded and stood up, letting Dolin take my seat and making my way to the door. I paused there and turned back with my hands on the doorframe. I took one final look at Mithras, then made my way down the hallway, feeling Joran close at my back. I wasn't ready to sleep, knowing in my heart that I couldn't, so I took to the gardens of the stronghold. That's where I found Amethyst.

The violet, mauve, blue and silver scaled dragon lay under a large tree by a rock pool near the back wall, her wings closed up at her sides. She raised her head to look at me as I approached, leaving Joran to watch me from the undercover walkway I had entered the gardens from. Her molten orange eyes locked on my face as I reached her, twisting my hands together uneasily.

"You've grown so much," I said to her, the Dragon just tilting her head at me silently. "I can't believe how big you are."

I knew she could sense my pain, that she could understand me, though I wasn't sure how. Besides, right now it wasn't the company of anyone else but my kindred soul that I craved, and I knew that was her.

A terrible flooding wave of grief struck through my heart like a thunderbolt and I nearly started to cry, covering my face for a moment and almost collapsing to my knees but I somehow saved myself.

"I don't know what to do!" I sobbed. "I can't stand the thought of losing him too! I just can't take it!"

I opened my eyes and faced her, clutching my arms around my aching midriff, feeling as if my sides were tearing apart. She met my gaze, her face seeming to almost look sadly sympathetic for a few moments.

Knowing what I needed, she opened her left wing up and turned her face to point at her side, looking to me expectantly then.

I took her hint and moved to lay with her, curling up into her side, half sitting with my knees up and my cheek resting against her scaled body. Her left arm came up to rest over my hips and stomach, and her wing closed around us to shield me from the cold winds blowing through the garden.

I started to cry, cuddling her massive wrist as she watched me with those soulful, loving eyes.

"Oh, Amethyst," I wept, huddling into her gigantic shape, "what do I do?"

She let out a soft, low sound that wasn't a growl, but more a murmur to a dragon, trying to comfort me.

"I wish you could speak," I whispered to her, snuggling into her warm body. "I wish I could understand you."

Then I felt something; a feeling of reassurance, of comfort and love. I knew it was her projecting it to me, not really caring how I knew or felt this, just grateful for her presence.

I lay there and closed my eyes, letting myself rest at my dragon's side, and trying to find some measure of peace in the turmoil that swirled within my heart.

* * * * *

For the next day I slept, though it was a disturbed and uncomfortable sleep. Nightmares plagued me, but they were distant and unrecognisable. I woke several times in the night, worrying for Mithras, fearing this new threat in the form of this man they called the Revenant, grieving still for my lost family, and dreading the thoughts of my dark pursuer.

My fingers curled instinctively around my pendant and its chain at my neck, squeezing it for comfort as the Shadow Lord entered my thoughts. I feared his sudden appearance in the darkness of the room, imagining the black cowl harbouring those sinister glowing green eyes as his broad shouldered, black wrapped form towered over my bed. But the shadows didn't change, and the darkness didn't stir, the light from the window shedding a pale, ghostly illumination through the room to reveal that I was still alone.

When morning came, I dressed and found myself once again lost to my aimless wanderings through the ancient castle. There was a comfort in this, a familiarity, like being back in Castle Arvon, though it was vague.

I went to check on Mithras to find that Ellora now sat with him alone, singing in a soft Elvish melody.

She didn't notice me, her eyes shut as she held Mithras' hand and sang her mournfully beautiful ballad to the air: "U, Hirrialey, woondey neydasar tu thros ish lov, ris nu ra rishini ishar stro sai thas ish mai retor. U, Cherriss'un, hom il helsodey, ishar cas'sar shail ish, ya, haase brintil ish tis grassiv'intu. Mai Gaya tul'lurilish, mirialey, ra brii ish swisi haleil. Bo fi ish shil pa fro lii'lurr, tin mai ish frai paic'ee ne Tulir'rael. U, Hirrialey, knir thas ish hivar domar vell, ish hivar gevin tu ishar hert t'i siv shee hool matar'mor t'i ish. Ris ra fainor, darairialey, fai il shil sharale ishar borsarn, ra shil ishar lii'sou daimar, knir thas il wey stirnd wath hirr, ra ish shono'beyfar."

I have no idea what any of those words mean, but it sounds so beautiful, I thought as I let out a sigh.

Deciding it was best to let her sit with him, I began wandering in another direction through the castle. I lost myself in my thoughtless numbness, aimlessly pacing the stone halls and walkways. I was so engulfed in my emptiness that I bumped straight into Carden and Tallinn, nearly knocking them over.

"Princess!" Tallinn cried out in shock as Carden caught me, stopping me from falling. "Are you alright?"

"I'm so sorry," I snapped out of my mindlessness and returned to them. "I wasn't paying attention."

"It's alright," Tallinn assured me. "Given everything that has happened, I don't blame you for being absent from the world."

"How is Mithras?" Carden asked softly, almost hesitantly.

"Ellora's with him," I murmured, crossing my arms around me and sighing. "He's... he's still not awake."

Tallinn and Carden exchanged a soft look with each other, then turned back to me.

"Why don't you come with us, Princess?" Tallinn suggested.

"Where?" I asked so softly I might as well have thought the word.

"We're going to the Great Hall to meet with the other Guardians," Carden explained. "Fawkner is about to undergo his initiation to join the Order."

I frowned: "Am... am I even allowed to see this?"

"The initiation is not a secret," Tallinn said gently, pulling her cloak further around herself. "Not the ceremonial parts anyway. There will be other non-Guardians present, so you should be fine."

"You said you were always fascinated by our Order, Leander," Carden reminded me.

"I did," I agreed quietly with a gentle nod.

"Perhaps it will offer you a much needed distraction for a while," Tallinn suggested.

I nodded again. "Alright."

I followed them and we soon came to the Great Hall where we had first met Riordan and the remaining Coastwatch Guardians. Entering the chamber, I was amazed at how different it looked; all of its furniture in their rightful places, no damage to be seen, no injured and frightened people occupying the spaces. It suddenly felt like a real fortress of safety like the others had described it to be.

Fawkner and Joran were near the door into the room with Tristan and the Dwarves as the Guardians were preparing. Fawkner didn't look very confident, nervously adjusting his shirt and jacket to make himself more presentable. Aldwyn stood with him, trying to reassure and prepare him for the ceremony.

"It is only the asking," the Mage was expressing evenly. "You've nothing to be fearful of."

"And what of these tests?" Fawkner demanded gravely. "I've heard that few survive the trials to become a Guardian."

"We've all undertaken them, Fawkner," Aldwyn replied. "Just rely on your skills, your mind and your true sense of will, and you'll make it through this."

"Gods take you for conscripting me," Fawkner soured, shaking his head.

"I will perform the rites for your passage should you fail, my friend," Joran pledged stoically.

"Oh, shut up," Fawkner rolled his eyes then faced us as we entered. "Come to see me die, girl?"

"No," I shook my head. "To support you."

"You can support me right out the front door and back to Lorveren," he chuckled.

I smirked at him and shook my head. "You'll do great, Fawkner. Don't worry."

"We're ready," Aldwyn drew us back to the room.

I moved to stand with Tristan, Dolin, Holger and Joran, watching on with them as the three Guardians joined the rest of the Order, Fawkner staying at Aldwyn's side.

All of the surviving Guardians from the Revenant's attack were there, dressed in their cloaks and ceremonial robes, which I then noticed Aldwyn, Carden and Tallinn were also wearing. The thirty or so men and women stood in a large circle around the brazier burning in the chamber's centre, Riordan in the space opposite the doors.

Riordan cleared his throat and began: "We have come together on this day to test a new potential and see if he may become one of our Order. Master Aldwyn, bring forward your recruit."

Aldwyn took a few steps forward with Fawkner at his side to stand between the brazier and Riordan, their backs to the fire. They both bowed their heads and received the same in kind from the Guardian Warden.

"Master Riordan," Aldwyn addressed him, his staff in his left hand, his right to Fawkner, "I present to the Order my newfound recruit, Fawkner of Lorveren."

"Have you witnessed skills and talents in this man that may earn him a place with the Order?" Riordan asked sternly.

Aldwyn nodded: "He has overcome many poor choices to act with courage and truth in order to save the life of an innocent young woman. He singlehandedly defeated a Shadow Knight, and he has bravely faced down a Shadow Lord."

The silence of the room became a nervous din, which quickly vanished as soon as Riordan gestured with one hand to the civilian audience surrounding us.

"Facing down a Shadow Lord," the Master Guardian considered, "may be seen as either brave or incredibly foolish. Yet, this is the very purpose the Guardians were once created for," he looked to Fawkner solemnly: "Fawkner of Lorveren, you have been sponsored by Master Aldwyn to join our Order, and have displayed many qualities that are held in high esteem by the Guardians. Will you accept the requirements to become a full-fledged Guardian of the Order?"

"I am willing and ready," Fawkner replied respectfully, if a little curtly.

"Since our Order was founded over four thousand years ago," Riordan played clearly, this speech very well practiced, "we Guardians have enacted the Tests of Initiation, both in honour of the trials faced by the first Guardians, and to find those most worthy to join our ranks. We have always sought exceptional individuals who exhibit the skills, talents, courage and morals our Order embodies: the protection of those who are innocent, vulnerable and in need, the upholding of justice and honour, and the willingness to fight for what is right. Sometimes we find potentials who have lived in the darkness of the world where they have done terrible things to get by. But it is their willingness to do what they must for noble reasons, like stealing bread so that others may survive, or acting out some terrible crime to protect those they love most, that make them worthy of becoming Guardians."

I noticed Fawkner's face soften and his eyes suddenly become teary as Riordan said that last part. That had touched him in some way, but I couldn't be sure of how.

"So, we do not turn them away, but redeem them," Riordan went on without stopping. "And *that* is the purpose of these tests."

"Sounds like a religious cult to me," Tristan muttered under his breath, his arms crossed.

I frowned at him disapprovingly, then turned my attention back to the scene before me.

"Fawkner," Riordan turned to the man solemnly, meeting his gaze. "You will journey to the nearby island off the coast that we call the Dragon's Crest and enter the Gauntlet beneath its rocky skin to face your challenges. You have five tests before you: The Test of Endurance, the Test of Awareness, the Test of Faith, the Test of Wits and the Test of Will."

"And... am I to face these tests alone?" Fawkner asked in his typically abrupt way.

Riordan answered: "Like the first Guardians before us, you will journey in a pair," he looked to Aldwyn. "Who would you send with your recruit?"

"My apprentice, Carden Highever," Aldwyn responded clearly and precisely.

My heart skipped a beat and my eyes darted to Carden as I heard Aldwyn's words. The young man didn't even flinch, striding forward with a sweep of his cloak and moving to stand at Fawkner's side.

Why? Why are they sending him? I couldn't deny the panic crushing around my heart like a stone claw.

"Carden Highever," Riordan addressed him in his very official tone, "you are an apprentice level Guardian and so you have been nominated by your Master to undergo the Rite to become a full Guardian. Do you understand what is expected of you?"

"Yes, Master Riordan," Carden replied with a gentle nod.

"You will go as Fawkner's overseer, to stand beside him as his companion in this test, and to assist him where needed," the Guardian Warden explained. "But you will *not* solve the problems nor face the enemies you encounter for him."

"Understood," Carden nodded.

"And just as the first warriors who became Guardians underwent such trials with a charge to defend, so too must you," Riordan turned his attention to all those gathered there. "I must now ask for a volunteer from those of you who are not members of our Order. We ask for one who is willing to go into the dangers of the Dragon's Crest with our brothers and serve as their charge."

Suddenly, it made sense to me why non-Guardians were present, my eyes searching the small crowd curiously.

"I volunteer!" Holger stomped forward brashly, smirking and crossing his arms. "I'll go with these boys and help them push back all the timorous beasties that wait to rip us apart! I'll smash 'em with me hammer!"

"I must ask, Master Dwarf, if you think you are able enough to undertake such a task?" Riordan was studying Holger's roughly bearded face curiously.

"What's that supposed to mean?!" Holger demanded. "Is this about my height?!"

"No," Riordan replied, "but it is in regard to your willingness to allow another to defend you, to surrender all of your weapons and go to the island vulnerable."

"No one parts a dwarf from his weapon, least of all me!" Holger growled violently.

"I suspected as much," the man shook his head gravely.

Dolin grabbed Holger by the arm, pulled him back and muttered at him: "You're such a hot head, Holger. Keep your mouth shut."

I watched the two of them for a moment past Tristan's hip, frowning at their behaviour. Then I glanced at Tristan, the Wanderer giving me an uneasy look before the two of us turned back to the Guardians.

"Is there another?" Riordan asked, but no one stepped forward. "Truly?" he looked disappointed. "Are there none here willing to serve as the charge for these men?"

As the silence deepened and the Masters looked around for someone to join Fawkner and Carden, I found myself drifting into a strange thoughtfulness again.

Why will no one go with them? Are these tests really so dangerous? I started to wonder vaguely. *If no one goes what happens then?*

"I'll go," a familiar voice broke me from my silent thoughts and I suddenly realised as I stepped away from my companions that the voice was *mine*.

Everyone in the chamber was staring at me in shock as I stopped just in front of Tristan. He grabbed my arm, trying to pull me back as Joran suddenly had a look of horror in his violet eyes, the first I had ever seen there.

"Lass, what are you doing?" Tristan demanded in a near hushed whisper.

I pulled my arm free and took a step out of his reach, facing the bewildered room: "I'll go with them and stand as their charge."

Stunned silence crushed down on the room and I could have easily imagined that it was a room of statues that I now faced instead of living, breathing people. Then, from the silence, Aldwyn moved towards me briskly with Tallinn stepping out of the circle beside him.

"Your Highness, I must protest," Aldwyn told me sternly, almost scolding me.

"You need someone to go with them," I reasoned.

"Not you, Princess. Someone else."

"Why not me?"

"You are already under the Order's protection," Tallinn said seriously in her soft voice. "That is why we are with you."

"Your uncle and father asked us to ensure your safety," Aldwyn added gravely, his flustered tone a few levels down from anger. "You are contradicting their wishes by offering to put yourself in needless danger."

"I have been in needless danger for months," I responded lowly at him, managing to keep my calm. "I have been threatened, kidnapped, attacked, tortured and nearly forced into a false marriage all because of the wishes of other people. I would just rather that if I am to be in danger that I be allowed to choose *which* dangers I face for once."

"Your Highness..." Aldwyn went to say, but I turned to face Riordan.

"No one else has volunteered," I pointed out, speaking clear enough for the entire room to hear me. "And I'm guessing that no one else will. Would you refuse me because of my nobility, or because I am under Guardian protection already?"

"Tradition is clear," Riordan said in a reluctant tone and let out a deep sigh, "we cannot turn away the only willing and appropriate volunteer to be the charge in the tests. Step forward, Princess."

I glanced at Aldwyn and Tallinn, the two of them staring at me with worried, helpless expressions as I stepped up beside Carden and Fawkner. I tried to ignore the two men's gazes being thrown my way, focusing instead on Riordan.

"I am required," he said, "to ensure that you understand that you face very *real*, very *deadly* dangers in the Dragon's Crest. Your survival will rely *entirely* on Carden and Fawkner."

"I understand," I assured him, flashing the two men a sideways glance, then adding: "I trust both of these men with my life."

"Then I accept you as the charge for the tests, Princess Leander, daughter of Ewan and Caralyn," Riordan declared, looking between the three of us. "Go now, rest and prepare yourselves. The tests begin at sunset."

The room began emptying and I turned to the frowning, worried and disapproving expressions of my companions. At least none of them tried to argue with me. Instead they went off to do what they needed to, Tallinn coming with me to help me prepare.

* * * * *

Sunset came with red, gold, orange and deep purple in the sky, the sea taking on a bronze tinted black form as it roiled against the rocks and cliffs below the castle. The air was cold, and the wind was gently gusting across the battlements and walkways as dark clouds hid the sinking sun and rising moons from sight.

I joined the others at a dock just below the lowest seawalls of the castle, a boat moored there and lanterns glowing amidst struggling torches. There weren't any civilians when I arrived, only the castle's Guardians, all in their black and silver cloaks, along with my companions.

I sheltered under the hood of my purple cloak, pulling the folds of it around me and grasping the sides of my green and pale blue skirts.

Carden and Fawkner were heavily armed, Carden strapping a large belt of throwing knives around his waist as Fawkner checked his sword and a dagger he kept at the small of his back. Both men had been given light armour, Carden's in the colour of the Guardians and with the shield and sword emblem over the chest plate's heart, Fawkner's more basic and browner in hue.

"I've never been more worried for you than I am right now," Aldwyn was telling Carden as I approached, then glanced to me. "For all of you. After all the dangers we have encountered in the last few months it is the tests that give me the greatest worry."

"I don't think you were even so worried during my tests as a recruit," Carden said.

Tallinn hugged him tightly. "Be careful, brother. Please return to us," then she hugged Fawkner. "May the Seven watch over all of you."

"Lest the Daemon God-Kings get their claws into us," Fawkner agreed, hugging her tightly.

Ellora turned to me from beneath her hood, her turquoise eyes severe and her arms crossed. "I must say that I disapprove of this, Princess. Just as I know Mithras would."

"Look after him for me, Ellora," I said, hugging her tightly.

"And if he should wake?" she asked.

"Tell him I'll be coming soon," I replied.

"The Carethanes command that I should accompany you, Sarissi," Joran declared deeply as I stepped back from Ellora's embrace. "I have keravas to ensure your cavara."

"The Tests of Initiation are restricted so that only the three involved may go," Carden pointed out to the Storvari. "Whether Leander wants you to come with us or not, you cannot follow."

"Just stay here with Ellora and take care of Mithras for me, Joran," I instructed him gently, looking up into his face.

Slowly, he nodded and bowed his head, remaining silent.

Riordan stood before us in the waning sunlight and drew our gazes as he began to speak. "This boat will take you to the Dragon's Crest to begin the test," he explained to us. "But I must warn you that once you enter the Gauntlet that you will be alone. The three of you must rely on each other to survive, and you will *not* be able to go backwards."

Maybe this wasn't such a good idea, a small voice in my head muttered at me, but I ignored it.

"Carden Highever, Fawkner of Lorveren and Princess Leander Aldrich," Riordan said solemnly, "I wish you well and hope that the Seven will see fit to bring you back to us alive."

With that, we made our way to the boat where two Guardians waited, Fawkner and Carden drawing their hoods as we reached the water's edge. I could feel the spray of the sea spitting up onto my face and neck, and smell the scent of the salty water, the chilled air making me shiver deeply.

Carden boarded the boat first, he and Fawkner helping me in before Fawkner joined us. We settled into the rocking boat and pulled our cloaks tightly around us as the two armoured Guardians cast off, then took the oars and the rudder.

We started away from Coastwatch Keep slowly, the heavy waves dipping the small boat up and down roughly. I had to close my eyes to stop myself feeling sick as we made our way out into the darkening twilight.

In half an hour we had left the castle behind us, a large shape of hazy details and lights flickering in the ever-increasing darkness that was pushing the golden glow of the sun behind the horizon. The lantern on the boat's bow was all that lit our path as we rowed south-east towards the looming black shape that was rising up like the crest of a dragon's head before us. Obviously, that's how the island got its name.

I stared up from beneath my hood at the island, apprehensive as its dark mass of sand and rock loomed ever nearer to us. The knots in my stomach were growing tighter and I wondered more loudly in my mind if I had made a foolish mistake by coming with the Guardians to this mysterious water locked place...

Chapter Thirteen
The Gauntlet

The turbulent waves were relentless as we brought our small boat closer to the sandy and rocky shores of the Dragon's Crest. I was battling my growing seasickness as hard as the men battled the waves, holding in deep breaths as I looked down at the floor of the boat and at the brown toes of my boots.

Carden was sitting close to me, pulling me under his own cloak to shield me from the deepening chill coming up off the sea. The cracking of the waves against the rocks was like thunder and at first, I thought a storm was blowing up. But I soon realised that this perilous strait along Aldegaad's southern shores must always be choppy and turbulent.

"Are you alright?" Carden asked me softly, his green eyes focused on my suddenly pale face.

I nodded. "I've never been in a boat in these conditions before. I'm feeling a little sick."

"Oh, wonderful," Fawkner rolled his eyes, watching us from where he sat facing us. "Not even on the island and already we seem to be a member down."

"Pessimism will not grant us safe passage through these trials, Fawkner," Carden advised him, though he sounded a little too harsh to me.

"Nor will the girl's weak stomach," came the older man's response.

"I'll be fine," I said, trying to reassure myself as much as them.

"You're mad coming along with us," Carden half laughed, half cringed as he looked into my eyes, trying to see me in the darkness beneath my hood. "You know that, right?"

"No more than you," I replied in a sickly murmur, looking up at him as my arms squeezed instinctively across my churning stomach.

"I have no choice in the matter. You do," he pointed out solemnly.

"Carden's right," Fawkner agreed. "Why did you decide to join us, Leander?"

"I... I just felt like I had to," I tried to explain, not really understanding it myself. "It's like there's something here I'm supposed to see."

"Like in Galvenin?" Carden asked.

I looked to him and gently nodded. "Yes... sort of. I don't understand it. I just feel... *drawn* here."

The only way to describe what I was feeling was a strange pull within me, like there was an undertow current in my chest trying to sweep me towards that mysterious little island in the strait. There was no understanding the sensation or the reason, which was as unyielding as the tides surrounding us at that moment.

It took another twenty minutes of navigating the choppy swells around the rocks to make our landing. The piloting Guardians used the rudder and oars to bring us right up to a small wooden dock that had been haphazardly built over the sandy shoals and rocks. One of the men awkwardly balanced to the front of the boat and took the rope from the floor. He aimed and timed the rising of the small wooden vessel just right, hooking the rope around the post jutting up from the surface of the dock.

"Alright brothers, your Highness," the older of the two who sat nearest the rudder addressed us, "this is where we leave you."

"You're leaving us here?" I asked in a voice that was more shocked than I would have liked.

"To go around to the other dock on the far side of the island," the Guardian confirmed with a nod from beneath his greying hair and his black hood. "We can't stay here or else you will not be able to reach the keep."

"The exit from the Gauntlet is on the other side," the second Guardian explained. "It is a short trip down the hilly cliffs to the shore, and that's where you'll see us."

"And where is the entrance to this Gauntlet of yours?" Fawkner asked as the winds were picking up and the rain was beginning to hit us more rapidly.

"Follow the lights," replied the old grey-haired Guardian.

Fawkner climbed up from the boat and onto the dock, the lantern swinging on the dock's highest post the only light we had to see by now that night had fully fallen. He turned and reached down, taking both of my arms and pulling me up as Carden helped lift me. I nearly slipped into the water, letting out a frightened cry, but Fawkner pulled me into his arms.

I clung to his chest for a few moments, his voice gentle in my ear as he said: "It's alright. I've got you."

We stood there as Carden joined us, the rain growing heavier and wetting our cloaks.

"You three be careful in there," the old Guardian called up to us as Carden freed the rope and tossed it back into the boat. "Especially you, young lady. The Gauntlet has claimed many an unwary man and woman. Just remember the virtues and you'll make it out alive."

As the younger of the two men tended the oars into the water and the boat turned away, I felt deeply uneasy. Trembling in Fawkner's arms I looked between him and Carden, the cold biting my skin through my slowly soaking clothes.

"I think maybe I *do* regret coming with you," I admitted in a small voice.

"It'll be alright," Carden said, turning and leading us from the dock.

It was a very short walk from the edge of the dock to the rocky and sandy path leading along the shore. We were almost immediately surrounded by an intimidating wall of rock on either side of us, torches glowing in alcoves that had been cut into the walls.

Carden was leading the way, Fawkner following behind with me kept between the two of them for my safety. All I could do was lift the hems of my velvet and linen skirts and try not to trip on any jutting up rocks or sink my boots into the deep soggy sand.

"Not a very well-travelled path I see," Fawkner commented, his hand on his sword's hilt. "Very little clear sight too. This would be the perfect spot for an ambush."

"I don't think we'll come under attack here," Carden called back over his shoulder. "Not outside the Gauntlet caverns anyway."

The shallow canyon led down a slope of sandy rocks and to a long beach, the sea lapping up out of the near perfect darkness across the sand. It rolled into the weak torchlight, then swept away back into the unyielding black, only to return with that same gentle rushing sound.

Following the torches brought us then to a large sea cave of volcanic rock, the entrance open to the air and flanked by torches set into the walls. We paused here as Carden and Fawkner took unlit torches from their belts and set them alight from the permanently fixed ones on the grey rock walls. Flames danced across the fresh torches as the two men shone them down the passage to try to get a clearer look at the way ahead.

"Carden," Fawkner said quietly as he peered into the dark with his torch above his head, "you've gone through these tests," he turned over his shoulder to the two of us. "Any ideas as to what we might face in there?"

"None," Carden replied, shaking his head. "I was tested in the caverns beneath the Citadel, not here. The basic elements should be the same, but I have no idea what order the five virtues will be in, or what the tests will consist of."

"Then why send you to guide us?" Fawkner demanded with a stern expression. "What's the point in you leading us through this if you don't know what the challenges are?"

"The Order never sends a Guardian into the same testing Gauntlet twice," Carden explained. "When you're sent through to graduate to Junior level like I am now, you won't know what you, the recruit and the charge you're with will be facing either. It keeps it honest."

"You mean *if* I'm sent through another Gauntlet," Fawkner replied gravely. "We could all die here tonight."

"Huh... now I'm *really* regretting coming," I said, trembling and twisting my hands together nervously.

"Well, no time like the present," Fawkner sighed and started forward, drawing his sword in his right hand and holding his torch in his left.

Carden directed me to follow, watching the way around us ardently at my back, but didn't draw his sword.

The tunnels were very close, and the walls made our breathing sound louder than it really was. The rocks changed and the way sloped down until it reached some closely walled stairs, making me feel more like we were going down into a tomb rather than a cave.

I felt a heat rising through me, my throat tightening as the fear of those close walls crept in through me.

It's just a tunnel, I tried to reassure myself mentally. *Just a very tight, dark tunnel. It's alright. It'll open up soon.*

After what felt like an eternity of climbing down those stone steps through that dark, close tunnel, the walls opened up and we were faced with a wider tunnel. I was able to breathe without panic again, my racing heart easing its terrible thunder as I pushed my hood back just as my companions did. I had tied my hair back from my face with a basic tie, the locks in a neat, loosely braided, low to the neck ponytail, dark strands still framing my face.

"Look for some kind of a marker," Carden advised us. "It should have the Guardians' seal. It will indicate where the first test will be."

"It won't be sprung on us then?" I asked quietly, trying not to show that I was uneasy.

"We're always given some warning," he confirmed with a nod. "These tests can be lethal."

"How considerate of the ancient Guardians to give us a warning," Fawkner said in a sarcastic tone.

We continued walking through the widening chamber until I saw the marker just as Carden had said. It was the Guardians' crest of a shield with two long swords crossed behind it carved into a narrow archway.

"Here," I murmured, looking over my shoulder, the two men coming over to where I stood.

"Through here, then," Fawkner nodded and tilted his torch forward above him, his sword held at a low angle.

We passed slowly through into another chamber where there was a wider archway flanked by two glowing torches. The two men were ready as we walked across the sandy floor and towards the opening.

I suddenly had a deep feeling of growing dread choking me. *They said these tests are lethal. Oh gods, what was I thinking?! I should have stayed at the keep!*

Beyond the doorway was a larger, rounder stone chamber with a domed ceiling and a number of torches set evenly spaced on the walls. Scattered across the sandy floors were rocky structures that looked to have been naturally formed, though they could easily have been moved there. Directly opposite the archway was a large, heavy, ancient looking door. It was round and just at a glance seemed to be covered in ornate carvings in five ringed sections that went from biggest at the edge, to smallest in the centre. I could only guess that it was some kind of ancient lock.

"Careful," Carden warned from behind me, drawing my quick glance over my shoulder, my ponytail flicking past my neck with the movement.

Fawkner went through first, each step he took laboured and hesitant. I followed him, nervously grasping the edges of my skirts, my ankles crossing subconsciously as sand crunched beneath my boots. I continued forward, my steel blue eyes surveying the space nervously as I waited for some terrible thing to happen to us.

"Argh!" Carden cried out from behind me as a shuddering, warping bang echoed through the chamber.

I spun around to see him lying on his back on the other side of the archway, dazed and looking as if he had been smashed in the face.

"Carden!" I ran forward and collided with something, falling backwards to the sandy floor, the room's torch lit, arching walls swirling in my swimming vision.

For a few moments, as Fawkner called my name and crouched beside me, I felt like I was being hurled through the air like a rolling ball. Then, my senses returned to me.

"Are you alright, Leander?" he asked me, helping me sit up, then stand.

"What was that?" I mumbled, moving to the archway cautiously, still a little dazed.

Carden was standing now, reaching out one large hand towards the empty space between us, his palm pressing into thin air as if it was touching glass. A strange ripple like the skin of a bubble swam from his hand and outwards to every edge of the archway.

Awestruck, I reached out and felt a solid surface that seemed to wobble like a wave beneath my hands, then harden like stone.

"What is this?" my panic was clear in my voice.

"It's a magical barrier," Fawkner assessed gravely, elbowing it, then turning his light grey eyes to Carden. "We can't get back through."

"There is *no* going back," Carden reminded us of Riordan's earlier warnings, "only forward. But I can't go forward and there doesn't seem to be a way around these walls."

"What now?" I looked between the two men nervously for an answer.

"Is this part of the test?" Fawkner mused.

Carden shrugged, backing away and surveying the walls around the barrier methodically. "Maybe. I remember from my test that the apprentice was separated from myself and the charge when..." he suddenly went silent and his eyes widened with terror. "Fawkner, protect Leander!"

"What?" Fawkner looked shocked.

"You're about to come under attack!" Carden cried in an almost hysterical yell.

There was a grinding sound that was like rocks crumbling down a cliff face, a section in the wall above the door opposite the archway opening and a large hourglass appearing in an alcove. With the whirring of mechanical gears, the hourglass began turning so that its full chamber was at the top instead of the bottom, and with a resounding click it stopped, the sand beginning to pour into the empty chamber.

Fawkner pushed me behind him, dropping the torch off nearer the wall and readying his sword.

My heart was racing, and my eyes were darting around looking for whatever was about to attack us. No monsters and no soldiers came out of the large round room or its strange volcanic rock formations. For a few tense moments the only sounds were our panicked heavy breathing and the rustling rush of the sand pouring in the hourglass.

Then, there came a loud crack and one of the largest formations of rock in the centre of the room began to open up. Instinctively, my hands grabbed at Fawkner, my fingers curling into the fabric of his cloak as I stared past him at the changing rock that was now glowing with a fiery light beneath its crusty shell.

Fawkner backed me away as the rocks moved and began to rise; large leg-like shapes straightening up and enormous arms extending to the sides of the thick, broad body. A stone head rose on a long neck, the red glow of lava shining through the gaps in the black rocks.

The creature stood above us at nine feet tall, seeming to sniff the air before letting out an angry, molten rock dripping growl as it locked the glowing holes that served as its eyes on us.

"What in the world...?!" Fawkner was moving me back behind him, his sword aimed up at the thing, his eyes locked squarely on it.

"It's a Golem!" Carden cried out in terror.

"How do I fight it?!" Fawkner asked, starting to move me around the chamber behind him.

Carden shouted: "I don't know!"

The Golem stomped towards us, grinding, growling roars escaping its strangely shaped rocky head. The ground shook with each step it took, dust raining from the ceiling with its shuddering passage. Without warning, it let out a bellowing roar as it opened its fiery, lava spewing mouth. It raised one enormous stone arm, the lower part that would be the fist the widest like the base of a tree's trunk.

It aimed straight at us, Fawkner throwing me away and just barely leaping out of the strike's range. The ground cracked with a thunderous boom from the creature's punch, sand exploding up from the ground in a cloudy storm that lasted only moments.

Fawkner leaped to his feet and swung his sword at the creature's face, the blade shedding sparks in a brilliant shower of golden bronze light as the metal skidded across the rock. The Golem just looked at him and roared, snapping its mouth down on the blade and melting it into a shattered molten mess of steel.

The powerful force of the sword breaking made Fawkner stagger, his awkward recovery leaving him staring at his ruined blade.

"Fawkner!" I screamed from where I lay on my hands and knees on the sandy floor.

He jumped towards me as the Golem swung at him with both massive arms and roared violently, the impact exploding with not only sand and rock this time, but a barrage of burning embers and coals.

I grabbed onto Fawkner as we pulled ourselves to our feet, running and ducking as the Golem leaped forward and pounded the ground again, lashing out with another blast of exploding rocks and flames. I felt the heat of the strike as we skidded past one of the rocky formations away from it, trying to take cover.

More cracking and grinding echoed behind us and a second golem rose from the black rocky formation it had been posing as, this one glowing with a purplish energy instead of the fiery sheen of the first.

"Blast! Another one!" Fawkner exclaimed, pulling me away as the second immediately barrelled towards us and landed a punch where I had been standing.

We narrowly escaped it as purple energy bolts exploded through the air and across the rocky surface of the formation it had struck. It turned and bellowed out a howling roar that crackled with purple electricity across its black jaws.

"They're Elementals!" Carden called to us from where he watched on helplessly. "The first is a Fire Golem, the second a Storm Golem! They're powerful magical constructs!"

The Fire Golem struck at us again, the two of us falling away and slamming into a large rock formation that instantly started shaking and rising with a cracking sound. There was a deep biting cold coming from the rocks and Fawkner threw me with him to the ground away from it as the third golem rose. This one had whitish blue ice energy swirling in its rocky shell's openings like a self-contained blizzard.

"Let me guess!" Fawkner exclaimed. "An Ice Golem!"

The Ice Golem threw its arms back and lashed at us with its deeply bellowing roar, cold icy air smacking us in the faces. We darted away from it and quickly jerked in another direction as the Storm Golem struck at us with an electricity charged strike that bounced harmlessly off the rocks, barely missing us by inches.

I was breathing so fast and my heart was cracking through my ribs, a sudden strike from the Fire Golem hurling the two of us into the air with shards of rock only heightening my discomfort. I hit the ground hard, coughing from the blow of the floor meeting my body, stones and rubble raining down around me. For a moment I managed to get a glimpse of Carden, seeing him smashing himself against the barrier desperately as he tried to reach us.

I looked up and let out a startled scream as the Ice Golem tried to stomp on me, just barely avoiding its crushing foot as I rolled to my left. My back smashed into one of the rocky formations and I slipped into cover behind it as the icy breath of the monster shot at me in a gale force gust, ice coating the rock where the strike hit.

"Leave her alone, monster!" Fawkner shouted, throwing a rock and hitting the Golem in the head.

It turned and snapped at him as the Fire Golem took a swing and missed him by inches, the man dropping behind another one of the formations.

"Use the formations, Leander!" Fawkner shouted to me, out of my line of sight behind the rocks. "They can't break through them!"

I looked around frantically, seeing an opening under a large formation and hurling myself forward. I slipped under it just as the Storm Golem crushed its fist down on the ground where I had been, tongues of violet energy licking at my body with scorching, painful heat. I dragged my feet in just in time as the Golem stabbed its arm after me, drawing a terrified series of hysterical screams from me as I looked away, shielding my face into my shoulder. I pulled my knees close to my chest tightly, just narrowly avoiding the grasping finger-like extensions of rock on the creature's hand.

"Fawkner! Help!" I screamed.

His footfalls smashed the sandy floor as he ran, the sound of his body crashing to the ground as he was thrown from his feet with the strike of one of the golems echoing off the walls. Through a gap in the rocks I could see him and tried to squeeze my way between them to reach him. It was a tight fit and I struggled against my waist, squirming to get free. Panic filled me as I realised that I was stuck, even as lithe as I am.

"Leander!" Fawkner rushed into my sight and reached out, grabbing both of my hands.

We struggled for a moment, then he pulled me free just as the Storm Golem nearly grasped my left ankle, my foot slipping away from its rocky fingers.

Fawkner grabbed my wrists, throwing his left arm around me as we ran from the golems striking at us. I looked up at the door, my eyes finding the hourglass, its sands nearly run out now. I was suddenly hit with realisation.

"The hourglass!" I cried, looking to Fawkner.

We paused and turned together to look at it. His frown became an expression of sudden knowledge and he nodded.

"This is the endurance test!" he realised with some excitement. "We just have to outlast them!"

"Look out!" I shrieked, both of us being struck by one of the brutes an instant later.

I cried out in agony as stone collided with my ribs and the room spun around me. I hit the floor hard, letting out another sobbing cry as my body crumpled. I then rolled onto my side to see that the Ice Golem was the closest, its roar terrifying as it stormed towards us.

"Fawkner!" I screamed, grabbing his jacket and trying to pull him with me. "Come on! Please!"

He recovered and pushed me down into the cover of one of the large formations just in time. The rocky ceiling above us was instantly shaking and thundering as the three golems converged on us and attacked.

We curled up together, pressing ourselves to the floor. Fawkner pulled me close into his arms and held me as I closed my eyes. I cringed against a heavy strike, squeezing my eyes tighter and covering my head with my hands.

"The hourglass should only be running a few more seconds!" he guessed from what he had seen, his hands and arms tight around me. "We just have to hold on! It will be alright, Leander! It will!"

I kept my eyes shut, plunging myself into a deep darkness. I didn't want to see the monsters as they killed us, fearing what being torn apart by stone fingers would feel like.

Suddenly, there was just silence and the shaking stopped. I opened my eyes and looked up from under my now messy hair, every detail of the rocks above us vivid to my vision.

Fawkner turned his gaze to me, then tilted my chin so that our eyes met. "Are you alright?"

"Yes," I half whispered.

He led the way and we cautiously crawled out of our hiding place. We looked around the room's torch lit expanse to see the three golems lumbering back to the places they had started in and settling down on the ground. They folded their bodies back up and closed their shells, the glow of their strange energy fading into the black of their rock skins.

I turned my eyes towards the hourglass in time to see the last few grains trickle through the narrow passage between the chambers to meet the rest of the sand.

Fawkner turned and I followed his gaze just as there came a wobbling sound like a flimsy sheet of metal being shaken. The barrier in the archway flickered with its bubble sheen, then erupted like someone had poked it with their finger.

Carden frowned at the archway, stepped through cautiously, then hurried towards us, his cloak flying behind him: "Leander!"

"Carden!" I threw my arms around his neck and buried my face into his shoulder as he pulled me into the tightest hug we had ever shared.

"Gods, I thought I was going to watch them kill you," he let out a slow breath, trembling as he held me, then looked to Fawkner. "Are you alright?"

"A few bruises and aches. My armour did a lot to deflect the force of their strikes," Fawkner answered.

"Ah!" I cried out as I settled back onto the flats of my feet, pulling Carden's hand away from my side quickly. "My ribs hurt!"

"Here," Carden quickly dug around in the satchel he carried at his hip, then pulled out a small bottle with a blue liquid in it. "Drink some of this. It's a poultice

Aldwyn gave me before we left. It should help you heal and take away some of the pain."

I gratefully took it and drank some of the contents, handing it to Fawkner so he could drink some too. Almost immediately the pain started to fade, and my breathing became easier.

We were all startled then by the grinding of metal and stone, turning to the far door. The five rings in the door were turning, each in a different direction to the others. They unlocked, slid back a few inches, then the door opened in half.

"We've passed the first challenge," Carden noted, taking the empty bottle from Fawkner and stowing it again as the older man recovered his torch.

"Are they all going to be as strenuous and deadly as the last?" Fawkner grumbled as he re-joined us. "I haven't got a sword to fight with anymore, remember."

"I've never heard of a gauntlet that contains nothing but battles," Carden glanced at him, then to me. "I don't think we'll face anything else like that."

"Now what?" I murmured, hugging my aching body tightly as I flicked my gaze between them.

"We can't go back, right?" Fawkner looked to Carden, who nodded gravely. "Then we continue forward."

With the torch held up he led the way, Carden hugging me gently as we followed through the large door. As soon as we stepped through into the darkened corridor beyond the heavy doors closed up and sealed us in. Our only light came from the torches the two men carried.

So... definitely no going back now. I grimaced at that thought as the locks fell into place loudly.

I turned my eyes up to Carden nervously, receiving a reassuring, but small smile from the young man. He squeezed my shoulders a little, then led us forward with his torch ahead of us.

It didn't take long before we had passed through those darkened tunnels, Fawkner suddenly halting our progress as something caught his eye.

"Another marker," he indicated the Guardian seal carved in stone on a pillar in the wall, lighting it up with his torch.

He turned over his shoulder at Carden and I, the torchlight illuminating his face in the near dark.

"We're coming up to the next test," he surmised in a calm tone. "Any thoughts?"

Carden shrugged and shook his head. "It could be any of the remaining four. But given how dull the light is here, my guess would be the Test of Awareness."

"Alright. Then we'll be cautious," Fawkner nodded, then gestured to Carden's weapon as he unsheathed his large dagger. "Have your sword ready just in case."

Carden nodded and unhooked his arm from around my waist to draw his sword. He nodded for me to follow Fawkner, and I did as I was instructed, staying close to them both.

We turned around the corner of the stale aired corridors, coming face-to-face with a long hall wide enough for five people to walk arm-in-arm. At the far end was another of the large circular ring lock doors, its stone shape closed and waiting for us. There were only two torches glowing on the walls, one near us and the other at the locked door; nowhere near enough light to easily see the long space between.

I walked beside Fawkner as Carden cautiously watched the way behind us, our footsteps slow. I began fiddling with the silk lining of my wide, long over sleeves, finding that touching the fabric helped to calm my nerves. My eyes were starting to sting as I strained to see through the extremely poor light, the large stone block walls overhung with weeds and vines growing from the floor and ceiling.

There would have been a time a few months ago where this would have been the adventure I'd wanted... well... I guess it is still kind of exciting.

I stepped with my right foot and suddenly screamed as rock broke and the floor vanished beneath me. I was falling, the world rushing around me.

"I've got you!" the voice startled me as much as the arms that were abruptly tightly wrapped around my torso.

I grabbed backwards over my shoulders at Fawkner, grasping his hood and hooking my fingers behind his neck as I struggled not to fall into the deep dark that had appeared beneath me. He pulled me back and my feet scraped against the floor before the two of us staggered and nearly fell. Carden was right there, bracing us to stay standing.

My chest was moving as fast as a rabbit's, my breathing laboured and loud as I stared wide eyed down at the hole that had opened up where I had stepped.

"It's definitely awareness," Carden noted gravely.

Fawkner let go of me after giving me a silent look to see if I was alright. I just nodded and he moved forward, crouching to the floor and picking up his torch. He held it over the stone tiles, and I could now see some very distinctive designs on each one. There were six symbols in total: a shield, a half circle with a line running up from its straight edge, a line with a triangle at each end, something that looked like some kind of flower, a square with a cross in the centre, the last symbol simply five vertical lines.

Fawkner prepared his dagger and he cautiously moved forward with it in both hands. He kept looking up at the ceiling and walls nervously, like he was waiting for something to hit him. He picked the nearest flowery looking symbol and stabbed it with the dagger, pulling back quickly. The room became bright all of a sudden as a blast of flame erupted from either wall over the stone, missing Fawkner by inches. It only lasted a few moments before the dark closed in on us again.

"Don't move," he directed with a hand towards us. "The tiles are pressure plates for booby traps."

He ran his eyes over the symbols as Carden and I edged closer to get a better look. He selected the nearest to the wall on our left that had the cross on it and stabbed the dagger into it. The tile crumbled and dropped, just like the one I had stepped on in the centre right of the line.

"What about the shield?" Carden suggested, pointing at the centre tile. "It looks like the tiles with the cross will drop."

Fawkner nodded and stabbed the shield plate, but nothing happened. After a few seconds, he stabbed it again, and when nothing happened, he stood on it. A smile spread over his lips behind his neat beard.

"The shield is the steppingstone," he indicated, looking then at the way ahead with his torch. "We'll have to watch ourselves. These stones are farther apart than most of the others."

"Leander will really need our help to cross," Carden said, then looked to me and added: "Your legs aren't as long as ours and you're wearing a dress."

"You're right," I conceded with a shrug.

Fawkner carefully hopped to the next shield stone, then turned and beckoned to me: "Alright, Leander. Follow on but be careful."

I nodded and lifted the hems of my dress to just above my leggings clad knees. My right foot touched the shield stone tentatively, then I put all my weight down and skipped my left foot to join it. I was amazed that for once I had managed to keep my balance instead of falling flat on my back.

This will definitely be the worst place to fall over.

I kept following Fawkner's path along the steppingstones, my eyes adjusting to the poor light enough that I could now keep track of the markings.

Suddenly, there was a click from behind me and I turned as Carden swore and leaped across against the wall. A huge sweeping pendulum blade glided out of a hidden gash in the wall right through where he had been standing only a second earlier. He looked up at Fawkner and I with wide eyes and an extremely white face.

I gulped against the hard lump that I hadn't realised had been forming in my throat. *A **very** bad place to fall over.*

I turned and slipped my foot, jerking back and bracing both hands against the wall to avoid the tile that cracked and fell between me and it. Through the tile I had slipped on, a metal spike sprung up from the floor, another mirroring it from the ceiling and two more from the wall only inches from my palms.

I felt my heart skip a beat as I stared at the spikes that would have impaled me if I hadn't stepped back, my body nearly paralysed with fear. As they retracted into the rock surfaces, Fawkner reached out to me and took me by my right arm. He led me carefully through the traps as Carden followed along behind us.

We soon reached the last tiles and managed to get across, my foot catching on one of the trap tiles in the process, but the two men had me away from it just as a barrage of arrows filled the air behind us. The sound faded and there came the heavy clicking and clanking of gears as the second door opened.

"That's two," Carden muttered as we passed the door and started down into the next tunnel.

Once again, the door sealed behind us and we were left to make our way by only the light of our torches. This corridor was a straight and long one that ended up leading us to a set of stairs reaching down towards an archway where the glow of torches could be seen.

We reached the bottom of the steps and entered another round chamber with a domed ceiling and curving walls of dark stone, torches glowing all around us. There were six tall human shaped statues that looked like knights with shields, their insignia that of the Guardians. Directly in front of us was a rectangular archway that looked as black as the darkest coal dipped in the thickest tar. I immediately had a dreadful feeling rising in my chest and up my throat at the sight of that terrible blackness.

"What do you think this chamber is?" Fawkner asked as he slowly paced the edge of the room, looking at the statues.

As I started towards the stone object in the centre of the room Carden answered, remaining by the door: "I haven't got the slightest idea."

I reached the object as Fawkner was investigating the doorway with his torch. It was a large stone altar, not big enough for someone to lie on, but large all the same. It had the Guardian symbol carved into all four sides of it, the top made of a smooth grey marble.

I turned my gaze to the doorway as I touched the altar, Fawkner moving his torch into the black. For a moment the light seemed to dance on the blackness as if it were a reflective gluey surface. Then, Fawkner pulled back... and only half the torch came with him, the rest of it eaten away by the blackness.

"What in the Void is that?!" he cried out, dropping the ruined torch as Carden quickly approached.

Carden studied it for a few moments then slipped a throwing knife from his belt and pressed the blade into the surface of the blackness. Again, the surface seemed to pull around the blade, and when he withdrew the weapon, all but the handle had been dissolved.

The two men exchanged worried looks, then studied the doorway uneasily.

I turned my eyes to the altar and noticed that there was a carved plaque attached to it.

"Look at this," I called quietly, the two of them moving to flank me.

They both studied the plaque as I leaned my face closer to it, the pair of them seeming more on guard around me after the last two tests.

I read the words aloud: "With naught but clothing enough for modesty's sake, or else to your death will you it take. With neither armour, nor shield, nor arms, with no magic, items or charms. With even light will you find a dread fate, your only course now lies with faith," I looked up from the carving and to the two men with a curious frown. "What does that mean?"

"It's the Test of Faith," Carden surmised, turning his green eyes to the black gateway.

"Oh. I see," Fawkner nodded as realisation and understanding struck him like a lightning bolt. "The poem is literally a warning. If we enter the doorway with naught but our clothing, we will make it through, but torches, weapons, armour and magic charms will immediately draw that... *whatever* that is in the doorway to kill us."

"So... you have to take off your armour and weapons?" I guessed, crossing my arms and looking to the altar. "Then what's the altar for?"

"Our equipment," Carden said, starting to take his armour and weapons off. "We leave it here and we can progress."

He and Fawkner placed all of their items on the altar, Carden putting out the remaining torch by scrapping it on the floor. Soon the two men only wore their clothes, boots and cloaks, all of their weapons, armour and Carden's supply bag resting on the altar.

"What about Leander?" Fawkner asked Carden as he set his bracers down.

"I don't have anything," I pointed out.

"The Pendant," Carden said lowly, crossing his arms and moving to stand over me. "It's a magical item used in defence."

I stared at him numbly and shook my head as I staggered one step behind me. "N-no... I won't leave it."

"Leander," Carden put his large hands on my shoulders and looked down into my eyes kindly. "You have to, or you won't pass through the black."

"But I..." my chest was heaving with a painful tightness.

"Just have faith that it will come back to you," he urged me softly.

I took a deep breath and reluctantly nodded.

Shrugging out of my cloak, I reached up to the chain around my neck. I unfastened it and coiled it in my hand as Carden set his cloak and mine upon the altar. Staring at the Pendant, I moved towards the altar, running my thumb over the coolly warm stone and the smooth silver, coiling, flowery designs. Every instinct I had was screaming at me not to give it up, my heart feeling like it was burning in my chest.

Are the Dragon Pendants truly such powerfully addictive things? Or is this just because I'm connected to it? With a sigh, I turned my hand down to the altar and set the Pendant there.

Carden and I stepped away from the altar and moved to where Fawkner waited for us by the doorway. I glanced over my shoulder at the Pendant, the fire light of the room seeming to dance on its sparkling silver shape. I desperately longed to keep it with me, not to leave it behind like this, but I knew I had no choice.

Fawkner's voice drew me away from my necklace and back to reality as I faced him and Carden again. "I think we should hold onto one another," he was suggesting as he glanced at the black doorway. "The doorway's too narrow to walk side-by-side, so I'll lead. Leander, you hold onto me, and Carden, you hold onto her."

"And whatever happens, we don't let go," Carden advised us.

I curled the fingers of both my hands into the back of Fawkner's old, thick leather belt and held tightly. Carden grasped my hips with both large palms, drawing my over the shoulder look of unease. He nodded and smiled at me, trying to silently tell me that we would be alright.

We all took a few breaths, then Fawkner led the way, vanishing into the tar-like surface of the blackness. My hands followed, and for a moment the gluey thickness of the substance closed coldly over my wrists, making me fear losing my hands. Then it was over my elbows, the blue sleeves of my dress disappearing next. In moments my chest and arms were following, and I instinctively closed my eyes as the pressure of that gooey darkness slid over my face.

All light vanished and I held my breath...

Chapter Fourteen
Riddles and Gold

For the first few moments I kept my eyes shut and held my breath, then I felt the gooey tar sensation fade away from my skin, like my body had passed through some kind of dense filmy substance. I took in a breath and opened my eyes, and while breath came as naturally as it ever had, my sight did not return, and all remained black.

I didn't dare to speak, listening instead to all of the sounds surrounding me. Boots scrapping against the stone floor, the two men breathing around me, my own softer, feminine breaths sounding like a melody next to their bass tones. Clothes rustled in the black and there was the tiniest echo of the wind in the distance.

My fingers curled tighter around Fawkner's belt, catching the fabric of his shirt near the small of his back. The pull of his body was strong enough that I had to keep moving before I fell and lost him in the black.

The pressure of Carden's hands around my hips did little to help my growing dread; the feeling of his fingers both comforting and a little distressing considering how tightly they gripped me.

After what felt like hours in that sightless world of blackness – for darkness wasn't the right word to use to describe it – I began wondering if we would ever find our way to the other side. All I could do was focus on the sensations running through my body and limbs, every pulsing beat and ache seeming enhanced by the loss of my sight.

What if this passage never ends? the grave part of my mind asked quietly. *What if we're trapped here in this blackness forever? Well, I suppose the people that are after me won't ever find me again,* it occurred to me as I stumbled and managed to catch myself.

Behind me I heard Carden murmuring in the black and listening closely I managed to pick up a few words.

"...Compassion towards the weak. Protection to those who are defenceless. Truth ever to be spoken," Carden was reciting as if he were praying, though I doubted his words were part of a prayer.

I turned back to my own thoughts: *We'll get out of this. Fawkner and Carden are two of my truest friends, and I believe that if anyone could get us through this that it is them. I don't think I've ever believed in anyone as strongly as I do in the new friends I have now come to cherish so dearly.*

Abruptly, there came another feeling of passing through a thick, but watery and oily skin. Suddenly, light blinded me, and I let go of Fawkner to cover my eyes with both hands. I stopped moving, Carden letting go of me, and for a few moments I could only feel the stinging behind my eyes as they were bombarded by light.

Slowly, I lowered my hands from my face and took in our surroundings. We were standing in a room identical to the round and domed stone chamber we had left to enter the portal. Throwing a glance over my shoulder, I noticed that the black portal was shimmering now, Fawkner and Carden both turning to watch it with me. The black wavered and convulsed as if it were a living thing, then abruptly vanished and we were left facing an empty stone alcove that was bricked up and solid.

"What magic was that?" Fawkner sounded as if he had seen a ghost.

"It was a portal of some kind," Carden assessed, moving and pressing his hand to the stone wall inside the alcove. He tested it with a few strong shoves of his left hand, then looked back to us: "The wall's solid. It wasn't an illusion."

"Now what?" I asked, twisting my hands together in front of my stomach absentmindedly.

Fawkner turned around the room and I followed him with my eyes as he moved straight towards a third huge round door like the two we had previously passed through. He pushed both hands to it, but it didn't open, and he looked back to me with a frustrated expression.

It was then that we noticed the altar in the centre of the chamber, every detail of this room the same as the last except for the large door that stood locked. To my surprise, the altar was shimmering with a white glow that faded as our belongings appeared. My eyes caught a silvery shimmer amidst the folded cloaks and I quickly took my pendant in my hand, holding it for a moment and just staring at it in relieved wonder.

"I told you you'd get it back," Carden smiled down at me as he now stood at my side. "Here, let me."

He took it from my hand, and as I lifted my hair, he fastened the chain around my neck again. I let my hair fall to my shoulders and back, the tie having slipped so that while the strands remained bound, they now sat loosely.

My right hand touched to the smoothness of my pendant's purple stone, the light of the torches shimmering through the facets of its shape to give it an inner shine. I suddenly felt calmer and so much safer.

"We'd best equip our armour and weapons," Carden suggested as he pulled on his black and silver leather jacket. "Two tests yet remain."

"Did either of you pray?" Fawkner asked softly, drawing our frowning expressions. "In the passage I prayed that Isnari and Maveria would watch over all those I care for should Azmerath take me," then he placed a hand on my shoulder. "And I asked Thringar to safeguard you from this place, Princess."

Carden nodded: "I was reciting the Guardians' Oath, for courage. Leander, what ran through your thoughts?"

I confessed: "I... I thought that if I were to be in such a terrible situation as that blackness, that I would only ever want to go through it with both of you. That if anyone were to get us out of that passage and all other trials here, that there was no one I believe in more than the two of you."

A deeply resounding grinding and clicking suddenly overwhelmed us and we turned to see the door opening. Within moments it had beared the way into another tunnel where the light of a single torch glowed brightly.

"It seems that we also had to pray to pass this test," Carden surmised as he stared at the door, then faced us. "It wasn't just about blind faith, but about the faith in our hearts."

"Then let's not stand around here having a theological discussion," Fawkner said as he grabbed his cloak and remaining weapons. "I am eager to pass these final tests and return to Coastwatch Keep."

Once we all had our cloaks on again and the two men had donned their armour as well as taken all of their equipment, we passed through the door and into the new tunnel. Like the two before it, the door sealed as soon as we had passed, and we had no choice but to continue onwards through the Gauntlet's passages.

Carden now carried the only torch we had between us and lit our path in that dark place. I was thankful for it until we found a charred and broken body slumped against a wall. I stayed back beside Fawkner as Carden crouched over the body with his light and inspected the damage.

"This was a challenger," he guessed, still studying the armour and the remains. "The apprentice judging by the seal on the armour. The bones and clothing are heavily burnt."

"A hint of the test still to come?" Fawkner suggested gravely.

I swallowed hard against the lump in my throat but kept my hands at my sides as I looked past Carden at the corpse.

Carden looked up at us from where he crouched with a calmly worried expression: "Or there's something else down here. Something *not* part of the tests."

"Another Fire Golem?" Fawkner offered.

"I don't know, but you'd better take this," Carden took the long sword lying on the ground and passed it to Fawkner as he stood. "Stay on your guard, Fawkner," the young man then looked to me. "And you stay close to us, Leander."

I nodded uneasily. "Alright."

We started forward again, making our way slowly through the tunnels and their twists and turns. They led us down to another stairway opening up beneath the island and into a great drop into darkness. I could hear the ocean crashing on the rocks below, knowing that there had to be a break in the cliffs somewhere to let the water in.

The stairway brought us to a narrow walkway that had the three of us pressing ourselves against the stone wall. The two men were obsessively protective of me as we crossed this and wouldn't let up until we were at last safely across the drop. We then had to climb another steeper and more awkward stairway. We had to crawl on our stomachs up the incline and once again I found myself relentlessly cared for by my two companions.

At last we made it to the top, Fawkner reaching the landing first and turning to help me. He grasped my wrist and pulled me up as Carden supported my back. My feet touched the flat ground of the ancient stone landing and I gazed around at the cavernous ruins we now found ourselves in. They were the remains of castle towers and battlements sunken beneath the rocks, almost like the Dragon's Crest had swallowed up a fortress and dropped it down into its depths.

"This place is ancient," Fawkner noted as we walked through archways of human make and natural formation. "How old must it be to have been swallowed by the earth like this?"

"I'll bet Ellora would know of other places like this," Carden said as he stared in wonder at the ruins. "How much must she have seen in fourteen hundred plus years of life?"

We continued through the ruins and up into another series of caverns. It was so intensely dark that Carden had to take the lead with the torch now, the flames struggling to light the way.

As our passage curved around a corner, there suddenly came a light through the parts in the rocks; a dull glow of a yellowish sheen. It was not intense light, but warm and beckoning to us as we silently turned the last corner.

"By the gods..." Fawkner gasped in wonderment as his grey eyes widened at the bewildering sight.

"Incredible," Carden whispered in astonishment.

I could say nothing, just walking between the two men as we traversed the steps down to the main floor of the gigantic cavern. My breath caught in my chest for a moment as I stared at the immensity of it all.

High above in the central ceiling of the cavern there shone the light of night down through a great hole that was too high to reach. With it and the torches set on the many natural columns surrounding us, the chamber was so brilliantly illuminated. But this wasn't what drew our wonder.

Piles upon mountainous piles of treasure clogged the arteries of this great natural chamber; chests laid open to bare their riches as vast fields of gold and jewels stretched on seemingly forever. The immensity of it all would drive many a greedy man to insanity as his eyes set upon such unadulterated wealth.

I just stood still at the edge of the great sea of precious gems and metals, staring and silently wondering why it was there.

Suddenly, a low growl echoed in the depths around us and our wonder faded away.

"What was that?" Fawkner drew his sword, looking around nervously as Carden did the same.

They pushed me between them as the growl reverberated off the cavern walls again, this time louder. I froze, listening and waiting. Then I heard the clinking of a wave of coins, my eyes finding the source of the sound as something seemed to swim beneath the great hoard's surface.

The two men turned to follow my gaze as the shape began to rise from the golden seas, horns and scales appearing out of the great mass of coins. Two enormous wings spread up into the air, raining coins and jewels down all around as clawed hands of brown, teal and pale blue scale clutched at the piles.

The men took a few steps back, pushing me behind them further as they went, their eyes locked on the behemoth rising before us. All I could do was stare up into the long snouted face of scales and its vibrant molten eyes.

The golden rain of coins settled with the trickling of metal on metal as the great tail swayed back and forth a few times, then coiled around one of the piles. We were face-to-face with an enormous brown and green scaled dragon, six great horns rising from its head, spines jutting up with large scaly plates across its shoulders and back. It was twice the size of Amethyst.

The Dragon locked its eyes on us, the irises looking like they were glowing in the shadows of the cavern. Its nostrils flared and its wings arched as it grimaced with razor sharp pointed teeth peering from beneath its great lips.

Wonder drew me to it as it sniffed at us, and I slowly slipped past my protectors.

Carden seized my arm to stop me, making me turn my face to him. "Leander?! What are you doing?!"

"It's alright... trust me," I urged him, placing my hand on his and gently unhooking his fingers from my arm.

I approached the great being and stood before it, looking up at its majesty and grace. The Dragon lowered its face to me so that our eyes met. I had never felt smaller in my life before its immense greatness. It sniffed deeply, pulling in my scent, my hair and clothes being sucked towards its face so forcefully that I had to plant my feet to save myself from falling into its snout.

"Hm..." a low, rumbling voice spoke as the Dragon moved its mouth. "You are the first in many a century to approach me with wonder, not fear, human woman-child."

"The beast," Fawkner was staggered as he watched on, nearly falling backwards, "it speaks."

The Dragon turned his head to the man and glowered at him. "It is most arrogant to believe that I cannot speak," the Dragon said wisely. "All things that live have speech. It is in your understanding of their words that limits you with this view, human."

"Forgive me," Fawkner apologised, looking like a frightened child before the Dragon. "I did not mean to offend you."

"Offense is a mortal word, not a word we Elder hold," the Dragon responded evenly. "Still, courtesy *is* something we value, and I would ask it of all of you."

"What courtesy would you ask of us?" Carden enquired, never blinking as he stared at the Dragon's enormous molten eyes.

"What courtesy be given?" the Dragon asked.

I stepped forward, drawing his gaze from my companions while feeling so insignificant next to him. I took in a breath, but not out of nerves, meeting his gaze and keeping my hands at my sides.

"My name is Leander," I introduced myself to him. "It's a pleasure to meet you."

"Ah!" the Dragon sat up more, his eyes widening with delight. "Where the men tremble at the sight of me, the woman-child grants me a greeting with manners!" he lowered his face to me again, ensuring that we were almost eye-to-eye: "I am Eamnonn the Wise Protector. It is a pleasure to meet you as well, Leander the human woman-child."

"How long have you been here?" I asked with curiosity, studying every facet of the creature's great face.

"This has *always* been my home," Eamnonn answered me earnestly. "I have dwelt below the breast of this island since first I left my life-giver's brood. It has been centuries, even a millennium in your words."

"That's... wow... that's so long," I mused, trying to imagine what it must have been like for him to live there in that place for such a length of time. "And you've always been here?"

Eamnonn nodded his horned head once. "Yes. I have outlived many ages of humanity," he looked to the two men then, considering them for a moment before speaking: "You are Guardians; the ones to defend the world of mortals and immortals alike."

"We are," Carden nodded, sheathing his sword and directing Fawkner to do the same as they realised that there was no threat here. "How do you know of our Order?"

Eamnonn made a sound that reminded me of a chuckle as well as a tone of deep thought: "When first the Guardians before you came to this place to forge their trials of worth, they came upon my great chamber and looked to me with both fear and wonder as all of you, except the woman-child, now do," he explained. "They beseeched my blessing and my assistance in exchange for their protection."

"Why would a beast such as a dragon need the protection of people?" Fawkner asked, almost scoffing at the idea.

"*Some* mortals, *many* mortals, fear my kind," Eamnonn answered with sorrow behind his strength. "I saw my kin driven from the world by men who called themselves "*Dragon Slayers*" many centuries ago, and so I sought my own refuge here in what you call the Dragon's Crest," he thought for a moment, then mused: "A fitting name for the island I call home, now that thought lends itself to consideration."

"It sounds awful," I murmured sadly, sitting on a nearby rock, my knees up, elbows resting on them and hands together. "Seeing your race nearly extinct."

"Indeed," the Dragon agreed, folding his wings closer to his back. "Apart from one other, I have not seen another dragon in near twenty long centuries past."

"It sounds lonely," I said, meeting his gaze again.

"Yet another reason for my willingness to aid the Guardians," Eamnonn continued his story. "I swore to help them test their recruits and apprentices to determine if they are worthy to join the cause. In exchange they have safeguarded my home from all those who would mean me harm. Truly, the Guardians live up to the name which they have forged for themselves."

"Defending everyone in need," Carden smiled faintly as he nodded and folded his arms, "no matter their race, creed, religion or status... Even a dragon."

Eamnonn almost seemed to smile as he regarded the young man. "You seem to embody such virtues, young Guardian. What are you called?"

"Carden Highever," Carden introduced himself and gestured to Fawkner. "This is Fawkner."

Fawkner nodded his head lowly, still obviously a little unsettled. "H-hello."

"I am an apprentice of the Guardians," Carden explained to Eamnonn as he would to any human, no longer as afraid as he had been. "Fawkner is our mentor's latest recruit."

"Then you have come to be tested on this island," Eamnonn realised. "That you made it past the golems, the trap hall and the blackness is already a testament to your dedication and virtue."

Then he turned his left eye to look closely at me as he took in my scent again, studying me thoroughly. I staggered from the strength of his inward breath, managing to catch myself again and meet the Dragon's gaze.

"But you... Your voice, your look, your dress, even your scent is different to those with you," Eamnonn mused as he tried to figure me out.

"She volunteered to be our charge," Fawkner stepped closer to me as if anticipating trouble. "She is under our protection."

Eamnonn glanced to him for a moment, then faced me again. "Yet, there is more than that... You are of noble blood. Tell me, woman-child, what title does human-kind gift you?"

I felt a little uneasy, but never took my eyes from his: "My full name is Princess Leander Idona Aldrich."

"I was not aware that human-kind had long life spans like dragons," the Dragon mused, nodding. "You must be twelve centuries old by now."

"I'm not *that* Princess Leander," I tried to clarify for him. "I'm her descendant, the second of our family to carry the same name."

"But you carry the heart of a dragon around your neck," he had seen the Pendant.

I glanced at it, then looked back to him. "It was given to me by my uncle. My ancestor passed it down through our bloodline. I am the first to inherit it since her."

He sniffed me again and his eyes filled with realisation: "You have lived only eighteen cycles. I should have sensed as much. Just as I should have sensed the other."

I frowned. "The other?"

"She is bound to you and you to her through the heart you wear," Eamnonn explained, lifting one massive clawed finger towards me.

He touched the tip of his talon to my chest and I fought the urge to pull away, afraid that I would anger him. The claw was both rough and smooth, and while I was sure he could tear me apart with it if he decided to, I knew that he wouldn't. He simply caressed the Pendant then withdrew his hand to settle it on the pile of gold before him again.

"It is all that shields you from those who would harm you, Princess," he said, distant and staring without seeing. "I have sensed them of late; the foulness wafting into my caves from the world beyond," he turned his fiery eyes towards me with sorrow: "I smell death upon you, woman-child, and it makes me yearn to weep."

"You know what has happened?" I asked, feeling as if this great wonder would bring me to tears with him.

He nodded solemnly. "Innocent blood has been shed in a great river by the oldest mountains. Fires have burned and ravaged the birthplace of your bloodline, and your kin is cutting a murderous swath through his own flesh and blood."

Eamnonn threw back his head and let out a powerful, bellowing roar, flames leaping from his jaws and into the air. The blast illuminated even the darkest places of the cavern, the heat burning the cold away for only a few moments.

The sound nearly threw me off my seat, Carden and Fawkner staggering as waves of gold swept down the greedy metal mountains in torrents. But just as suddenly as he had roared, the hurting dragon turned his head down and the flames went dark.

"He... he hurt you, didn't he, Princess?" the Dragon sounded so incredibly sad.

I felt tears filling my eyes and nodded, wiping them away with my pale blue sleeves. "Yes."

"I can read it in your eyes and scent," Eamnonn confessed gravely, bringing his face closer to me; so close I needed only to reach out my hand to touch his horned nose. "So much pain is in you. Why? Why must one so young carry such a mighty burden?"

"How can you know what she's feeling and what she's been through?" Fawkner asked the Dragon.

"We dragons can see things for what they truly are," Eamnonn explained to him. "I see the grief and the conflict in you, Falcon-Lord. What was taken and what you can never reclaim, and what you did to this innocent girl for noble intentions. Were that you had stayed that path I would feast on your bones," he snarled, then spoke more softly: "But you are redeeming yourself, so I will not."

Fawkner was trembling, his eyes shining with tears. I could see that the Dragon's words had struck him just as they had me.

Eamnonn looked past me to Carden: "And you, young Guardian. I smell the affliction within your blood. You battle it as you battle the name you were given by your King and the heritage of your bloodline."

Carden stared at him with a calm expression and remained silent. His eyes looked darker and for a moment I could have sworn that they had turned red. But I guessed that that was only the light.

Eamnonn turned back to me sadly. "I feel so much anger and hatred in the world beyond my home. It pains me greatly."

"Is... is that why you stay here?" I asked him softly, meeting his gaze.

"Oh..." he said mournfully, staring at me with ever saddening eyes, "poor child... If only we dragons had been peaceful amongst ourselves, then perhaps humans would not destroy one another."

"What do you mean?" I frowned.

"There are no other races like our two," he expressed slowly. "Do you know why only humans can carry the Dragon Pendants?"

I shrugged. "I... I honestly hadn't really thought about it."

He moved his nose closer to me and I could smell the sulphur on his breath, the odour making me edge back further on the rock I perched on, my hands now behind me.

Eamnonn told me: "It is because humans and dragons are alike at our very hearts. Where elves hold beauty, dwarves hold strength, orcs hold aggression, and giants hold great calm, it is humans and dragons that possess all emotions and attributes of living sentience, but most of all imagination. This is what makes humans capable of possessing and wielding the greatest strengths our kinds ever forged. It is because we share the same hearts and life energy. And so, you hold one of the Pendants now, and thusly you and your Amethian protector are bound by your hearts forevermore."

"What kind of dragon are you, Eamnonn?" Carden asked as I digested the Dragon's words.

"I am an Aquari Dragon," Eamnonn answered proudly. "My species is one of those joined with a pendant, though I myself am not honoured enough to be a protector."

A question struck me, and I had to ask it: "What happens... uh... what happens if either Amethyst or I die?"

Eamnonn answered gently: "The one who does not will grieve the loss of the other. Your heart bond does not join your lives to the same death, only to understand and care for one another."

I nodded thoughtfully, looking down at my hands where they rested on my knees. *Well, that's good to know... I guess.*

"Forgive me," Fawkner drew our attentions as he walked forward to stand beside Carden and I, "I know that you must relish speaking with people who come here to breach your loneliness, Eamnonn, but we *have* come here to complete the Guardians' trials."

Eamnonn raised his neck and head, reclaiming his composure: "Of course. Forgive my indulgence. It is so rare that I may converse as only challengers pass through these caves, and I never see any who leave again."

"And... what became of those who *didn't* leave?" Carden asked the dreaded question.

As if he had a theatrical flair and a desire to impose fear, Eamnonn lowered his gaze to Carden and sniffed in deep.

"They failed the test I gave," he answered ominously, "and *I* had a hot meal."

I swallowed hard and looked to the others uneasily. Suddenly the Dragon's wonder and beauty had vanished with that one sentence and I found myself wanting to leave as fast as possible.

Eamnonn looked at me, his next words adding an extra cold shard of fear to my spine: "I've never tasted nobility before. Nor untouched innocence."

I gulped.

"What is this test of yours?" Fawkner drew the Dragon back to the business at hand, crossing his arms firmly.

"Ah... yes..." Eamnonn sat up straight, his long neck raised high so his head was looking down on us. "I will test your wits with *three* riddles. Answer correctly and you may leave. Answer wrongly and... well... need I say more?"

"Riddles?" Fawkner looked to Carden and I with astonishment, then back to the Dragon. "And you'd kill us for a wrong answer?"

"I will," the Dragon confirmed.

"Alright," Carden agreed, pulling me from the rock and pushing me behind him to shield me. "We'll play your game, but Leander is left out of this. She goes free no matter the outcome."

The Dragon's eyes flared brighter and he brought his face closer to us, snarling lowly.

"*Three* riddles for *three* lives," Eamnonn declared sternly, his voice booming in the caverns. "Either *all* of you leave or *none* of you do."

"It's alright," I touched Carden's shoulder, drawing both men's eyes to me. "I'll stay."

"Leander..." Carden went to argue, but I stopped him with a hushing sound.

Fawkner nodded and turned to Eamnonn. "Ask your riddles, Wise One, and we will answer."

Eamnonn seemed to brighten up and smiled – or what passes for a smile to a dragon.

"Very well," he cleared his throat and held one large scaled hand to his plated chest. "Answer: I am vast, both wide and deep, the largest of my kind. My skin is dark, but it may also shine, the earth itself the bed on which I lie. And no matter how cold I may get; I will never complain of being wet. What am I?"

Instantly, my mind began working to solve the riddle, recalling everything I had learned in my life. The memory of my grandfather sitting with me when I was six winters old before my uncle became king returned to me. I saw him reading a book of riddles and having me solve the answers by thinking them through.

"It sounds like a body of water," Carden was analysing as he looked to Fawkner and me. "The wet part makes that clear."

"It could very well be a lake," Fawkner considered.

"Is that your answer?" the Dragon narrowed his eyes at us.

My mind clicked. "Not a lake!" I turned to Fawkner, grabbing his arm. "Listen to the words. He said vast, wide, deep, largest and wet. They are the key words. A lake would be too small."

"Then what?" Fawkner frowned at me, his bearded jaw clenching.

I thought for a moment, crossing my arms in front of me. "There are two answers we could give."

"But either could be wrong," Carden warned.

"Then we choose the largest of the two," I suggested with a shrug.

Fawkner turned to Eamnonn and said clearly: "The answer is Ocean."

"Yes... very good," Eamnonn prided us. "Sea and lake would have ended your lives, but you chose wisely," he closed his eyes and took in a deep breath. "Here is your next riddle," he warned us. "Standing beneath the midday sun, I will stay with you however far you may run. By day I live, by night I die, always to return with the ever-brightening sky. What am I?"

"I know this one," Fawkner smiled. "I used to read this to... uh... I mean..." he looked to Carden and I, our frowns drawing a blush, then a paleness to his cheeks. He coughed and turned back to Eamnonn. "You are a shadow," he answered with quiet confidence.

Eamnonn seemed impressed: "Final riddle, my friends. Speech is my Father, the Soul my Mother too. Joy is what I bring, from the Heart I test if you are true. I am held by many, by bird and by mortal too, but not all may carry me. Am I carried by you? What am I?"

Silence followed the Dragon's words as we all considered the riddle deeply. It was a hard one, there was no doubt, some of its words clearly misleading.

"This is like the first," Carden finally said after a few long moments of silence. "It's full of clues, but some of the words could be literal or figurative."

"Speech... Soul... Joy... Heart...Carry... Hm...." I creased my brow hard and I racked my brain with everything I could imagine. "I can think of two answers," I told the others carefully. "Tune and Song."

"But which is right?" Fawkner asked gravely.

"Only *one* will I accept," Eamnonn prodded, flashing that toothy dragon smile again.

Twisting my hands, closing my eyes and biting my lip, I struggled with the answers.

"Fine," Fawkner decided as I opened my eyes again. "I'll say s-"

"Tune!" I cried out, stopping his answer and looking to the Dragon. "It's Tune! You can't carry a song, but you *can* carry a tune! That's the saying!"

"Do you agree with your charge, Guardians?" Eamnonn enquired of the two men.

Carden nodded to Fawkner, who answered: "We'll go with what Leander says, yes."

Eamnonn lowered his face towards us and I held my breath as we waited for him to deliver his decision.

"You... have passed," he said, and we all relaxed as he sat up and gestured with one clawed hand to the treasure surrounding us. "Take whatever prize you will from this trove and return to your keep through the tunnel behind me. You are victorious and are now a Guardian Apprentice and a Guardian Junior."

"Just like that?" Fawkner eyed the Dragon suspiciously. "Can *you* even state such things?"

Carden shook his head: "I was initiated back at the Citadel after I returned from my trials. This doesn't sound right."

They were right. I could feel that the Dragon was up to something, glancing around at the treasure surrounding us.

"What kind of dragon," I looked up at Eamnonn curiously and sceptically while remembering all that I had read about his kind, "would willingly give up part of its treasure hoard to humans?"

"You have earned a prize," the Dragon replied and gestured to the gold piles again. "Please, claim what you will."

"You're trying to trick us," I realised, remaining very calm as I stepped up onto one of the piles and faced him, his snout right down to me again. "Dragons *don't* share the gold they hoard. I know this from all the books that I've read my whole life."

"The girl's right," Fawkner came up behind me, facing Eamnonn with a hand to his sword's hilt. "You try to deceive us, dragon, but without gain. This is another test."

"And you have passed it," Eamnonn nodded proudly. "You have proven yourselves to be just and true. There is no greed in your hearts."

"It was the Test of Will," Carden stared in wonder at the Dragon, then looked to Fawkner and me with a small smile forming on his lips. "Greed was the temptation. If we had accepted his offer..."

"He would have killed us," Fawkner realised and faced the Dragon again.

"But you did not fall to temptation," Eamnonn prided, smiling a dragon's grin and straightening his back majestically. "Only true Guardians can recognise and resist temptation as you have, and only true Guardians may leave these caverns alive."

He turned and stood on his four legs, his tail swinging up over us, the wind the movement caused rushing through our hair and clothes. He came to sit on his back legs and tail beside a large opening, pressing one huge hand to the wall within to reveal a hidden passage only big enough for humans to pass through.

"*This* passage will take you back to the surface and the dock where your boat will be waiting," Eamnonn explained as we reached him. "I believe that you will hold the mantle of Guardians well, Fawkner and Carden."

"Thank you," Fawkner smiled and nodded to him kindly.

"And you, Princess," Eamnonn turned his head down to me one last time. "I offer you and your companions a warning: the one you call the Revenant is striking at the Custodians of the Past. *All* of them."

"And you want us to stop him?" Carden guessed.

Eamnonn kept his eyes on me: "What is written in stone must always be so. Success is on his side as it is for the one who haunts your waking thoughts, woman-child."

"The Shadow Lord," I breathed slowly, nodding and meeting the Dragon's gaze. "He's coming for me."

Eamnonn nodded gently. "I worry for you, Princess. So much grief and pain is yet to come, and my heart burns at the thought of tears filling your eyes," he indicated my pendant with his talon again. "Keep your dragon companion close to you just as you should the Pendant. You have great power, woman-child. You need only learn to wield it."

"I wanted to ask," I chose my words carefully as I finally put forward the question that had been hounding me since first seeing him, "why is it that you speak in the common language, but Amethyst doesn't?"

Eamnonn chuckled lightly and studied me for a moment as he considered the answer. "She does not speak in words you understand because she has not been taught to do so by another dragon. Yet, you speak with her through your heart, do you not?"

I smiled and nodded. "Yes... I do."

"I wish you well, Princess," he bowed his head to me, and I curtseyed in return to him. "I feel that we shall meet again one day. Until then, may you find the happiness that you deserve out of this terrible darkness."

I reached out and laid my cheek against the horn of his nose, hugging his snout as best I could: "Thank you, Eamnonn. Goodbye."

"Goodbye, Princess," Eamnonn said warmly as I joined my friends and we entered the passage.

I took one final look over my shoulder at him as he sealed the wall again, then, with my friends at my side, started up the stairs towards the smell of fresh, cold, salty air and the sound of crashing waves.

Chapter Fifteen
Honoured Friends

We climbed the stairs and reached the opening at the end of the caverns, the torches marking the entrance flickering against the late-night wind. Just as we had been told, there was a path down the sloping rock face back to the beach which led us straight to a second dock. The boat was waiting with the two Guardians who had brought us here sitting there playing cards. They were both surprised and glad to see us.

In moments we were in the boat and making for the mainland again, the rain thundering down harder now than when we had first entered the trials. Carden smiled at me and slung one arm around my shoulders as we huddled away from the rain together. I rested my head on his shoulder, feeling so exhausted from our ordeal. This, being in his arms, felt right.

The passage through the rocky straits took longer on the way back than it had to the Dragon's Crest. The winds were riling up the seas and causing the waves to grow in size. Then, out of the dark came flickering lights and the looming black shape of the mainland. The towers of Coastwatch Keep came into view as silhouettes, the lights on the battlements and in the windows our beacons to safety.

It took near half an hour for the men to bring the boat to the undercover docks of the keep, every instant spent battling the winds and tides. But soon we were climbing from the drenched boat and up the stone steps of the keep to the Great Hall.

When we entered the large double doors, we found ourselves faced with almost the entire population of the castle. The civilians were all gathered – man, woman and child – their eyes set on us with admiration. In the centre of the room around the brazier as before were all the remaining Guardians who had stayed behind. Riordan stood at the head of the group, his hands at his sides, dressed in his armour and black cloak. To his right stood Aldwyn and Tallinn, both now dressed in light Guardian armour similar to what Carden wore.

We walked into the centre of the room and stood with our backs to the brazier as we had before, facing the steps that Riordan stood on. I was grateful for the heat at my back, shivering from the cold of the rain and sea that had left my clothes and hair sodden.

"You have returned victorious," Riordan smiled, proudly nodding. "Tell me, Carden, how did your companion fair in his task?"

Carden replied: "He demonstrated a great willingness to defend our charge on his own, even without weapons. He fought with the endurance to face his foes. He sought a path of safety for us with unyielding awareness. He looked into the black with true faith, used his wits to overcome a dangerous challenge, and proved himself true when he was offered temptations," he smiled at Fawkner and placed a hand on his shoulder: "I would be honoured to count him as one of my Guardian brothers, Master Riordan."

Riordan nodded and gestured with both hands. "Fawkner. Step forward."

Fawkner smiled at me and I nodded to him, offering my own smile. He turned and knelt on one knee before the Guardian Masters as Carden and I stepped back to watch on.

Riordan moved to stand before him as a young Guardian woman and Aldwyn walked beside him. Aldwyn handed him a bowl of watered-down oil and Riordan dipped his thumb into it. He wiped the oil across Fawkner's forehead, lips and chest before handing the bowl back to Aldwyn. He then turned to the woman, who carried an ornate silver and black sword bearing the markings of the Guardians, and held it point up in front of him.

"By the ways of the Old Guardians, passed on before us, and by the honour of the Eldest Ones, watching over us from their refuge in the world, speak true and find your place amongst our brothers and sisters," Riordan declared and met Fawkner's gaze. "Do you accept the responsibilities of a Guardian?"

Fawkner nodded his head. "I accept."

"Then speak the Oath of our Order."

Fawkner closed his eyes for a few moments as he composed himself, then spoke: "Loyalty to all and to none. Justice upon the wicked. Compassion towards the weak. Protection to those who are defenceless. Truth ever to be spoken. From all nations we come. To no nation are we devoted. To all peoples are we in service. We serve with honour. We serve all, from highest king, to lowliest beggar. So we make our pledge, Guardians forevermore."

And there came a great din of voices as all the Guardians surrounding us – including Carden, Aldwyn and Tallinn – responded: "So shall it always be, from life in service, from service into death. A Guardian forevermore."

Riordan lowered the sword and gestured to Fawkner: "Please rise."

Fawkner stood and two Guardians came forward. They took off his cloak and helped him remove his armour and jacket. They then gave him a black and silver leather jacket similar to that which Carden was wearing and dressed him in Guardian armour. They threw a black and silver cloak across his back and bowed their heads to him.

Riordan took a second sword that was sheathed and turned to Fawkner with it held on the palms of his raised hands. Fawkner took the sword reverently, then bowed his head as Riordan placed a medallion with the Guardian seal carved into it around his neck.

The Warden stepped back and said: "You now stand as one of us and are granted the level of Initiate. Welcome, Brother Fawkner."

The room erupted in applause; Fawkner never having looked prouder as long as I had known him.

Then came a hand on my elbow.

I turned to see Dolin and Holger looking up at me, both with solemn expressions.

"Dolin? Holger? What is it?" I asked softly, still smiling as I ran a hand through my damp hair.

Dolin drew in a shuddering breath, his voice breaking. "You'd...eh...you'd better come, lassie."

My smile vanished. Dread and panic filled my heart and I looked over my shoulder back to the others. Fawkner was smiling brightly as the Guardians were surrounding and welcoming him. He and Carden turned their gazes to me, their expressions instantly dropping. Behind them, Tallinn and Aldwyn had already noticed my dread and now wore dark, worried stares.

"Lassie," Dolin urged me.

I tore my gaze from the Guardians and gathered the edges of my skirts to hurry as the Dwarves jogged to keep up with me. As I ran up the stairs with the Dwarves, I felt like the world was slowing down around me. Every movement took an eternity to make, every breath agonising to draw into my lungs. My cloak slipped from my shoulders and it seemed to flow in a slow wave of purple cotton weave, barely settling to the stone floor as I kept running.

The way ahead seemed to stretch on forever, my breathing and footsteps sounding so strangely long in my ears. I reached out one hand to grasp the doorframe, throwing myself around and into the room.

I skidded to a stop, Dolin and Holger halting right behind me. Ellora looked up with tears in her turquoise eyes from where she sat, grief striking her face. She saw me and nearly began to weep.

No... gods! No! I was screaming in my head, but my voice had stolen away, and my body petrified where I stood.

"I'm sorry, Princess," was all she said.

I glanced around to my right and left. Tristan was sitting with his eyes on the floor, his face hidden behind his long red hair, his elbows on his knees. He lifted a flask to his lips as he tried to chase away his sorrow, but it remained on his face. Joran stayed standing with his head bowed and his hands together as if he were praying. His violet eyes were closed, and his hard expression was harder still.

I turned to the bed, every agonising step cutting through me like an icy dagger, tears threatening me. Ellora stood and moved aside for me to get through, stepping past me to stand with the others.

I felt numb.

Mithras lay still, his chest motionless, no breath issuing from his lips.

My breathing started shaking as tears fled my eyes. My knees trembled and gave way. They hit the stone floor and my hands clung to the bedcovers. My heart shattered and I lay my head beside him as I cried. I felt as if I had been torn open and left to the cold of winter. The icy touch of his flesh as my fingers curled around his hand only made this worse. I could say nothing as I sobbed, my lungs burning with my grief.

"Vashabaravan Karvarn," I heard Joran say deeply from behind me as hurried footsteps and clinking armour drew from the hallway.

"Oh gods!" Tallinn gasped as the sounds of metal and cloaks settled into silence.

I closed my eyes tightly as I half lay on the bed and half kneeled on the floor. The world suddenly became dark and all I felt was the crushing grief and loneliness of his passing.

A hand touched my back and I glanced up through my tears. Carden crouched beside me with tears beading his cheeks, his green eyes filled with great sorrow and sympathy. He said nothing but kept his hand to my back as I laid my head into my arms and cried.

I closed my eyes tighter, the rain and the thunder, the chill of the room, all of it biting my skin and tearing my mind apart as my tears continued their unrelenting march of agony. Even Carden's touch couldn't soothe this pain away from me.

All seemed to fall into shadow and where I had felt pride and joy now only grief remained. And in the distance, as lightning flashed and thunder bellowed, there came a mournful howling. I knew Amethyst stood in the courtyard garden letting out her sorrow to the stormy skies above as I wept beside my friend's deathbed, the Dragon's call echoing all around me...

* * * * *

Light shone through the curtains over the arched stone window, the shadows of the steel framing the glass dancing across the floor. But it was a cold, grey light that came into the room, bringing no warmth or comfort with it.

I lay in bed wrapped in the thick bedcovers and fur blankets, staring at the window aimlessly. Tears still pooled from my eyes, though my sobs had slipped gradually from their mournful howl to a silent catching of my breath.

I could feel Fawkner's presence as he sat beside the bed, his pale eyes locked on me where I lay. He didn't try to speak to me, simply stroking my hair and shoulder the way a father would his heartbroken daughter. He had sat with me for what seemed like several ages of the world, silent and simply there.

The others were attending to the... *arrangements*. It was Ellora who had taken on the task as she had known Mithras the longest. I had heard them talking, but had stayed out of the discussion, and though I fully agreed with the decision in how best to honour my dearest friend, it was all a wound that dug too deeply into my bleeding heart for me to really do more than grant my grieving approval.

The fourth day after Mithras' passing, I woke to dark clouds and thunder on the horizon. Tallinn came into the room and tried to get me to eat, but I took only a little bread and water. She had taken my clothes and had them cleaned, now returning them to me. Once I was dressed and had my cloak on, we started from the room and down to the front courtyard of the castle. I had drawn my hood to shield my face from all the people that lived there, in no way wishing to see their looks of sympathy and sorrow.

The cold winds were like a hard punch as we stepped into the courtyard. I looked up to see that repairs were well underway from the Revenant's attack and that the Guardians were now strengthening the fortifications.

Amethyst was the first of my companions that I saw, and I immediately crossed to her. She lowered her long, scaled snout down to me and I reached up with both hands to stroke it. She looked to me with those beautiful, glowing, fire orange eyes, but they were so sad, seeming more like embers now than the blaze they should have been.

She let out a low, mournful sound and edged her face closer to me.

"I know," I whispered, pressing my forehead to the top scales of her snout. "I miss him too."

I opened my eyes and glanced to my left. The others were busy preparing for the journey north, but Aldwyn was nowhere to be seen.

Joran was hitching a large, stout workhorse to an open topped, four wheeled cart, a large doe skin leather coat now pulled on over his otherwise sleeveless armoured jacket. Beside him, Dolin and Holger were checking the supplies that I assumed they would put in the cart, but they were attaching them to two more horses instead. Ellora, Fawkner and Carden were saddling more horses, six in total; one paint horse in shades of chestnut and white, two chestnuts, one black and two white horses. They had all donned their cloaks, Ellora's pointed ears and long crimson locks hidden beneath her sage green hood.

Tristan passed Tallinn and I with a bag of supplies on his shoulder and a gathering of scrolls tucked under his arm. He wore his long brown coat now, the length of it swirling around his ankles as he walked. He reached the cart and set the scrolls down on the driver's seat, then went about attaching the bag to his horse.

I moved from Amethyst to stand close to him, touching his shoulder and drawing his brown gaze.

"Now there's a face I've not seen in a few days," he tried to be cheery, but I couldn't smile.

"You're coming with us, Tristan?" I asked so quietly I might as well have not even spoken.

He nodded. "Aye, lass, that I am."

"Oh," was all I said, leaning my back against the cart and crossing my arms.

He studied me for a few moments before stopping what he was doing and turning towards me fully. He looked down at me, so much taller than I was.

"Look, lass," he said gently with sympathy in his eyes, "I won't pretend to know how you're feeling. And I won't try to talk about any of this until you're ready," he sighed and closed his eyes for a moment, then looked to my face again. "But I know what it is to lose everyone you love. There's no cure for that pain. And I don't think there should be."

He reached out one coarse hand and touched two rough fingers to my chin, making me meet his gaze.

"But you won't do this alone," he swore softly with a gentle expression. "We're here for you. Alright, lass?"

I nodded with closed lips, fighting my tears and managing to stop them from flowing again.

He flashed me a faint smile and nodded his ginger head: "That a girl," and he turned back to his work.

I sighed silently and turned my eyes to the doorway of the keep. Amethyst was watching on where she sat nearby as Aldwyn and Riordan came walking out. Aldwyn carried his staff in hand and his sword at his hip, dressed in the Guardian travel armour like Carden, Fawkner and Tallinn now were. I could see that they were increasing their protection and so mine as well.

"I don't see why you should leave," Riordan was saying as they walked through the wet cobblestone yard towards us as rain dusted the air. "It is not a wise decision."

"Mithras was a good man and someone we had all come to count as a friend," Aldwyn explained without halting his pace, his staff clicking on the ground with his footsteps. "He deserves to have his final wish fulfilled. Besides, it is the Princess' request that we do so as well as his."

"She's a child in mourning," Riordan stated a little too coldly for my liking as they stopped near me, clearly having not seen me yet. "Her decisions are not being made from a place of wisdom."

Aldwyn nodded, facing him. "Maybe so, but regardless of her youth she is still Aldegaad's princess. *Your* people's princess. *And* your rightful queen."

Riordan put a hand to Aldwyn's plated shoulder, pausing his movements: "If the events of the past months are anything to go by, then the Princess is the focus of several deadly plots. Not only are traitorous elements of Aldegaad's nobility after her – including her remaining uncle – but she has also drawn the gaze of a new Shadow Lord," he shook his head gravely. "You cannot tell me that this journey is worth more than her safety. Especially with the Revenant's appearance."

"We cannot be sure that he has any involvement in these affairs, or any interest in the girl," Aldwyn reasoned as he leaned on his staff. "His focus was *this* stronghold, and since he left just as we arrived it was the artefact he stole and *not* the Princess he sought, or else he would have engaged us," he drew up closer to

Riordan, staring into his eyes in a more serious way, shaking his head: "And this journey is worth far more to her than doing nothing for Mithras. As much as it is to honour our fallen friend and ally, it is to give this poor heartbroken child some measure of peace. She needs it."

Riordan fell silent and just nodded. Aldwyn turned and saw me where I looked out from around the edge of the cart, nodding once to me, then moving with Tallinn to the horses.

"Come, Sarissi," Joran's voice drew me to him as he towered above me. "We must depart." He reached down and lifted me the way he would a child, placing me in the front seat of the cart.

I turned my head and braced my right arm on the top of the seat as I looked into the back of the cart. They had laid a plush pile of furs there to form a bed and had set Mithras upon it. He had been cleaned up and now only looked deathly white, but no longer ill or in pain. He had been dressed in his newly cleaned clothes and his silvery armour had been restored to him, his sword clasped by the pommel in both hands, the point between his feet.

Dolin and Holger were climbing into the back with him with what few supplies the horses couldn't carry. Dolin gave me a sympathetic nod and a reassuring half smile from behind his neat, but thick black beard.

Joran climbed into the seat beside me, taking the reins of the horse in his gargantuan hands, his own hood drawn over his head. I glanced up at him, then looked forward at my feet.

"Take care my brothers and sister," Riordan was saying to the four Guardians with us. "Be mindful and watch the roads. The Regent's forces will be searching for you."

"Once we reach Mountain Falls, the Knights of Draconia will help us protect the Princess as they have already pledged. Ser Callenhad will be pleased to see us again," Aldwyn assured him, then bowed his head in farewell. "Goodbye, Riordan."

"May your journey bring you safely to your promised destination," Riordan replied with a smile.

Amethyst flapped her wings as the Guardians nodded their goodbyes to Riordan and the gates opened. She launched herself into the air and was flying up and out of sight in moments with Farsight at her side, only her roar telling us where she and the falcon were as we started out.

* * * * *

The journey would take six days where the trip to Aneuran from Mountain Falls had been nearly two full weeks. We would be entering the mountain roads heading north at the Alstan Forest bridge less than a day from Braybrook, cutting time off our trip and avoiding the town and castle of Alstan.

It was a cold, slow journey along the paved and gravel roads. We reached Farlight easily enough, then after a short stopover made the trek north. It would be a day and a half before we reached Braybrook, passing through the empty plains and patchy trees of the eastern-most Coastlands.

I kept finding myself looking to Mithras where he lay, half expecting him to wake up and smile at me. But he didn't and I felt my tears flow and my breaths becoming soft sobs once again.

"Sarissi," Joran spoke lowly after an hour or so of watching me from beneath his brown cowl. "Why does it rain down your face?"

I glanced at him through my tears, Carden staying close by and listening as he guided the chestnut horse he was riding: "What?"

"Your cheeks have been growing wet since first I met you," the Storvari stated as callously as if he were studying dirt. "It has made me curious."

"You mean crying? Why am I crying?" I asked him, my heart cracking hard in my chest again.

He nodded. "Yes. What is this... *crying*? What is its function?"

"I'm sad," I told him incredulously, staring up at him in bewilderment. "When I'm sad I cry. You must have cried sometime in your life."

He shook his head, his violet eyes set forward: "Storvari do not cry as humans do. We are beyond such things."

"Oh right!" I snapped at him. "I forgot! The great Storvari don't have emotions like us pathetic humans! You won't do anything you see as weak! You just say a few words when someone dies and get over it!"

I slumped my head down onto my arms where they rested on my knees, crying while trying to ease my heaving, aching chest.

"Forgive me, Sarissi," Joran said gently, but still without emotion, "I did not mean to offend you," I looked up at him with puffy eyes as he sighed. "I have never cried before because Storvari cannot cry."

"Why not?" I asked, wiping my tears away with my sleeve.

"Our eyes do not have the parts that cause humans to cry," he explained. "We do not show emotion because we are not the same as humans, though we look very alike to you. Our faces are crafted differently. It is like our words," he looked to me from the way ahead again. "They are precious to us, as are our emotions. My people cannot outwardly express emotions beyond anger, aggression and reverence either through our faces or our voices because we simply lack the ability. Yet, that does not mean that we do not have emotions like sadness, joy and love."

"You do?" I blinked away my tears as I stared at him. "I'm... I'm sorry I snapped at you, Joran. It was unfair of me."

He bowed his head to me: "It is alright, Sarissi. You are grieving, so I will excuse your outburst."

I sighed and sat back as I felt like I might cry again all too soon. "I just... I miss him so much."

"As do I," the Storvari said reverently.

I nodded and huddled under my cloak more snugly. I now understood the Storvari people more and I couldn't hate Joran for not showing his emotions. It was enough to know that he had them and that he understood mine.

* * * * *

It was early in the morning when we drew near the monastery after a night in the shelter of an outcropping of rocks. Amethyst had re-joined us when we had passed high enough into the mountains and now walked beside the cart on my left. Carden stayed on the cart's right as Tristan and Fawkner followed on their horses at the back, leading the supply ponies behind them. Tallinn, Aldwyn and Ellora had the lead, their hoods drawn to guard against the cold as snow was wafting down on us in the faint glow of sunrise.

Suddenly, Ellora held up her hand, stopping our group on the road. Joran pulled up the cart, the sudden movement bringing me out of my near frozen sleep as I opened my eyes. I was tired from my bad nights full of the old nightmares and had been dozing beside him.

"What's going on?" I murmured as I woke more fully, blinking away sleep.

"Something is wrong, Sarissi," Joran told me.

I looked to Amethyst, the Dragon sniffing the air with agitation, her eyes more ablaze as they studied the peaks around us.

"Ellora?" Aldwyn was addressing the Elf. "What vexes you?"

Ellora turned over her shoulder to the rest of us, her fair face framed by her red locks and green hood. I had seen that look in her eyes over a month ago when we had arrived at the Citadel and immediately, I felt a new worry inside me.

"Something is not right," she said gravely, listening to the winds with her sharp ears. "The mountains echo of ill deeds. I believe danger is nearby."

"Alright," Aldwyn nodded seriously. "Let's make for the monastery with haste and get behind their walls before this unknown danger comes upon us."

We started forward again, making our way along the road and around the cliffs. But with each meter we travelled I felt a shadow growing in my heart and mind, a familiar energy crackling in the air.

Amethyst suddenly let out a low warning snarl as we came into view of the monastery's walls. I frowned at her but said nothing. It wasn't until we were coming to the large main gates that this unease I felt, and my dragon's agitation made sense.

The gates to the monastery lay cleaved in four on the snowy ground and against the walls, splintered as if struck by some great monstrosity. Beyond there was nothing but devastation. I felt lightheaded as the strong scent of blood breached my nostrils and went straight to my stomach.

"What is it?" Tristan called from the back of the group.

"The monastery has been attacked!" Tallinn called back to him, then faced Aldwyn. "What should we do, Aldwyn?"

Aldwyn looked so deeply conflicted. He frowned his already lined brow and set his bearded jaw as his dark eyes roved the ruin before us. He threw a gaze over his shoulder back to me, staring at me with a haunted and apologetic expression.

I was fully awake now, every part of my core aching with this new fear of whatever it was that could have done this.

Finally, Aldwyn decided: "We take it slow as we enter. Let's try to ascertain what has happened here."

He led the way on his black horse through the gates, his staff at the ready. Ellora and Tallinn followed close behind him and we were all soon inside the courtyard. Joran pulled the cart to a halt and stepped down to the snowy ground. He reached out and helped me from my seat as the Dwarves leaped to the cobblestones with the clank of their armour. Looking at all of my companions in their armour – except Tristan – I suddenly felt very out of place.

Joran set me to the ground and drew both of his enormous curved blades, looking so much more impressive and frightening with his face shielded under his hood. The golden marking covering the left side of his face glinted in the early morning light, his violet eyes shimmering with a severe fire as he began searching the way around us.

I stood there watching as the four Guardians dismounted their horses, Fawkner and Carden drawing their swords as Tallinn prepared her bow with an arrow and began moving through the ruins cautiously. Carden's left hand moved to the throwing knives around his waist, his green eyes focused and hard, his sharp jaw set.

Holger and Dolin remained by the cart with Joran, their weapons at the ready. Holger looked out from under his heavy helm with aggressive agitation, brandishing his massive hammer while Dolin held two smaller, single bladed axes, his battle-axe across his back. Between the Dwarves and the Storvari our escape was secure should the need arise.

Ellora and Tallinn strode in flanking movements through the courtyard with their bows ready, both women scouring the wreckage for any signs of what may have done this. Behind them, Aldwyn walked with his staff in hand, his left palm resting on the pommel of his sword. His long hair flickered from beneath the rippling silver and black of his hood as he inspected the damage.

I stayed near Amethyst as Tristan moved out ahead of me, my dragon following me as I slowly walked through the scene, my teal dress trailing behind me through the snow. All around us there lay brown robed monks and golden armoured knights, each with a weapon near them, each with horrible fatal wounds.

This is just like the Citadel, I thought gravely, my heart trying to speed up as I looked at the dozens of dead. *Gods, how can this be the same?*

Fawkner gave voice to my thoughts, turning over his shoulder to the other Guardians: "This is just as it was at the Citadel. We arrive only to find our safe haven in ruins and all who dwelt within dead."

"It seems we have been countered again," Dolin agreed darkly as he edged closer into the mess.

"Was it the Shadow Lord who did this?" Tallinn wondered, though I doubt she was actually looking for an answer.

"It's impossible to say for certain," Aldwyn was pacing slowly through the bodies. "I see only monks and knights. There is no sign of the enemy which they fought."

My eyes turned to the monastery itself, the front of it in ruins, part of the roof having collapsed into the central hall and destroyed the stairs to the courtyard. I could smell burnt wood as smoke still rose lightly from parts of the sanctuary into the grey, snowy sky.

Then, Amethyst turned her head and let out a strange sound that wasn't a growl but was like a curious moan. She strode towards the wreckage of a wooden building and I followed her curiously as Tristan looked up from the body he was checking. He was at my side in only a moment, the two of us following the Dragon to her find.

Amethyst sat back on her hind legs and braced her massive clawed hands into the base of the fallen roof. She lifted it with a snarl and pushed it back into place with a snapping grinding sound that drew everyone's attention. Beneath it were some of the knights and monks, still alive, but injured. Amongst them was Ser Callenhad, one of the few living who could stand under his own power.

"Princess Leander," he gasped as he saw me, standing up as Amethyst settled the roof and returned to all fours.

"Over here!" Tristan turned and shouted to the others. "We've got survivors!"

Callenhad slumped to the ground and braced his back to a wall with exhaustion, clutching one armoured arm to his chest. The plates were cracked and bent; his arm most likely broken.

I dropped to my knees beside him, pushing back my hood so he could see me clearly as I tried to steady his uninjured shoulder.

"Are you alright?" I asked him worriedly, staring at his mangled arm. "Your arm..."

"Is broken," he confirmed with a seethe of pain. He looked from his arm and back to me, smiling softly. "You've returned to us, Princess."

I nodded, fighting my grief as it tried to push against me again. "I said I would."

"Ser Callenhad," Aldwyn had practically run over to where we were, crouching down beside me as Tallinn and Fawkner started tending to the other survivors.

"Master Guardian," Callenhad nodded as Aldwyn started searching through his satchel for something. "If not for our current circumstances, your visit would be greeted with glad tidings. Yet, it is still a welcome event nonetheless."

"Here," Aldwyn produced a bottle of blue liquid and gave it to him, "drink this. It will help with the pain and begin mending your bones."

Callenhad drank the potion, then looked around as he handed the bottle back to the Mage.

"Where is Mithras?" he asked, and I felt a stabbing of ice through my heart. "I would speak with him at once."

"He's... he's dead," I choked out, closing my eyes and slumping to sit on my haunches.

After a few moments, I opened my eyes to see the white-haired knight staring at me in shock. He said nothing, so I decided to try and explain, though tears began slipping down my cheeks and my voice shook violently.

"He was killed by a wound he took in Aneuran," I had to fight with all of my strength not to scream. "He died... saving my life."

"He passed in Coastwatch Keep nearly two weeks ago," Aldwyn took over as Tristan knelt beside me and placed a hand on my shoulder, pulling me into a loose hug. "We've brought his body to lay to rest."

"There are many of our brothers and sisters who will be laid to rest this day, sadly," Callenhad declared as he managed to stand, Aldwyn, Tristan and I following him.

"How did this happen?" Aldwyn asked as Callenhad stumbled past us, recovering his strength and limping towards the ruins of the sanctuary.

"At sunset last there came a traveller on the road," Callenhad recounted as he stared at the ruins with the conviction of a true warrior and leader. "He was clad in black armour and crimson robes, his face concealed behind a grizzly masked helm where behind terrifying eyes did glow."

He turned around and looked to us as the others were beginning to help the injured out of their hiding place and to the shelter of one of the few structures still standing.

"He stood for some hours in the snow as night fell, never moving until he suddenly called out in a demonic voice, stating his wish to speak with the head of our Order," Callenhad explained. "I came to him and when I asked what he wanted he declared that he had come for the Cradle."

"What's the Cradle?" Tristan asked, frowning at me, to which I only shrugged.

"Knowing not what this was, I told him to depart our walls and never return," Callenhad drew in a painful breath, his voice growing quieter. "Then foul words spewed from his mask in a language I had never heard, but only read. It was Gorth'lakian."

"Gorth'lakian?" Aldwyn stared at him with a severe frown. "Are you sure, Ser Knight?"

"What's Gorth'lakian?" I asked, fearing what they might say.

"It is the language of the black land of Gorth'lak in the far north-east of High-Realm," Aldwyn explained ominously, turning to me. "It was spoken in only three places of our world: Gorth'lak, the Blackfelds east of Gorvenna, and in the Domain of Arnath in the heart of Dorvana."

"Arnath?" I frowned, remembering the attack on Coastwatch Keep instantly. "Then it was..."

"The Revenant of Arnath has struck the Sanctuary," Aldwyn nodded gravely, turning back to Callenhad. "Did he resurrect your dead to fight against you?"

"No," Callenhad shook his head. "Aside from the Heroine's Tomb, no bodies remain here. We commit our dead to the flames and the mountain air, for that is the way dragons die, and so we do as well."

"What else happened?" Aldwyn continued investigating.

"With not but his dread words, the Revenant tore our gates asunder," Callenhad went on in answer as he sat down on a bench near a burnt tree. "When he entered the grounds, we fought him with all our might, and he smote many with only his first strike. He cut a violent swath through our Order with his dark magic and his cold blade..." he shook his head as he stared blankly, remembering. "Never in my life have I seen one man stand against so many and take not even a single scratch upon his armour, let alone his flesh."

"One man did all of this?" Tristan snorted as he looked around at the ruins, but I could hear the unease in his voice and see it in his eyes.

"The Revenant is no mere man," Tallinn said quietly as she approached, the Dwarves now helping Fawkner with the injured as Carden and Ellora moved towards us. "He is a living corpse of great malevolence, once a necromancer in life, slain for his crimes by my people and the High Elves, now a monster of his own sinister making. None have ever faced him and survived... save one."

"The Heroine of High-Realm," Ellora stated, looking to me. "Your ancestor defeated him over a thousand years ago during the War of the Shadow."

"If he has come here as he did Coastwatch Keep," Tallinn looked so distressed, "then nowhere could be safe."

"Tallinn, breathe," Carden advised her, drawing her hazel eyes to his green ones. "We can't afford you passing out again."

She closed her eyes and drew in some deep breaths, her golden hair flowing freely around her cloaked and armoured shoulders like yellow waves in the breeze.

"How many did he slay?" Aldwyn looked back to Callenhad.

Callenhad gestured to the dozen and a half people Fawkner and the Dwarves were tending to. "All that remains are those you see before you," he turned to us gravely. "We are less than a fifth of our number. He declared that he would leave only so many alive once he claimed his prize."

"The Cradle," Aldwyn nodded. "How long ago did he depart?"

"Some hours past," replied the Knight. "He took some of our dead unto him as resurrected servants, and they scoured the ruins of the Sanctuary for an incredible time. Then there came a terrible cracking, and all was silent. Minutes passed and the Revenant came before me as I tried to fight him once more," Callenhad winced in pain as he touched his arm that Tallinn was now putting into a makeshift sling. "He shattered my sword and my arm, then told me that he had his prize. He said that people would come to us and that we were to give them a message."

"What is the message?" Aldwyn was stroking his beard as he listened, deep in thought.

Callenhad looked to me darkly: "The Custodians have failed in their duty and *all* the artefacts will be recovered," he hesitated. "And the descendant will come to where the ancestor lies as the Lord is restored."

"W-what does that mean?" I felt myself tremble as ice slid through my spine and spiked my heart again.

"It sounds as if the Revenant is planning something," Tallinn murmured, her arms at her sides, her eyes to the ground. "I think it means that he has fully reclaimed his power."

"So, now we not only have the conspiracy in Aldegaad and the Shadow Lord to deal with, but also the Revenant of Arnath pushing against us," Carden sighed and shook his head, his arms crossed. "How many more enemies will array against us before this is done?"

"Our first priority is protecting the Princess," Aldwyn started saying, but his voice faded away from my hearing. "Only then can we set about determining what it is the Revenant came for..."

The world faded away from me and I looked past the shadowy versions of my friends at the glowing figure before me. A tall, dark haired Elf stood amongst the wreckage, seemingly glowing with an otherworldly light that shone from her gold and emerald robes.

Illuminil, I realised, recognising the Galvenin Elven Enchantress. *How is this possible? Is this magic?*

Illuminil looked to me but did not speak. All the same her voice swam through my head in that melodious tone she had used in Galvenin: "*Travel to the Cradle of your Ancestor, from the Citadel, across the Great Bridge, into the Calian Mountains. Take to the Mountain Falls and seek her. Only then will you know your path.*"

I closed my eyes as I heard her voice, and in that strange twilight world where it seemed that the shadows were flickering as flames, I saw the tomb in Mountain Falls. The torches were glowing around the Dragon statue within and there lay the stone covering of my ancestor, her likeness captured perfectly as she lay in eternal sleep beneath the hard skin of the tomb.

I opened my eyes and Illuminil was gone, the light and shadows back to normal, and colour having returned to the world. I felt as if I had awoken from a strange dream, though I hadn't been asleep.

Horrified realisation struck me, and I turned on my heel, sprinting away from my friends. I heard their calls, but I didn't turn, running as fast as I could around the ruined sanctuary into the great memorial garden.

I slowed my pace, passing the ruins of the angel statue and walking into the tomb. My heart broke, my legs fell away, and I slumped to the wall, finding my place sitting there.

The Dragon remained untouched, but the tomb was shattered in the middle, only its two ends left intact. Pieces of stone were scattered across the floor, the lid that had the carving of my ancestor completely obliterated.

Tears were running down my face, but no sound came out of my lips. I just stared at the empty space where my ancestor should have been, her body long gone, the meaning of the word "cradle" so clear to me now as I sat in silence.

Hurried footsteps approached and I watched Ellora pass me by. She dropped to her knees, covered her face and began weeping without words as she saw the ruined tomb of her long-passed friend. It was a pain we could share, much like losing Mithras.

"What is this place?" I heard Tristan ask, seeing him, Callenhad, Tallinn, Carden and Aldwyn standing in the archway just outside the tomb.

"The tomb of Leander Aldrich the First," Callenhad replied in a saddened and defeated tone.

"It was the Great Heroine's remains the Revenant was after," Aldwyn stated darkly, his face glum as I turned my gaze to the ruined sarcophagus while Tallinn moved to comfort Ellora. "We should have expected this."

I gazed aimlessly at the ruined stone case through my long dark hair. I didn't feel the cold of the floor or of the icy air, nothing but the overwhelming amount of grief that had been forced on me since turning eighteen.

My mother. My father. My aunt and uncle. My closest friend and protector. My home. My birthright. Now my ancestor's remains... Gods! How much more must I lose?! How much grief must I endure?! I closed my eyes tightly, certain that my pain was registering on my face. *When will this nightmare end?!*

"It seems that there will be no refuge found here," Callenhad sounded apologetic. "The monastery has fallen, and we have failed in our duty. We are too few now to protect the girl."

"So what do we do?" I heard Carden murmur, uncertainty in his cold voice.

No one answered as none of them knew what to say. But I knew. There was only one thing to do and it took all of my strength to be able to say the words necessary to make it happen. After all, even in grief I had to be strong because that was the Queen that I was supposed to be, and the Queen that Mithras had died for.

"We do what we came here to do," I said without looking at them, sucking in a wavering breath as I felt another tear slide down my cheek. "We lay Mithras to rest."

Chapter Sixteen
The City of Eilath

There was no recovering the sanctuary itself, and only a few of the Dragon Knights remained living. Carden, Fawkner, Tristan and Joran aided the knights with setting pyres for their dead while Aldwyn tended to the injured with the help of the knights' one remaining healer.

I sat in the cart with Mithras' body, huddling from the cold as I stared at his face. There were so many things I wanted to say to him, but none of them mattered anymore. To speak them now would only serve to make me feel worse.

When night fell there was only one pyre left to build. The four Guardians tended to it, constructing the pyre's wooden platform and stuffing it with hay. The knights then carried Mithras to the pile and laid him on top of it. He would be set in his Aldegaadian armour, but he still had his Order of Draconia ring and sword.

I stood between Carden and Tristan with Fawkner and Joran at my back. Aldwyn, Tallinn and Ellora stayed to our right as Dolin and Holger took to our left, Fawkner holding Farsight on his arm. The falcon remained silent, twitching her head as she watched on.

The remaining knights bowed their heads in reverence as Callenhad touched a torch into the lowest part of the pyre. Flames instantly spread throughout the gaps and their tongues started licking at the wood, filling all the empty spaces with their orange glow. In mere moments the fire had surrounded Mithras and was devouring him.

"A Dragon Knight never truly passes," Callenhad declared reverently. "Like the Eldest Ones, in fire we ascend."

I closed my eyes, the glow of the flames spreading a red light through my eyelids as I sniffed against sobs. The only warmth I felt came from the blazing pyre and from the fresh tears quietly and slowly rolling down my cheeks.

I felt Carden's arm encircling me as he looked at me from beneath his own hood. Meeting his eyes with tears in mine, I let him hold me close.

Something pressed into my back and I glanced over my shoulder, Amethyst now moving her large head and long neck up beside me on my left. She let out a soft sound as she looked at me with her right eye, pressing her scaled cheek against my shoulder.

I reached up under her long jaw and stroked her snout with my left hand, the Dragon growling softly and sadly. I sighed and faced the flames again, blinking away my tears as I watched my protector pass into ash.

* * * * *

Far into the night, after the fire had burned until there was nothing left, we sat in silence in our makeshift camp amongst the ruins, the knights doing the same nearby. Food had been cooked, but few of us had the stomach to take much of it. We were all feeling defeated and helpless, even the Guardians.

Finally, after so long in silence, it was Dolin who spoke, sitting nearer the entrance to the monastery gates.

"So..." he considered slowly, chewing his pipe and puffing out smoke rings, "what are we to do now?"

"We need to find a safe haven," Aldwyn muttered as he stared into the small campfire before us. "Our mission remains the same: protect the Princess."

I grimaced as I heard him, staying as far from the group as I could while remaining within the safety of their gazes. Amethyst lay near me, her head on the ground, her neck and tail nearly coiling a half circle around the ten of us. I just cuddled into her side, finding a deep comfort in her presence.

"And where would you suggest we go, Master Guardian?" Holger asked gruffly, taking his own pipe from his lips. "Back to your stronghold in the south?"

"The Regent's forces have begun setting up checkpoints along every safe path we might take," Tallinn said coldly as she wrapped her cloak further around herself. "I fear the road back to Coastwatch Keep is now lost to us."

"We could make for Galvenin," Carden suggested hopefully. "The Elves *were* welcoming. Surely they'd help us."

"The path back is crawling with Scourge, remember," Ellora looked up to him. "We would never make it there. Besides, the bridge across the chasm between the Calian and Nartarn'lath Mountains now lies in ruins. We cannot hope to pass that way again."

"Then we go back to Hecturn," Holger offered, relighting his pipe. "We dwarves will give these foes a mighty battle indeed."

"No brother," Dolin shook his head as he stroked his beard and smoked. "Lord Eilan bade us to take them from Hecturn. Our people fear another attack from Shade Seekers, and for that very reason the lassie isn't safe there."

"Not to mention the goblins in the tunnels, and that... *thing* we fought," Tallinn recalled, shaking her head. "Gods, is there nowhere we can turn?"

Silence fell amongst us, everyone sitting there in thought. I couldn't even imagine where we could go, all hope of safety seeming far gone now.

"I have an idea," we all turned to where Fawkner sat feeding Farsight on his arm.

He looked up at us from his bird, taking in each of our faces and ensuring that we were all paying attention before deciding to continue.

"Since there is nowhere in Aldegaad we can go, there is but one course left to us," he stated.

Tristan nodded as he realised what the older man was saying. "We leave Aldegaad."

Leave Aldegaad? I was alarmed as I heard those words. *But... but I've never gone beyond Aldegaad's borders!*

"It is a thought," Aldwyn was considering it and I was sure he could not see my shocked stare under the shadows of my hood. "The question is, where do we go?"

"Lorveren," Fawkner suggested evenly and with certainty. "We could head for my city."

"Which city is that?" Ellora asked.

"Eilath," came Fawkner's response, "the ancient capital of Ranhart before Vorhalaas and Lorveren were formed."

With interest in his severe eyes, Aldwyn leaned forward, his hands clasped together with his elbows on his knees. "It is a possibility to consider."

"We stand mere days from my homeland," Fawkner explained evenly, "the path through the mountains to the town of Lorso clear to us. And, unlike Aldegaad, there are no corrupt nobles hunting the girl in Lorveren."

"But Eilath is near the border with Vorhalaas," Tallinn pointed out with a calm worry in her voice. "Historically, your people have not shared peace of any kind with the Vorhals for more than a couple of centuries."

"It is an uneasy peace," Fawkner agreed with a nod, "but we are at peace nonetheless."

"How safe will the Princess be in Eilath?" Aldwyn enquired seriously.

Fawkner met his gaze: "Safer than she is here. You have my word."

"I would not agree to anything without the Princess' approval," Aldwyn turned his gaze to me. "Your Highness, does this course of action suit you?"

I glanced over my shoulder at him and shrugged half-heartedly. "I don't see that we have any choice."

"Then we'll depart in the morning," Aldwyn declared and stood up. "Everyone get some sleep. We will need all our strength for this next journey."

So, this is the way my life goes now, I thought sadly. *I lose almost everyone I love, get deposed as queen, become a fugitive in my homeland, and am suddenly forced into a neighbouring nation. Gods... how did this happen?*

* * * * *

At day's break we rose to another frozen storm, packing the tents into the cart as quickly as we could and stowing our supplies as well. We gifted the two spare horses to the knights to help them since they would soon leave Mountain Falls in search of their brethren elsewhere in High-Realm. We said our goodbyes and made our way out through the blizzard.

I sat on the same horse as Carden, wrapped in my cloak and hood, the young man seated behind me and guiding the reins. It was the only comfort I could find as we set out once again.

The Dwarves and Joran took the cart while Tristan, Aldwyn, Ellora, Fawkner and Tallinn rode the remaining horses, Fawkner casting Farsight into the sky to watch our way. Amethyst walked beside mine and Carden's horse, staying close to me out of a deep need to protect me, which I truly appreciated.

By midday the storm had gone, and we were faced with the clear mountain air, the snow finally settled upon the ground. Still, the cold did not let up, and we kept our faces shielded and our hands wrapped against the frost.

It was a two-day journey from Mountain Falls to where the passage through the mountains would lead down into Lorveren's verdant green fields. The way was easy despite the uneven rocky ground and the heavy snow that powdered the way.

Hours after leaving camp on the second day we were nearing the border with the sun slowly setting in front of us. Carden and I were following the cart now with Tristan at our backs and Fawkner's horse clopping at our side.

From here I could see the far-reaching yellows and greens of the Knolling Plains beyond the Alstan Forest. To our left the Great River Arvon snaked its way west, shimmering as it flowed to meet the Crestian Sea. And far in the distance to the south-west there gleamed the white city of Aneuran in Albion Bay, surrounded by the patches of woods and rocky rises that made up the Coastlands.

"Leander?" Carden halted the horse as he noticed my distant gaze. "What is it?"

"I've never been outside of Aldegaad before," I confessed in a quiet voice, my hair catching in the wind and my hood hanging over my shoulders freely. "I'm afraid I'll never get to come home."

"You will one day," Carden promised me, looking into my eyes over my shoulder, touching his thumb and finger to my chin reassuringly. "When this ordeal is behind us and your safety is assured, we will bring you back and you can reclaim your birthright as Queen of Aldegaad."

"I hope you're right, Carden," I murmured.

"Come," Fawkner drew our eyes to him as he and Tristan led their horses up to us, "we have a long way still to go ere the night falls."

I nodded as they started past us, turning my eyes back to Aldegaad's distant beauty. I drank deep the view of my home before leaving it behind me, my heart full of a new sorrow.

In less than an hour, as the sunlight was dying and the night was closing its cloak of darkness over us, we came to the border where a stone marker waited. It pointed an arrow west that read **Aldegaad** and another east which said **Lorveren**, both words chiselled in stone.

Another day was spent traversing the mountain path only to rest for the night amidst some rocks before setting out down the slopes the next day. We found ourselves arriving that following night in the small farming town of Lorso.

In three days, we journeyed via the road next to the Emerald River southeast along the borders of Haven Forest, and on the fourth day we came upon the vast green and gold grassy plains that stretched all the way to the southern coast of Lorveren. After camping for the night, we set out again, and by late afternoon we were riding up a tall hill only to halt there and gaze at another ancient majesty.

I stared in wonder at Eilath, a great historical city, one of the three oldest cities to live beyond the War of the Shadow. The other two were Aneuran and Nargilith, the capital of Gorvenna. I couldn't help wondering how this ancient city had lasted so many centuries before the war as well as so many after.

It was set on a large rocky rise jutting up highly from the plains, stone walls surrounding the wooden log houses that stood within. They all had thatched roofs, which was common enough to see in most towns and cities, but it was the largest structure standing at the pinnacle of the city that surprised me. Like the other buildings, this one was made of carved wood with stone supports, multiple thatched roofs reaching around its grandeur. It looked like the great hall of an ancient warrior king long since passed on into the Beyond.

"Eilath," Fawkner declared with pride in his eyes, Farsight now on his arm once again, "ancient capital of Ranhart. And at its centre stands the Hall of the Plains, once home to the great Horse Lords of Ranhart and their Kings," he turned his head and smiled at me, peering under my hood. "In all of Lorveren you will find no safer refuge than that which resides within Eilath's great walls. Fitting also that it is the ancient home of your ancestor's maternal bloodline, Leander."

I nodded but said nothing as we admired the view for a few more moments, very aware of my family's origins in ancient Graphtar and Ranhart.

The Guardians soon urged our horses forward, and, with Fawkner leading and Amethyst high in the skies above us, we began a gentle trotting gallop towards the city.

I looked up at the great walls to see sharpened logs pointing up in a stockaded top around the lowest parts, armoured men in scale chest plates over green and brown tunics pacing the walls. Upon the posts above the gates flew two great green banners trimmed in gold, the avatar of a golden falcon with its wings outstretched in the centre. They flew high, flickering on the breeze like green and gold flames.

Fawkner trotted his horse to the gate and called up to the guards: "Open the gates!"

They hurried as they recognised him, one of them shouting: "Open the gates! The Lord of Eilath returns!"

I turned my gaze to Fawkner and frowned, but he didn't even acknowledge me, simply leading the way through as the gates were opened.

Beyond the gates we were greeted by a city that was beautiful in its own way but was certainly more gold and brown in colour than what I had expected. There were very few green plants and aside from sprigs of lavender growing from a few places, and vegetables in the outermost gardens, there was only dried grass.

The streets were paved in light cobblestones, the houses close together and smaller than what I had imagined. They all had golden roofs and hard wooden doors with small barred windows. Their clay and wood walls were carved in ornate images of horses and smooth twisting designs, supported by thick upright log beams.

Green cloaked guards patrolled the streets with falcon emblazoned shields and tall spears, swords at their hips, their faces hidden beneath helms. Their chainmail and scale armour clinked and rattled as they walked, their long hair flowing from beneath their helms in shades of red, brown and blonde.

The people weren't really similar in appearance, though almost all of them had the same grey eyes that Fawkner had. The women wore simple dresses with bodices bound at the chest, their hair in plain styles. The men left their hair untied and wore typically basic pants, boots and corded tunics over long sleeved shirts.

They stared up at us in wonder as we passed by, their comments sounding all around us. I remained hidden beneath my hood, watching out at them as they stood gawking at us.

"Guardians! They're Guardians!" I heard one man say to his friend.

"They come with elves, dwarves and giants," a second was commenting with unease and awe. "Unbelievable."

"What would Guardians be doing here?" a woman was asking her husband.

"It seems we've drawn quite a bit of attention," Carden noted as we continued past.

Children were staring up at us and I met their small, innocent eyes from beneath my hood. They were as curious as their elders were, fascinated by the strangers in their midst. Even the guards were whispering to each other. *I remember feeling like that when the Guardians first arrived in Arvon...*

Fawkner led us towards the Hall of the Plains, the large mansion-like fortress house where several guards were waiting to welcome us.

"It appears that we are to meet the Lord of Eilath," Aldwyn observed as we began dismounting.

Carden helped me down from our horse after dismounting himself, a guard coming up to us and taking the horse's reins as movement from the stairs up to the hall drew my gaze.

A tall man with brown hair that was heavily silvered came walking towards us. He wore armour like the guards, but his cloak was black and topped with fur like the other Fawkner had worn. His face was bearded with streaks of light brown amongst grey, his eyes bright as he approached Fawkner.

"Ah!" Fawkner smiled brightly, taking the man by the forearm in greeting. "Oddvar, it is good to see you."

"And you, my Lord," Oddvar bowed his head respectfully to him. "I have attended to my duties in your absence, but Eilath has sorely missed her leader."

"And I have missed my beloved Eilath," Fawkner replied.

" ahem," Tristan coughed and Fawkner turned.

We were all staring at him with incredulous expressions, some of us with our arms crossed in front of us, others just staring in shock. Only Joran remained untouched by what we were seeing, but since he had been with Fawkner longer than the rest of us, I was sure that he knew everything.

"Who are these?" Oddvar asked with a frown, then looked to Fawkner. "You bring guests to Eilath, my Lord Fawkner?"

"My travelling companions and I have come a long way, Oddvar," Fawkner told him. "We are in need of rest. And I must see them."

"They wait for you, my Lord," Oddvar replied and gestured to the stairs. "Please, they will be overjoyed."

He and Fawkner started up the stairs, the rest of us exchanging puzzled expressions.

"What the Void?" Tristan swore lightly.

"It appears Fawkner has some explaining to do," Aldwyn stated and immediately started up the wide stairs.

I looked to Carden who shook his head and opened his mouth to say something, but he was far too bewildered. I shrugged at him and turned to the stairs, taking the hems of my dress in my hands and following Aldwyn.

We reached the wide flat porch before the great wood and stone carved manor, guards standing at the doors into the hall with shields and spears, their cloaks and hair catching in the winds coming up from the vast grassy plains. The majesty of the Great Hall was not lost on any of us, all of us staring in wonder at this historical place.

"Papa! Papa!" a tiny voice cried out.

I dropped my eyes to the door as a little light brown-haired girl ran from the doorway with a stuffed toy doll held by the arm in one hand. She was no more than four or five with a beautiful round face and grey eyes. She was clothed in a green and gold dress with simple shoes, her long hair done up with braids and flowers running through the length of the untied strands.

She excitedly ran towards Fawkner, who, laughing with joy, ran forward a few steps, dropped to one knee and scooped her up into his arms. He hugged her tight as she giggled happily.

"I missed you, Papa," the little girl said, looking up at Fawkner so innocently.

"And I missed you too, my little Freda," he told her, cradling her in his arms. "Have you been a good girl while I've been away?"

She nodded vigorously as only children do: "Yes, Papa, I have."

Fawkner chuckled and nodded. "That's my beautiful girl."

She just kept hugging him as a tall, light brown-haired woman came from the doors in a flowing white and green dress, carrying a baby in her arms.

He has a family! It all made sense to me now, the mystery that was Fawkner finally being unravelled before my eyes.

"Ah!" the woman beamed as the baby cooed. "My beloved husband at last returns from his travels."

Fawkner stood, reached out an arm and pulled her close, kissing her on the lips lovingly. They embraced and separated their faces to gaze into each other's eyes, drinking in their visages deeply.

"I began to wonder if I should ever lay eyes upon you again, my love," she told him softly, smiling warmly. "I am glad to see that my prayers to Isnari have not been made in vain."

"I have dreamed of your fair face each long night, and thought of your loving heart each passing day, Erika," Fawkner smiled at her. "To see you and my children again was all that kept me warm in the darkness of these past months," then he smiled and looked to the baby, poking a finger into its hand as it gurgled happily. "And my son... how big he grows. My little Bran."

His wife, Erika, looked past him and frowned. She studied us with a harsh expression, then turned her gaze to her husband, the length of her hair and the silken sleeves of her dress swaying with her.

"Who do you bring with you, Fawkner?" she asked in a shocked voice. "Where are the others?"

"Only Joran and I return, Erika," he said solemnly. "Jarvis, Davis and Morgan were slain by... well..."

"I see," she nodded with a severe expression, glancing at us and taking in our appearances. "Those three wear the trappings of the Guardians."

"They *are* Guardians, my love."

She glared at him. "And you! *You* wear their armour!"

"Erika..."

"You've joined the Guardians then?!"

"With little choice," Fawkner assured her, his expression sincere. "My life was forfeit to one of the royals of Aldegaad. The Guardians with us recruited me to the Order to save my life."

"Please, my Lady," Aldwyn stepped forward and nodded to Lady Erika as she cradled her baby.

Fawkner held his daughter to his hip where she clung to his coat as she watched on with curious eyes.

The Mage bowed his head: "I am Aldwyn Draken, Master Guardian of the Order," he gestured to the two younger Guardians. "These are my juniors, Tallinn Landrace of Dorvana and Carden Highever of Gorvenna. What your husband says is true. We did indeed save his life by recruiting him."

She just nodded, eyeing Fawkner and shaking her head. "Well... I would not be much of a hostess if I did not welcome you to our home, Master Draken."

She turned and stared in bewilderment as Fawkner started the introductions. "Allow me to introduce the others, Erika," he said. "This is Tristan of Ivansten, a Wanderer."

"My Lady," Tristan nodded politely, a gentleman despite his rough appearance.

Fawkner went on: "Ellora Snowleaf of the Galvenin Wood Elves."

Ellora bowed her head, her hood pushed back, and her ears now displayed where they poked up from under her thick red hair.

"And the Axton brothers from the City of Hecturn," Fawkner turned to the Dwarves, "Dolin and Holger."

"It is an honour to be welcomed into your great house, my Lady Erika," Dolin said without any concern of standing down ceremony, bowing deeply, then smacking his brother to do the same.

Erika raised an eyebrow at Fawkner: "Elves and dwarves have come to Eilath in your company?"

"Ahem, that's *one* elf thank you very much," Holger said, holding up his forefinger. "One pointy eared bitch is enough for me."

Ellora immediately kicked him in the backside and the Dwarf staggered, then spun around and glared at her.

"What do you think you're doing, She-Elf?!" he demanded, fuming with rage, his face bright red.

"Taking exception to such insulting phrases, toadstool," Ellora replied in a very casual tone, raising one sharp eyebrow at him.

"Toadstool...? Toadstool?!" Holger bellowed.

"Brother," Dolin warned him, grabbing him by the collar and meeting his gaze sternly. "We are in the company of Ladies. Let us behave to our very best, shall we?"

"But... eh... ah!" he shook his head, then nodded. "Oh, very well, brother."

"They're funny!" Freda giggled, clapping beside her father's leg.

Dolin nodded to her and smiled. "Ah ha-ha... indeed we are little Lady."

"Well, at least Freda will have some new friends to keep her entertained," Erika smiled and turned her gaze to me. "And who is this?"

I pushed back my hood and immediately her eyes widened, and her jaw dropped. I blushed instantly, the heat in my cheeks making me glance to the ground as I tried to push it back.

Even outside of Aldegaad I'm recognised, I grumbled in my head.

"I know her face," Erika breathed, taking a few steps closer as Oddvar stared at me along with the few guards surrounding us.

"Erika," Fawkner put his arm around his wife and faced me, "allow me to present her royal highness Princess Leander Idona Aldrich of Aldegaad."

I immediately dropped into old habits from everything my mother and my deportment and etiquette tutors had taught me: "It is a pleasure to meet you, Lady Erika," I reminded myself of the name as quickly as I could, managing to sound flawless as I spoke. "Thank you for welcoming us to your home."

"Please, your Highness," Erika was taken aback, "the honour is mine. Never before have we hosted someone of your social standing from your country."

"I get that a lot," I murmured as I looked down at my hands where I was twisting them together in front of my stomach.

"Wait a moment," Erika turned to Fawkner, "if she's here then that means... Oh Gods!"

Fawkner placed his hands on her shoulders and reassured her: "It's alright. His attentions are no longer upon us."

"But..."

"I'll explain later, my beloved," he promised her, "but for now let us attend to our guests."

Erika blinked and nodded. "Oh... uh... yes, of course. Oddvar," she turned to the man who I had now determined was Fawkner's steward. "Would you be so kind as to show our guests to quarters? And provide the Princess with rooms in the royal wing of the house."

"As you wish, my Lady," Oddvar nodded and turned to us, gesturing with an open arm to the doorway. "If you would follow me."

We were taken through the Great Hall of the house, which was once a large throne room, a long rectangular fire pit set into the centre of the stone floor where servants were already hard at work preparing a meal; the banners of Lorveren hanging on the high walls as sunlight shone from the windows set into the ceiling. Great carved columns ran in pairs through the length of the room, leaving enough space for a large opening in the centre. Long tables were set around the pit, two on each side, a shorter one set opposite the entryway with six chairs bearing heightened backs.

From there, Oddvar led us each to quarters, Aldwyn telling him that it was important that the Guardians' quarters be kept close to mine for my protection. I grimaced as he said this, but I knew he was right.

The room I was given was on the second floor facing east, overlooking the gardens to the back of the manor. Warm rugs were set on the bare wooden floors while thick linen curtains framed the two large windows that poured light into the room on either side of the balcony doors. There was an old closet, a chest of drawers, and two night tables flanking a large four poster bed dressed in green covers and curtains.

I was advised that dinner would be in two hours as well as told that I would have some new dresses made to replace my ruined and lost ones, then left to my own devices.

I took the bag that Carden had carried for me and set it on the bed, opening it and studying what belongings remained to me. I had only my night gown and my ill begotten wedding dress from Aneuran left. The only other option I had was a cobalt and purple battledress I had taken the night Arvon had been attacked.

"Perfect," I grumbled, shaking my head and tearing through the bag. "Have I nothing else I can wear?"

Aside from the undergarments I had packed, I began to think I had nothing left, but a shimmer of blue caught my gaze. I reached in and withdrew my mauve long sleeved dress and my blue and purple over dress that were identical to the teal, purple and blue ones I was currently wearing.

I smiled for what felt like the first time in ages and slipped out of my clothes. I washed, grateful for the bathtub that had been provided for me in the next room, dried and dressed in the second pair of leggings that I had, then the fresh dress. I adjusted the long flowing over sleeves, then brushed my hair straight again. At least now I looked presentable.

I left the room and returned to the hall to find the others all waiting there. I was directed to a seat beside Carden where he sat with Tristan and Tallinn; Ellora, Dolin, Holger and Aldwyn set across from us. There were also a number of well-dressed men there that I could only guess were city officials.

Fawkner – like the other Guardians – had exchanged his armour for more comfortable clothing, dressed now in a long, dark green velvet tunic and a brown shirt, the sleeves unbuttoned at the wrists. He looked so different as he sat there with his wife and children, nothing like the man I had first thought him to be.

As I entered, the entire room stood and turned their gaze to me.

"Oh great," I murmured to myself, "back to royal protocols."

I sighed and crossed to the seat Oddvar had pointed me to, pausing and looking around at everyone before taking my place. As I had expected, once I had sat down the rest of the room did too and the servants began serving our meals.

While we ate, the pleasantries were completed, and the officials began speaking of city business to their newly returned lord. I sat there absentmindedly picking at my food and eating slowly, lost in my thoughts. I had never really listened to courtly business all that much while dining with Father and his advisers, so it wasn't strange for me to be mentally absent at that moment either.

"Now then," Fawkner said once his advisers were finished and as he drank from his wine goblet, sitting back comfortably in his seat, "I do believe I have some explaining to do, my friends."

"Yeah!" Holger agreed loudly with a mouth stuffed full of food, scraps of meat covering his beard. "Like how come you're a lord all of a sudden? Weren't you just some mercenary scum?"

"Holger!" Dolin hissed at his brother, shaking his head and taking some mead from his stein.

I sat back and crossed my arms, turning my gaze to Fawkner and watching him in silence.

"I *did* say that I was a mercenary," he confirmed with a nod, "but given what my task was then, I was not willing to reveal my lordship to the people of Aldegaad."

"There is wisdom in concealing one's identity when undertaking a dangerous task," Joran's deep voice came from behind me, leaving me shocked that I hadn't seen him there.

"And you did not wish to incite a war between Lorveren and Aldegaad," Aldwyn determined with an even nod.

Fawkner nodded with shame. "Yes... It was my hope that my task would be completed, and I could return home without revealing my true identity to anyone in Aldegaad."

"Your task was to kidnap the Princess for a monster," Tallinn spoke quietly, but her tone was harsh as she glared up from under her blonde hair. "You risked the life of an innocent young girl."

"I did," Fawkner nodded and looked to me earnestly. "As I told you when I took you from Arvon, Leander, I wish I'd had another choice. I really didn't want to bring you to any harm. That is why I helped you escape in the end."

I just nodded and let my long hair frame my face to shield my gaze from everyone around me.

"So, you're a Lorveren noble then?" Tristan asked as he set his mug down, his mouth wet with alcohol.

"I'm the eldest son of the Caradoc ruling house," Fawkner declared quietly as he swallowed some food he had picked from his plate. "We are maternal cousins of the current Lorveren King, Haral son of Harcourt. Our line is one of the oldest noble bloodlines in High-Realm, excepting that of the Aldrich Family."

"Ah, well, what do you know? A princess *and* a lord," Tristan smiled, holding up his stein, maybe having had a little too much to drink now that he was on his fifth. "I'm becoming quite the fancy man of the world with the noble company I seem to be keeping nowadays. Eh?"

"You're drunk," Tallinn shook her head.

Tristan nodded; his words slurred. "Maybe just a wee bit, yeah."

I flicked my eyes up at Fawkner from the spot I had been staring at on the table, my arms still crossed as I was slowly chewing my teeth together behind my closed lips.

"Why didn't you tell me you were a lord?" I asked softly, but volume or not all eyes were on me again.

"For the same reason I kidnapped you for him," Fawkner answered evenly and honestly, "to protect my family."

"You could have said something after we started travelling together," I murmured.

He frowned and leaned towards me, making me look him in the eyes: "It was not my intention to deceive you, Leander. Truly, I *am* sorry."

"I understand," I nodded with raised eyebrows, feeling that I appeared harsher than I had meant to. "Your deception about who you are is nowhere near the sin of your actions against me in Aldegaad."

"Surely you can forgive him, your Highness?" Erika looked to me as she cradled her son.

I just nodded and faced her. "Your husband has already redeemed himself to me," I shrugged. "I have no more to ask of him to gain my forgiveness. He already has it."

She seemed satisfied with that answer.

I just sat back and stared at the table again, trying to lose myself in my thoughts, but finding it impossible.

"I suppose the next question," Ellora said as she rested her clasped hands in front of her on the table, looking around the room at everyone, "is what should our next step be?"

"The Elf's got a good point," Holger pointed at her rudely as he shoved more mutton into his face. "When do we start fighting and carving through some enemies?"

"We don't," Aldwyn replied with a sideways glance to the Dwarf. "Our duty is to safeguard the Princess."

"She couldn't be safer anywhere else," Erika looked up from Freda, who was sitting eating her mashed-up food. "Eilath is the most fortified city in Lorveren, besides the capital. Our force will be more than adequate to protect her."

"The same was thought of Castle Arvon," I murmured, looking up at them.

"Your Highness, Arvon fell due to treason carried out by some of the nobility," Aldwyn reminded me, trying to be reassuring.

"Aldwyn's right," Fawkner agreed, meeting my gaze. "There are none in my city or our land with any incentive to go against you. You *are* safe here."

I nodded, not feeling wholly convinced. I didn't feel safe anywhere anymore, especially with Mithras gone. My heart twinged with pain and I closed my eyes for a moment to stop myself from crying again. It wouldn't do to bawl my eyes out in front of a foreign lord and his court.

"Well, what do we do then?" Carden asked as he leaned on his elbows, looking across the table at the rest of us. "We obviously can't just sit around doing nothing."

"I agree," Ellora said with more strength in her voice. "We have brought the Princess to safety but hiding here will only serve us for so long. We need to determine what it is the Enemy plans to do with her, then counter it."

"Know thy enemy," Dolin nodded as he set his stein down and sat back. "And if we are to protect the lass, then such knowledge would see that our task be easier."

"I think it is a prudent plan," Aldwyn agreed as he took a clay pipe from the table and started filling it with herbs to smoke. "Once we know what it is the Shadow Lord seeks, we will be able to prevent any further harm coming to the Princess. In the meantime," he looked to me in all seriousness, "you *must* remain here, your Highness. Within the walls of this manor house."

I just nodded, not having anything else to say. Then I remembered my dragon. "What about Amethyst? She won't come near the city without me saying so," I told them.

"Who is Amethyst?" Erika looked to Fawkner for an explanation.

"Oh, I forgot to mention," he said, "we have a dragon in our company that is protecting the Princess."

"A really real dragon?!" Freda smiled brightly where she sat between her mother and I. "Wow!"

"We'll bring her to the gardens behind the manor," Fawkner assured me. "I'll take Ellora and Carden tonight and we'll retrieve her."

"Thank you," I felt at ease with his assurances, sitting back more comfortably.

"There is something else," Tallinn sounded uneasy as she spoke. "What about the Revenant? He seems to be a new threat after the assault on Mountain Falls. Can we afford to ignore him?"

"We cannot rule out that he may have sided with this new Shadow Lord," Ellora added gravely, looking to Aldwyn and Fawkner. "He was once known to have cooperated with the Shadow Dominion during the War of the Shadow."

"Identifying the Shadow Lord might help too," Carden said lowly as he swirled the drink in his cup, studying it casually.

"Where would we find such information?" Tallinn asked with a shrug as she crossed her arms.

"My only care now is in finding my bed. Goodnight," Tristan said, standing up and staggering away, Oddvar ordering a servant to go with him.

Fawkner thought for a moment, then smiled and nodded: "I think perhaps there is something that might be of worth to us that you should see," he stood and looked to me. "I think you should come along, Leander. It might be of interest to you as well."

I gave him a nod, then stood and started following him as the others joined us, Erika remaining with the officials and her children.

Behind us, Holger shouted: "You lot go! I'm about to challenge this mutton to a contest!"

Chapter Seventeen
The Custodians

Fawkner led us from the Great Hall and down a corridor to a set of large double doors. He pushed them open and stepped aside, turning to me and gesturing for me to enter first. Stepping through, I felt myself fall into deep wonder as a gasp escaped my lips at what lay beyond. The others followed and I heard their similar intakes of surprise as we were faced with one of the most incredible libraries I had ever seen.

It was two thirds the size of the main hall and covered two floors entirely with a high ceiling above us supported by intricate arch work. There were eight carved columns reaching up to support both the second floor and the ceiling arches, three heavy sculpted iron chandeliers hanging from the ceiling's highest point.

At the far end opposite the door there was a large fireplace of stone flanked by the carvings of rearing horses with a great falcon set above the mantle, its wings widely outstretched. The fire was low in the hearth and offering a warmly inviting space where two velvet armchairs were placed beside a low, round table.

In the centre of the room was a long oak table with twelve chairs set around it, a silver candelabra set on either end flickering with three golden flames. It stood over the enormous gold trimmed green rug that reached almost the entire length and width of the central space.

Massive bookcases covered almost every wall of the ground floor, books of all genres choking them near to spilling. The second floor could be reached by narrow stairways on either side of the doors and were so close to the ceiling that the bookcases were touching its lowest edge. Where no bookcases stood there were pedestals and display cases, each one safeguarding one or more intriguing and ancient artefacts or books. On the few bare sections of wall there hung several paintings and tapestries, each just as rare and old as the encased objects.

For the first time since I had been forced to flee my home, I was standing in a place where I felt no fear, or dread, or grief, my mind instead racing with the possibilities of what exploring these shelves might bring to me.

Wow... This place... it's so... I felt myself smile very softly as I began moving through the room, gazing around at all that lay there. I was dimly aware of the others doing the same, yet my eyes were blinded to all but the art and knowledge surrounding me.

"Quite the collection you have here," Aldwyn was studying the library in its entirety, leaning close to a shelf and reading some of the titles aloud. "*The History of*

Old High-Realm, the Ancient Lineage of Ranhart and Graphtar, the Lore of the Plains: A Compendium of Ranhart's folktales... Hm. A lot of history."

"More than just history," Fawkner responded, hands clasped at the small of his back, smiling as he met the Mage's gaze. "The collection contains a great many books on magical theory and lore, instructional guides ranging over a vast quantity of subjects, a goodly amount of fiction, and much, much more," he then turned his attention to me: "So... what do you think, Leander?"

I turned from a bookcase full of fiction that I was looking at, my hand resting on a couple of the books' spines as I had been reading the titles. I couldn't help my awed smile as I met his gaze.

"Where did you ever get so many books?" I wondered aloud.

"The whole library was passed down to me from my father, as it was from his father to him," Fawkner explained, gazing fondly at the room. "My family began gathering this collection nearly twelve hundred years ago after the War of the Shadow. It was my ancestors, Doran and Fairlor Caradoc, brothers from Nargilith, who started this library."

"Doran and Fairlor?" Ellora turned from where she was studying one of the display cases. "They were your forebears?"

Fawkner nodded. "Indeed, they were."

"I knew them personally," the Huntress said with fondness and nostalgia. "We travelled together long ago with the Princess' ancestor."

"Really?" I was surprised.

She nodded to me. "Yes. They were just and good men who were ever loyal to the girl who became Aldegaad's first Queen."

"Incredible," Dolin had sat himself in a velvet armchair that was positioned nearer the doors, his pipe in hand. "What are the chances that the two of you," he gestured to Fawkner and me, "would come to know each other and travel together with Ellora just as she once did with your ancestors?"

"It is a rarity of fate to say the least," Aldwyn commented, now standing with his own pipe to his lips as he faced us.

"I would venture far enough to say that perhaps it is destined that we three should meet," Ellora stated profoundly.

"This... this is the famed Caradoc Library, isn't it?" Tallinn drew our attention to where she stood by the large table, a book open in her hands, wonderment filling her hazel eyes. "I have heard so many tales of this place, but I never knew it existed. How did it come to be here?"

Fawkner explained: "Long ago, when ancient Ranhart fell, our family brought the library with us from where it was once held in Nargilith for safekeeping. Then, when the Vorhals of old broke into Lorveren and the New Vorhalaas, my ancestors of that age were a part of the uprising. As our King built the Emerald Capital to reside there, my side of our family kept our lordship over the city of Eilath and maintained our residence here in the Hall of the Plains to watch over our city, but also this library. And here it has remained for more than six hundred years in our keeping."

"Even the College of Mages in Safferan is lacking a library of such intellectual and historical wealth," Aldwyn commented, puffing at his pipe.

"This library is not the most comprehensive in High-Realm," Fawkner declared. "That honour lies with the Elemental Brotherhood's sanctuary itself."

"Who are they?" I asked, the name vaguely familiar to me.

"They are the Five Wizards who watch over all of High-Realm," Ellora explained, now at my side. "Each Wizard embodies an element and wears colours to reflect these. They are some of the wisest living beings to hold guardianship over the world."

Carden moved up between Tallinn and Ellora, his arms crossed, his eyes set on Fawkner with all seriousness. "You said you were going to show us something that would help us protect Leander," he reminded Fawkner evenly, but with a hard expression.

Fawkner nodded. "I did indeed. As I said before, knowledge of one's enemies is a powerful strength to have."

"And you think your family's library can be of help," Tallinn guessed.

"This library has books, parchments, tomes and scrolls that date back over four thousand years," Fawkner explained, pacing slowly as he spoke. "One of Doran and Fairlor's chief concerns when they began compiling this collection was to ensure that future generations would be able to defend themselves should a threat come again from the Shadow Dominion, or others like them. So, they sought out copies of all the documents they could find relating to the Shadow Lords, the Darkest Shadow and any others that could threaten High-Realm as far back as they could find."

"And now it seems we face just such a threat in our own living days," Dolin was stroking his beard, nodding as he said this.

"Surely this library cannot be complete," Tallinn pointed out as I started looking at the display cases. "Four thousand years is a long time to preserve such knowledge. Reason states that there will be inconsistencies and mistruths."

"Of course," Fawkner agreed. "Yet, that should not mean that we will be unable to at least glean some sort of defence against the foes we now face."

"One should think so. Especially considering the forbidden texts you seem to possess," I looked up to see Ellora glaring at Fawkner, her turquoise eyes sharp and hard, her pointed ears seeming to twitch with aggravation.

She was standing beside a large display case with a book inside that looked very, very old, this obviously the source of her outrage.

I moved closer to get a better look. The book's spine was at least thirty centimetres tall, its cover hard and thick, wrapped in a binding that seemed eerily like it was once flesh, though now it was almost black like coal. It was trimmed with silver corners, the pages looking like such ancient parchment that I felt touching them would make them crumble to dust. On the cover there was an eerie symbol of two sinister snakes coiling through the four outer points of an inverted pentagram star, their mouths hissing out towards the edges of the book, their tails meeting at the downward point. Set into the centre there was etched an evil looking eye of emerald amidst all the silver and obsidian designs.

"How did you come to possess this?" Ellora almost seethed with silent rage behind me, never blinking as she stared viciously at Fawkner.

"Ellora..." he started, but she cut him off quickly.

"This monstrosity was left in the Wizards' Sanctuary under their protection and that of the city of Silvervale, home to the High Elves of High-Realm," she said calmly, though her true rage burned in her eyes. "I knew the man who took it there myself. *Why* is it here?"

Before an answer was given, I felt suddenly hypnotised and fixated on the black thing glaring up at me through the glass. I could have sworn that the green eye began to shimmer with some kind of supernatural energy, though it could have just been my imagination. But what wasn't my imagination was the strange, dread filled feeling that was starting to invade my heart.

"Sarissi!" Joran's voice snapped me out of my dazed awareness just as two strong male arms clenched around me.

My hand slid across the glass of the case as I became aware of the world again, the eye flickering and going dark as I was pulled away. I looked over my shoulder, breathing hard and finding myself staring up into Carden's jade eyes, his face filled with a deep worry. He held me so that my wrists were crossed together above my collarbones, my right hand's fingers instantly scratching for my silvery pendant.

"C... Carden?" I stared at him as if I had just awoken from a strange dream.

"Are you alright?" he asked me uneasily, his voice shaking.

I felt dizzy: "I'm not sure... I feel... strange..."

"I am hardly surprised," Ellora said, stepping between me and the strange, evil book. "This is the Nempanarth."

"The... the what?" I frowned at her through my unsteadiness as I held onto Carden.

"The Nempanarth," the Elven woman explained darkly, crossing her arms as she glared down at the book. "It is the ancient grimoire given to Gorth Lavelle, the original Shadow Lord, by the Darkest Shadow itself. It contains the most sinisterly evil spells, incantations and black rituals the world has ever been cursed by. Upon his death, Gorth Lavelle ensured that it would always pass to the next Shadow Lord in line for Gorth'lak's Black Throne."

I felt a new nausea fill me as she turned her gaze to me, Joran having moved to stand by Carden and I from where he had been by the door. The Storvari was staring sternly at the book, his massive greyish arms at his sides.

Ellora went on dreadfully: "And with *this* book the Shadow Lords would rule the evil that spewed forth from the Serpent's Maw - the Gates of Gorth'lak - to wreak such terrible and torturous havoc on our world for nearly three thousand years," her eyes grew darker as she stared at the black thing glaring up at her from its casing: "For any but a Shadow Lord or their disciples to open it, the Nempanarth casts a spell of bewilderment upon the mind as it calls out into the darkness, yearning to be found and returned to its dark masters..."

"It's alive?" Tallinn looked horrified.

"It is the most powerfully evil thing in all creation," Ellora clarified coldly. "It is even rumoured to possess the means to restore the lost powers of a Shadow Lord... and darker still... to resurrect one from the Netherworlds."

"Resurrect?" I felt this horrible fear fill me. "Do you mean like... like if he were a... a ghost?"

"Do you know something, Princess?" Aldwyn asked, moving to stand near me.

I nodded softly, fearfully. "The Shadow Lord was at Aneuran working with my uncle, as you know. But what you don't is that he couldn't touch anything... like he was a ghost..."

"A dead Shadow Lord returned from the grave?" Dolin stared from his seat with shocked eyes. "Is it possible?"

"Historically, it is," Fawkner confirmed. "I have heard of three such cases in the past with use of various artefacts."

"What do you mean?" Carden looked paler than normal as he still held onto me, though I was glad he did, as my legs were still weak.

"Three Shadow Lords have been restored to life in the past," Fawkner explained gravely. "Shadow Lord Heskath, two hundred years before the War of the Shadow, then Shadow Lord Everild fifteen hundred years earlier. The first to achieve such a dark thing was Shadow Lord Gorth Lavelle, who was first resurrected three thousand years ago, then again four hundred years later, and a third time a further one hundred and fifteen years following that. He is the *only* Shadow Lord to have been resurrected more than once."

I shuddered and fearfully thought: *If the Shadow Lord can be resurrected, then this might never end for us. Even if we defeat him, he could just come back again...*

My breath caught in my throat and I clutched my pendant even tighter to my chest, trembling in Carden's arms. He must have felt this because he hugged me even tighter to try and comfort me.

"So... can... can the Shadow Lord be resurrected?" I asked in a small, shaking voice.

"Not without this book," Ellora replied, glaring at the display case icily. "As long as it remains in the safekeeping of those not aligned with the Shadow Lord, he cannot use it to restore himself."

"How did it come to be here?" Carden looked up from cuddling me, his eyebrow arching curiously.

Fawkner nodded and cleared his throat of a light cough before answering. "When I was a young boy the Green Wizard came to visit my grandfather and father.

He had been sent on behalf of his Order with the Nempanarth in his possession, as he was the one member of the Brotherhood to have the most contact with those of us outside it."

"The Green Wizard? He came here?" Ellora was calmer, her face softening with her surprise.

Fawkner nodded. "Since they were keeping possession of a number of Gorth'lakian artefacts, it had been decided that the Nempanarth would be sent to my family's library for safekeeping. It was the Wizards' belief that should an enemy arise in search of such artefacts that it would be safer if the book be somewhere they would not consider looking."

"Perhaps a wise decision," Aldwyn nodded thoughtfully.

"But if these artefacts are from Gorth'lak," Carden said, finally letting me stand on my own, "then how is it that they are here?"

"When Queen Leander was seventeen and had begun building Aldegaad, she led a crusade against the remnants of the Dominion," Ellora explained distantly.

"You sound like you were there, Lady Elf," Dolin observed.

"Indeed I was," she confirmed with a nod of her fiery haired head. "We made our way into Gorth'lak where we wiped out the remaining Shadow Disciples and six Shadow Acolytes in a fierce battle at the foot of the fortress known as Grishk'kinnar, which translates into Common as 'the Black Doorway'. It was on the steps and mountain battlements of Grishk'kinnar where we fought the Scourge and the Shadow Knights in a bid to wipe the Dominion from High-Realm once and for all. Yet, with no fully powered Shadow Lord to lead them, the remaining forces soon fell to our swords or retreated underground. We even pursued many of them through the Labyrinth of Dol Amor that surrounds Gorth'lak to the very edges of the Forests of Arnath, but we could go no further. Under the deathly rule of the Revenant himself, the Labyrinthine Fortress of Arnath had become the last bastion for evil beyond Gorth'lak..."

"Or so it was thought," Dolin commented gravely.

Ellora went on: "Victorious, we searched Grishk'kinnar for any others that lingered, and for anything the Shadow Lords may have left behind. We found many artefacts and Queen Leander saw the danger they could present if we left them where they dwelt. So, as she had the Guardians and the Dragon Knights, she created a group whose purpose it was to safeguard these artefacts..."

I suddenly remembered our arrival at Mountain Falls and the message Callenhad gave us from the Revenant: "*The Custodians have failed in their duty and all the artefacts will be recovered. And the descendant will come to where the ancestor lies as the Lord is restored.*"

A chill ran through me as I thought of Eamnonn in his cave beneath the Dragon's Crest, sitting atop his piles and piles of gold treasure. I could see the Dragon's aqua, teal and brown scaled form as he spoke the same words he had to us in those stone depths.

*"I offer you and your companions a warning: the one you call the Revenant is striking at the Custodians of the Past. **All** of them."*

"The Custodians of the Past," I murmured, everyone turning to me as I looked up at the man and woman before me. "That's you, isn't it?"

Fawkner and Ellora looked at each other, then back to me with surprised, but calm expressions.

"Eamnonn, the Dragon in the Dragon's Crest, spoke of a threat against the Custodians. And at Mountain Falls, Ser Callenhad was given a message from the Revenant for them," I recalled, everything suddenly so clear. "*You* are the Custodians..."

"Not just them," Aldwyn stepped forward, putting out his pipe and setting it on the table. "We have ties throughout all of High-Realm, just as Queen Leander commanded."

"Aldwyn?" Carden looked like he had just been beaten with a stick into confusion. "Are you saying the Order is a part of this?"

Aldwyn shook his head. "Only a small group of us are, myself and Master Riordan included."

"Why would you keep this from us?" Tallinn looked so deeply betrayed as she moved to confront him. "Do you not trust Carden and I?"

"It isn't that, Tallinn," Aldwyn tried to reassure her gently. "The Grand Masters decided that the members involved in the Custodians' tasks should remain few and secret should we ever come under threat."

"And how long have you been one of these Custodians?" she demanded angrily.

He let out a slow sigh: "Almost twelve years..."

"All this time you've been hiding this from us!" Tallinn pushed herself away from him, staring at him in disbelief.

"You should have told us," Carden snarled lowly.

"I would have when you graduated to the level of master," Aldwyn said earnestly.

"How many Custodians are there?" I asked, turning to Fawkner and Ellora more calmly.

"We do not know," Ellora confessed in all honesty. "Your ancestor did not wish us to know so that we could not give away the location of the other Custodians should an enemy ever begin searching for the artefacts."

"Which it now seems is the case," Fawkner said darkly. "After all these centuries it is the Revenant who strikes against us, not the forces of Gorth'lak."

"The question is, what could the Revenant want with Gorth'lakian artefacts?" Aldwyn mused, turning back from Tallinn and Carden, who were both still looking very hurt.

"Not all that the Custodians protect are Gorth'lakian in origin," Ellora pointed out. "Without knowing what he has taken or how many Custodians there are, it will be all but impossible to determine what it is he seeks."

"He took my ancestor's remains," I said softly, almost coldly. "I... I don't know why he did... but maybe that's somewhere to start."

"It's as good a place as any," Fawkner agreed. "I suggest we make use of the library and see if we can't at least find some answers towards the Shadow Lord's plans and his identity, as well as what the Revenant's designs are."

"And I suppose you'll be cutting us out of this now?" Tallinn glared at Aldwyn with her arms crossed.

I had never seen her so angry in the few months I had known her.

"I can only apologise for my deception," Aldwyn placed a hand on Carden's and Tallinn's shoulders, "to both of you. I swear that I did not mean to betray you, however, now is not the time for such things. Our duty is to the Princess and her safety, and this library may hold the key to her protection."

"You're right," Carden nodded, patting the other man's forearm firmly. "Our duty comes first."

Tallinn nodded without speaking and they turned to the rest of us.

"Where shall we begin?" Aldwyn asked of Fawkner.

"I would suggest that we divide our efforts and research both the Revenant and each Shadow Lord recorded," Fawkner advised them, pointing off to one section of shelves. "That section is the historical biographies. I'll see if I can find any records on the artefacts and the Custodians, and we'll search for any possible motives based on the histories of each person we locate."

"I will write to Master Riordan and see what it was that was taken from Coastwatch Keep," Aldwyn stated and gestured to Carden and Tallinn. "You two begin with the biographical histories."

"Alright," Carden nodded and led Tallinn to the appropriate section as Aldwyn left the room.

"I will see what I can find on possible rituals," Ellora moved towards the magical books section. "Perhaps we should also send word to the Wizards?"

"I shall attend to that," Fawkner stated evenly.

"Well, this is where I won't be much use," Dolin slid from the chair and started for the doors. "I'll let my drunken ass of a brother sleep, then tomorrow we'll get started on maintaining all our weapons and equipment."

"That's a good idea, Dolin. Thank you," Tallinn said to him, looking up from the book in her hands.

As the Dwarf left, I turned to Fawkner: "What can I do?"

He looked genuinely surprised. "Perhaps it is best that you leave this to us, Leander. You have enough on your mind. But by all means, help yourself to any book that takes your fancy."

I nodded as he headed for a row of shelves, though I felt a little annoyed at being excluded from helping in the search.

I made my way up the stairs to the second floor and started glancing through the titles. Fawkner did have a point and I doubted that I would be of much use in searching for any information on the Shadow Lord or the Revenant, despite being extremely well read and academic. Still, I didn't like not being helpful, especially since I was the one the Shadow Lord was after.

I found myself glancing at a large painting on the wall that I recognised from my history lessons. It was the artistic rendition of the battle between my ancestor and Lord Morod. The two figures were wielding swords and backed by great dragons as a shadowy monstrosity hung above them that had to be the Daemon, their respective forces battling behind them.

Turning from it, I started flicking through a book I picked up from the shelf without looking. There were many pictures and words in it, but my eyes soon found a page with a figure wearing black, my focus falling to the strange item around his neck. It was a pendant with a black stone at its heart, the page before it an image drawn of all thirteen Dragon Pendants.

I thumbed through the book then set it back when it seemed like it was nothing more than a book on the myths of High-Realm, finally picking a fictional romance story and glancing to where the others were gathering books at the table.

A bad feeling crept its way into my heart and I felt certain that something terrible was going to happen...

* * * * *

At first, we were all on edge as we had become accustomed to falling under attack when we stayed put for any length of time, but this fear we shared faded away after the first week or so. I finally had the time to rest and let my building grief free in complete safety. And soon, I had brought myself from my sadness, finding that I was able to once again enjoy the changing seasons and fresh air of this beautiful ancient city. I was able to watch the others more closely now too, curious about them and what they were doing.

At first the others were confining themselves mostly to the library in search of their intellectual prize, but this didn't last more than two weeks. Not long later they had each found their own activities: Aldwyn studying in the library, Fawkner attending to his duties as Lord of Eilath, Tallinn and Carden keeping guard, Ellora exploring the gardens, Tristan spending much of his time in the tavern, and the Dwarves working in the smithy.

With the complete lack of threats, I found myself wandering the halls on occasion looking for something to do. When the rains hit, I took to the library and cuddled up to the fire - though summer brought no real need for the hearth, and I often played chess with Joran, the Storvari able to defeat me easily within a few moves each time. When the sun came out or when the days were cloudy, but dry, I would find a place in the gardens to gather myself and bask in the peace of this place.

On one such day I sat on the Hall's side porch overlooking the training yard, perched on the rounded wall surrounding the great sycamore tree that grew there. I sat with my back against the tree's trunk, my knees up and my boots' soles planted to the top of the stone wall. My hair was tied back at the nape of my neck, draped now over my right shoulder and against my chest, the gentle summer breeze tugging at the auburn strands. I was buried in the latest book I had picked from the library, halfway through reading the story of romance and adventure, losing myself in its pages as I used to before this all began.

Amethyst was sitting on the paved porch beside the tree's surrounding wall, spending time with me as we had been doing for months now whenever I sat outside. I felt like she could have been guarding me as much as Joran, but I didn't mind; the Storvari at that moment lumbering around the yard with his arms crossed, his violet eyes flicking to me periodically.

Slowly, as I finished the paragraph, I looked up from the book to survey the view. To the north were the distant purple shapes of the Nartarn'lath Mountains, their peaks hidden under the fluffy white and grey clouds, which only became visible when the blue sky poked through. At their feet were forests and the wide expanse of rolling golden green hills and rocky crags. To the east were more plains and fields stretching towards the border with Vorhalaas, what they called the Great River Impasse snaking off from the south to the north in the distance.

I took a moment to consider the majesty of this place, imagining what my ancestors who built Eilath as Ranhart's capital must have thought.

If this were my home, I would never want to leave. It is so beautiful here.

Turning my eyes back to the yard, I studied the other people there aside from the green and brown clad guards patrolling the walls. Ellora was basking in the gardens, taking the time to literally stop and smell the flowers. She looked so at home, filled with the love for nature that I had imagined all Wood Elves must have.

Down the steps from where I sat were Fawkner, Erika and their children. Erika was playing with her daughter, Freda chasing butterflies with orange wings towards the garden. She caught one and ran excitedly to show it to her mother, who smiled and viewed it with enthusiasm for her child.

Meanwhile, Fawkner was crouched by the stone bench on the grassy ground of the garden with his son. Bran had grown so much in the last few months, well past his first year and beginning to learn to walk and talk. He was trying to walk to his father, standing on his own and wobbling unsteadily. He would fall and sit, giggle and try again, finally making it into his father's waiting arms as his mother and sister re-joined them.

Fawkner picked Bran up with the biggest smile stretching across his bearded and scarred face, so very proud of his son.

As I watched the happy family, I once again found myself longing to be back with my own. Though my sister and I had been in correspondence now, and she knew I was safe, I didn't feel much better. I longed for family, my sister now the only one I had left that I could trust completely, but the distance between us was far too much, and there was little that a handwritten letter could do to alleviate that longing.

Amethyst must have sensed my feelings because she lifted her head towards me and started brushing her scaly cheek and snout against my arm. She cooed and looked up at me with those warm molten orange eyes.

"I miss my family," I confessed to her softly, feeling a little teary. "I feel so alone without them. I've lost almost everyone I love."

She clucked at me, raising her head a little and cocking it to the side.

I smiled and set my book down: "Of course you're my family too, Amethyst."

I ran my right hand over the top of her larger dorsal scales, their surface so smooth, but strong like steel all at the same time.

"I don't know what I would do without you," I told her gratefully, smiling faintly. "You're my best friend."

She seemed very content with that and brushed her head against my hands and arms, her long, smooth horns touching my shoulder lightly. She then settled back beside me and lay her head down, her wings pressed to her sides as she rested.

I turned my gaze back to the training yard, my eyes falling to the lone figure standing there.

Carden was focused on his fighting skills as he faced a straw stuffed training mannequin, his sword in his right hand, a belt of throwing daggers around his waist. He had taken off his black and silver jacket and set it down on a nearby stone bench, his teal green shirt left open a little from his collar. His nearly black hair was a little messy and damp on his brow, sweat gleaming on his warm, lightly olive skin, his shirt darker around his neck and under arms with his perspiration. His green eyes were narrowed on the targets of the mannequin, his sword ready in his hand as his left was poised to snatch a knife from his belt.

He moved suddenly, lashing out with two knives, one after another, and lunged in to strike with his sword almost immediately. The knives hit their marks on the target's chest, Carden slashing twice with his sword at the hand targets a few seconds later, before delivering what would be a killing blow to the mannequin's head, then stabbing with another knife into where the ribcage would be.

I was fascinated by him; the way he moved, the poise of his fighting stances, the skills he used, everything. There was just something about him that I liked more than I could ever explain, and I found myself nearly obsessed with thinking about him.

Did he have those skills when he was growing up in Nargilith? I wondered as I clutched the book close to my knees. *Or did he learn all of these when he joined the Guardians? Either way, he really is amazing.*

He was taking the throwing knives from the target and returning them to his belt, my eyes searching the shape of his tall, broad shouldered, athletic body. My gaze dipped to where his shirt lay open, exposing the fine contours of his masculine chest.

Oh Gods... I would love to see what he looks like without that shirt... I startled myself, thinking quickly with alarm: *Wait! What?! Oh, come on Leander, you're supposed to be better than that!*

My heart fluttered as I looked at him, some new feelings I had never known suddenly filling my very core. He was turning from the target and making his way back to the mark where he had started. As he was walking, he turned his gaze up to me, a lopsided grin spreading roguishly across his handsome, sharp jawed face as our eyes met.

I felt myself blush, smiling at him softly and sweetly, then looking down at my book as one hand started absentmindedly playing with my tied back hair.

Oh, but he is so handsome...

I felt something nudge me and looked up to see Amethyst staring at me, her neck and head raised to nearly stand as tall as me while I was sitting.

"What is it, Amethyst?" I asked her, glad for the distraction.

She turned her nose scale towards the training yard and nodded in that direction, grunting for me to pay attention. I followed her gaze to see Carden returning to his training, then frowned back at the Dragon. Suddenly, I thought I knew what she was saying.

"Wait... Are you suggesting...?"

She nodded and snapped her jaws in response, gesturing emphatically with one clawed hand towards him.

I shrugged and shook my head. "No... It wouldn't work..."

She gave me what I can only describe as a questioningly doubtful look.

"Social standing wouldn't allow it," I said.

She snorted and rolled her orange eyes at that.

I half breathed, opening my mouth and feeling my jaw twist a little as I stared at her incredulously: "He's a Guardian and I'm a Princess..."

She shook her horned head and stared at me even more firmly.

I was trying so hard to find the reasons against what she was suggesting, but my heart was telling me that there really were none, even despite my continued attempts.

"He's... he's protecting me?" it sounded more like a question as it slid from my lips.

If I were to describe her expression, I would say that if she'd had them, she would have been raising her eyebrows at me. It seemed to me that she had won our debate.

"Oh, alright," I groaned and set my book onto my knees, running my hands over my hair and digging my nails through the strands. "You're right. I have no excuse."

There was no more hiding from what was true for me. I had to just admit to myself that my feelings for Carden were as real as all the world around me.

"What should I do?" I turned my blue eyes to her uncertainly. "I've never... I mean... How do I do this?"

What she did next was as close for a dragon to what I could call a heavy shrug as could be, as if to tell me that she had no idea. She cocked her head to one side as she watched me lower my arms and slump my shoulders back against the tree.

"Right," I nodded and sighed. "You'd have as much idea about this sort of thing as I do."

I let my head fall back to touch against the tree as I closed my eyes, drifting away from the warm summer breeze and into the safe darkness behind my eyelids. I let my heartbeat fill me up and I took in a few breaths as I tried to decide what to do.

I have to tell him. I just have to talk to him and tell him how I feel...

"Leander?" my eyes flashed open and I sat up straight to the call of my name.

Carden stood in front of me, his black jacket slung over his shoulder, his sword in its sheath in his opposite hand. He was breathing a little faster than normal, but no more than he would immediately after exercising. His near black hair was catching in the warm breeze and starting to dry off the sweat that clung to the strands.

I felt my heart swell again and my depths yearned like I had never felt before. I had to crush back the feeling out of fear of acting on it without knowing what I was doing.

"Carden," I thought that I sounded too surprised as I greeted him, righting myself to hold my knees close to my body, my hands pressing to the top of the wall on either side of me.

I didn't know what else to say.

"May I sit?" he gestured to the wall at my right.

I looked to it for a few seconds, feeling dazed and out of sorts, then turned back to him: "Um... oh... Yes. Of course."

He set his jacket down and moved to sit beside me on my right. His scent caught in the wind coming up off the plains and I felt instantly drawn to him without knowing how to even describe the sensation. There was a nervous air between us, and it felt like neither of us could find a way past it. We both just gave each other half smiles and shy glances, not really sure what to say.

"So..." Carden broke the unease, looking to me out of the corner of his eye as he rested his elbows on his knees, "how are you?"

I brushed a hand through my hair and nodded: "Good. Good... And you?"

"Good..." he nodded.

The awkwardness returned, as did the smiles, and I knew I had to find a way to break through it.

"You... uh... you looked pretty amazing in the training yard," the words came out on their own and I was sure I would blush with embarrassment.

He raised one heavy eyebrow sharply, a half grin on his face. "Were you watching me?"

I felt flustered, the heat rising in my cheeks and leaving me blushing.

"No... I... uh..." I sighed and nodded. "I only meant that I didn't realise that you were such a skilled warrior."

"You've seen me fight before," he reminded me.

I shrugged: "I never actually saw you fight. We were always too busy trying to stay alive."

"True," he nodded thoughtfully, then looked at the book I had set down at my side. "What are you reading?" he picked it up and read the title, smirking a little with amusement. "*Of Rose and Flames*... I didn't take you as the sort of girl to be into romances."

I smiled softly and shrugged. "I like all kinds of stories... Romances happen to be one of my favourites. I guess it's because I've never known romance in reality, but I love how two people come to confess their shared love and embrace a life together."

He nodded. "I completely agree."

At first, I wasn't sure if it was real, the feelings so foreign to me, but I knew it had to be.

He reached his left hand to my right one where I had it pressed to my seat on the wall, curling his large, coarse fingers around my smaller, softer ones. His touch was warm and so comforting, his grasp strong but gentle.

I looked from our hands to his eyes, losing myself in their jade hue and feeling almost hypnotised. I couldn't draw my eyes back from his, all else fading from me, my vision even losing focus as his irises seemed to change to red for a second, though I knew that was just my mind playing tricks.

"Can we talk about something?" he asked me gently, looking to our hands for a moment and breaking the hypnotic gaze he had on me.

I nodded. "Of course, Carden."

"Do you remember when we were on the *Black Asp* nearly five months ago?" he asked me, looking deeply into my very soul as he lifted my hand and held it with both of his. "There... there was something I wanted to talk to you about."

"I wanted to tell you something too," I confessed, sucking in a shaking breath at his touch.

Don't stop touching me, Carden. Please, never stop... Please...

"Had we not been interrupted I would have confessed my very soul to you that night," he admitted so quietly, his face showing his longing. "Leander..."

"Yes, Carden?" I held my breath, waiting for the words I was hoping to hear, the words I had longed for since I had first learned of my true feelings.

He spoke softly: "I..." but before he could continue, the moment shattered around us and my hope crumbled to the floor.

"There you are, Carden," Tallinn approached us, her blonde hair hanging free. "My apologies for my interruption, your Highness," she nodded to me.

I just nodded, hiding my annoyance with the grace I had been taught. Carden didn't try to hide his as well or even at all, however. The expression on his face was cold as he glowered at once again being interrupted.

He turned his eyes sideways towards Tallinn, not taking his hands from mine: "What is it?"

Tallinn didn't even seem bothered by his harsh tone: "Aldwyn wants to see you."

"Can't this wait?" he asked, turning his gaze to her sternly.

She folded her arms firmly. "You know *this* can't wait, Carden."

I frowned as I looked between them, completely lost in their meaning. Carden was still glaring, but he reluctantly nodded.

"Alright," he said, letting go of my hands. "Just let me wash up first."

"Carden?" I drew his gaze back to me, my voice barely sounding more than a murmur.

"It's alright," he flashed me a warm smile. "We'll talk again later."

I sighed and nodded, watching him stand and take his jacket from the wall. He looked to me once more, then followed Tallinn back through the porch doors.

My heart sank in my chest and I sighed dismally as I hugged my knees. *Isnari... are you determined that we should always be so close to speaking our hearts, only to be interrupted? Damn it all. Why can't we get a break?*

It was then that Amethyst reared her head and turned her gaze back towards me. I had almost forgotten about her during my short conversation with Carden, which seemed impossible with a thirteen-foot-long dragon.

She brought her nose close to me and I rested my hands on her scaled snout and neck.

"This just keeps happening," I told her glumly. "It seems that there's another conspiracy. But this one is to keep Carden and I from talking about what lies in our hearts."

She cooed at me and stroked her head against my neck and shoulder lovingly, much like the way a cat would. I just hugged into her, hating that I had once again been so close to the truth and yet so very far.

I couldn't help but wonder grimly: *Will I ever get the chance to tell him that I'm in love with him?*

Chapter Eighteen
Truest Truths

My interrupted moment with Carden was haunting me, leaving me with an unrelenting unease. I found myself longing even more and more to hear what he had wanted to tell me, and to confess my true feelings for him in return. I just hoped desperately that there would be another chance to do so.

I tried to find some way to distract my mind from these thoughts, to separate myself and find some calm in the swirling storm that had become my emotional turmoil. But it was beyond hard. A horribly dark thought had long ago entered my mind, something I had found myself thinking more and more often as the days had turned to months: *The Shadow Lord was right... He was right about us... As he was right about almost everything...*

After the evening meal, I left the Great Hall and made my way upstairs to my room. I felt the sudden need for oneness, which I was certain was because of the unwavering stares I had been given at dinner - minus those of the three absent Guardians. Only Fawkner had been present while Aldwyn, Tallinn and Carden were nowhere to be seen.

I entered the upstairs corridor, my sights met with the brilliant, artistically carved wooden columns and the arched beams that supported the roof above. As I walked, I lifted my right hand to my neck, massaging my fingers into my nape as I began feeling the familiar ache of tiredness. The longing I felt to find my rest and sleep that night was stronger than any of the unease and anxiety I had felt all day, my thoughts now bending towards the ecstasy of crawling into bed.

A sound of rustling clothes and clinking jars suddenly drew my attention, my fingers sliding free of my neck and grazing the silkiness of my tied back dark auburn hair. The origin of the sounds was the door that I recognised to be Aldwyn's room.

Curiosity took me and I found myself - without thought - moving to stand by the partially open door, my back against the wall. I glanced around the corner and through the opening, trying to get a full view of the room. It was set up much the same as the other rooms of the manor, other than those used by nobility.

A strange herbal scent drifted from the room along with the sound of bubbling water. Set on the table's top were a number of glass jars, canisters and vials filled with various plants and herbs. A small controlled flame burned as a part of an alchemy apparatus, the smell originating from what was simmering in the glass above it.

Aldwyn leaned over the table, dressed in his brown suede mage's robe, dark trousers and grey long-sleeved shirt. He had his back towards the door, lending me no view of his lined face, and only a little of the silvery streaks that dusted the sides of his long dark hair. He was mashing herbs up in a mortar with a pestle, deeply focused as he worked. Carden and Tallinn were also in the room.

They didn't retreat to this room all those hours ago after Carden and I were in the garden, did they? That doesn't make much sense. I edged myself into a position where I could see them more clearly, somehow determined not to be seen myself. Something told me that this was a moment not to be interrupted.

Tallinn was by the window, both arms crossed firmly below her breasts, her blonde hair left untied and hanging past her shoulders, though not as long as mine. Her hazel eyes were harsh and watchful, her expression hard as stone.

Carden was seated at the table, not quite side on with the door I stood at. He didn't have his black jacket on, and his dark green shirt's left sleeve was rolled up firmly. His eyes looked strangely dark and there was a hint of something there beneath their jade hue, something unnerving.

There was another scent. This was acrid, like copper and salt, burning my nostrils and bringing dizziness to my eyes and head. I felt like I was going to faint but braced my shoulder and back to the wall as the urge to be sick flooded me. After eight months of this strange new life I had come to find myself in I could easily identify the smell of blood as soon as it hit me.

The source was Carden, a strange length of tube inserted beneath the skin in the crook of his arm, the other end drizzling droplets of blood into a glass container. He didn't seem uncomfortable, his expression that of someone who had done this - whatever this was - many times before.

What are they doing with his blood? I was both curious and a little sickened, especially given that it was my protectors acting out this strangeness.

"It has been quite some time since last I mixed this medicine for you," Aldwyn was speaking to Carden. "It seems that your tolerance to your affliction is growing, as is the time before your need for your next treatment. And yet, I worry for you."

"I'm fine," Carden insisted quietly and evenly, glancing to the older man. "I haven't felt like it's been a problem for a while. Not until recently. I've been trying to use my willpower to hold it back should the need arise where I would be unable to get my treatments for a long time."

Aldwyn looked at him with a very disapproving expression, starting to undo the tube from his arm. "Carden," his tone was severe, but calm, "that is incredibly dangerous. Your affliction is not historically one that has bent to the wills of its victims. It is almost always the reverse."

"I know," Carden sighed grimly as Aldwyn took the jar of blood and wrapped a bandage around his arm.

"When we took you into our Order, Tallinn and I promised Varel that we would ensure the maintenance of your condition to prevent you causing harm to yourself or others," the older man said as he tended to the younger's arm, "I know you do not wish to have this condition, however, you were born with it and cannot simply be cured."

Carden just nodded, remaining silent as Aldwyn took a sample of the blood and mixed it in a vial with some kind of solution from another. He began swirling it and watching it for any kind of change.

"When did you have your last treatment?" the Mage asked very evenly, sounding so much like a physician.

When Carden shrugged uncertainly it was Tallinn who answered for him: "When first we arrived at Castle Arvon to meet with King Aric," she expressed in a direct and even tone, not moving from where she stood.

"Ah yes," Aldwyn nodded thoughtfully, a twinkle of an impressed light in his dark eyes. "It has been eight months then. Quite the improvement from your previous treatment."

"I find the cravings and impulses greatly diminished after taking my medicine," Carden admitted freely.

"And what of the months following?" Aldwyn asked with a narrowed perception, his gaze severe.

Carden sighed and shrugged. "The effects are so gradual that I often don't feel them until they are upon me," he glanced to Tallinn as she moved to stand at his side. "Were it not for Tallinn's vigilance I would succumb to my affliction before I would think to take treatment myself."

"Is that why you leave it so late?" Aldwyn queried, though it sounded like he was certain of what he was asking.

Carden just nodded. "In part."

Aldwyn turned his gaze to the vial, studying the now changing colours within the glass. The blood was slowly shifting and churning, its hue darkening to become a deep, nearly black tainted crimson. Amidst this dark swirl of human life essence there swam strange silvery shimmers, glinting in the flames of the candles. They almost looked alive as they stroked and swept through the vial, trying to spread and engulf all other hues.

Shaking his head with deep gravity, Aldwyn turned back to his work with the herbs, taking the rest of Carden's blood and adding it to the simmering contents over the alchemy flame.

"The conversion is trying to progress," he said darkly as he began stirring and crushing herbs. "Your blood is battling the enzyme, however, without treatment the change will be inevitable," he turned over his shoulder to look at the young man as he continued to work. "How long has it been since the cravings started?"

"A little over a week," Carden admitted reluctantly.

Aldwyn was shocked: "So long? Why did you not tell me?"

He shrugged. "I thought I could will it back. But it got worse today."

"When?" the Mage frowned.

"I was in the training yard, practicing with the target mannequins," he recalled carefully, narrowing his eyes as if trying to see his memories from a distance. "I felt fine. I mean, I could feel the cravings, but they were under control," then his face softened as desire and something far more beautiful appeared in his eyes, a tiny smile tugging at his lips: "Leander was there."

"The Princess?" Aldwyn raised an eyebrow at him, momentarily halting his movements with the pestle.

Carden nodded: "She was sitting under the sycamore tree with Amethyst. She was reading, of course," he half laughed admiringly as he said that, then became lost in his memories. "I caught the smell of her hair in the wind. My Gods, she looked so beautiful with her hair tied back..."

I felt myself blush. *He thinks I'm beautiful? Really?*

"They were speaking when I found him," Tallinn told Aldwyn evenly. "He had *that* look in his eyes we've seen before."

"What did you feel when you were near her?" Aldwyn asked Carden seriously.

Carden shrugged, still lost in his thoughts: "So many things. I was so... drawn to her, so lost in her..."

"I think perhaps the Princess may have unintentionally affected your condition," the Mage surmised.

I stared at them in shock, not comprehending what he had just said.

Carden snapped back to reality and stared at Aldwyn incredulously, his eyes growing momentarily darker. "Wait... Do you think I would try to hurt Leander?"

"I am saying that she has a power over you that not even she realises she possesses," Aldwyn clarified as he started combining ingredients. "And if you do not maintain caution, then you may be unable to prevent causing her harm..."

"I would *never* hurt Leander!" Carden growled loudly and angrily, standing up and nearly knocking his chair over. "*Never*! I couldn't!"

"You wouldn't mean to, Carden," Tallinn put her hand on his shoulder, trying to settle him back down into his seat. "But the two of you have a *very* close connection, and it is clear how strong it is. If you do *not* take care of your affliction and control it..." she hesitated, her face suddenly very worried. "Well, you may be the next threat that the Princess must face... and we would have to stand against you to protect her... To whatever end..."

"It won't come to that," Carden said lowly, almost hissing through his teeth.

"As long as you keep taking your medicine," Aldwyn agreed, making up two round bottles full of liquid as he spoke, "then I do not see any harm. But I warn you, Carden, your affections for the girl may be your undoing."

"I don't believe that," Carden said with quiet conviction, almost standing over the Mage.

"Pursue this if you must," Aldwyn said sternly, "but do so without risking her life. She has no idea what lurks within your blood," he pushed the completed poultices across the table to him. "Keep one poultice close at all times should you need it, and do *not* allow yourself to give in to those urges while you are near *her*."

Carden slowly took his seat, sighing and nodding as he picked up one of the poultices. "I should tell her the truth about my condition then."

"No," Aldwyn shook his head, drawing Carden's green eyes to his face quickly. "No, you should not. If it cannot be avoided, then do so if you must, but there is no need to involve the Princess in this. It will be yet another concern for her to worry about, and I think a girl of only eighteen winters should not have any more problems than those which she already faces, for they are too many as it is."

Carden sighed again, sadness filling his eyes: "Telling her may only make her afraid of me anyway. She would never want anything to do with me once she knew the truth..."

I didn't stay to listen any further. I just pulled away from the door, moving as quickly and as quietly as I could towards my own room. I could feel tears threatening to burn down my cheeks as I hurried, my footfalls nearly silent as my pace increased. I reached my room and threw open the door, darting inside and closing it without any conscious thought. In seconds, I had my back to it and was sitting on the floor, my face buried into my forearms, my knees to my chest as I fought the painful urge to cry.

Does he really think I'm so shallow?! I would never condemn a person for something like that! I felt heartbroken and disillusioned as I squeezed myself so tight that I felt like coal becoming a diamond. *He's sick... So that's what he wanted to tell me. How could I be so blind and stupid?*

Suddenly, a loud sound broke me from my hurt and I looked over my shoulder towards the door. I could hear hurried footsteps and raised voices, a man and a woman arguing. Once again, I found myself an unintentional spectator in the conversation of others as I peeked through the gap I opened in the doorway.

"I've had enough!" Lady Erika was furious as she stormed down the hall, her long light brown hair swaying at the small of her back, her green and gold dress trailing behind her ankles.

"Erika..." Fawkner was hurrying behind her, his voice calmer and more even, though his movements were decidedly less so.

"No, Fawkner!" she snapped at him angrily over her shoulder, still moving. "This has gone on for *far* too long! I want them *gone*!"

Fawkner reached her, seizing her arm gently, causing her to stop and glare at him. He gazed at her through his collar length hair with deepest care, but also concern.

"Not so long ago you were saying what an honour and a privilege it is to have such respectable guests staying in our home," he reminded her.

"That was before I learned that they would be staying here for so long!" she retorted angrily, and I knew exactly what her tirade was about.

"Come now. Be reasonable..."

"I *have* been reasonable!" she nearly screamed as she glared at him, drawing nearer to him so that they were only inches apart. "I have let this charade go on for long enough! For *months* we have been sitting here with targets upon our backs because of that... that... *girl*!"

I gasped, realising she meant me.

"She is no threat to us," Fawkner defended.

"Oh wake up, Fawkner!" she snapped, glaring daggers of brimstone. "Can you not see the danger that lingers behind that girl?! *He* pursues her even now, hunting her as he did when he came to you! Do you think for one moment that he has given up his pursuit of her?!"

"He cannot sense her," Fawkner explained to her evenly, trying to keep his calm. "The pendant the girl wears shields her from his all-seeing eyes. He cannot find her, save by chance, and even if he did, she is protected by *four* Guardians *and* a dragon..."

"Is there truly any such power as can defeat a Shadow Lord?" she sounded hopeless in her anger. "Do you not remember what he did to Will and Brie? Have you so easily forgotten the pain he inflicted on us when you refused him?"

Fawkner fell silent, grief shielding his pale eyes, his bearded jaw loosening and his shoulders slumping. Erika turned from him, crossing her arms and sighing as she calmed herself.

She now spoke in a gentler tone: "When you told me that you had agreed to work for that monster, I was... I was so... so certain that you could not do what he asked."

He placed his hand on her shoulder and she flinched very slightly but put her hand over his fingers.

"I knew in my heart that my beloved husband could never bring harm to an innocent girl," she went on quietly. "Not after all we lost. And yet, in your absence as you travelled to enact his dark will, I found myself praying that you would succeed, if only to protect our children."

She gazed at him and turned fully into his arms, letting him hold her close to his crimson velvet clad chest.

"In my shame... I... I hoped that you would turn one child over to a monster to save the lives of your own, and help us escape the terrible wrath the Shadow Lord would wreak upon us should you fail him..." she shook her head, teary and breathing hard: "Out of fear I gave in to that monster and wished pain upon someone so innocent..."

"Shh," he placed his finger to her lips softly, comforting her. "You are no more shamed than I. I understand your fears for our children, but I swear to you that *He* will *not* find the girl here."

"How can you even know that?"

He looked her in the eye: "In all the months since I departed for Aldegaad have you seen even the slightest flicker of his eyes, or the black of his shadows?"

She thought about it and shook her head as realisation struck her. "No... no I haven't. But are there no other places she can be taken?"

"I have sworn an oath as a Guardian, as a lord and a warrior to protect the Princess," Fawkner said with quiet conviction. "I cannot forsake her now. Will and Brie would not expect me to."

That seemed to have an effect on Erika, her face softening. "It is because of who she resembles, isn't it?" she nodded as he smiled at her. "Of course, you're right. We cannot turn her away. I am sorry for my outburst."

"It's alright, my beloved," Fawkner assured her. "Your fear is justified, but we *are* safe. And I love you."

"I love you too," Erika smiled and they embraced in a passionate kiss.

I turned away, feeling deep guilt in my chest. I was beginning to think that I had a lot of misconceptions about the way I was seen, which had never been something that I had been all that concerned with before. All I did was try to be good, but now even that wasn't enough.

I closed the door, moving to the bed. As I began unlacing my dress' bodice I felt nothing but the overwhelming urge to sleep. Inadvertently hearing these two separate conversations had hurt more than I could have expected. These truest truths had brought only pain and all I wanted now was to escape into my dreams.

There was a knock at the door, and I grimaced with my back to it, my fingers tightening around the cords of my dress.

"Come in," I called quietly, the door opening a few moments later.

"So, I take it you heard all that," I didn't need to turn to know it was him.

I just nodded as I refastened my bodice, drawing in a slow, deep breath.

"Leander, can we talk?" I looked over my right shoulder to see Fawkner gesturing to the open double doors leading out onto the balcony.

I nodded and we made our way together out into the gently cooling summer air. The sound of the slow wind and the crickets chirping was strangely calming, as was the spectacular view of the plains and the mountains. We came to the barrier of the balcony and I rested my elbows there, letting my wrists hang close together over the edge of the rail as Fawkner placed both hands on it and stared out across the plains.

"It's beautiful is it not?" he said, gazing across all that lay before us. "I find it very soothing to take in the view on a summer's night before retiring to my bed."

"I'm sorry that I'm causing so much trouble for your family," I murmured, feeling so numb that I wasn't even sure that I had actually said it.

Fawkner looked to me sympathetically: "Leander, you have done nothing of the sort."

"Haven't I?" I met his gaze from under the few strands of hair that had loosened themselves from their tie. "Erika is right."

"What?" he was incredulous.

"I'm cursed," I said sadly, accepting it. "I bring ruin to every life I touch."

"That's ridiculous," he commented quietly.

"Is it?" I asked. "In the last eight months every turn we have made, every path we have taken has ended in some kind of tragedy," I stared numbly out at the ground below: "The Shadow Lord will *never* stop hunting me. How many more people are going to be killed because of me?"

"Listen to me," he leaned closer, but I would only look at him out of the corner of my eye as he spoke, "you are *not* the cause of all these deaths. You are as much a victim as anyone that monster has touched. Don't blame yourself for what *he* has done."

"Who are Will and Brie?" the question was out of my mouth before I realised I had even asked it.

Fawkner suddenly looked haunted, like a terrible apparition had arisen behind me to frighten him anew. He looked out across the grounds of the estate and the silent city beyond as he considered my question, remaining as composed as he could manage. But he now had the look of a man once tortured in the darkest of ways, and I truly regretted asking my question.

"I once had four children," he confessed. "Only my youngest remain. Will was nearly fifteen winters, and Brie was the same age as you," he smiled at me. "She had hair the same colour as yours and that same adventurous, but loving spirit that you have."

"What happened to them?" I asked softly.

"A little more than a year past," he spoke as if he were reciting a well-known tale of fiction, "a man ventured into my city. A man in a black cloak and hood."

His look to me told me all I needed to know, dread filling me instantly.

Fawkner continued: "I met with him in the main hall as I am accustomed as Lord of Eilath. At first, he tried to play on my vanity, telling me of my so-called prowess as a warrior and greatness as a leader. I bade him to simply tell me what it was he sought. He told me that he had a desire to acquire something he needed; something precious and beyond value that dwelt in Aldegaad's northern foothills. When I asked what he sought I was... disgusted..."

"And, yet, you agreed," I guessed, knowing how we had met.

"Not at first," he responded to my surprise. "When I learned that he meant for me to abduct a helpless young girl, I, of course, refused. Never mind that such an act could cause war between our two countries, I could never harm someone so innocent."

"What did he do?" I was almost afraid to ask.

"He made me a promise," Fawkner answered darkly. "He vowed that as long as I denied him that I and my family would know not but misery..." he covered his mouth, tears swelling behind his eyes and gleaming in the fading moons' light. "I did not see Will watching from the doorway," he confessed, grief stricken and heartbroken, nearly on the verge of weeping. "He saw the monster threatening me and took up my sword to defend me. As I cried out for him to stop, he struck," he turned to me with such a horrible look in his eyes: "The Shadow Lord barely blinked as he shot a bolt of lightning through Will's heart..." his lip shook and he started to quietly weep. "My son... my son, slain by a monster who wanted me to hurt an innocent girl. Murdered for my refusal to serve."

"Oh my Gods," I gasped, horrified and so desperately sorry for him.

"As I cradled Will's lifeless body in my arms and screamed for help, the Shadow Lord told me that this was only the beginning of my pain. He said that he would return when I had learned my error, then vanished as if he were nothing but smoke in the wind. We buried Will two days later. Erika... she was beyond grief and would not speak to me for near a fortnight."

"But it wasn't your fault," I said softly.

"Will died with my sword in his hand whilst in my presence," Fawkner reminded me. "To Erika that was blame enough. But the worst was yet to come," he took in a slow breath, trying to console himself. "In the weeks that followed, Brie began to grow ill. She would cough blood and struggle to draw breath. Her limbs grew weak and thinned, and the skin around her eyes turned black. She could not leave her bed and soon she lost the use of her eyes, which turned white as pearls..."

"That's horrible," I just stared at my hands as I clasped them on the rail together in an effort to keep them from shaking.

"I sent for every physician in Lorveren, and many from other nations, but none could tell us what was wrong with her," Fawkner sighed deeply, blinking back tears and nodding. "Then, the Green Wizard came. He identified Brie's ailment as Shadow Sickness, and he told us there was no cure. All he could do was cast a spell and craft us medicines to ease her pain," he leaned down over the rail, fighting his tears as they slid free: "It took three months for her to pass from the time of her reception of the illness. Only eighteen years old and buried beside her brother who hadn't reached his sixteenth year."

There was nothing I could say, my sorrow for him and his family beyond my own reckoning. Now it was clear to me why we shared such a kinship.

He managed to compose himself: "The night of Brie's funeral, I took to the library alone, needing solitude. And as I sat like a worn-out old dog in the chair by the fire, I felt the darkness close in behind me. He came from the shadows, wreathed in evil and reverent as if he were paying his last respects to my dead children," Fawkner cringed, his eyes very shadowy now. "His gloating was soft, quiet and subtle as if it were simply fact falling from his foul grey lips. He told me that I had brought this horror upon us and that more would come if I continued to refuse him. I told him that he wished me to commit evil for him, that what he asked me to do was cruelty incarnate. He reminded me of what he had done, and when I demanded to know why he simply replied, "Because it is within my power to do so.""

I shuddered, instinctively running my hand across my warm neck and cleavage to grasp my pendant for security.

He went on: "It was then that he promised me compensation of wealth for my services and for those of the men I selected for the task, as well as the safety of my wife and my two youngest children. Bran was newborn and Freda..."

"It's alright," I tried to reassure him, placing a hand to his shoulder. "You did what you had to."

"And nearly forfeited my soul in the process," his voice was little more than a murmur. "When I took you to Averet I was convinced that my family would die if I did not."

"Why did you help me then?" I was curious now that I knew his motives for kidnapping me in the first place.

He smiled at me and stroked my right cheek gently with his rough, warm hand: "Because of Brie. When first I saw you brandishing that sword at me, I instantly saw her. She was as much a fighter as you. Then, as we travelled to Averet, I came to know you and I could not allow him to harm you."

"But don't you worry that he will make good on his threats?" I asked.

He shook his head. "Once he saw you that was all that took his focus. Besides, if there is one thing I know about Shadow Lords it is that they are not petty creatures. If there is nothing to be gained by his actions, then he will not make them."

"So... you aren't worried for your family?" I was surprised.

"I cannot change what fate has in store for us," he said wisely. "My choices are made and thus the die is cast. I have learned that there are no certainties in life beyond those we make ourselves. All we can do is treasure the time we have and never hide our truest truths from the ones we love most."

I nodded as I took in his words, the wisdom there so incredibly flawless. I then became painfully aware of the stare he was giving me.

"Perhaps that is a wisdom you and Carden should put into action," he suggested knowingly.

I looked up at him in shock. "How do you know about that?"

"Do you remember when we sailed on the *Black Asp* that you asked me about the bruise on my face?"

"You said you and Carden had an argument," I recalled.

"It was about you," he admitted.

"Me?" I was stunned.

"Your capture at the hands of your uncle and the other traitors left Carden distraught," Fawkner explained in all honesty. "He was certain that we could not reach you and had all but given up. I accused him of letting you rot intentionally, that clearly his vows as a Guardian meant very little, but that his care for you meant even less."

"And he hit you? Why would you provoke him like that?" I was utterly bewildered by this.

"Because I knew it would make him recover from his inaction and want to save you. Which we did."

I sighed glumly, slumping my shoulders and leaning on the rail of the balcony again: "I'm not sure Carden feels as he did in Aneuran."

"Why not?" Fawkner asked.

I shrugged, feeling that twinge of pain in the depths of my heart as I confessed: "I overheard him speaking with Tallinn and Aldwyn earlier. Did you know that he has some kind of illness?"

"No," he was genuinely as surprised as I was. "Is it serious?"

"Apparently he needs to have some kind of treatment Aldwyn mixes for him, or his symptoms worsen," I explained, then paused as I stared at nothing below where my hands hung. "He seems to think that I won't accept it if he tells me about it; that I will be afraid of him and never want to see him again."

"That doesn't sound like you."

"It isn't," I replied with another slumping shrug as if my shoulders were suddenly coated in lead. "I could never condemn someone for such a thing," I thought for a moment as I stared blankly, remembering my encounter in Aneuran. "The Shadow Lord was right..."

"What do you mean?" he stared at me with a dark frown curling his seasoned brow.

"The day my uncle intended me to go through with that farce of marrying Tibain the Shadow Lord came to me," I admitted in a quiet voice. "He told me that by allowing them to force me into that marriage, regardless of my intentions, that I was betraying not only myself, but also the man I love."

"And that is Carden," Fawkner realised, nodding to himself. "Tell me, how *do* you feel about him?"

I smiled very lightly, blinking as if I was going to cry, though there were no tears. "What I feel for him is more than love. I didn't know it at first because I had never felt such a thing," I shrugged and nodded to myself. "I *am* in love with him. He's the One. I don't know how I know... I just... I just know."

Silence fell between us for a moment as I let myself revel in what I had just admitted. Gods, it felt good to say it aloud. Then, Fawkner pressed two fingers beneath my chin and turned my face so that I was looking up at him.

"Then, you need to tell him," he said.

"I've tried," I replied almost hopelessly. "But every time we get a chance to speak privately someone always interrupts us. It just feels that there is nowhere for us to go where that won't happen."

"I know of a place," he said thoughtfully. "Not but an hour or so walk from the city to the north-west there is a grove that can only be reached through a break in a rocky crag beside a great oak tree. It is a beautiful place where the trees have leaves the colour of ivory and flowers that gleam like gold. And the pooling water is the clearest of blues, and so fresh that it can quench any thirst. And in summer it is the coolest, most refreshing water to swim in."

"It sounds amazing," I said, awestruck by his description.

"It's called Ivory Leaf Grove," he told me, smiling as he recalled how he came to find it. "It is where I met Erika. I was young and stumbled upon it by accident... She had flowers in her hair as she sat by the pool, singing."

"How do I get Carden to go there with me?" I wondered, a little concerned. "Besides, I doubt Aldwyn will allow me to go beyond the city walls. He is so certain something will happen to me outside of his view."

"Leave Aldwyn to me," Fawkner stated, "though I am certain he will allow you to go provided that someone goes with you, and if you take Amethyst as well. As for Carden, he will follow you anywhere."

"Then what?"

"Tell him how you feel, and I will pray that Isnari smiles on you both," he said.

I smiled and kissed him on the cheek. "Thank you, Fawkner."

"You're welcome, Leander," he returned the smile and led me back into my room. "Now, if you'll excuse me, I will retire to my room and my wife's company. And I suggest you get some sleep too."

"Alright. Goodnight, Fawkner."

"Goodnight," he smiled as he stopped at the door, nodded to me, then left and closed it behind him.

* * * * *

I awoke the next morning with a renewed enthusiasm. I washed and dressed in a deep lilac dress and dark blue velvet and purple silk main dress that left my arms bare except for a small sleeve, my leggings and boots underneath. For once I made an effort on my make-up, ensuring that I looked as natural as possible, but flatteringly attractive. Then I brushed my long hair free of tangles and left it hanging down my back. I was determined that I would make this work today.

When I went to the Great Hall for morning meal, I found myself suddenly disappointed. Carden and Tallinn were nowhere to be seen and I learned from Ellora that they had gone to gather supplies from the markets.

Sometime after midday, the two Guardians returned with a cart, Tallinn guiding a large work horse at its front. I stood on the main porch at the front of the manor watching them bring it up, smiling as Carden flashed me one of his handsomely roguish grins.

Fawkner came out of the main doors and went to join them as Dolin and Holger started helping to unload the cart. After a short discussion with them, he came walking back up the steps and to my side.

"I've spoken with Aldwyn," he told me. "He has agreed, though begrudgingly. You're ready to go. Good luck."

"Thank you, Fawkner," I smiled at him and started down the large steps to the cart.

I moved to the others; my eyes locked on Carden as my nerves tried to overwhelm me: *I can do this. I can. This will work.*

"Carden," I called gently as I reached him.

"Leander," he smiled, turning to me.

There was an awkwardness similar to that which had been between us the day before when we had sat together. At first, we just smiled at each other, my cheeks feeling hot as I suppressed a blush and my nervousness.

"So... uh... Fawkner told me of a place called Ivory Leaf Grove," I told him, saying the only thing I could think of. "He said Aldwyn is alright with me going for a walk there as long as someone goes with me. Oh... and Amethyst too..." I could feel myself getting even closer to blushing. "Would... would you come with me?"

"Absolutely," he smiled eagerly, then looked to the others uncertainly. "That is if I'm not needed here."

"We can handle this, Carden," Tallinn assured him, giving him a nod. "Go with her."

He turned back to me and shrugged. "Alright. It sounds like an interesting place to explore."

As we turned away together, I heard Holger mutter to Dolin: "More like the girl just wants the young Guardian to explore her nether regions..."

I glared over my shoulder at him and growled through my teeth: "Shut. Up."

Dolin slapped his brother and shook his head, disgusted at him as Carden and I walked away. If Carden had heard the comment, he didn't make mention of it.

Once we had left Eilath's gates Amethyst re-joined us from the air, settling onto her four feet and closing her wings to her sides as she walked with us. It was warm enough that we did not need our cloaks and also why I had chosen a short-sleeved dress, Carden also not wearing his jacket, but not so hot as to make us perspire either. The sky was grey with summer rain clouds that threatened to pour over us, but I was determined not to let anything ruin this.

As Fawkner had told me it took us over an hour to reach the crag under the oak where the opening to the grove was, the scent of flowers and fresh water wafting up from inside on the winds.

Carden paused with one hand to the wide opening, gazing down inside, then turning to me: "Is this it?"

I nodded. "I think so. That's the tree Fawkner mentioned," I indicated the oak.

"Alright," he said and took my hand.

I drew in a sharp breath, glancing at our hands, then to his face. He smiled at me, drawing my own smile across my lips. As he led me into the opening, I looked over my shoulder at Amethyst, the Dragon following close behind; only just managing to slip through the gap with her wings closed.

We entered the sun-drenched grove, the trees surrounding the small lake with their ivory coloured leaves and golden flowers gleaming just as Fawkner had described.

"This is incredible," Carden breathed, lost in the awe of the place as much as I was. "I have never seen trees like these."

"Neither have I," I admitted, my feet now touching the beautifully soft green grass.

We came to the water's edge, the sound of the waterfall so soothing, the splashing droplets hitting my skin coolly. I became so lost in the wonder of the small cliff surrounded grove that I almost didn't notice Carden watching me.

"So," he said, smiling at me wryly, "I know why you wanted me to come here with you."

"You do?" I felt suddenly nervous.

He nodded. "You want to continue what we started yesterday without interruption."

"Um... yes... I do," I admitted.

He became suddenly solemn. "I... I have to tell you something..."

"I know you're sick," the words came out of my mouth before I had time to think.

He stared at me curiously, one eyebrow arched below his gently messy hair. I felt instantly embarrassed and foolish, looking down at my feet as I twisted my hands together.

"How do you know that?" his voice was cold.

I confessed, meeting his gaze sheepishly: "I'm sorry... I-I overheard you speaking with Aldwyn and Tallinn."

"You did?" he looked pale and worried suddenly.

I just nodded.

He groaned and turned towards the water, running his hands through his hair in exasperation. I was suddenly very worried that I had crossed the worst line I could possibly have.

"Carden... I'm... I'm *so* sorry..."

"It's alright," he said, looking down at his hands as he flexed his fingers. "In truth, I'm glad you know."

"You are?" I frowned.

He turned to me and I froze, watching him while twisting my hands together nervously.

"I wanted to tell you for a while now, but Aldwyn thinks you have enough problems to contend with," he moved closer to me.

"What *is* your condition?" I asked, staring up into his eyes, feeling almost hypnotised by their green hue. "What does it do to you?"

"It's a rare blood affliction," he explained evenly, never taking his eyes off mine. "Its name is better not spoken. Without treatment my blood changes. There are other physical changes too... and mental ones."

I felt my back hit a tree and jolted in shock. I hadn't even realised that I had been backing away until that moment. He didn't even flinch at my startled reaction, just coming so close to stand over me now that he could easily have kissed me... and I desperately wished he would.

"The problem," he said darkly, staring at me in such an inhumanly predatory way, "is that it can make me dangerous. I... I can hurt people... I *have* hurt people."

"And you think I would be too scared to want to know you because of this?" I found myself studying every detail of his handsome face.

"Aren't you?"

I shook my head. "No."

"Why not?"

I shrugged. "It doesn't define you. You're still Carden Highever to me."

He looked suddenly pained, his hand reaching out and caressing my cheek, brushing my hair over my ear. My eyes fluttered at his touch and my chest heaved beneath my bodice.

"What are you afraid of then?" he urged me gently.

I met his gaze with my steel blue eyes again, completely lost in this feeling for a few moments as thunder crackled overhead and I felt the first droplets of rain hit my cheek.

"I... I'm afraid that I'm going to lose you," I admitted in a small, low voice, not taking my eyes from his. "I've never known anyone who makes me feel so... so... real," I felt my breath catch in a tiny, invisible laugh as I at last said what I had always meant to.

"No girl has ever made me feel so alive before you," he told me, his face changing into a pained frown. "But I'm *not* like other men, Leander. I'm... dangerous."

I shrugged and shook my head. "I don't care. I just don't want you to disappear on me."

He looked at me incredulously, shaking his head in bewilderment, a tiny smirk tugging at his lips. "Gods... you're such a foolish girl."

"If it's foolish to be in love," I said with all the honesty and truth I had ever known, "then let me be a fool."

He was taken aback. "You're... in love with me?"

I nodded. "I am."

He smiled, all his fear and worry just melting away like the last of winter's snow in spring's early breath. He moved closer to me, so close that our faces were nearly touching.

Then, he whispered to me as if I were the only other person in all existence: "Then let me be a fool too."

His right hand held to my left cheek, so cool to the touch, a sharp breath staggering into my lungs. My eyes fluttered shut as the rain began to fall, almost like Isnari herself was crying for joy. My left hand touched to his and my right pressed to his firm chest as he drew me closer to him.

It felt like an eternity that I had waited for this moment, my heart burning with delight at its final arrival. His other arm curled around my hips and I let myself fall into the embrace. At long last... we kissed.

I couldn't begin to describe what I felt, only knowing that it was perfect and right. Our embrace was passionate and filled with the deepest, truest love I had ever known in all my life. *This* was the first kiss I had always desired.

Then, suddenly, the rain stopped. We both opened our eyes and looked up to see Amethyst giving us the most approving gaze she had ever expressed, her right wing held up to shield us from the storm.

I turned my eyes back to Carden through my wet hair and smiled the biggest I could remember in all the months since first we had met, a small giggle of joy escaping my lips. He smiled too, but more subtly, and once again we kissed, safe in each other's arms, our love blossoming under the watchful gaze of my proud dragon protector.

Chapter Nineteen
Ghosts of the Past

I had never known such happiness before in my young life, wishing that these moments would never end. My heart finally felt as if it were filling the gaps within it once more with this greatest love I had ever felt, taking it in to become a part of me. I no longer felt empty.

I felt a large hand caressing my cheek, smiling as my eyes fell shut. My hands took his and brought it to my lips where I let preciously soft kisses fall to his rough, warm skin. I opened my blue steel eyes again and gazed dreamily up into those handsome green ones, my smile staying as my heart fluttered.

Carden smiled down at me, his near black hair a little damp from the rain that was managing to get past Amethyst's wing. He was sitting with his back against the Dragon's side, keeping me resting in his arms where I lay, his right hand the one I was holding. He had never looked more content as he lay there with me.

"I wish we could always stay in this moment together," I confessed my secret longing. "I don't think I have ever known such loving bliss as this."

"Nor have I," he replied, stroking my hair with his right hand once he had reclaimed it from me. "I feel truly blessed to have a girl of such kindness and beauty gift her heart to me."

I felt myself blush as I smiled at him. "You think I'm beautiful?"

He nodded. "Ever since our first meeting. And I will continue to say so for eternity and beyond."

"Even in my waning years?" I asked softly as he leaned over me, my left hand grasping his right wrist. "When my hair is no longer dark, but white as the snows, and when my skin is creviced like the mountains' faces? If my mind wanders from the waking world and into the realm of dreams while I see with my living eyes?"

"Yes," he confirmed. "And so too shall my love for you go on without boundaries or confines."

I felt so gladdened by those pledges as my heart harboured the same truths for him. Yet, another concern filled my thoughts and made my chest ache.

"Though I will never lose my love for you either," I told him honestly, "there is something that makes me fearful."

"What is it?" he asked softly, gently running a hand across my forehead to brush my hair from my eyes.

I looked up at him with a desperate uncertainty inside every part of me as my fingers tightened on his wrist.

"Will we be allowed to be together?" I gave voice to my fears, the same ones I had dreaded since Aneuran.

"You fear our stations will prevent our union?" he guessed.

"Will they not?" I asked him seriously with a concerned frown.

"The Guardians have never restricted their members from forming romantic relationships," he explained very evenly and simply. "Occasionally such partnerships *have* formed between a Guardian and their Charge, just as it has between us," then he looked into my eyes, having me turn onto my stomach and meet his gaze as my hands lay on his strong chest: "But it isn't the Guardians' you fear."

I nodded and sighed. "I'm... I'm nobility. The aristocracy is incredibly strict on matters such as relationships like ours. Social stature, class and birth mean a great deal in the world I was born to..."

"Are you regretting this day?" he frowned.

I sat up and looked at him, shaking my head fervently: "No. No, I couldn't *ever* regret this day, or what we have confessed here."

"Then what is it?" he asked quietly.

I shrugged. "I'm... I'm worried what will happen if I should ever be able to return to Aldegaad..."

"When you become Queen," he noted, nodding with disappointment.

"Many of the noble families won't accept me choosing to be with you," I glared at the grass with frustration. "I hate that such snobbish ignorance and petty perceptions still linger after so many centuries," then I murmured thoughtfully: "Yet, were my father still alive he would tell me to ignore such ill will and follow my heart."

There was a short silence between us for a few moments as the words lingered on the edge of my thoughts. I considered what my father would have said and felt a sense of comfort from that knowledge.

I looked up to Carden and smiled. "Having you in my life and now sharing this love we have gives me the reason I was searching for," I murmured honestly as he held me close. "I feel that there's nothing we can't face together."

"I feel the same," he smiled at me.

I gave in, letting him have control as he guided my body back into the grass. My heart fluttered and skipped, my breathing staggering as my breasts heaved beneath my dress' velvet blue bodice. My head and shoulders lay in a silken veil of my dark auburn hair, my hands reaching up his arms as he placed them on either side of me.

His face leaned closer to mine and I felt another shaky breath fill my lungs as my eyes struggled to remain open. I sensed so many urges rushing through my body, my need for him growing to intensifying proportions. I felt as if I would die if he stopped touching me, my want and yearning so powerful that I feared my heartbeat *only* because of him.

"I love you, Carden," I told him, my voice a faint whisper, my eyes opening so I could see his face, "with all my heart."

"And I love you, Leander," Carden replied, smiling softly at me, my hand on his chest now, letting me feel his heart beating through his shirt.

With a slow, careful movement, as if I were made of glass, he leaned into me and brought his face to mine. I felt our lips touch and begin to caress passionately, but softly. His arm was around my shoulders as both of mine hooked together in a ring around his neck.

I let myself fall into this powerful embrace, every tiniest unseen fragment of my being releasing itself so that we two might become one. All thought escaped me, and I found myself focused on nothing but the moment as his lips continued their powerfully gentle hold with mine.

I wanted him to never stop kissing me, to never take his hands away from my body. All I wanted more than anything else was him, and my heart, mind and body were in complete agreement on this.

His lips left mine, allowing me to draw breath and pausing this beautiful embrace.

"It... it will be getting dark soon," he murmured reluctantly. "And the rain has been growing heavy..."

I nodded, feeling a sort of sadness fill my heart at saying goodbye to this moment. "We... we should return to Eilath."

"We should," he agreed, but still made no attempt to move from me.

"Do you think the others will be happy for us?" I wondered without meaning to ask the question aloud.

"They already know, I'm sure," he gave me that handsome lopsided grin. "Were our feelings for one another lights on the coast they could guide wayward ships to land."

I laughed a little and nodded. "You're right. Only a blind and deaf fool wouldn't have seen the truth in us."

"Come," he stood, taking my hand and helping me to my feet. "We'd best not linger, or Aldwyn will send the city guards in search of us," he gathered his weapons belts - which he had laid on the ground - and put them on, then took my hand in his with a smile.

We were soon leaving the grove, the three of us pushing through the cliff passage and into the now lightly raining plains once more. The sun was sinking towards the horizon and with it was coming the night as the ever-fading triple crescent moons rose from the west.

With Amethyst at our back, Carden and I walked hand-in-hand, my free fingers clutching my skirts so as not to let them drag, my black legging clad shins feeling the cooling breeze that was blowing across the grassy lands. I kept turning my gaze to Carden through my wind swirled, sternum length, auburn strands, studying him with all the love I had until now hidden. He just smiled back at me; no words needed.

As we neared the city, I longed for this happiness to last. Then, Amethyst became agitated, her orange eyes glowing wildly as the fires within her body swirled and lit the cracks in her underbelly's scales. She didn't let loose flames from her jaws as she still wasn't old enough to do so, but smoke rose from between her teeth and out of her nostrils all the same.

"Amethyst?" I frowned at her as we came to a stop. "What is it? What's wrong?"

She was glaring towards the city, snarling the way a hound might when an intruder approaches its home. I followed her gaze towards the ramparts and walls of Eilath, the dulling twilight making it difficult for us to see. Smoke was rising from the city and screams echoed on the wind as the smell of fire reached us through the rain. I felt suddenly sick as a familiar and terrible sensation hit me, my thoughts returning to our arrival at Coastwatch Keep.

"Oh, Gods," I gasped, clutching Carden's hand.

"Come on, hurry!" he directed me, drawing his sword as we fell into a short sprint down the hillsides to the gates, Amethyst launching into the air above us.

It felt like time had vanished and I was soon walking beside Carden into the city, fires burning on some of the houses around us as citizens were desperately working to put them out and save their homes. There were injured soldiers being dragged and carried out of harm's way, shouts and the sounds of battle drawing us a little farther up the hill towards the Caradoc home.

We ran together towards the hall, desperate to re-join our friends as the city was ablaze around us. And that's when we saw him. A single terrifying figure stood with his back to us, robes of a wine-coloured crimson hue billowing around his frame in the smoke and rain choked wind, a black and silver crown adorning a crimson hooded head. A sinister black sword was held in his gauntleted right hand, the point to the cobblestone street, his left grasping a breathless Eilath guardsman by the throat. There was a horrible cracking and the guard was dead in the figure's black and silver hand, suddenly being tossed aside like a ragdoll a moment later. All around the figure were the bodies of fallen soldiers, some still alive with grievous wounds while others lay dead.

"Leander..." Carden snarled in a low, threatened voice, his eyes locked on the attacker, sword at the ready, "Get behind me... Now."

I didn't disobey, slipping behind him and watching past his green clad shoulder at the horrifying creature that towered before us.

The figure turned his head towards us, and I saw the visage that lurked beneath his hood. I couldn't see his face since it was shielded by a horrible silver and ebony mask that resembled an enraged skull whose skin had stretched tight and become smooth metal. The mask was attached to the crown and set over the close-fitting hood, the points of the crown sharp and sinister. The only skin visible on this monster was corpse-like and cracked, seen through the gap in the collar beneath the mask's jaw.

I felt instantly terrified as he turned his black eyeholes towards us, and I was certain that I could just make out dead white eyes in the shadows lurking beneath the mask.

"Ah..." he breathed with a deeply resounding voice. "What is this...?"

"Carden..." I was terrified.

"Stay back, monster!" Carden shouted, brandishing his sword angrily.

"Foolish boy," the voice spoke from beneath the mask, my mind running wild with fearful imaginings of the visage that lurked beneath it, "you know not whom you face."

He started striding towards us, the crimson cloak sweeping around him in the wind, a horrible blood red energy crackling across his free hand's fingers like a static storm. I felt nauseous and staggered, Carden swinging his left arm around my waist and catching me before I could fall. We tried to back away, but I was more a hindrance on Carden now, my feet struggling to keep strong against the ground as my head swam with dizziness.

The monster kept striding towards us, slowly gaining ground. Then, a roar echoed from the sky and Amethyst rushed him, but her strike was instantly defeated. To my unimagined horror, he sent a shockwave of evil red energy towards her and my dragon howled in pain before crashing to the ground some fifteen feet behind him.

"Amethyst!" I cried out, trying to rush to her and nearly hitting the ground as Carden fought to keep me standing.

She was breathing, but she looked as if she had been knocked unconscious by the strike.

"The Dragon protects you, girl," the monster turned to me from Amethyst. "*You* are the one I seek..."

"You will *not* touch her!" Carden nearly screamed as he tried to keep me standing, putting himself between me and the monster.

"*You* cannot stop me, young Guardian," the masked monstrosity told him with no threat, only truthful promise. "Arnath has come forth for its prize..."

Suddenly, an arrow whistled through the air and struck him in the left shoulder close to his throat. He cried out in pain through his mask, staggering back only one step before another arrow hit his throat, but still he didn't fall.

"Carden!" the voice called from the rampart nearest us as a blonde-haired figure raced into view.

Tallinn rushed from our left some nine feet away with her bow already firing another arrow to strike at the monster. She laced a fourth as he staggered and roared, aiming and losing it in mere seconds.

"Keep the Princess away from him!" she commanded, Carden immediately trying to help me back away.

As Tallinn fired another shot Joran rushed from out of nowhere, passing by us and swinging his twin swords as the Guardian drew her own blade.

I slid to the cobblestones, Carden crouching on one knee beside me, my body shuddering and my stomach retching inside of me. I turned my gaze towards the battle as more flashes of that evil energy appeared.

The figure had turned to fight them, his black blade clanging with an eerily sharp resonance as he met Tallinn first. She ducked away and he swung up at Joran, catching both of the Storvari's blades. There came a flash of light and Joran was thrown off his feet, his eight-foot form crashing into a house's wall where he slumped to the ground and lay still.

Then, the attacker turned on Tallinn, panic now filling the Guardian girl's eyes as she weaved and ducked away from him. He slashed at her with twin serrated blades that were mounted to his gauntlets, his sword turning to take hers from her hands. She rolled backwards and came up to fire another arrow, this one lodging into his hip. With one hard strike across her face from his fist, she was catapulted to lie only a few feet away from us, her consciousness retreating quickly. Now, the monster was turning towards Carden and I.

Carden stood like a stalwart sentinel, turning his sword's point to the ground as the figure cast the arrows from his body.

"Carden... no..." I reached for him, but I couldn't stay up, my mind a haze with this strange sickness that had suddenly overwhelmed me.

He didn't have more than a few throwing daggers, losing only one at first, which was enough to cause the masked monster to be slightly distracted. In seconds their swords were meeting, and they were parrying and striking at each other hard. A horrible ear-splitting shriek sounded from the mask as the creature struck, demonic and harsh.

Still, Carden fought on, determined to defeat him... to protect me. But after a few more evasions, he suddenly grunted in pain as he was stabbed in the side, my scream muffled in my ears as I saw him being backhanded. He hit the ground near Tallinn and that's where he lay still on his back. At least he was breathing, though blood was seeping from the wound in his side.

I don't remember getting up only that I was suddenly crouching beside both of them to see if they were alive. I thanked the Gods that they were, my eyes then turning to the monster, who was now focused solely on me.

"Your protectors have failed you," he said in that harsh, deep voice as he drew nearer. "I came here for one prize, yet I find two, and I will *not* be departing this mortal city without *you*, Princess..."

"No..." I shook my head as he reached for me, awaiting the touch of those cold metal fingers.

As if it could sense my fear, the Pendant's heart-stone started to glow purple. The monster was cast back with smoke rising from his gauntleted hand as a shield of purple light surrounded me, my hands up in instinctive response.

What is this?! What am I doing?! I stared in shock at my hands as I pulled myself unsteadily to stand, seeming to know what to do without conscious knowledge.

I pushed with my hands as if I were shoving a door, the shield of light surrounding Carden and Tallinn too as the monster shrieked in rage and let loose a continuous blast of that terrifying reddish energy from his left hand. It hit the shield with a snapping bang, and I felt it as if it were a powerful arm trying to knock me down. I screamed in shock as it hit, but quickly recovered.

I won't fall! I told myself, pushing all the strength I could manage into my willpower, mind and heart, thrusting into the shield with all the energy I had. *I won't let him win! I won't! I won't! I WON'T!*

The shield grew stronger in its colour and seemed to thicken as I plied myself with these thoughts of power, only the rain passing through to wet my hair and clothes. The Pendant felt hot on my skin and it stung me as its heart-stone glowed brighter and brighter. My arms started hurting and I dropped to one knee, struggling to hold up under the immense weight that felt to be crushing in on me. The shield began wavering slightly, the Pendant fighting with as much power and determination as I was, both of us like two joined souls battling this fearsome foe.

"You have considerable power, girl," he observed, striding awkwardly towards me as if our opposing powers were pushing him back. "Though you have learned to use your pendant, you cannot hope to subvert me. You are weakening with every passing moment and will soon fall, as will your shield."

I could feel my energy fading, nausea trying to take over again as what reprieve the shield had given me from his magic was disappearing with the fading glow of my pendant's power.

I saw Carden's eyes open as Tallinn looked up at me groggily. They were regaining consciousness, both so badly hurt that they couldn't have helped me. Now it was their turn to watch on in bewildered horror as *I* fought the monster to protect *them.*

"You have overexerted yourself," the monster told me, drawing slowly nearer, the sparking of his magic against my pendant's shield deafening and blinding. "Had you only shielded yourself you might have lasted longer..."

I gritted my teeth, my whole body burning with pain as I slumped to both knees, my hands wide apart as I fought to keep the shield up. My hair whipped around my face and shoulders, my limbs feeling as if they would break under the strain.

I felt Carden's hand on my thigh as he murmured my name: "Leander...?"

I turned my eyes back to the monster. He seemed victorious as he stood only two metres from me, his crimson lightning strikes increasing in intensity. I cried out in pain, closing my eyes tight and clamping my mouth shut as I struggled to keep the shield up.

I... I can't give in! I can't! I was practically screaming at myself in my head.

"You have made a valiant effort, girl," he told me coldly, "but your resistance is all in vain. In moments your shield will fail, and I will take you."

I knew he was right, feeling like I wouldn't be able to hold on much longer. I felt like my body was splintering under the weight of an entire mountain, my vision growing hazy with green and black spots filling it, and my head spinning as my body filled with a nauseating heat.

Then, there came a sudden blast of green light amidst the darkness, and the monster shrieked in pain, his powerful glowing crimson strike evaporating. My body released and I felt myself fall as the purple glow faded into shadow. My pendant now shielded only me in an invisible field that I could feel on my skin, its stone still alight.

Two arms were snapping around me as I fell, turquoise eyes meeting my gaze as red hair billowed over two pointed ears in the wind.

"Ellora?" I felt so weak and my voice was near a rasping croak.

"It is alright, Princess," she assured me as she cradled me in her arms. "I have you."

I turned my attention to the battle that was still continuing, the monster shrieking as he was struck by bolts of emerald green energy. Fawkner rushed past him with Tristan, Holger and Dolin at his side, weapons in hand, the four of them reaching us and taking up defensive stances. Aldwyn suddenly appeared, standing with his back to me, his staff at the ready but not the source of the strikes.

I held Ellora's sleeves and bracers with both hands, watching the monster battling a lone figure who was now pushing to stand between us and him.

The figure was an old man with long white hair and a flowing white beard. He was dressed in robes of varying greens and browns, a brown hood hanging down his back, a pointed green hat with a wide brim planted on his head. He carried a silvery sword in his right hand and a gnarled looking staff in his left, a crystal glowing green in its top. He was battling the armoured monster and pushing him away from us, glowing flashes of crimson and emerald energy being exchanged between them.

"Be gone from this city, Foul One!" the old man shouted at him. "Dead things such as you have no place amongst the Living!"

"Do you truly think you can stand against me, Wizard?" the monster demanded, slashing with his sword and launching another energy strike.

The Wizard simply deflected it and met the monster with his own blade.

"Go back to the dark forests and ruins of Arnath!" he commanded powerfully, striking with sword, staff and magic. "Return to the Blighted Darkness from whence you came, Necromancer Wraith!"

Their battle continued and the Wizard pushed even harder as Fawkner commanded his soldiers to surround them and aid our new ally. But my eyes were failing, and I was losing myself, only lights and garbled sounds filling my senses now. I could feel Ellora holding me tightly as my hands lost their grip and fell.

There was an enormous flash of green and a horrible shrieking sound, then I lost my hold on the waking world...

* * * * *

I opened my eyes to find myself lying in the softly lit bedroom I had been given in Fawkner's house. The wood beamed ceiling was darker in hue than normal above me, the heavy green curtains drawn back from the windows, and the double doors open to let in the fresh air and pale rainy sunlight. I was dressed in my nightgown, its sleeves close around my wrists, my shoulders bare except for the shoelace thin straps that held it there. The blankets had been pulled up over me and the pillows set to ensure my comfort, leaving me nestled in a soft cradle of linen.

I noticed almost immediately that there was a figure sitting to my right, and I stared up at him in wonder as the scent of smoking herbs caught in my nostrils, trying to clear my vision enough to see him without my sleepy haze. The Wizard sat back in the chair with one leg crossed over the other knee, his left arm in his lap, his right clasping the edge of the pipe he was smoking, his hat and cloak now removed.

"Ah," he smiled beneath his white beard as he saw me awaken. "Finally, your eyes open. Good. I must admit that you gave us all quite the scare, young lady, but it is clear you have some fight in you."

I squinted against the candlelight, then looked back up at him. "Where... where am I?"

"You are in the Hall of the Plains, home of Lord Fawkner and Lady Erika Caradoc," he explained. "It is the late afternoon of the Fifth Day of Autumn."

"What?!" I was shocked. "It's... it's Autumn?!"

"Indeed," he nodded. "You have been asleep for near to eight days and slumbered through the last of Summer's time for this cycle."

"H-how have I slept for so long?" I just couldn't grasp the thought of how such a thing was possible.

He shook his head thoughtfully as he put out his pipe: "When I came with the other Custodians to your aid, you had spent much of your strength battling our enemy. Had we not arrived when we did, you might be awakening in a cage in a far worse condition than you are now."

"I... I was fighting?" everything that happened after our return to the city was a blur.

He nodded. "You harnessed the power of your Dragon Pendant and wielded it to defend yourself and your friends. However, you were not prepared for the toll it took on you, and your strength rapidly drained," he seemed to study me with a fond curiosity as he mused: "Intriguing... Never in all my time in this living world have I ever encountered a Holder who was able to command a Pendant's powers so quickly, even to such a degree. You must be a very gifted girl... Quite astonishing..."

I frowned at him. "Who are you?"

He raised an eyebrow and smiled at me. "Who do you imagine I must be?"

I shrugged, shaking my head vaguely: "I feel like we've met before..."

"We may very well have," the Wizard conceded with a slight nod, clasping his hands together and leaning his elbows on his robed knees. "I was summoned here by Lord Fawkner, though his letter reached me some months past and it took time for me to arrive..."

"You're the Green Wizard," I felt like it was obvious. "But your name..."

"For now," the Wizard stated, "you may call me friend. Rest, child, for you have much recovering to do after facing the Necromancer Wraith."

"The Necromancer Wraith?" I repeated worriedly. "Was that the creature who attacked us?"

His face was dark with a cold expression of severity, his voice grave as he spoke: "He is known by another name, one more commonly used by High-Realm's fractured nations: The Revenant of Arnath."

A cold chill spiked down my spine and I felt sick as flashes of the monster's ghostly image slashed through my mind like a blade wielded by a madman.

The Wizard went on: "He has been hunting the secrets of the Custodians for nearly one year, though, for what dark purpose I do not know. His encounter with you gave him pause, and his focus shifted from this house to you."

"Is... is he going to come back?" I was certain that I sounded like a frightened child.

He shook his head. "I have cast some very powerful protection spells over the entire city; the same ones that shield Galvenin and Silvervale. He will be unable to breach this city again. For now, you are safe here, Princess."

I gasped: "My friends! My dragon! Are they...?!"

"Fine, fine," the Wizard assured me with one hand held up lightly. "The Storvari and the Guardian girl have some bruises for their trouble but are ultimately unscathed, the Guardian lad a stab wound that is healing well, and your Dragon is recovering nicely in the gardens under Ellora's care. It was you who was the most gravely injured of all, though not by any wound of the flesh. And so, you must try to gather some more rest."

"I need to see them," I moved to sit up, but became suddenly dizzy, the Wizard catching me and laying me back in the bed.

"You are not yet strong enough to stand," he told me sternly, but gently. "Your accessing of your pendant's powers was too much too quickly. Please, try to rest."

I breathed deeply and nodded as I lay back.

"You shall not be wanting for company very long, however," the old man smiled at me and called to the door. "Come in, lad."

I looked up and couldn't help the small, weak smile that managed to spread over my lips.

Carden walked in, looking a little dishevelled and favouring his left side where he had been stabbed, but otherwise alright. He wore a light grey shirt now that hung to his thighs, his dark brown pants underneath.

"Carden," he smiled as I said his name.

The Wizard stood: "Well, I shall leave the two of you to your privacy. Please, try to rest, Leander," his use of my name surprised me, then he placed a hand on Carden's shoulder and said close to his ear more quietly: "Make sure she does."

"Of course," Carden nodded, then watched as the Wizard left the room. "It's good to see you awake, Leander," he sounded relieved, sitting beside me gingerly. "I was worried about you."

"I was worried about you too," I told him, reaching out and taking his hand in mine. "How badly did he hurt you?"

"It looks worse than it is," he confessed, seething as he moved the wrong way. "The Wizard healed me, then he and Ellora worked together to help you."

"Was I hurt badly?" I asked.

He shrugged. "Honestly, I don't know. What was that power that you used? I thought you weren't a mage."

"I'm not. It was the Pendant," I replied uncertainly. "The Wizard said that I somehow managed to access its full power, but that I didn't have enough control over it. That's why I got hurt."

"He seems to know a lot of things," Carden considered as he glanced to the door. "I only wish we knew his name."

"I feel like I know him," I said, still trying to recall how. "I just... I can't figure it out."

Carden reached out his other hand and started to stroke my hair back past my ear, smiling at me softly. "Perhaps - just for now - you can let it wait and try to rest. I would hate for my beloved girl to be in pain."

I smiled at him. "Back to where we left things?"

He nodded. "I think so."

He almost lay beside me as he leaned down to me, the light casting such beautiful shadows and glows against our bodies as we stared into each other's eyes. He set his lips to mine and kissed me softly, all else silent as we embraced again, injured though we were. As if by some miracle of the Gods, the pain I felt was all but gone, the sweet sensations of our love all that remained.

He pulled back and gazed long into my blue eyes, his smile only a ghost, but there all the same: "Try to rest, my love."

"Will you stay with me?" my voice was the tiniest whisper.

He nodded. "Of course," and sat on the bed at my side, holding his arms around me.

I turned gingerly onto my right side and curled up with my head on his chest, my left-hand palm down against the fabric of his shirt.

We just lay staring into each other's eyes for what felt like the longest time, his arm curled tightly around me, his other hand stroking my hair and caressing my aching back and shoulders.

Slowly, I let my eyes fall closed and I listened to the beating of our hearts. As if it was because of our closeness and our shared feelings, the two beats that started out of time slowed and began to beat as if they were one heart between two people, no longer separate, but a part of one another.

* * * *

I caught my own reflection in a mirror, stunned by how I looked. I had my hair pulled back and hanging down my shoulders with braids securing it, my face bearing a hard expression of determination. I was wearing plate armour over chainmail, a sword held in my hands, its blade shimmering with an otherworldly white light, its hilt and pommel so uniquely carved. My pendant lay around my neck still, sitting on the steel chest plate of my armour, its stone glowing purple.

My blue gaze turned to the stairs and I started up them, a figure moving at my side. He was tall and handsome with dark hair and grey eyes, dressed in armour too; carrying a shield on his arm and a sword in his hand. It wasn't Carden, but he felt familiar to me.

We walked the stairs cautiously, the ashen smell of the air from outside reaching us as pale daylight choked with smoke shone towards us. At the top was a terrifying black throne room, the entryway facing the balcony, the throne itself to our left.

Sitting on the horrible black throne was a figure that didn't seem like it was even there, a shadowy form with eyes glowing of evil green flame; those same flames licking and lapping across its shadow robed body. The flames and shadows grew like a great presence behind it, and my heart felt as if it would explode from fear.

The other figure at the first's side I immediately recognised as the Shadow Lord, his eyes glowing, a black sword that smoked with shadows the way ice smoked with cold in his hand. Almost as if he had a sudden burst of superhuman speed, he moved towards me, swinging his sword, my arms flashing up to bring my blade to meet his.

Shadows and light clashed and swirled between each other, creating a terrible storm that burned in mid-air. The collisions of our swords were colossal, the world feeling as if the sound would break it apart. My arms hurt with each impact, but I wasn't going to give up, some strange knowledge filling me that the fate of the world lay on the outcome of this fight.

I clashed with him once more with great force, both of us grasping the other's forearm as we clutched our swords, sparks bursting from the grinding blades.

A flash of colour drew my eyes to below his collar and I saw it. There, hanging around his neck, was one of the Pendants. It was not like mine with its silvery flowered curls and loops, but instead a black star set with a golden backing, each inward corner of the star having a silvery black point slipping up from behind it. At its centre was a stone as black as midnight but glowing with a light the colour of dark blood.

His face had become calmer as he studied me, our pressure on our swords never letting up. It was like he and I were taking on the roles of someone else, but we were separate from them.

"I know who you are..." my voice was mine but sounded so foreign and strange as I half whispered, and half choked the words.

His eyes blazed brightly, and he sneered evilly before he pushed me back and swung with his sword. I tried to block him, the clang of the swords ringing as the figure behind him stood and my eyes locked onto it. Suddenly, I felt as if it had flashed forward inside my eyes and invaded my mind, flames, shadows and a terrifying black face with fiery eyes burning as they stared at me...

I woke up in terror, jolting where I lay beside Carden as a yelp of panic slipped from my lips. He shifted and looked down at me in alarm, his arms still tightly coiled around me. My breathing was hard, as if my chest was being crushed by a great stone hand, my body aching now with terror instead of pain. My hands clawed at his arm and shirt, my fingers looking for some security and comfort after the terrible nightmare... or vision.

"Hey! Hey, it's alright!" he was calling to me, grasping my struggling, thrashing body and trying to calm me. "Leander, relax! You're safe!"

"Carden?" my voice was less than a murmur.

"It's alright, it's me," he confirmed, holding me close to him. "You're safe. You were having a nightmare. That's all."

Certainty filled me and I stared at the still open doorway, knowing exactly what I needed.

"I need to go to the library," I said and pushed myself past him, out of the bed and through the door without really feeling it, struggling against the weakness in my limbs.

"Sarissi?" the deep voice came from the towering figure outside the door, repeating with a little more urgency: "Sarissi?"

I hadn't even noticed Joran, sweeping past him without a second thought, knowing that he would be hurrying after me in less than a moment along with my lover.

Bare foot, I hurried along the carpeted wood floor of the corridor, my silken night dress flowing around my ankles, my fingers grasping at the cuffs of the sleeves. My naked upper arms, shoulders and neck felt the cooling autumn air, but I didn't shiver, somehow oblivious to such sensations at that moment.

Carden was jogging behind me, his left hand holding the still painful wounded area on his side. He caught up to me quickly, worry plastering his handsomely sharp, young features.

"Leander, what is it? What's wrong?" he asked, but I didn't answer him.

We burst into the library; the room completely deserted. I swept past the pillars, pausing as I looked towards the display case that imprisoned the Nempanarth. It seemed to glare at me with that sinister green eye through the night light, daring me to fight against the evil it held within its pages.

Turning from it, I started scouring the bookshelves, but I couldn't quite remember where I had seen what was now burning like an inferno in my mind.

"Sarissi, are you distressed?" Joran demanded as he stood close by, Carden pushing past him.

"Leander? What is it?" he repeated more sternly.

"There's a book here," I replied, pushing away from the shelf and rushing to another one where I started yanking books out to check their pages before shoving them back when I found nothing. "It showed me something that was in my nightmare."

"What?" Carden frowned as I remembered and moved to the stairs to the second floor of bookcases. "What are you looking for?"

I turned over my shoulder to him, my right hand resting on the banister. I drew in a shaking breath before answering, knowing how terrible the truth that I was about to utter truly was.

"I know who the Shadow Lord is," I murmured the words so quietly and hoarsely they might as well have been inside my head.

Carden stared at me with wide, horrified eyes, his jaw clenching and unclenching as if he wanted to speak but didn't know how to. His body had become rigid and he looked like he had just been turned into petrified wood by some terrible, dark spell. Behind him Joran suddenly had an expression of curiosity, but also dread.

I rushed up the stairs with both men following, Carden at speed and Joran at an easier pace. In seconds I was tearing through another bookshelf, desperately seeking out the tome I needed, my eyes flashing over all the leather spines.

"Here," I said, pulling the book from the shelf and turning back to the others.

I held it with my left hand while my right flicked the pages, dimly aware of Carden standing to my right as he tried to see what I was looking at. The pages thundered past as my eyes desperately hunted for the image in my mind. Then... it appeared.

I flipped back and looked at the coloured image I had found months ago of all thirteen Dragon Pendants. I recognised mine without any effort, the others all fairly similar, but only a few like the one I wore. Inevitably, I found myself staring at the gold and silvery black star with a black stone at its core that I'd dreamed about.

"The Obsidian Pendant," I murmured, then turned the page and found what I had searched for.

Like a ghost of the past the image rose from my nightmares, a monstrous face with grey skin hidden beneath a black cowl and wrapped in dark robes, the Obsidian Pendant hanging around his neck. Beneath the face of the man who had haunted me since the day I had turned eighteen was written a large amount of text, but the single line directly under the engraving made my blood turn to ice and my breath turn cold in my lungs.

I felt myself tremble and a whimper escaped my lips as I read the words aloud: "An engraving of the last known Holder of the Obsidian Dragon Pendant: the servant of evil, Right Hand of the Darkest Shadow, Shadow Lord Morod..."

Chapter Twenty
Darker Truths

My mind raced with so many thoughts, the knowledge of the terrible secret I had just discovered leaving my heart cold. The strange familiarity of my nightmare made sense now. I had seen the final battle almost twelve hundred years ago when Leander the First faced Lord Morod and the Darkest Shadow. It was as if my grandmother from twenty-three generations ago had come in spirit through my dreams to help me see the dark truth.

It's him... It's really him, my thoughts were colder than winter and harder than the ice of the mountains. *But how can it be? He's been dead for over a thousand years...*

"Did... did you say what I think you said?" Carden looked so pale, fear bleeding through every pore in his skin as if it were a solid, tangible thing.

I looked at him, feeling very drawn and sick as I held the book with my shaking hands. I felt like I couldn't close my eyes, the image of that great monster forcing them to stay open.

"The Shadow Lord we've been fighting to stay away from...," I murmured in response to his terrified question, "is Lord Morod..."

"But how can that be?!" Carden asked, giving voice to my cold, fearful thoughts. "That monster is dead! He died centuries ago! Your ancestor killed him!"

"I know," my voice didn't go above being a tiny whisper as I looked down at the book. "But somehow... it's... it's him."

"This Hessiik must have terrible power to cheat the Benarvorn," Joran considered gravely with dark eyes.

I knew that there was only one thing we could do.

"We have to tell the others," I said, closing the book and holding it to my chest. "Joran, do you know where they are?"

"They were in the Great Hall, Sarissi," Joran told me evenly, his arms firmly crossed in front of him.

"Come on," I grabbed at the side of my dress and hurried down the stairs towards the library doors.

The three of us made our way quickly through the corridor and towards the Great Hall. As we approached, we could hear voices in heavy discussion, their tones calm, but their words filled with significance.

Fawkner, Aldwyn and Ellora were in deep conversation with the Wizard and - to my surprise - Enchantress Illuminil. I paused at the doors and listened carefully with a curious frown.

"The Dark Ones all have their own agendas," Enchantress Illuminil said in her misty, transparent way, seated at the table in her flowing gold and emerald robes, guarded by Wood Elves. "Whether these agendas intersect is unknown, though dread plans are being laid even as we speak."

"Enchantress Illuminil is right," the Wizard agreed, looking around at all those there, pacing with his staff in hand. "The Revenant is a powerful necromancer who once sided with the Shadow Dominion long ago, however, he is also very proud and egotistical. All I can say for certain is what my trip to Gorth'lak revealed," he took a steadying breath before going on: "I could not go beyond the Black Peaks where the Labyrinth of Dol Amor reaches Gorth'lak's Maw. The three gates have been rebuilt and the watchtowers set to the mountains surrounding the Grey Wastes anew. Even Dread Mountain belches forth flame and ash into the sky once more, and the emerald storms have returned," his expression was grave as he paused. "I am certain that the reawakening of Gorth'lak is related to the rising of this new Shadow Lord."

"What can be done?" Fawkner asked, leaning further forward on his elbows where he sat at the table, trying to remain calm, though I could see the fear in his eyes.

"We must make preparations and be steadfast against whatever assault may come," the Wizard stated strongly, his experience clear in his articulate voice. "Far too many portents of the return of Gorth'lak have come to light in recent years... Chief among these is the girl's birth..."

I frowned and looked to Carden. He had a hard expression, his brow deeply creased with confusion.

Do they mean me? I couldn't help wondering.

"I won't entertain such thoughts," Fawkner shook his head, disturbed by the discussion. "Leander is an innocent in all of this."

"I completely agree, Lord Fawkner," the Wizard nodded softly, one hand to his hip, the other on his staff. "Yet, we *cannot* ignore the truth of *what* she is."

"*What* she is, is a vulnerable, grieving adolescent girl!" Fawkner snapped. "She is not some sign of the End of All Things!"

"I didn't say that she was," the Wizard replied calmly. "She is an innocent who is trapped by fate, and we *must* protect her."

"And your foresights, my Lady?" Aldwyn queried of the Enchantress with one eyebrow raised. "Does she not figure strongly in them?"

"Her birth was foretold," Illuminil said softly, distant as if remembering the past. "The return of the Shadow Lords will be preceded by the birth of a girl-child of the Heroine's line, her likeness incarnate. And her lifetime will be set to bring with it the rise of a darker evil long forgotten, and the Shadow's return from the Void to begin Its war anew," she turned her gaze to the Wizard, still dreamily absent in her way, though present: "My foresights have never lied. You know better than most the power and sway they hold, which is why the Scrolls *must* be consulted, as once they were with the girl's ancestor..."

"Those days are long past, my Lady," Ellora spoke with a quiet, almost frightened voice. "This girl is *not* the Great Heroine..."

"So it would seem," Illuminil stood and turned her gaze to the doors. "Please, come in, Princess Leander, Master Carden and Joran of Vorash Jaaktar..."

I looked to Carden, surprised that she knew we were there. He shrugged, growing ever paler the more of this he heard. I just took in a deep breath and pushed one door open, entering with him and Joran right behind me.

The other Custodians were surprised as they looked up, their expressions ranging from shock to awe, and even exasperation from Aldwyn. The Wizard remained fairly even, though there was a knowing gleam in his eye, almost as if he too had expected my sudden appearance.

"I think it only appropriate that you should join us, Daughter of Aldrich," Illuminil faintly smiled as she bowed her head reverently and as Fawkner stood and turned to me. "It is good that our paths have once more crossed."

I simply smiled at her before Aldwyn drew my attention. "Your Highness," his tone was one of discretion, "perhaps your attire is not appropriate..."

"I doubt the way I'm dressed matters right now," I said a little more sternly, feeling heat rising inside of me as I stared into his eyes. "It seems that you've been keeping a lot of secrets from me, Aldwyn."

"Leander..." Fawkner started, but I threw him a swift stare that made him fall instantly silent.

"Did you know anything about this before tonight, Fawkner?" I demanded in an even tone, glaring at him.

He shook his head with nothing but honesty in his eyes: "I swear, this is the first I have heard of this."

"How much have you heard, my dear?" the Wizard questioned me in a low, quiet tone.

"I heard you speaking of foresights that some of you think means that I will bring back the Shadow Lords," I replied coldly.

"Understand, Princess," Aldwyn spoke up, his eyes focused intentionally on my face alone, "that none of us think any such thing. We simply believe that you are a figure of importance in this time, a clear marker as to *when* the Shadow Lords would return. Nothing more."

"For better or worse," Ellora turned her gaze to me with soft sympathy, "you are involved now, not because of your birth, but because of the new Shadow Lord's interest in you."

I fell silent, swallowing back hard as I ran their words through my head. I knew what I needed to tell them, but I felt as if trying to even think the words I needed to speak was like climbing the greatest of mountains or swimming the widest and deepest of oceans.

"You carry some dark knowledge, child," Illuminil perceived, her turquoise eyes delving deep into my heart and mind. "A knowledge we have been seeking ever since the beginning of these dread events."

Then, I heard her voice in my mind, as if she wanted to speak to me alone without the others overhearing: "*Yet, you cannot bring your physical voice to speak the horror that screams in your mind and heart... I see him where he lingers now in your thoughts, a plague upon you of the worst kind.*"

I locked my eyes with hers and felt a peaceful kind of strength reaching out to me. I could sense a warming, comforting light coming from her and began to feel safer, though still disturbed.

"*It is alright, Princess,*" she assured me in thought. "*Take the strength I gift to you and speak the name of the monster we both know has returned from the Dark Places to violate this world once more...*"

"Come, child," she said with words now, continuing her urging. "Give voice to what you know."

As if she had broken some terrible spell that the name of our enemy had cast on me, I felt my body relax.

"I know who the Shadow Lord is," I murmured, my voice croaking a little.

The Custodians all stared at me - save the Elven Enchantress - curiosity and fear mixing in their eyes.

"And who is he?" the Wizard asked, moving to stand close to me. "Who is the foe we now face?"

I set the book down on the table in front of me carefully, hesitant to touch the cover. I opened it and slowly turned to the pages I sought. The Shadow Lord's face sneered up at me in all his horrible glory as that familiar chill shattered through my spine again. I felt Carden's hand on my back, grateful for my lover's touch as I fought my fear and pushed myself to meet the Wizard's gaze.

"It's Morod," I said quietly, but clear enough that all the others there heard my words. "The Shadow Lord we're facing... is Morod."

I looked around, seeing the terror on their faces and feeling it thick in the air as if it were some kind of choking miasma. None of them spoke, but nearly all - except a very solemn Illuminil - looked like they could die from fear.

"It cannot be," Ellora seemed as if she could start to cry, covering her mouth with both hands.

"Princess," Aldwyn was cold, his expression making me feel like I was being judged for pulling a tasteless prank, "you must be mistaken. Lord Morod has been dead for over one thousand years. He can *never* return..."

"He's not really alive," I told him, squeezing my eyes shut in thought, then shaking my head before looking at him again. "As I told you before, he is some kind of spectre or ghost."

"How do you know that this enemy we face is Shadow Lord Morod?" Aldwyn asked darkly.

I turned to the book and pointed to the image of the Obsidian Pendant, the Wizard facing me and laying his gaze to the page.

"He wore this around his neck," I said, looking into the Wizard's hazel eyes. "At first, I didn't think anything of it, but when we were fleeing the basilica in Aneuran he lifted his hand to it. That's when that enormous black dragon attacked us."

Carden drew my gaze as he said: "I remember. That was horrific..."

"The Obsidian Pendant," the Wizard took the book from me and studied both the image of the thirteen Dragon Pendants and the engraving of Shadow Lord Morod. "Yes... of course. It all makes perfect sense..."

He took in the faces of every person there before speaking. I could see he was uneasy, but strong, his resolve unbroken.

"Only *one* Shadow Lord ever gained control of one of the thirteen Dragon Pendants, and that was Lord Morod," he expressed sternly. "The Obsidian Pendant was the one he took, and so, knowing this, and knowing that the current Shadow Lord carries it means only one thing..."

"So... you believe me?" I asked, looking up at the Wizard as he stood right over me.

"Of course, Princess," he assured me. "There can be no doubt in my mind."

"Nor mine," Fawkner agreed and I looked to him thankfully.

"Now then," the Wizard stepped away from me and back to the others, "we must act quickly and counter Lord Morod before he can achieve his plans. There is still much we do not know."

"Given what we know of the Revenant's activities, we must assume that Eilath is still a target," Fawkner surmised, clasping his hands together behind him. "The one Gorth'lakian artefact we possess is the Nempanarth, and I think it is safe to assume that *this* is his target. Especially since Shadow Lords require it to resurrect themselves from the state this one is in."

"As the book is a target, so too is the Princess," Aldwyn stated, looking to me sternly. "Your Highness, I would have you return to your room and continue to rest. We have much still to do."

"But what about the Shadow Lord?" I asked in an urgently worried voice.

"We shall do what we can to counter him," the Wizard assured me. "For now, our best action against him is ensuring that he never reaches you. Regardless of all else that has occurred of late, Lord Morod's gaze is still focused on you, my dear."

"Carden," Aldwyn called to the young man. "Stay with the Princess, keep her near you at all times," then he added quietly and knowingly: "I know that it is a task you are more than happy to take on."

"Understood, Aldwyn," Carden responded, then turned to me. "Let's go, Leander."

We left the Great Hall, Joran following close behind us. In only a few short minutes we were back in my room and I found myself standing by the windows, looking out on the slowly growing light of the triplet moons.

I felt fear clutch me and I whispered: "He'll never stop... He'll... he'll keep coming for me. I can feel it..."

Carden turned me around so that I looked up into his eyes, our bodies fully facing each other now. I felt so small and fragile next to him, like a tiny mouse before a great lion; so easy to crush under foot. Yet, I had come to feel no stronger safety with anyone else in my life. As he reached out one hand and touched my face, his fingers under my long hair, I knew for certain that this was true.

"It *will* be alright," he promised, pulling me into his arms and laying my head on his chest. "We'll keep you safe. He will *never* get his hands on you."

There was nothing I could say, just closing my eyes and hoping with all my heart that what he pledged would be true.

* * * * *

It took a couple of weeks, but both Carden and I were soon healed, finding our bodies able to move once more without the aches from our encounter with the Revenant. It was little comfort though as the knowledge of the Shadow Lord's identity continued to plague me, my lover's presence all that relieved such ill thoughts of my heart and mind.

One grey, cloudy day, I walked on to the main porch with Carden, dressed in my teal, purple and pale blue dress, my hair left hanging long and free. Carden had donned a replacement green shirt and his black and silver Guardian jacket now that the autumn air was becoming more chilled, his sword at his side. We had come to farewell our friends who were now preparing to uncover the truth behind the Revenant's designs.

They hadn't told me much, but what little I had learned of their plans meant that the Custodians were going to have to travel in order to confirm some rather sinister suspicions. They had been in talks ever since the night I revealed the Shadow Lord's identity, ardently making plans in order to counter him.

And so, I was conflicted, both yearning for the answers and fearful of being left without some of my strongest defenders. But at least Carden would remain with me.

"I trust that you shall make haste with your investigations," Enchantress Illuminil stood at the steps with Ellora, Fawkner and Aldwyn, her hood drawn, her gowns and cloak swirling in the breeze. "We cannot be idle now that the Enemy is revealed."

"We will be cautious and vigilant, Lady Illuminil," Aldwyn assured her, carrying his own staff just as the Wizard did. "We will make for the ruins of the Citadel and ascertain if our concerns are correct."

"If they are and the remaining Orbs of Darkness are not still sealed away beneath the Citadel," Illuminil said darkly, "then we are assured of the Revenant's new alignment with his old commander."

I had never heard of such artefacts as these orbs, but, then again, there were so many things that I didn't know. Whatever they were, however, they must surely have been sinister and powerful for the Custodians *and* the Guardians to hide them away so diligently.

"It will take us nearly two weeks to reach the Citadel," Ellora was saying as the Wizard came to stand with them. "Though so much time has passed since the night it fell, we shall be cautious should the Scourge yet linger there."

"You're really leaving?" I asked, surprised by this as Lady Erika came out to join us, carrying Bran with Freda at her side.

Fawkner turned to me and nodded, pulling his Guardian cloak further around him: "We are. Joran, Ellora, Aldwyn and I are to depart for the Citadel's ruins. The last two artefacts of Gorth'lak, other than the Nempanarth, were being kept there according to Enchantress Illuminil. And ascertaining if they are still consigned to the Citadel's keeping will determine whether we face two separate foes, or one allied front."

"So, you do think the Revenant and the Shadow Lord are working together?" Carden asked, standing right behind my shoulder.

Fawkner shook his head uncertainly. "I cannot say before searching the Citadel's ruins. However, once we have, we will return with an answer."

"Carden, Tallinn, while we are gone you are the only protection the Princess has," Aldwyn told the two younger Guardians solemnly. "Whatever the circumstance, stay by her."

"We will not shirk our duties, Aldwyn. I swear to you," Tallinn assured him with a serious expression and a light nod.

"I worry for you, my love," Erika told Fawkner, moving with the children to meet him. "You were gone for so long, and now you are to return to where you once faced terrible danger."

"It will not be more than a month before I return to your waiting arms, Erika," he pledged, then kissed her.

"I'll miss you, Papa," Freda reached up and hugged him as he crouched to embrace her.

"And I you, Freda," he replied, then kissed Bran on the head. "As I will you, my son."

"Just come back to us safe," Erika urged him.

"Come," Ellora called to the two men and the Storvari, "we must depart ere the daylight escapes us."

They started to move, Joran bowing silently to me, then joining them. The four started down the steps as Enchantress Illuminil paused and turned to me.

"One final word to you, Princess Leander," she stated in her even, but beautiful voice. "Caution must not be cast aside so readily. Know that there are still threats abundant around you, even if the Revenant and the Shadow Lord are not. Be aware, for *some* dark truths are *still* to be revealed."

With that, she bowed her head and turned away, following the others with the Wood Elves that had accompanied her. They left on horseback, the Wizard gazing up at me from beneath his hat, nodding his farewell, then turning and following my friends and the Elves.

"What did that mean?" Carden asked me.

"Elf gibberish," Holger snorted grumpily, his arms crossed firmly. "It's best we're rid of her."

As Lady Erika was leading her children inside, Tristan came hurrying up the steps from the city, his expression urgent, his fleecy red hair tied back behind his shoulders, his cloak flicking up behind him.

"You've been gone quite some time, lad," Dolin observed as the five of us faced him. "Drinking at the tavern all night again?"

I couldn't help eyeing Tristan uncertainly. He *had* been disappearing more and more in the last few days since learning of the Shadow Lord's identity, and I found myself wondering what it could possibly be that had him so interested in being absent from us all of a sudden.

"Bartering a deal for some information that might help us," Tristan replied to the Dwarf, following as we started into the Great Hall and took to a small seating area near the doors.

"And what kind of information might that be?" Tallinn asked as I took a seat, Carden standing with his arms crossed at my side.

"What's the one thing we don't know right now that we need to?" Tristan asked, standing before us and mirroring Carden's pose, the Dwarves both seating themselves as he spoke. "In the last few months we've learned a lot about the Custodians, the Revenant, and now we know who the Shadow Lord is. But what *don't* we know?"

"Why you're suddenly such a distant vagabond going off to taverns all the time?" Holger suggested, then added gruffly: "And why you're not inviting me when there's drink to be had?!"

Tallinn eyed the Dwarf and turned her attention to Tristan, pacing slowly with her arms crossed. "You *have* been very absent of late. One would wonder why."

"As I said," Tristan repeated, "I've been bartering a deal for some *very* valuable information."

"And that would be?" Tallinn stopped moving and raised an eyebrow at him.

"The one thing we haven't been able to find out about the Shadow Lord," he gestured to me, "is what he wants with the girl."

I sat up straighter, staring with a surprised gaze at him. "You know why he's after me?"

"Well, no, not yet," Tristan admitted with a slow shrug. "But I've been talking to someone who says he has found out."

"And how do we know we can trust this man?" Carden asked suspiciously, his eyes narrowing and his jaw tightening.

"I've made a lot of friends during my travels through High-Realm," Tristan explained. "Most of them can find out some interesting information and bring it to me for a favour or a price. So, this friend of mine came to me in the tavern a few days before the Revenant attacked and told me he had heard some rumours. He said that there was talk of a man people are whispering about being a Shadow Lord looking for a young noble girl from Aldegaad. Naturally, I asked him if there was any truth to what he was saying, and he told me that he could find out what the evil bastard wants with the lass."

"And he's just willing to give up this information?" Tallinn was very clearly doubting this.

"Well, he wants money, obviously," Tristan replied, "but he came to me last night and we went to have a drink. That's when he told me he had found out some information about the Shadow Lord's plans."

He turned to me, his body language telling me that he was about to say something that made him feel awkward.

"He... uh... he wants to meet you, lass," he said uncertainly.

"Out of the question," Tallinn shook her head with vigour. "Aldwyn left specific instructions to keep the Princess out of danger. She is *not* meeting this man."

"Look, I don't see any danger from him," Tristan tried to convince her. "He's not a low life or anything like that, but an honest merchant who hears some interesting information in his travels. He just won't tell *me* directly."

"And why not? Doesn't trust you?" Carden asked harshly.

"What are you saying, boy?" Tristan rounded on him slowly, his voice low and annoyed.

"He's saying what we're all thinking," Holger chimed in roughly, having lit up a pipe and now puffing away heavily. "You're a hard man to trust, Wanderer."

Tristan turned to me imploringly: "Haven't I given you reason enough to trust me, Princess? After all that I've done since Aneuran?"

"*I* trust you, Tristan," I said, drawing the others' incredulous stares and ignoring them as I kept my eyes on his face. "I just... I'm worried that I'll end up in more needless danger."

"I wasn't suggesting we go alone," he told me, determined to plead his case. "I told Fawkner just as they were leaving, and he said to speak to you and to *only* go through with it as long as *all* six of us go."

"Your Highness," Tallinn looked at me with severity, clearly unconvinced, "I'm not sure that it is worth the risk. This man might be luring us into a trap."

"One man alone against us six," Tristan pointed out more clearly. "And we don't have to leave the city, so there won't be a problem there. If there's any threat, we can call to the city guardsmen."

Tallinn sighed reluctantly. "The choice is yours, Princess."

I sighed, secretly wishing that they wouldn't leave all the decisions to me. But the truth was that the possibility of learning the Shadow Lord's plans for me was too strong to just refuse to take the chance.

At least this way we can help find out more for when the others return from the Citadel. Besides, once we know what he wants me for we can better defend against him.

"Alright, Tristan," I said, looking up at the man with quietly serious curiosity. "Where and when are we meeting him?"

"At midnight in the warehouse district," Tristan explained with more enthusiasm now that I had accepted, though his voice was still calm. "I've chosen that area because of its high frequency of city guard patrols."

I nodded. "Alright. Then, we'll *all* go and meet with this friend of yours."

"But if there's any trouble," Tallinn warned him harshly, "we will not hesitate to act."

"Which is exactly why I came to you, Lady Guardian," Tristan stated.

The details were discussed, and we went about our normal daily activities. I could see that Carden and Tallinn were uneasy about this, but we needed to take the chance that this mysterious friend of Tristan's could truly have found some information we would need. In truth, maybe I was being reckless, but the desire to finally know why the Shadow Lord wanted me was just too hard to ignore.

* * * * *

When night came, we gathered on the porch above the city, all dressed in our cloaks and hoods to shield us from prying eyes. With twenty minutes to spare, we started down the steps and made our way into the city, Tristan at the lead with Tallinn still suspicious at his back. Carden and I stayed close together with Holger and Dolin walking behind me, their heavily bearded faces glaring from under their dark blue hoods. They were making a concerted effort to hide their weapons just as Carden and Tallinn were.

"Are you sure about this?" Carden whispered to me as we entered the warehouse district on the eastern side of Eilath. "Something just doesn't feel right to me."

"No, I'm not," I confessed, looking up at him from under my hood. "But we can't just let this chance pass us by."

"I hope for all our sakes that you know what you're doing, lassie," Dolin remarked coldly from behind me.

"So do I, Dolin," I replied, looking to Carden and receiving a light squeeze of his arm around my shoulders.

We came to a darkened section of the district, the heavy guard presence doing little to lift my unease. Tristan led us down an alleyway towards a side door into a warehouse, a lantern struggling to burn there in the darkness and the breeze.

"This is it," he said, looking out from under his hood at us. "We should be cautious how many of us enter."

"What are you saying?" Tallinn's voice was hushed, but still harsh, her eyes narrowing at him.

"I'm saying let's not intimidate the fellow," Tristan said. "The Dwarves can guard the door, so no one follows us in."

"It is a good idea, Tallinn," Carden conceded in a hushed voice. "It ensures an escape route in case things don't work out."

"Very well," Tallinn almost groaned, then looked to me. "Stay close to us, Princess."

I just nodded.

"We'll watch yer backs," Holger muttered, revealing his massive war-hammer as Dolin took out his battle-axe from under his cloak.

Suddenly, there came a frantic snarling and yelping as Amethyst slipped from the shadows, her eyes wide with worry.

"Amethyst! What are you doing here?!" I reached her quickly, stroking her long snout and trying to comfort her.

She gestured her head to the door, growling and snorting with urgency. I could see that she didn't want us to go in.

"Something's wrong," I looked from her back to the others.

"We should leave," Tallinn said in a low, cautious tone, her hazel eyes prowling the shadows around us.

"We might not get another chance at this," Tristan countered as he stood at the door, then looked to me. "Lass, tell your dragon to stay out of sight. She'll be great backup if the need to fight and flee should arise."

"Princess..." Tallinn stared at me incredulously.

Against my better judgement, I turned to Amethyst and said: "Do as Tristan says. We'll call if we need you."

Amethyst was reluctant, snapping with her scaled lips at my cloak and trying to pull me away from the warehouse. She was more than insistent; her demeanour having completely changed to one of unyielding unease.

"It *will* be alright," I tried to reassure her, pulling my cloak free. "I promise."

She sighed and nodded, rubbing her head against my chest and shoulder affectionately. I couldn't help thinking that it was almost like she was a child worrying that her mother wouldn't return.

She pulled away and, with a beating of her wings, was airborne and out of sight.

"Ready?" Tristan asked me and I nodded.

The four of us passed the Dwarves and made our way into the warehouse. There were two rooms we would have to pass through before the main floor, the lamps cold and the smell of various cargos reaching my senses. It was so dark that I was finding it hard to navigate my way through the narrow spaces, Carden walking with his hand around mine to keep me close.

Slowly, we entered the largest part of the warehouse, a wide loft opposite us stacked with barrels. The room was stocked with two dozen shelves and had stacking areas filled with crates and sacks. There was one lamp at the door we had entered through, the light of the moons shining weakly through the hatches in the ceiling.

"Well," Tallinn turned to Tristan sourly, "where is this man?

"I don't understand," Tristan looked around in the shadows anxiously. "He *should* be here."

Carden stopped and suddenly pulled me close to him. I frowned up at him, seeing that his gaze was locked ahead of us. Hesitantly, I turned my eyes to follow his line of sight, gasping in shock and clinging tighter to his shirt and jacket.

A man was lying on the floor, his eyes wide with a deathly stare, his chest still and no breath issuing from his lips.

"I think we just found him," Carden mumbled direly.

Chapter Twenty-One
The Serpent's Snare

I felt so sick, the smell of open veins rancid in my nostrils, my fingers tightening as I held onto Carden's shirt, staring wide eyed at the scene before me.

"Is... is this your friend, Tristan?" Tallinn's voice was small and fretful now, her eyes paling at the sight of the corpse.

Tristan nodded slowly and numbly. "Aye... This is him," he crouched down to examine the body as Tallinn took her bow from her shoulder in anticipation of an attack.

I couldn't keep looking at the body, my eyes closing tightly and my head touching Carden's shoulder faintly. I drew in deep breaths through my mouth, so I didn't have to smell the blood. I could feel how tense Carden was, his breathing slow, but heavy, his heart racing in his chest like a thunderstorm against my ear. I opened my eyes and looked up at him, his expression hard and his jaw set as if it were made of stone. His green eyes were blazing, and I could feel him shaking as if with fear... no, not fear... rage... silent and unrelenting rage.

"His throat's been torn out," Tristan observed, pushing his hood back to clear his sight. "There's... there's a lot of blood."

"Not as much as there should be," Carden snarled under his breath, not even blinking as he stared at the corpse.

"No blade did this," Tristan murmured, then looked up at us with a paling expression.

"Carden?" I almost whispered as I stared worriedly at him, clinging to his clothing. "What's wrong?"

"There's only one creature that could do this," Carden stated, looking over his shoulder at Tallinn.

She nodded her agreement but said nothing.

"W-w-what did this?" I was trembling as my mind raced through all the monsters and beasts I had read about throughout my life.

"We need to get out of here," Carden said urgently, drawing his sword and grabbing me by the arm. "Now."

He dragged me towards the door abruptly, my hood falling back at the ferocity of his pull. His grip was so tight it actually hurt, and I wanted to yank my wrist free of his crushing fingers, but I couldn't. Then, he stopped, Tallinn and Tristan freezing behind us at the sound of footsteps.

"Someone's coming," he said coldly.

"Damn it! Hide!" Tristan ordered.

He and Tallinn darted off into the dark as Carden yanked me towards the far end of the room. I staggered to keep up with him, losing sight of the other two swiftly. He dragged me behind a heavy grouping of crates and made me sit on the floor.

"Carden..."

"Shh!" he hissed at me in a whisper. "Be quiet, Leander! Don't make a sound!"

I swallowed hard and nodded, looking over my shoulder and between the crates, my back pressed up against one of them. The lantern by the door suddenly went out and the only light left to us was the pale glow of the crescent moons. My eyes flicked frantically across the room, searching for some sort of movement. I couldn't see anything, but I could sense someone there with us, someone with harsh, predatory eyes.

There's a killer in here! my mind was screaming frantically. *Oh Gods! What should we do?!*

I glanced up at Carden, his brow furrowed and his eyes searching thoroughly and tirelessly through the darkness. He had never looked so intense before, never so ill at ease. It was like this was all too familiar for him, and I realised then that there was much more he hadn't yet told me.

A loud bang nearly made me yelp, my hands slapping over my mouth immediately to keep my voice from sounding. I closed my eyes tight, trembling, my heart racing and my blood curdling in my veins.

Slowly, perilously, I opened my eyes and looked to Carden again, his hand now on my right shoulder.

"Leander," he whispered, turning to me and meeting my gaze. "Stay here and don't move."

"Where are you going?" I asked in hushed panic.

He took up his sword and tried to force a smile for me, but it was more of a worried grimace. "It's going to be alright."

"Carden," I pleaded, but he silenced me with a deep, long kiss.

He broke the kiss and said: "I'll be right back," then he stood, moving from our hiding place.

"Carden!" I quietly called, grabbing for him and missing. "Don't!"

He vanished from my sight and I sat there, breathing hard, panic racing through me like a thundering river filled with rapids. I turned and peeked through the gaps between the crates, watching as Carden moved slowly with his sword ready in hand. He was studying the darkness, his eyes carefully seeking out any signs of movement.

"I know you're here," he called in an even, calm tone. "Show yourself..."

I squinted through the darkness, trying to get some sense of what or who he was talking to. Then, I saw a figure standing in the shadows off to his right.

"Come now, Adriana," Carden spoke with a faint smirk on his handsome face, addressing the killer by name to my utter terrified surprise. "Don't think that I wouldn't know it would be you. This all reeks of your style."

With deliberate grace, the figure slipped from the shadows to reveal herself. She was incredibly beautiful; a woman in her early thirties, her jet-black hair hanging to her shoulders and her skin like flawless alabaster. She wore a black velvet hood over her head that was attached to the collar of her clothing. She was clad in a black dress jacket with corsetry in the front, her white breasts perfectly still beneath it as if she wasn't breathing. Her legs were wrapped in dark coloured leggings with impeccably clean but worn black knee-high boots. At first glance she looked like a Gorvennan, but her eyes were gold, not green, her perfect lips parting to reveal her teeth, two pointed fangs gleaming in the moonlight.

"You always know when it's me," she smiled, her hands at her sides under her wide sleeves' cuffs. "Don't you, Carden?"

"Well," he turned to face her fully, "you've always been very theatrical."

"I'm not the only one of my kind to use such parlour tricks to intimidate mortals," she stated, moving a few steps forward and looking up at him.

"Why have you come here?" he demanded coldly.

"What's this? No warm greeting?" she mimicked being hurt, still smirking. "I thought you would be more accommodating for your own *mother*."

I gasped and covered my mouth in shocked horror. *She's his mother?! How?! She's so young... and I thought he was an orphan!*

Carden glowered at her, gripping his sword tighter, his other hand ready to snatch at his daggers.

"You're *not* my mother," he snarled.

"Of course I am. I birthed you after all," she said with the illusion of care in her supernatural eyes.

She reached out to stroke his hair, but he pulled back abruptly, glaring at her.

She laughed: "Still trying to deny your birthright, I see. But tell me, does *she* know?"

"Who?" he glared.

"Don't play coy with me, my son," Adriana turned and paced casually as she surveyed the room. "I know that you've found the love that you won't accept from your own mother in the arms of some sweet little Aldegaadian girl," she turned over her shoulder to him, smiling wider: "A princess, no less."

Carden shrugged nonchalantly and looked her in the eye as she strode towards him: "I don't know what you're talking about."

"Come now, Carden," she mewed. "Do not try to hide the truth from me. I can smell her scent clinging to you just as she was not more than a few minutes ago. You even have her *taste* on your lips..."

I cringed, unable to take my eyes off this foul woman claiming to have given birth to my lover. Carden just shook his head and said nothing as she leaned closer to him.

"Where is she?" the woman questioned him softly. "I know she's close."

"I'm not telling you anything," Carden glowered at her with a faint smirk of his own.

"Don't think," Adriana said softly and threateningly, "that one adolescent girl can escape *me*. Either tell me where she is, or I *will* find her *myself*."

He brought his face close to hers, trying to intimidate her. "If you try to lay *one* finger on her... I *will* kill you."

She smiled widely at his threat. "Go on. Try it," she shoved him hard with so little effort, Carden viciously lashing out with a throwing dagger.

Adriana bent her back and pulled her chest out of its path, Carden immediately slashing with his sword. Every vicious, powerful strike he threw she evaded, almost like he had been cursed by some kind of slowing magic, though it looked more like she was moving faster than was possible.

Suddenly, a black shape slammed into Carden and his sword clattered to the floor. A large man with the same colour skin and eyes as Adriana appeared, grabbing him by the throat and putting him to the wall. Carden coughed and choked, grabbing at the man's arm and stabbing him in the shoulder with one of his daggers. The man just glared at him and slammed him against the wall again, harder this time and stunning him.

I wanted to jump up, but made myself stay put, covering my mouth as I fought the urge to scream.

Don't let them kill him! Please, please!

Adriana sighed and kicked the sword away, turning her eyes to Carden: "I'm disappointed really. You're still trying to fight like one of *them*."

"I... I *am*... one of them," Carden choked in response.

Something fell from one of the lofts and hit the ground, a second, slighter, skinnier man landing on his feet a few seconds later.

"Look what I found, Mistress," he chuckled and kicked the body over.

Tallinn lay there, unconscious with a gash in her forehead. She was still breathing, but she was pale, and her wound looked deep.

"Tallinn!" Carden cried out and was slammed against the wall again, pinned there hard by the large man's hand.

Adriana eyed her and threw a savage look to the slighter man: "This is the other Guardian. She's *not* the girl we're after."

A hand suddenly clamped over my mouth and I struggled, clawing at the skin frantically.

"Shh, it's just me, lass," Tristan whispered in my ear and I immediately relaxed, his hand slipping from my mouth as soon as I released my tension. "Here," he handed me a short sword. "Take this. And follow my lead."

I nodded, grasping the grip in my right hand and turning back to the scene before us. It didn't even occur to me to question the sanity of charging three seemingly supernatural beings with a short sword. In truth, at that moment, seeing my friends in danger, there was no questioning such actions. And so, I just stayed low and waited for him to make his move, turning my eyes back to the horrible scene before me.

"Do you see how weak they are?" Adriana was asking Carden, gesturing to the unconscious blonde girl sprawled before them. "Why would you *ever* want to be one of *them*?"

"Because... ahem... I *don't* want to be like *you*," Carden hissed and spat in her face.

The large man backhanded him with a crushing, horrid sound, then put both hands around his neck in response to him spitting at his mistress. Adriana just wiped her cheek and put her heel on Tallinn's neck, the blonde girl gagging in her unconsciousness.

"Tell me where the girl is, or I'll kill your friend," she dictated to Carden coldly and maliciously.

Tristan nodded and we both moved, weapons at the ready.

"Stop!" I shouted, pointing the blade of my sword towards the pale woman, drawing all of their gazes as Tristan did the same to my left.

Adriana raised an amused eyebrow at me and smiled. "Well now. What's this?"

"Let them go," I ordered, brandishing the blade steadily at her.

"Or what?" she asked. "You can't fight us with swords, girl."

"That's why I have this," I put my left hand over my pendant. "If you know who I am, then you know what this can do."

I was not certain I could repeat what I had done with the Revenant, but I was willing to bluff at least. And it seemed to pay off. I could see the unease in her eyes as her smile faded.

The cruel woman took her foot away from Tallinn, her amber eyes unflinchingly locked on the Pendant.

"Let them go... or I'll use it," I threatened, hoping I sounded convincing.

Adriana smirked victoriously, but said nothing, edging towards me slowly.

"I mean it!" I raised my voice, trembling but trying to stay strong. "I *will* use the magic in this necklace!"

I suddenly felt something sharp and cold touch my right shoulder, freezing as the point of a blade poked into my neck.

"Lower the sword, lass," Tristan told me firmly. "Throw it away. Alright? Be a good girl."

I closed my eyes as realisation hit me, hating myself for trusting him. I threw the sword away, silently cursing in my head at him as it clattered on the wooden floor some feet to my right.

Tristan moved closer to me, the blade now within my peripheral vision. My chest was heaving as I tried to steady my breathing, my heart freezing momentarily and forcing a new paralysis over my limbs.

"Take it off," he tugged at my cloak.

My hands shot to my neck and released the clasp, the purple fabric slipping from my shoulders into a pile on the floor. I shivered, but not from the cold.

"I meant that pretty little necklace of yours, girl," he spoke lowly into my ear, his breath hot and his voice making my hearing on my left vibrate. "Take it off and hand it to me."

His left hand came around my shoulder and I just glanced at it. My eyes darted to Carden where he still struggled, his boots' heels scraping on the wall.

"Leander! Don't!" he cried out, the man squeezing his throat and silencing him as he choked harder.

"They'll kill him if you don't hand it over," Tristan warned me. "Best do as I ask."

I just nodded with short breaths sounding from my lips, tears threatening my eyes. Both hands reached under my hair and fumbled with the chain's clasp, releasing it. The necklace slid down my chest and I took it in my hands, staring down at the silver pendant and its purple heart-stone.

Reluctantly, I placed it in Tristan's outstretched palm. He stashed it in a pouch on his belt then put his sword across my throat, looping one arm under my left shoulder and pinning the blade against me with both hands.

I couldn't help the whimper that slid from my lips or the tightening flinch of my body at the sudden pressure being plied to my neck.

"Now, there's a good girl," he whispered to me.

"I trusted you!" I said with a shaking, scared voice, my hands balling up at my hips. "How could you?!"

"It's nothing personal, Princess," he replied softly, almost with shame. "But I want what was promised me, and you're how I'm going to get that."

Adriana turned towards me as she moved to Carden, touching his chest as he squirmed.

"She's a pretty little thing, Carden," she said with a vicious smirk. "I can see why you fancy her."

"I'll kill you!" he screamed, struggling against his captor. "If you hurt her, I swear to the Gods that I will tear you apart!"

Adriana lashed out and knocked Carden unconscious, my heart aching as I saw him slump to the floor.

She eyed the two Guardians off and nodded to her men: "Take them to the carriage. Restrain and gag them. They'll make for good insurance should we have any trouble with the girl."

I shied away from her as she moved towards me while her men dragged my friends from the room. She reached out and grasped my chin, her fingers so cold that I instantly whimpered and shuddered hard as she forced me to look at her.

"I can see why you're so appealing to so many," she commented, studying my eyes, her gaze drifting longingly to my neck. "Your scent is... *intoxicating*. I wonder if the Master will be willing to allow me to partake of your taste."

I cringed at that eerie comment, feeling like a dinner course rather than a human being.

"Who... who is your master?" I asked in a trembling voice, my body straining against Tristan's hold.

"I believe you've already had the pleasure of meeting him. And you shall again soon enough," Adriana said cryptically, turning and heading for the door. "Bring her, Wanderer."

He pushed me forward, never taking the blade from my throat. I struggled, digging my heels into the floor to try to slow him down, but it was no good. He was soon leading me out into a side alley on the opposite side of the warehouse to where we had entered.

"So, this has been your plan from the start. Even when you claimed to be helping me," I scorned him.

"I don't have to explain myself to you," he said and shoved me further down the alleyway. "Adriana. What about the Dwarves?"

"They won't be a problem," she called back to him as they led me through the dark. "Nor will the Dragon. I made sure to drug it before we entered."

Hearing that, I started struggling harder, worrying what they might have done to Amethyst: "If you've hurt her..."

"Quit your thrashing!" Tristan snapped at me, tightening his grip and forcing me to hold still, cutting off my enraged threat.

We came around the corner to where a cargo carriage was waiting. The two other men were already there along with a large, nearly seven-foot-tall hooded figure. Tristan brought me to him, and I froze as I stared up into his fierce yellow eyes.

Black hair hung around his face in thick clumps, a heavy ridging of bones rising from his forehead. His skin was thick and leathery with a horrid purplish brown colouring like he had been bruised all over, two large jagged ears visible beneath his hair and hood. I knew immediately that he was a Gathlork disguised as a masked wanderer, my muscles tensing and my heart shrieking inside me.

"Is this the one the Master seeks?" he snarled in a bestial voice, glaring at me like I was food.

"She is, Vorgak," Adriana confirmed. "Bind her wrists then gag her. We can't have her calling for help."

Tristan shoved me to the ground, and I lay there in a sitting position, staring up at the Gathlork fearfully.

"Be gentle with her," Tristan warned him and looked to me. "And you be a good girl, or he might break your arm off."

Vorgak stomped forward and snatched me up by my arm, his fingers crushing around it hard. I tried to struggle, but he just tightened his grip, making me cry out in agony. He shoved me against the back of the carriage, my feet on the ground, my chest and stomach pressing to the wooden floor. He then yanked my arms back behind me, causing me to scream out of shock and pain.

"Hold still, woman-child!" Vorgak snarled down at me, pressing me hard into the carriage floor. "The Master wants his meat in one piece when it arrives."

"Get off me!" I screamed and howled as he twisted my wrists hard, bringing tears to my cheeks. "Uhnh! You're hurting me! Please!"

"He will not be pleased but keep resisting and I will break you!" the Gathlork roared like a beast into my ear.

I felt him force my wrists together, a coarse leather binding being pulled tightly around them. He wrapped it firmly then grabbed me between my neck and shoulder, forcing me to stand up and face him.

"Much better," Adriana smirked and nodded to the carriage. "Put her in."

Then, there came a shout and we all looked up as two figures rushed forward from the other end of the alleyway.

"Unhand her, Scourge filth!" Dolin commanded, ready with his weapon.

"Dolin! Holger! Help!" I screamed, the Gathlork slapping his hand over my mouth as I struggled.

Vorgak roared and a small number of Gathlorks rushed from the shadows, all in disguise. They bellowed and howled, swinging their ragged, rusted blades as they attacked.

"Finally!" Holger roared with delight. "A *real* fight worthy of a Dwarf!"

The Dwarves started fighting the Gathlorks, only Vorgak and four more remaining back as the battle erupted around us. It was clear to all of us that the Gathlorks were falling quickly to the dwarven weapons and my captors were obviously not pleased, moving quickly to complete their task.

"We're leaving," Adriana snapped her fingers to Vorgak and jabbed a hand at the carriage before ordering Tristan silently to follow her.

Vorgak took a white cloth from his belt and quickly gagged me before throwing me backwards into the carriage. I landed hard amongst furs and linen, crushing my hands under my back and crying out in pain. The monster closed the door and locked it, the carriage moving within moments. I started struggling again, fighting my restraints, but the bindings were too firm and coarse for me to slip my wrists free.

I looked up to see Carden sitting with his back to the wall, his hands bound in front of him, his head slouching to his chest. Tallinn lay on her side opposite him, her wrists restrained behind her just as mine were. They were both bloodied and gagged, our attackers having beaten them after taking them from the warehouse.

It was obvious to me that there was no way out, no windows in the carriage apart from the barred one set into the door at the rear. Launching my feet into it proved useless, the door bolted firmly shut, but I kept trying, slamming the heels of my boots into the wood desperately and relentlessly.

Come on! Break! I have to get us out of here!

In only minutes the glow of Eilath's lights faded away into the dark sky above and there was only the silence of the roads and wilds. There were gaps in the walls of the old carriage, and I could see figures walking outside, most likely the Gathlorks escorting us, though the darkness and their dress made it impossible to tell.

I don't know how long I lay there after my struggles had fallen into stillness, the time feeling infinite. All I could do was try to shift so that my hands weren't being crushed beneath me, then lie there staring up at the shuddering ceiling.

Where are they taking us? I worried, pushing the cloth with my tongue, my jaw aching from the tight knot wedged into my mouth. *The master they're talking about has to be the Shadow Lord. The Gathlorks make that clear... Oh, Gods! What do we do?!*

I closed my eyes and tried to find mental release from this nightmarish state, but it was no use. Sleep came as easily as freeing my hands from the tight leather wrappings, so, not at all. I started contemplating our situation, specifically wondering why the Eilath guardsmen hadn't given chase.

There are a few options I can think of, I rationalised direly. *First, perhaps the Gathlorks fighting the Dwarves drew their attention away from us as a distraction. Or, maybe there were more of them ready to fight the guardsmen. The only other option I can think of makes me feel sick... Maybe someone was paid to look the other way while we were kidnapped... I truly hope not though...*

Hours felt to be passing me by, though I had no way of telling time. Outside the small barred window, I could see the colour of the sky lightening at last.

A groan came from behind me and I struggled to turn myself towards it. Carden was frowning deeply as he regained consciousness, his eyes blinking and squinting, blood staining his hair, left cheek, jaw and neck.

I let out a muffled sound and he looked to me, wobbling to his knees and grabbing my arm with his bound hands. Awkwardly, between the two of us, we got me sitting against the wall beside him, meeting each other's gaze as we breathed hard from the effort.

He reached out his hands to touch my face softly. I knew he was checking to see that I wasn't hurt, his gaze and his muffled voice confirming that.

I nodded that I was alright, and he seemed relieved as Tallinn sat up. She narrowed her eyes and frowned at our surroundings, instantly squirming against her restraints.

I looked up at Carden, feeling as if I could cry. He reached his arms out and slid them around me to hold me close, the ropes giving his wrists so little space to move. I rested my head on his chest, this embrace in bondage so bizarre. My sobs were quiet, but his awkward caressing on the bare skin of my shoulder blades was somewhat soothing, easing my fear as we now waited to see what would become of us.

* * * * *

Days and nights passed us with a deep, unyielding, stressful emptiness. All three of us were starving, but we were barely fed when the Gathlorks thought to feed us at all. Only once did Carden and Tallinn try to ask questions when our gags were loosened so that we could eat and drink. Vorgak simply glared at us and we were spoon fed the foul-tasting stew they had cooked up. I didn't dare to ask or even consider what it was made of.

Without any way to communicate, planning an escape had become almost impossible, yet the two Guardians still managed to find a way. Tallinn had been trying to work a large nail from the carriage wall with great difficulty, Carden having to take over since his hands were bound in front of him.

We were soon crossing a river bridge and passing along a thick forest road, the air growing colder. In another two days everything green vanished in the dark of night and jagged, pointed grey rocks surrounded us.

There came the sounding of a great horn unlike anything humans, elves or dwarves made, and some gigantic heavy iron thing began groaning. Those sounds woke us from the sleep we had fallen into, Carden holding me between his restrained arms again for comfort. The groaning of heavy metal sounded again as two great black watchtowers of demonic design appeared behind us, flanking a mammoth set of black iron gates.

Carden nodded to Tallinn and took the nail they had managed to pry from the wall. I pressed my back to the opposite wall and drew my knees close to my chest as I watched them work to pry Tallinn's restraints free with it.

Carden managed to loosen Tallinn's bonds and she pulled her hands free, letting the cloth that had gagged her hang from her neck. She quickly untied him, then they moved to me, taking the gag from my mouth first.

"Are you alright, your Highness?" she asked me quietly as Carden worked on my bonds.

I nodded. "Where are we?"

"I'm not sure," Tallinn admitted, glancing to the window as a third gate sealed with a heavy boom. "But it cannot be a good place."

"We've been heading north-east since the edge of the Nartarn'lath Mountains," Carden pointed out, finally freeing my hands to my relief. "There's only one place we might be going, though I dread to even consider speaking its name."

"What do we do now?" I looked between them for an answer as I rubbed my aching wrists and forced the feeling back into my fingertips.

"We're not more than four days from Nargilith, two from the river city of Orgilith," Carden theorised. "I think we should head for Orgilith and find a way to return to Eilath."

"We're in Gorvenna?" I was stunned.

He simply nodded.

"We should loosely tie ourselves again and make it seem that we are still helpless," Tallinn planned, having given this considerable thought. "When they remove us from this carriage, we let them think we're at their mercy, then we throw them into disarray," she looked to me. "When we make our move you *must* run, Princess."

"What about you?" I had a deeply unsettling feeling in my stomach about this.

"We'll join you as quickly as we can," Carden tried to reassure me. "Just find somewhere to hide and we'll find you. I'll also try to get your pendant from Tristan."

"Kill him if you get the chance," Tallinn snarled with disgust.

"Alright, let's get ourselves set up for this," Carden said and I let him retie my hands, though very loosely. I could easily slip my wrists free now.

He put the gag back in my mouth, then Tallinn tied his wrists again. He readied her as he had me and we sat in silence, Tallinn keeping the nail in her closed fist.

A putrid grey light filtered through the bars on the window, the air smelling of sulphur and ash. I felt like I could choke, my throat aching for water to drink despite the cold of this mysterious northern place.

Finally, we came to a stop and the door was flung open, the strange light blinding our unprepared eyes as Tristan and Vorgak climbed up into the carriage. The Wanderer took me by my shoulders as others reached in and grabbed at Carden and Tallinn. They took the gags off us and fed us cool, but tasteless water.

My boots touched a grey ashen ground, nothing green growing, the only trees surrounding us black and stripped of all leaves. The sky above was choked thick with strangling black ash clouds, green lightning striking violently with a hard crack. There was a large active volcano several miles to the west of where we stood, its fires glowing red at its peak. We were surrounded by jagged black peaks with sheer sides, pools of a green bubbling acidic liquid dotted about the barren landscape.

"Oh, Gods," Tallinn gasped in fear as a gathlork held her steady by her arms. "We're in the Grey Wastes!"

Carden looked to me with horror: "This... this is the Black Land of Gorth'lak!"

I wanted to scream and run, the nightmares I had suffered of stories of this place now threatening to come true. My chest was heaving hard enough that I thought it could crack as Tristan walked me around the carriage to face our ultimate destination.

Before us was a black iron and stone fortress that looked to have been built into the rocks. There were pointed battlements running through the cliffs hundreds of feet above us, sinister watchtowers rising from the jagged rocks. High above, there was a terrifying black tower reaching towards the sky with a smaller one connected by a walkway.

We stood before a long black bridge of steel and stone over a great chasm that encircled the front of the fortress, a gate and black guard walls flanking it on the far side from us. Beyond the chasm was an enormous wide staircase of black stone rising some fifteen feet or more up into the rocks to a gigantic set of black doors. They were flanked by four statues that were carved to look as if they were holding up the cliffs with their arms and shoulders, their faces deformed and their bodies straining under the weight.

Guarding the open doors of this evil place were the black armoured Shadow Knights, their faces hidden behind those skull-like masks, pikes in hand, swords at their hips and shields on their arms.

"Grishk'kinnar," Tallinn was shaking, terror in her eyes and voice. "The Black Doorway of Gorth'lak..."

I felt like I could die from the fear clutching at me. The thought of standing before the most terrifying fortress of the Shadow Lords was almost too much for me to take, my heart screaming and my mind numb, especially as I realised that I had dreamed of this place ever since I'd turned eighteen.

It was then that I noticed the two black haired women approaching us with their hoods drawn, Shadow Knights flanking them in a group of six with the Revenant right behind them. That only confirmed the Custodians' suspicions about the mysterious undead necromancer and his possible allegiances.

"My Ladies," Adriana bowed her head to them and smiled cruelly. "We have succeeded in our task."

"Indeed you have, Adriana," one woman spoke in a harsh, raspy voice, her skin white and tainted with greenish veins, her purely black eyes locking onto me.

She was with the Shadow Lord at Aneuran! I realised in horror as I recognised her. *The Witch that was there at the Basilica!*

"The Master will be pleased," the rasping woman strode towards me as I pulled back into Tristan's hold. "At last, the girl comes to us."

"She is rather pretty. Isn't she, Manth?" the other woman, who looked like the rasping woman's twin, spoke with a well-rounded voice, her skin more olive and her eyes green.

"She is," Manth hissed at me. "She looks almost exactly like her namesake. Do you not think so, Keilantra?"

Keilantra nodded with a cold smile. "I do, dear sister. His Lordship has chosen his victim well."

"Let us not keep the Master waiting," Manth looked to our abductors. "Bring the girl and her Guardian protectors to the throne room."

The two women turned their backs and started forward as we were shoved to follow. I looked to Carden and Tallinn, their focus strong and their conviction stronger. I saw the long nail from the carriage in Tallinn's hands, took a deep breath and braced myself.

Wordlessly, Tallinn shouted, snapping her hands free and stabbing the nail deep into the neck of the Gathlork holding her. At the same moment, Carden lashed out and took down his captor, landing a punch on another. The two Guardians snatched up the downed gathlorks' swords and began fighting the guards surrounding us.

I threw my foot back and caught Tristan in the groin, the man crying out as he fell to his knees as I slipped my wrists free of the ropes binding them.

"Princess, run!" Tallinn shouted at me and I threw myself into a sprint away from Grishk'kinnar's steps without a second thought.

"Stop her!" Manth screeched from behind me. "She must *not* get away! She must *not* be harmed!"

I ran hard and fast, my legs hurting and my body pleading for me to stop, but I knew I couldn't. I clutched the hems of my dress and forced all the strength I could manage into my legs, my mind blind to all but escape.

Suddenly, a terrible roar echoed above me and a great shape collided with the dusty grey ground before me, throwing a heavy, thick cloud of dirt into the air. I skidded to a stop as grey horns and crimson wings rose from the dust, a tail swishing at the dirt with a razor spiked tip.

I started to back away, breathing hard from running as a new terror clutched my heart. My widened stare stayed on the creature rising from the murky cloud, two glowing, molten orange eyes glaring down at me from its gargantuan form.

I turned to run, but I was stopped as a second shape smashed into the earth in the same way, cutting off my escape. Golden wings stretched out and clawed hands dug up the rocks as its terrifying glowing eyes snarled at me viciously. I had nowhere to turn, stuck between the two great beasts as they finally emerged from the dust clouds.

Two terrifying dragons glared and snarled down at me, both of them some twenty to thirty feet in size. One was golden scaled with six horns, largest to smallest from the centre of its skull down to its cheekbones, its snout short and rounded. Smaller horns of white bone ran down its neck and back, its tail tipped with an arrow shaped club. The second I had already seen during the fight in Aneuran; the same black armoured beast the Shadow Lord had summoned with his own Dragon Pendant.

"Well," he spoke in a deep, growling voice of great intelligence, "what have we here?"

I staggered back, darting my gaze over my shoulder as the gold dragon sniffed at me.

"A human woman-child," the gold dragon smirked. "How interesting..."

"Yes," the black dragon agreed. "An interesting little morsel indeed."

"I imagine she would taste divine, brother," the gold dragon chuckled, slithering his neck so that his face was close up to my right. "I haven't had noble-born human for quite some time."

A whimper escaped my mouth and I stumbled away, letting out a startled scream as the black dragon stomped its massive claw down behind me.

"Too small a meal, I'm afraid," he mimicked disappointment. "She could not satisfy *my* hunger."

I moved back, screaming and squeezing my eyes shut as the gold dragon stomped closer, both of them surrounding me so that there was no escape.

"The scent of her fear is intoxicating. Is not, Cathal?" the gold dragon asked the black dragon.

"It is, Kuldar," the black dragon agreed. "Yet, my Master would not be pleased to lose this one."

"Nor would my Mistress," Kuldar sighed. "But at least her attempted escape means we can toy with her."

"What do you want with me?!" I cried out in panic, looking up at them frantically.

"She demands an answer from *us*?!" Cathal questioned with amusement and laughed. "A spirited one, this human woman-child! How invigorating!"

"You... you serve the Shadow Lord?" I spoke in a softer voice, trembling uncontrollably.

"Why yes, little morsel, I do," Cathal confirmed, his face so close that his nostrils were venting his hot breath into my face. "And you... You are she; the doppelganger he seeks."

"I don't know what you're talking about," I murmured, gazing up at him fearfully.

"Does she lie, Cathal?" Kuldar snarled, making me stagger back again as he brought his face closer. "Or does she simply not know the Master's plans for her?"

"I think she lacks that knowledge, Kuldar," Cathal decided and stomped his right hand to the earth, dropping me to the ground with the shockwave.

I crawled on my back away from the sniffing maw of the Dragon, my hands scrambling behind me through the dirt, tears burning my eyes.

"Please," I pleaded, feeling so tiny as I stared into his glowing eyes. "Please... Let me go..."

"Do you really think pleading for your release will sway me, human?!" Cathal demanded in a loud, fierce voice, following me like a hunting predator. "If we so choose, we could end your existence with a burst of our fires! And *I* am he who holds dominion at the right hand of the Lord of Shadows himself!"

He snapped his jaws at me, and I screamed, throwing myself back in terror.

"I will not be commanded by some human woman-child!" he kept stalking towards me to my great panic, forcing me to scramble closer to his companion. "I will see you bleed for my Master, and you will beg for death before he is done with you!"

"Do you smell it, Cathal?" Kuldar came up on my right, my head only a few feet from his back legs now. "The scent of one of our kind lingers on her."

"Ah, yes. It does," Cathal sneered down at me. "But she does not come to help her young mistress. Without the heart-stone you are helpless, woman-child," he glared down at me, a look of disappointment in his glowing fire wrapped eyes. "But this little game has now ended, for I hear my Master's call for his prize."

I heard the crunch of boots on dirt and looked up to see the Revenant towering over me, impressive and terrifying. There really was no escape for me...

Chapter Twenty-Two
In Darkest Shadows

As the Revenant and I reached the great bridge with our dragon escorts, his hand squeezing my elbow, I saw the scene that awaited us. Gathlorks lay dead on the ground, but more were in their place, the Shadow Knights having stormed down from the black fortress to assist their allies. Adriana and Tristan were glaring at me, the man still seething from the low blow I had dealt him.

Keilantra and Manth stood before the bridge as the Revenant dragged me back to them, their eyes fierce and victorious. I couldn't help cringing before them.

I was yanked to a stop beside the Revenant, facing the two women, surrounded now by so many enemies. I gasped as I saw Carden and Tallinn, both battered, but alive, their hands tied behind them as they knelt on the stone ground with gathlorks holding swords to their throats.

Keilantra turned her harsh gaze to me and spoke coldly: "That was quite the surprise uprising the three of you tried to affect. Yet, it was ultimately fruitless. Now wasn't it, Princess?"

I just stared at the ground below her feet, my chest jolting with my harsh breaths.

"Let us take them to the throne room," Manth commanded in her hissing voice with a dark glare. "The Master grows impatient, and I will *not* keep him waiting."

The Revenant tightened his grip and led me across the bridge, my cooperation more out of numbness now rather than his forcefulness. I just lifted the edge of my skirt with my free hand so that I wouldn't slip and be punished for that too. Glancing over the edge of the bridge presented me the dizzying drop into the deep chasm, my head heating with a terrible ache and my stomach growing nauseous.

As we reached the stairs, I heard grunts from behind me and looked back past Tristan, Adriana and her men. Carden and Tallinn were being forced forward by the Gathlorks, the monsters showing them no mercy. I threw a saddened, apologetic look to Carden, his own regretful expression bringing me close to tears again.

As we stepped through the black archway and its open doors, I breathed in a loud, frightened breath and closed my eyes against fearful tears. I tried to convince myself that I was dreaming, but I knew better than that. This was too vivid to be anything but real.

The massive hallway seemed to stretch on forever, its highest points pitch black with deep shadows. Shade Seekers were floating through the halls, their glowing blue eyes staring from beneath their wrappings and shrouds, their ghostly hands drifting at their sides as they watched us pass in silence.

Being led up a long flight of stairs, we came to a massive hallway of black stone that was under the heavy watch of the Shadow Knights, two flanking the hall every few metres, each standing as still as statues. Black and crimson tapestries hung on the walls with the serpent insignia of Gorth'lak set upon them, lit only by what eerie light the sconces gave off.

We reached the far end and passed down another flight of stairs into an enormous cavern that seemed to go on forever above and below us. Only a long bridge gave us passage to the round platform supported by chains and iron beams set within the centre of the space. My heart sank as I recognised this terrible place of evil darkness from my nightmares; the same throne room I had seen the Shadow Lord occupying in my dreams now vividly present before me.

Manth gestured to the Revenant as she and her sister moved to flank the evil bat winged throne, the necromancer forcing me to my knees in the centre of the black marble floor. He pulled my arms behind me and I felt the cold iron of heavy shackles being locked around each of my wrists, a chain rattling loudly against the floor.

I looked over my shoulder to see Carden and Tallinn being made to kneel to my right, two Shadow Knights holding their black blades to their throats. Tristan, Vorgak and Adriana moved to stand to my left as the Gathlorks waited at the step from the bridge, the remaining Shadow Knights moving to surround us.

The Revenant stepped away and moved to stand behind me, leaving me to test my new restraints. I quickly learned that the chain was too short for me to stand up and bolted securely to the floor, keeping trapped submissively on my knees before the throne.

"Isn't this just perfect?" a familiar, sinister voice mewed from in front of me.

I looked up slowly, my heart freezing as I saw the black hooded figure sitting there upon the throne's red velvet seat. The Shadow Lord just smiled as he studied me with those glowing green eyes.

"Did I not tell you, Princess, that one way or another you would find yourself here as *my* prisoner?" he sounded smug, but I quickly decided it was more confidence in his voice than arrogance. "And behold how I was right, my prediction confirmed."

I was breathing quickly, my chest heaving and the muscles under the skin of my neck flexing rapidly. I was trembling, my eyes fighting back the increasing pressure of tears, my arms already straining and my legs aching from my position.

"Did you succeed in your second task, Wanderer?" the Shadow Lord looked to Tristan expectantly, his gaze cold and without mercy.

"I got it just as you commanded," Tristan nodded and opened his satchel, which I then noticed looked suspiciously heavy.

He withdrew the Nempanarth and I stared in shock as he handed it into Manth's waiting hands. The frightening woman ran her black eyes brightly over the evil book then twisted her dark lips into a smile.

"It *is* the Nempanarth, my Lord," she confirmed. "After all these centuries, it is returned to us."

He stole it! I can't believe this! I thought in dismay.

"And this," Tristan pulled my pendant from his belt pouch and held it up. "I took it from the girl just after we captured her and the two Guardians."

"Very good, Wanderer," the Shadow Lord nodded, smirking where he sat. "Hand it to Lady Keilantra, if you would be so kind."

Tristan paused as the other woman reached for it, hesitant to give it to her. "And what of our deal, my Lady?" he queried her suspiciously. "You swore to give me what's mine."

"And I shall," she assured him harshly, pushing her waiting hand closer to him. "*After* we return to my castle."

Slowly, begrudgingly, Tristan handed her my pendant and she clutched it tightly, staring at it like a greedy miser would gold.

The Shadow Lord turned his gaze to me, smiling as he savoured all of this. "I cannot begin to tell you how pleased I am to finally have you in my possession," he told me with what I could only describe as a sense of pleasure. "Too long have I waited for this very moment..."

"You... you don't scare me," I forced myself to sound strong as I glared up at him, flexing my aching hands behind me. "I know what you are now. I know *who* you are... *Morod.*"

Silence filled the chamber and I felt a haunted chill shredding my nerves, forcing a shuddering tremble to erupt through my body.

Morod smiled and leaned forward, his hands now on his knees: "So, you have learned the truth of who I am. Somehow, I knew you would, girl."

He rose to his feet and made his way down the steps, his dark robes trailing behind him with an evil grace unlike any other.

"In truth," he spoke softly as he studied my face, "I am glad that you know. It makes all of this that much easier for you to understand."

I shivered as he drew nearer to my shoulder, his gaze feeling like cold daggers cutting through my spine, right to my heart and freezing it solid.

"I assume you would now ask what it is that I wish from you?" he made sure I was looking up at him as he moved to one of the pylons at the edge of the platform and paused there, gazing at his fingers. "As you know, I do not possess a corporeal form. I am as the wind to the world; a living ghost in darkest shadows," he demonstrated his point, his hand passing through the steel pylon and emerging untouched. "With the items we have reclaimed from the Custodians of the Past," he explained, moving to my right side, making me shudder at his presence, "I can now be restored to the physical realm and reawaken all of my powers anew."

He knelt beside me and mimicked running his hand under my chin and jaw, the strange sensation making me shiver in disturbance. I managed to suppress my fear, staring him down with as much ferocity as I could muster.

"And that is why I have sought you since you were born," he told me, his eyes focused on my uneasy expression. "*You* are the only one who can bring me back from the Netherworlds in which your ancestor imprisoned me."

"H-how?" I simply asked, trembling uncontrollably.

"With your participation tonight in a ritual designed to do so," he answered evenly. "A resurrection ceremony of sorts. Will you consent?"

I stared at him in bewilderment. "Consent? You... you want my consent?"

He nodded: "In your consenting to the ritual and all it entails, the magic we use will be all the more powerful than if you were forced unwillingly."

I felt a smirk tug at my lips as a thought occurred to me, his need for my agreement to be involved never having crossed my mind before.

"And... what if I decide to refuse?" I met his gaze squarely and narrowed my eyes with a new strength.

Morod's expression fell and he stared at me with severity in his green eyes. I felt a small sense of victory as I watched him slowly stand and take a few steps back from me.

"You can't kill me," I reminded him. "You kept saying that you need me alive, so I know you can't."

"I could always torture you," he stated lowly, his every thought measured and deliberate, "force your compliance through pain, both physical and mental."

I almost laughed: "My uncle tried that, remember? And I didn't give in to him. I told you before that I *won't* give in to you either."

"I suspected as much," he said with a faintly cruel smile and snapped his fingers. "The boy."

"What?!" I lost my composure instantly as Carden was dragged forward by the Shadow Knights, immediately thrashing against my tight restraints.

Two of them pushed him to his knees and drew their black swords, the blades crossing in front of his neck so that they needed only to bring them together like a pair of sheers to do what I feared they were willing to.

"Don't do it, Leander!" Carden shouted as they held him steady. "Don't give him what he wants!"

In my peripheral I could see Tallinn struggling as a Shadow Knight forced her to stay put, its blade ready near her throat too.

"We are Guardians, Princess!" she stated sternly. "If our deaths can stop this abomination, then we will gladly die!"

Morod turned to me, standing between Carden and I, waiting expectantly for my answer as I kept trying to break free of the shackles on my wrists.

"If you refuse," he said with promise, not threat, "then my knights will kill the boy. If you refuse again, then they will kill the other girl," he held out his hands to his sides. "Regardless, you *will* participate, whether willingly, or by force once your friends are dead. The choice is yours, Princess."

I turned my eyes back to Carden, trembling as he breathed rapidly, struggling not to show his fear. He turned his green gaze to me and awkwardly shook his head, silently pleading with me not to give in.

Falling in love had never truly been something I had given much thought to any more than the thought of having to lose that love once I had it. Love had seemed so foreign to me, something I had only ever dreamed of; a beautiful concept within the pages of the books I adored reading. And now that I had come to know its touch, I never wanted to feel its absence again.

Where I had only felt pain and emptiness, he had shown me what it meant to truly be loved, and to love in return. I would do anything for him, because I knew in my heart – now and forever – that he was the One. He was truly my soul mate.

So, despite his protests, and my own dark, unrelenting fears of what the monster before us was proposing, I could make only one choice. After all, how could I possibly make any other? Especially if it meant losing him forever.

So, I chose the only alternative that I had left to me.

Alright...I'll... I'll do it..." I murmured, fighting back tears and ceasing my struggles as I glared at him. "But *only* on *one* condition."

"No!" Carden struggled, the Knights holding him back from me roughly. "Leander, no!"

"Go on," Morod eyed me, his interest piqued.

I tried to compose myself, trembling though I was: "I want your word that you won't kill Tallinn and Carden, or bring them any harm. You agree to this..." I felt sick as I vomited the last words out, "and... and I'll do whatever you want."

"Really?" he was intrigued.

"*Only* if you agree to this condition," I said firmly, though I was close to breaking down.

"What are you doing, Princess?!" Tallinn nearly shrieked from behind me. "*Don't* give him what he wants!"

I kept my gaze firmly locked with his, waiting for his response. He smiled faintly, holding his chin thoughtfully as he considered my proposal.

"You have my word," he said softly after a few moments of contemplation, nodding his agreement. "And a Shadow Lord's word *is* his *law*. I *cannot* break it."

A sort of hollow relief filled me as I let my head bow and my shoulders slump, the chains tightening against my back and wrists.

"The two Guardians are not to be harmed," Morod declared and nodded to his knights. "Secure them in the dungeons."

"Leander," Carden said hopelessly as he was dragged to his feet. "What have you done?"

I closed my eyes and sobbed behind the curtains of my hair, my heart breaking in my chest. I couldn't look at Carden and Tallinn as they were led away, shame filling me from the decision I had made.

They'll never forgive me for this, my heart ached at that thought as the room emptied and I was left alone to await my fate. *I've doomed us all...*

* * * * *

I couldn't tell how long I lay there alone in the silence of that dreaded throne room, shivering with the cold that flooded the air. My body shook and my teeth chattered behind my closed lips, my tears still wetting my cheeks even though my sobs had become less and far between.

The look on Carden's face haunted me in my loneliness, the disbelief and horror he had worn invading my thoughts. My heart ached as my mind raced with all that had happened since I had turned eighteen, and I thought that if there were any hope of changing all of this and starting again that I would take it.

I prayed to the God of Justice: *Thringar, please hear me. Save us from this nightmare... please. Stop them...* But after what felt like hours, I let my mind fall silent and I lay there quietly, waiting, staring at the floor in front of me.

I just want to go home! I thought for the millionth time since Arvon had fallen. *I want to see my parents again! Gods, I wish they were here...*

Then, as if in answer to my silent cries, there came a voice from the darkness. "Leander?" it was male and so familiar, my heart warming as soon as I heard it.

I looked up, my blue eyes searching the darkness, my chest and breath shuddering with silent sobs. I moved to my knees again, a figure catching my gaze as my heart skipped within my breast.

It... it can't be...

My father smiled at me, his greying brown hair hanging to his neck, his blue eyes bright as he saw me. He had on the same type of blue and gold tunic as he had most commonly worn, his princely crown set neatly on his head.

"F-Father?" I couldn't believe my eyes, tears of joy replacing the ones of fear that stained my cheeks.

"It is so good to see you, my sweet daughter," he moved forward and dropped to his knees, wrapping his arms around me. "By the Gods, I feared that I would never see you again. I prayed that I be given the chance to hold my little girl once more. And here you are..."

I was stunned, his touch so real and so right, his heart strongly beating and his breath warm on my neck. He was real. I started to cry and buried my face into his shoulder; his smell, his touch, all the same as I remembered.

"Shh, it's alright, Leander," he soothed, stroking my back gently. "I'm here."

"I thought you were dead," I sobbed, looking up into his face. "I mean, you died... in my arms..."

"Do not try to understand it," he told me, gazing into my eyes with love and care. "Just be glad that we are reunited."

I nodded, closing my eyes for a moment and taking some deep breaths. "I just... I can't believe you're really here, Father," I looked into his eyes tearfully. "I've missed you so much."

"And I you, my sweet girl," he replied and frowned sadly at me. "How it pains me to see you like this..."

I pleaded quietly: "Then help me... Please... Please, Father, help me... Before they come back... Please..."

He touched my cheek gently and gave me a sympathetic expression: "Oh, my poor daughter... if only I had the desire to..."

I stared at him in confusion, not certain I had understood him: "W-what did you say?"

He stood up and stared down at me, his expression suddenly very cold: "You've never lived up to my expectations, or your mother's. What sort of Queen sobs on her knees before one who could be her greatest ally?"

"I... I don't understand," I was trembling, his words like poison to my ears.

"Of course you don't," my Father said coldly, crossing his arms and glaring at me. "You'd rather play the child in your little storybooks than understand how the world *really* works. You weren't worthy of the name we gave you..."

"Who are you?" I demanded in a murmur, glaring through angry tears. "You're *not* my Father. He would *never* say such horrible things."

"You're right," he agreed, his eyes glowing that same evil green as the Shadow Lord's as he vanished, my Mother's face appearing in his place. "I am your mother, Leander, dear..."

I was breathing hard, trying to pull away as I stared at her, the chains rattling with my movement and tightening on my wrists. She looked like my mother, dressed and walked like her, even smelled like her, but she wasn't.

"There, there my girl," she reached towards me. "Everything is going to be alright..."

"Don't touch me!" I pulled as far back from her as the chains would allow, straining where I knelt. "You're not my Mother either! What are you?! Why are you doing this to me?!"

"Intriguing, is it not, Princess?" I looked over my left shoulder to see Morod's black form slowly stepping into my view.

"How are you doing this?!" I demanded of him; my chest so tight that I could barely breathe.

"This is not *my* doing," the Shadow Lord confessed, and I immediately knew it was the truth.

I turned to my mother and stared up into her eyes, trembling with fear at the thought of what I now faced.

"Who are you?" my voice was quiet, trembling just like my shoulders and spine were.

She changed again with the warping of black smoky shadows and I recoiled in haunted terror: "Perhaps I am an old friend, Leander," Mithras was standing before me, dressed in his armour and his blue cloak. "Perhaps I have returned to offer you guidance as I once did."

"Mithras?! No... no you're not him!" I shook my head, my mind and heart hurting.

"I am anyone I choose to be, child," Mithras said darkly, beginning to pace around me as Morod watched on with dark amusement. "I am all those who are both living and dead..." he turned to smoke and Aislinn appeared in his place, dressed in a beautiful blue and white gown, her dark hair hanging long to her hips: "Your dearly beloved sister..." she became Fawkner: "A trusted friend who has sought your forgiveness..." then, he became Joran: "A warrior pledged to your life service, Sarissi..."

I tried to pull away as he moved to my right and shifted through those shadowy wisps to become Ellora, the Elven Huntress eyeing me calmly.

"A once loyal companion and friend of your bloodline," she said, though her tone was strange and not like her at all.

She shifted again and Tallinn faced me with a severity and coldness that was unlike her, dressed in her cloak and full Guardian armour.

"Those who protect you," she stated in a grave, serious tone, "who swore to see you safeguarded against all evil."

Then she became Aldwyn, but he didn't speak, Holger appearing next, and last Dolin.

"Allies who pledge their skills to your needs," the Dwarf stated deeply and gruffly. "Aye, always at your side, lassie..."

"Please..." I begged in a whisper, trembling so hard now it hurt. "Stop this..."

His form shifted and Tristan's face stared down at me from beneath his reddish gold hair, his smile spreading beneath his neat beard.

"Even one you trusted who became your betrayer," he said with a cruel smirk. "I can be anyone..."

He shifted again and I started breathing harder, almost whimpering at the face before me.

"I am even the one you love most," Carden said, crouching down before me and touching his hand to my cheek. "The one person you would sacrifice yourself for. The *only* person you *have* sacrificed yourself for."

I jerked away and shook my head. "No! No, you're not him! You're *not* Carden!"

"That's where you're wrong," he said, standing as the black wisps covered him again.

I stared up at the new face this daemon wore in terror, the one face I hadn't expected to see before me.

The girl was dressed in a long flowing gown of black silk, a hood drawn over her face from the long sleeved, sheer, black over-robe that trailed behind her. Her skin was fair, her hair dark auburn, her face no older than eighteen winters. She pushed the hood back and met my blue eyes with those frightening glowing green ones, a cruel smile tugging at her *very* familiar lips.

"I am everyone," she said, "even you, Princess."

How is this happening?! She looks just like me!

The other, darker Leander looked down at me as Morod moved closer into my view, her grace and poise so demonically perfect, her appearance a near flawless copy of my own. She stood before me, as beautiful as she was terrible, making me feel lesser in comparison.

"W-what are you?!" I stammered in terror, unable to take my eyes off her face. "Why do you look like me?!"

She answered in my own voice: "I am the Darkness from which all darkness is born... I cultivate nightmares and destroy dreams... I bring Order to Chaos and command all the dark legions of the Void," she moved closer towards me, staring down at me as Morod stayed by her right shoulder. "I am the Shadow that rules all others," she continued, an iciness to her voice that mine didn't have. "I live in the hearts of all beings and urge them towards Evil's embrace."

She smiled coldly at me and I pulled back as she leaned towards me. Our eyes were all either of us focused on, hers cruel and confident, mine filled with nothing but fear.

"I *am* the Darkest Shadow," she whispered as if it were some terrible secret that could end the world.

I felt numb with a terror that surpassed even that which I knew in the presence of Lord Morod, now a helpless prisoner on my knees before the greatest demonic evil the world had ever known.

"What... what do you from me?" I whimpered, so scared that I was certain I could faint dead away.

"Just you," she replied, straightening up. "I thought I would offer you a chance to choose your fate. Join with us and I shall grant you *so many* rewards..."

"Why would I ever want that?" I demanded, though I sounded so tiny and weak.

"Would you not rather be on the winning side when all is said and done?" the Darkest Shadow asked, the mere fact that it was my face and voice before me beyond frightening and bizarre.

"I don't want any part of what you're offering," I told her, trying hard to reclaim some composure out of all of this. "I'm not evil..."

"There is Darkness in your heart," the evil Leander said, holding up her right hand to call forth the same flame in her palm as that which Morod used. "Imagine the power you could possess if you gave in to it. Think of all that you could have and achieve by siding with us," she closed her palm, snuffing out the flame and moving to Morod, turning her eyes back to me. "Think of all the *pleasures* you might enjoy."

She reached out her hand to Morod and somehow touched his hideous cheek. He smirked down at me as she turned to him, making sure I was watching. I cringed away as they kissed deeply and passionately, my stomach churning at the sight of my own face kissing his.

"Embrace this, Princess Leander," the Darkest Shadow turned to me from breaking their embrace. "Stand at Lord Morod's side as his greatest ally, and you will gain my favour. You cannot deny the evil within your heart..."

"I'm not evil," I repeated, my voice shaking and tears burning my eyes. "And I won't *ever* join you. You're not me... you're a daemon pretending to be me. I'm *nothing* like you..."

She closed her eyes and tilted her head back, drawing in a long, deliberate breath before looking to me again: "If that is your wish, then I will gladly grant it."

Morod gestured to the doorway behind me and six Shadow Knights surrounded us. Two of them moved forward and unchained me, brought me to my feet, then tied my wrists with leather bindings in front of me.

"I gave you the chance of aiding us willing," the Darkest Shadow said with all seriousness, locking her gaze with mine. "Yet, you have elected to remain weak and a victim rather than a powerful Queen of Darkness. How disappointing."

"The time has come," Morod moved past her to stare down at me. "The ritual is about to commence."

The Shadow Lord and the Darkest Shadow both swept past me, the Shadow Knights surrounding me and making me follow them.

We left the throne room and they took me along corridors and down winding stairs through what I could only guess was the cliffs that covered most of Grishk'kinnar. It felt like an eternity was passing me by, my nerves stinging inside of me as we travelled down through the rocky archways supported by black steel. There was no end in sight, and I couldn't help fearing what would become of me.

At last we came to two large doors of black iron and entered into another enormous chamber, this one more like some kind of rounded amphitheatre beneath the cliffs.

The room was full of Shadow Knights guarding the outer perimeters, forty men and women in black hoods and robes present around the central space, their faces shrouded by black and silver masks. Their presence was terrifying.

Morod and the Darkest Shadow led the way to the central space where eight black stone pillars were set to hold the domed ceiling, eight pedestals of the same material set before them. Attached to these pillars and seated on the ground were eight people, all gagged with their wrists chained above their heads. They were trembling with fear, each man and woman struggling desperately to get free.

In the centre of the space there were two black marble altars, one already occupied by something covered by a cloth. The second had a silvery cushion set at one end with shackles bolted into the top corners, another two at the other end closer together.

Manth stood beside a black marble throne, the Nempanarth in one hand and a sinister black staff in the other. The staff was topped with a bat winged design, an enormous emerald set into the centre of the black ring between them.

The Revenant moved forward from the opposite side of the chair and took my arm, the Shadow Knights turning and heading back to the doors to guard the entrance.

I took in all the faces around me nervously. Keilantra stood beside Manth with her hood cast back, a black-haired man standing at her left shoulder wearing the black and gold heraldry of a Gorvennan Royal Knight. Beside each of the eight prisoners there stood a loyalist to Morod. I could only guess that they were his highest-level disciples.

Adriana was clear to me, gazing out from beneath her hood beside a frightened young Ivanstenian woman, her fangs gleaming as she sneered at me. Across from her, I recognised the shrouded and armoured reptilian beast from the Under Roads that had called itself the Unseen. I could see its face as it was clicking its nasty, gnashing jaws, its red eyes surveying all the victims before it hungrily.

The other six I had never met before; one a very large, burly man with a distinctly wolfish quality to him. I immediately thought of the story of werewolves my grandfather had told me as a child. Next to him was a man who resembled an elf, but his skin was paler and almost luminescent, his eyes a deep red and his hair bright white. I knew instantly that he was a Dark Elf from the Blackfelds in the far east.

There was a man who looked like a smoother version of Morod, his nose a mound of white flesh with flaring slits for nostrils, his eyes a strange yellowish hue where they should have been white. A large orc stood beside him, dressed in heavy armour with a black hood and cloak. His upward pointing bottom teeth were sharp and yellowed, his greenish brown skin like leather.

Nearer the throne stood a man who looked to be made of individual rocks, his eyes glowing red and strange markings covering the exposed parts of his body. He was very large and reminded me of the golems in the Guardian Trials. On the other side of the throne, there was a figure dressed entirely in black, his hood drawn, and his face hidden beneath a cloth mask. What skin I could see was greying and corpse-like, his eyes completely white; a sword at his hip, and steel gauntlets hidden under his sleeves.

Too scared to keep looking at them, I found Tristan easily, standing just outside the circle of pillars, Vorgak and a number of gathlorks with him. On their knees amongst them were Carden and Tallinn, both gagged and restrained by the monstrous beasts.

"You said you wouldn't hurt my friends!" I turned to Morod angrily as we stopped by the altars.

"And I will not," he replied truthfully. "Unless *you* decide to resist."

He moved to stand by the throne, a giant black and emerald eye built as a frame behind it. The Darkest Shadow moved to stand there, my eyes looking back to Tallinn and Carden as she did. They were flicking their gazes between me and her with unrelenting confusion.

I know how they feel, I thought.

The Revenant released my restraints and moved to stand by the first altar with its strange grey shroud.

"The First and the Dire," Morod spoke calmly and gestured towards me. "Please secure the Princess."

Manth pointed to the altar as the golem man and hooded ghost left their place and came towards me. "Lay down, girl," she ordered me.

I threw a look to Carden and Tallinn, so much regret filling me at having consented to this. Hesitant, but willing, I sat down on the alter and lay back, resting my head on the pillow and letting my arms lie at my sides. The two haunting disciples came over and set to work, the ghost creature taking my left wrist and moving it to rest above my shoulder, my forearm kept straight. He started securing the cold shackle while the golem man removed my boots and placed my ankles into the two closely bolted restraints beside them. The ghost creature then secured my right wrist and the two of them moved away, leaving me with my knees bent and my legs together.

I looked to Morod apprehensively, moving my shoulders awkwardly to free my hair: "If you needed my consent to be here, then why do I have to be restrained?"

He moved to my right and stood over me, his gaze frightening and coarse as he smiled darkly.

"Because," he said softly, "we need you still for the ritual and you will not remain so unrestrained. Not when the pain starts."

I stared at him in horror as he turned to the other altar, immediately tugging at my restraints desperately.

"I am sure you wonder what the ritual entails, Princess," he assumed. "As you can see, there are eight disciples here beside the pillars; my eight most powerful and loyal followers below my inner circle. They have each brought me a sacrifice..."

"You're... you're going to kill these people?!" I stared at him in horrified disbelief.

He nodded: "Using the eight Orbs of Darkness, the Darkest Shadow will devour them to grant me my physical form."

"And what about me?" I asked uneasily, trembling at the described image of what he was planning. "Are you going to kill me too?"

Morod shook his head and stood over me again, mimicking running his hand over my face, neck and breasts, drawing sharp breaths of panic from my lungs.

"*You* will *not* die," he replied, stepping backwards to the other altar. "The ritual requires the presence of both the doppelganger descendant of the champion who condemned me," he sneered, "*and* the Champion herself..."

The Revenant removed the shroud on the altar, and I screamed, closing my eyes and turning my face away from the desiccated remains of Leander the First; grey haired, dusty and almost just bones.

"A sort of family reunion for you," Morod was enjoying how he was tormenting me with all of this. "It is almost like a window into your future, is it not?"

"Why are you doing this?!" I glared up at him, trying hard not to look at my ancestor's ancient corpse.

"Because it is necessary *and* it amuses me," he replied and moved to take his seat. "The rest you can learn as we proceed. Manth, if you would be so kind."

Manth moved forward, her hood drawn over her long dark hair. She handed the staff to her sister as she began speaking in a harsh, hissing language that I couldn't understand, the Nempanarth open in her left hand, her right held towards Morod. Then, the Witch moved to stand over my ancestor's remains and held her hand over the ancient skull. She uttered more of the demonic language before turning towards me. She stood at my head, my struggles against my restraints passing ignored by her sinister coal coloured eyes. She just held her hand above my face and spoke the unsettling hisses again before standing between the altars and facing Morod.

"Disciples," she hissed in her sinister, wispy voice, "place your orbs upon the pedestals before your offerings."

The eight disciples each took a small black crystal ball that fit easily in the palm from eight black hooded women that I guessed were like priestesses or lesser servants.

So, it's clear that the Citadel was attacked for these orbs, I thought grimly. *Fawkner, Aldwyn and Ellora are not going to be pleased... Gods, I wish they were all here...*

"Speak the words and offer your gifts to our Master," Manth instructed the disciples.

The eight spoke in Common language all at once, their timing perfect as they placed the orbs on the pedestals, their victims struggling and thrashing desperately to escape their fates: "To the One who has been chosen by the majesty that is our God-King, in honour of his greatness and his power, we offer these living souls of the World of Light to die that he may be restored to lead us once more. We pray to the Darkest Shadow; bestow your favour upon our Master, and restore his physical presence that he may offer us his blessings to serve him in conquering this weak, sunlit world for the Shadows..."

The Darkest Shadow moved from her place behind Morod, throwing me a coldly evil smile as she passed that made ice run through my spine. She stood in the centre between the two altars and faced Morod, her hands by her sides.

"By my power," she said in her dark version of my voice, her eyes glowing brightly as green flames started to slip up across her shoulders and limbs, "I accept these offerings of mortal souls to restore my most loyal servant to the physical world..." the voice changed and became more demonic as she spoke, the flames growing in intensity over her black clad form.

Shadows rippled around her and the evil copy of my face erupted into a terrifying concentration of supernatural green flame. My nightmares returned as I stared up at the black figure made of shadows and wreathed in green flames, the fires seeming to be growing out of its body rather than just around it. Where its eyes should be there were just these orbs of green fire burning with evil ferocity.

The Darkest Shadow uttered the same language Manth had been speaking in its harsh, guttural voice, which I guessed was Gorth'lakian. Flames exploded out from its body in eight terrifying pillars, passing through the orbs and burrowing into the eyes of the eight screaming victims.

I screamed and closed my eyes as their cries echoed through the chamber with the roar of the supernatural flames.

"My favour..." the Darkest Shadow spoke in a haunting, demonically evil voice, "has been granted!"

The flames retreated and engulfed it as I opened my eyes. The Darkest Shadow roared, and all the green fire was suddenly extinguished. The shadowy daemon closed its fire filled eyes, then faded away, leaving us there with the charred and smoking ruins of its victims still chained to the pillars, the eight crystal orbs glowing with fading energy.

Morod stood from his throne and Keilantra gave him the staff, the Shadow Lord somehow able to hold it.

Manth set the Nempanarth down on a black table, then took a sinister stone knife and an ornate black and silver chalice in her hands. Keilantra took a ceremonial water pitcher and stood ready as Manth approached my ancestor's corpse.

The Revenant held his hand over the remains and a bone drifted up with a sickening snap of old sinew as if it were being called by the sparking, rippling red energy surging over his gauntleted hand. He closed his fist and the bone ground itself into the chalice, turning to dust.

"The Bonemeal of a Great Champion, long since dead," Manth hissed as the last of the bone fell into the chalice, "to grant physical shape..."

She turned to me with the knife and I started panicking, trying to get free. The Revenant moved with her and grasped my right hand tightly in his metal clad fingers. As he untied my pale blue sleeve's ribbons to expose the skin from my wrist to my elbow my mind raced with all sorts of terrible thoughts and fears.

Manth pressed the blade into my inner forearm below my wrist and I screamed in agony as my blood broke free. She began collecting it in the chalice, tears burning my eyes as my shoulders pressed to the altar to arch my back against the agony.

"The Blood of her Doppelganger Descendant," Manth hissed viciously, sneering as she inflicted this slow agony on me, savouring my desperate screams, "to gain the Life Energy needed to exist in the mortal realms..."

She took away the blade and I eased back, breathing hard as I looked down at the deep cut that ran halfway towards my elbow, my snowy white skin stained red as my blood trickled to the altar's smooth top and my nerves burned with agony. It hurt too much to even try to move, even my pulse causing me pain.

Keilantra moved forward and poured water from the pitcher into the chalice as Manth continued her chant: "The Purest Waters of the World to cleanse away the incorporeal," she started stirring the mixture with the blade, "these three components together granting new life."

Morod stepped from his throne and brought the staff with him in his left hand as Manth held the chalice ready. I suddenly grew worried that the Revenant still stood at my head, fearing that they were planning to do more to me. I tugged at the shackles, letting out a painful whimper at trying to move my wounded right arm. She had crippled me with her cut in one easy movement, leaving me now with only one arm to defend myself, if I could even manage to get free.

"With the Staff of the Great Gorth Lavelle, first of the Shadow Lords," Manth declared as she stood before Morod, clutching the chalice with both hands, "you are granted the divine right to rule this Dominion. Drink, Lord of Grishk'kinnar, and you shall begin your restoration."

Morod smiled and nodded once beneath his hood: "As Lord Gorth Lavelle, Lord Everild and Lord Heskath were once restored from the Netherworlds before me, I now accept the Gift of Restoration."

She smiled and tilted the chalice so that he could drink the contents. I gagged and had to look away, trying hard not to think of what he was tasting.

"The Descendent of the Champion," Manth turned to me with the chalice, her eyes harsh, a cruel sneer now on her face, "has consented to her participation in the Restoration of Lord Morod. Princess Leander Idona Aldrich the Second: drink now and grant him the gift he seeks..."

"What?!" I nearly screamed. "No! No, I won't! I WON'T!"

"Hold her," Manth commanded and the Revenant secured my thrashing shoulders.

The Witch came towards me and pressed the chalice towards my lips, but I tried desperately to pull my face away. The Revenant held my head steady and I clamped my mouth shut, this action angering the evil woman. She dug her long purple nails into my wounded and bloodied right forearm, drawing a heavy scream from my lips.

They forced all that remained of the foul concoction into my mouth, tears blinding me as Keilantra held my sternum and legs against my struggles to aid them, the Gorvennan Knight helping her.

"Don't let her spit it out, Ulric!" she commanded.

"Yes, my Queen," the Knight nodded, covering my mouth with one hand as Manth took the chalice away.

I screamed through the foul powdery liquid, tasting my own blood mixed with my ancestor's bone dust. I could feel it burning my sinuses and feared that one cough would choke me and expel it from my nose, worsening this already horrific experience. I struggled, squeezing my eyes shut against painful tears, desperately screaming and crying for this to end.

"Make it easier on yourself, girl," Manth hissed viciously down at me, meeting my frightened, tear filled blue eyes with her sinister black ones. "Just swallow it and we'll be done."

I tried to scream "no" but that just helped the heavy mouthful of foulness to slip down my throat. I held it in my mouth, determined not to swallow it.

"Enough of this childishness," Ulric declared and put his other hand over my nose.

I stared at him wide eyed and tried to fight the pain that was building in my lungs. A pressure was mounting in my face and I squeezed my eyes shut to try to fight it off. Finally, I couldn't hold on and I reluctantly swallowed.

"There's a good girl," Ulric smirked at me as he let go of my face.

I choked and cried out in distress, the taste burning my tongue and fouling my throat as they took their hands from me.

"Oh Gods!" I cried, closing my eyes and spitting out what I could, still coughing as if I'd nearly drowned.

"Now," Manth took the Nempanarth and read from its black pages, "with this wine, two are joined to restore one. And with an intimate act, she will give of her essence, and the Lord of Shadows will be corporeal, and shall regain all the power he once possessed."

I looked up at her in terror, fearing her words. *Wait... What does she mean by "an intimate act"? He's not... They wouldn't... Oh, please, no! Not that!*

"My Lord," Manth turned to Morod and gestured to me. "Partake of her essence, drink deep her future and you will be fully restored."

Morod turned to me and started moving to the altar. I caught a glimpse of Carden and Tallinn, the Gathlorks holding Carden back as he violently struggled in their grasps. He was fearing that Morod would do the same thing I was, Tallinn averting her gaze with tears running down her cheeks.

I tried to break free, ignoring the cutting pain in my arm, but the shackles refused to give. I pinned my thighs together in anticipation, knowing that it was a defence these monsters could easily breach.

"Please... please, don't!" I cried frantically as I looked up at him, shaking my head desperately. "Don't do this!"

"Be calm, Princess," Morod whispered, leaning down towards me. "It will all be over in not but a minute."

I shook my head, tears streaking my face as my voice became softer: "Please, don't... please..." but my pleas did nothing.

I pulled back into the altar, his horrid visage so close to my face that I could feel the heat of his breath on my chin and cheeks. His hand reached out and pressed to my neck, his skin clammy and coarse. I sobbed helplessly as I felt his lips press into mine, my heart lurching in my chest as tears poured down my face.

My eyes closed tight, and I wished that I couldn't feel this violation, though it wasn't what I had expected. His other hand pressed to my right cheek, his fingers curling behind my nape to hold my head steady. That's when I felt the strange draining pull inside my chest, and I jerked against his foul intimate touch even more fervently.

I opened my eyes as pain filled me and I screamed against his kiss, the pain growing worse with each second of time that passed. He pulled back, his mouth open as a strange white energy began rising like mist from my lips and into his. I couldn't breathe and my head was spinning. I tried to resist, but it was useless, all of my attempts failing as my strength and energy reached their limit.

The last thing I saw was his cruel smile as he closed his lips and devoured the energy he had stolen from me, a heavy, dizzying, nauseating swell overwhelming my skull and causing my eyes to go dark...

Chapter Twenty-Three
The Mercy of Fiends

S lowly, the world returned, and I became aware of my surroundings. I opened my eyes to find that I lay staring up at a black marble ceiling, a large circular stained-glass window set above my head letting the glow of red, orange, maroon and gold light fall across my sheet wrapped body. I was nestled amongst silken crimson pillows and black sheets, still wearing my dress and leggings, but no boots, my feet left bare.

Sitting up in the bed, I didn't bother to worry when my right sleeve slid down my arm and my shoulder was exposed, my attention entirely focused on this strange room that I had come to find myself in. It was like palatial quarters in a palace, but with a sinisterly dark theme, crimson curtains with black ropes bunching their middles hanging all around. There was a carpet of black and crimson set on the floor at the edge of the large, beautifully carved ebony bed that I lay in, two chairs of the same make set there with crimson cushions.

A mirror was to my right, allowing me to see my reflection. I didn't look different, that much I could say with gladness and relief, except for perhaps looking a little thinner because of my lack of decent food and rest. My hair was messy, and I brushed it with my fingers to regain some control of the wayward strands, my clothing rumpled from my strange sleep.

I noticed then that there was a large archway that opened onto a balcony to my left. I turned my head to see a black tower partially visible from where I now sat with my left knee bent. In the distance, I could see the glowing maw of Dread Mountain, foul black smoke rising to choke the air, the Black Peaks a distant shadowy line farther away. The sky was reddened with the mountain's flames, but the air was cool, drawing a shiver through my shoulders and urging me to keep my feet shielded by the bedcovers.

I realised then that I was not alone.

He stood with his back to me, his grey hands behind him, the long fingers of his right-hand gripping around his left wrist. He was dressed in his dark sorcerer's robes, but not his hooded cloak. That was hanging on a coat rack beside the large black doors opposite the foot of the bed. His bald grey head was turning as he surveyed the view outside, his ears pointed, but not like an elf's.

I wanted to run, but I was afraid to even try to move knowing that he could so easily hurt me without effort. I must have breathed loudly or shifted and caused the bed to creak, because he straightened his back and spoke in his gently chilling tone.

"Awake at last," he observed with what sounded like quiet relief. "I admit I had worried that we had damaged you beyond repair. Yet, I was able to heal you."

I raised an eyebrow at him, not sure what to say or do.

"Your arm," he reminded me. "Manth was a little overzealous when she harvested your blood. She cut nearly to the bone, but I knitted your flesh back together."

I lifted my right hand, flexing my fingers experimentally and studying my white flesh with worried eyes. There was no pain and only a fading scar where the terrible wound had been torn into my skin.

"As for the rest," he went on, still staring at the sky, "I did what I could to lessen your pain, though I chose not to cure it. That will come in time."

He turned and I saw his face in all its terrible entirety. His irises were glowing as he studied me with a look of strange care and attraction. It made me shudder.

"Where am I?" I asked softly, glancing towards the door, my voice raw with my dry throat.

"My personal chambers," he replied, watching me from where he stood. "I decided not to condemn you to a dungeon after the strain the ceremony had on you," he analysed me for a moment before adding: "You must be thirsty after all that. Please. Permit me."

He crossed the room to where a silver pitcher was waiting beside two silver goblets. He took the pitcher in his hand, the mere fact that he could do so astonishing me. I could only watch as he poured water into one of the goblets, then set the pitcher back where it was. He scooped the goblet up in his hand and strode towards me in a sweep of black robes, offering it to me.

Seeing my uneasy expression, he said evenly: "It is not tainted, if that is your concern. It is merely spring water. Drink."

Hesitantly, I took the cup from him and drank slowly, the cool water both refreshing and stinging. I felt as if there were grains of sand trapped in the lining of my throat, scratching and grating with the passage of the water, itching inside me and making my voice hurt. Still, I needed this and I thirstily swallowed back all of the water.

He took the silver cup from me when I was done and returned it to the table. "There. That must feel better. Does it not, Princess?"

I didn't say anything as he turned back to the view, instead hugging my knee with both hands, feeling tense.

"Is it not beautiful?" he mused as he observed all that lay before us. "My land truly is the embodiment of Order brought to Chaos."

"That depends on who you ask," I said quietly, watching him as he turned to me again. "I think it's... grey... cold... and lifeless."

314

"Perception is what defines reality," Morod said as he approached me, running his right hand against one of the curtains, making it sway. "Until recently, my reality was one of immaterial existence. I cannot begin to tell you how it feels to," he chuckled lightly and looked to me with bright eyes, "*feel* again."

He sat down on the side of the bed, so close to me that I felt like he was invading on me once more and I had to suppress my urge to jerk away.

"In twelve hundred years I had forgotten the taste of food, the cooling relief of water, the caress of the wind," he reached out and ran his hand along my right wrist, "the touch of another living being..."

I pulled away and pushed myself further up the bed, turning my eyes to the covers.

"You fear me, girl," he observed, moving closer to me. "But you and I have already shared an intimacy I have not with any other in many centuries..."

My jaw shook though I tried to keep it still, my body trembling and my eyes watering with the disgust of what he had done to me. Though it hadn't been sexual, the mere fact that he had demanded my consent demonstrated how alike his actions against me were to rape. That thought made me tremble and fight the urge to let more tears flow.

"I never.... I never agreed to that," I murmured, on the verge of sobbing. "What else have you done to me?"

"Fear not, you remain pure," he promised, and I believed him because that was one of the few parts of my body that didn't hurt. "Though," he placed his hand on my thigh and I shuddered at the sensation with fear, "I must admit that the thought had *indeed* occurred to me..."

I shook my head, unable to speak for fear that I would start to cry and beg.

"Have you ever wondered what it is to taste carnal pleasures, Leander?" he asked me.

"Don't..." was all I could say, though it was barely a whisper as it escaped my lips.

"There are other meanings to such words," he told me, drawing nearer to me and forcing me to lie back, my hands in the pillows beside my shoulders. "Understand that I have not engaged in such things for so long..."

I tried to hold still as his right hand pressed to my neck and slipped the fabric of my dress from my left shoulder. His flesh felt dry on my softer, smoother skin, so coarse and without human warmth. A whimper escaped me as I felt his touch, leaving me trembling and feeling a pressuring sickness inside me at the thought of what he was planning to do. I couldn't even think, my mind numb with the simple fact that he had me alone in *his* bed, leaning over me as he contemplated forcing further intimacy on me than a mere kiss. The image of such a thing was like a horror story in my mind and I felt like I could scream at any second, though I didn't.

"It has been so long since I felt the warmth of a woman's flesh," he mused, more curious than aroused. "It is... so soft..."

His hand travelled over my collarbones to rest just beneath the edge of my dress, the cringe that went through me at his touch hurting me. I tried to blind myself to it, to imagine that it was Carden touching me instead. But it was impossible.

"Your heart is strong," he stated, drawing my nervous gaze. "It beats well beneath your breasts. Your unease, of course, is understandable."

"I don't want this," I whispered, trying to hold back tears from this new violation. "Not from you..."

"I could show you so much, Leander," he told me, meeting my eyes, his other hand touching to my cheek and neck as if he loved me. "I could gift you with so much more than what I already have."

I frowned at him, though it was more fearful than anything else, the wetness of my tears starting to push past my eyes. *Please, make him stop touching me!*

He stroked my face and I held still, my back hurting from the tightness of my muscles. My breaths shook and I felt like crying could come so easily.

"You are so young and beautiful," he considered me, savouring my appearance with so much appreciation. "To think of what ravages time could inflict upon such beauty is almost enough to make me grieve... However, time can never harm you now..."

I looked at him with a harder expression, my jaw trembling at his words: "*What* did you *do* to me?"

"I took away your time, your aging, your change and your future," he spoke such terrible words.

I looked at him in utter horror, wanting to pull away and escape him, but unable to move both due to fear and to his close presence.

"How?" I gasped, trembling.

"The gift you granted me returned my powers and my physical form," he sounded grateful, but it was a poison that choked my heart as more tears slid down my cheeks without sobs. "In return, you were gifted eternal youth and life."

I thought then of all that he had stolen from me. I would never change, or grow old, never know the joy of having children, or of spending my life as I should have with the man I love. I would never be more than a child on the verge of adulthood, a girl just beyond the reach of becoming a woman. My heart ached even deeper.

"Ironic, is it not," he said softly, "that three days' time would have marked the start of your nineteenth year? And last night you were saved from ever knowing the pain of growing old. That is a true mercy, Princess."

I closed my eyes and felt my tears' hot wetness fall through my eyelashes as hard, loud sobs broke past my lips, my face buried in my hands.

"Why do you cry?" he sounded confused, frowning as I looked at him.

"You've taken... everything... I've... I've lost what it means to be human," I sobbed in a murmur, my tears coming quickly. "Now what am I?"

He sat back, studying me curiously. "I would have thought you would be grateful for this."

"Take it back!" I pleaded. "Please, take it back!"

"I cannot," he simply said, then stood and turned back to the windows.

I curled up and hugged my knees, crying now over the greatest loss I had ever known. In deciding to save the lives of my friends I had let this monster destroy mine and leave me alive to suffer through it. *It would have been kinder if he'd killed me...*

"You have what you wanted from me," I said in a soft voice, staring at my feet. "You... you don't need me anymore..."

"I will *not* release you," he said so factually that I looked up at him through my long hair in numb surprise.

"Why not?" I sniffed against my sobs.

"I still have a use for you," was his cryptic reply. "And I am not in the habit of simply releasing my prisoners. However, you will not stay here. Grishk'kinnar can change a human and corrupt them beyond anything but lost souls. I do not want that for you, for you must remain pure."

He turned back to me as I just stared at him, feeling so defeated and grief stricken.

"What are you going to do with me then?" I murmured uneasily, sniffing back my sobs.

"You will be taken to Castle Ortagaad, a fortress on an island off the northern Gorvennan Coast," he decreed in a low, calm voice, his hands clasped behind him. "You will be placed in the care of Keilantra and Manth until such time as I have further need of you."

I just closed my eyes and slouched my shoulders in grief filled defeat. I couldn't even bring myself to plead with him now. What would be the point? He had won anyway and pleading with him wouldn't have changed anything.

"You have lost your freedom by your refusal to join with me," he told me as if it were my fault that he was doing this to me, tilting my chin with two fingers so that I had to look up at him. "When you awaken, you will be far from here and you will languish in the cold of a tower cell, wishing that you had accepted my offer."

I just stared at him as his eyes drew me in and made me feel so tired.

"Sleep, Princess," he urged me. "Sleep..."

* * * * *

The feeling of cold air and the smell of sea salt battering over my body woke me from my strange sleep. The sound of water flowed beneath me and the shadows around me were punctured by the paling of the three moons fighting to break the early hours of night's growing darkness. There were heavy clouds above and I saw a ship's sails dressed in black and gold with the emblem of a gryphon set over them.

I was lying on a wooden floor that smelled of many travels drifting through the seas and weathered from heavy use. The boat was small with one main mast and no below decks, this single deck all that kept me safe from the water below. There were men carefully moving around me dressed in the garb of Gorvennan soldiers and sailors, a few knights there as well. I felt a shuddering breath enter my lungs as I saw Ulric, the Knight who had been there during the ceremony to restore the Shadow Lord's powers.

"Leander?" a familiar male voice whispered, and I turned over my right shoulder.

My heart leaped joyfully in my chest as I saw Carden and Tallinn, both sitting with their backs against a wooden frame, facing the boat's bow. They looked tired and ragged, their clothes torn in places and crumpled badly, their skin bruised and stained with dried blood from the beatings they had taken. Both sat with a rope bound around their waists and fastened to the frame behind them, their hands tied behind their backs. That was when I realised that my hands were tied behind me too, the bindings tight and refusing to release.

"Carden," I breathed a sigh of relief and propped myself up awkwardly, a weak smile appearing on my face. "Tallinn. You're alright."

"We're alright," Tallinn agreed, studying me worriedly. "But you don't look well, Princess. You must have suffered greatly from what they subjected you to."

"I'm fine," I lied, knowing that I really wasn't.

"We saw what they did to you," Carden reminded me of their presence during the ceremony. "I... Gods, I just can't believe what you went through."

"It was gruesome," Tallinn agreed darkly, her hair so unkempt now, dirt staining her otherwise smooth and perfect skin.

"I... I don't want to think about it," I admitted to my disgusted unease. "I don't even want to think about what they made me do..."

"Have you had any ill effects?" Tallinn asked me curiously, but also out of concern. "I mean, did the ritual do anything to you as well?"

I thought about it as I looked at them, the Shadow Lord's confession of what had happened to me as clear in my mind then as it had been when he first told me. The pain of that knowledge was still too near and I wasn't sure that telling my friends that I had lost such a valuable, irreplaceable piece of myself was something I really wanted to do.

"Nothing, really," I lied. "I guess I just... I just felt so tired and weak afterwards."

"I am hardly surprised," Tallinn sounded convinced, but Carden's eyes were harder and more knowing. "Such a terrible violation would take time for you to recover from."

I just nodded, pushing myself up and leaning my back against another wooden frame like the one they were tied to, facing them fully. I looked over the edge of the boat's walls and out at our surroundings. It was colder than I had expected, the water deep and dark, stretching on for miles. There were ice sheets forming to my right, which I then guessed was east as I saw what I knew had to be the Black Peaks of Gorth'lak on the coast. The green lightning flashes and red glow of fire beneath the poisonous black clouds made it all too clear.

Ours was not the only boat making this icy crossing, two others visible on either side of us, the one to our boat's port side a little farther in front than the other.

What kind of boats are these? I wondered as I frowned at the scene before me. *What's going on here?*

"You're sure you're alright?" Carden questioned me, unconvinced by my lies.

I looked back to him and nodded, the wind tugging my hair to flick across my shoulders. "Yes. I am. Really."

He still didn't look convinced, but nodded and let the matter remain at that, to my relief.

"So, where are we?" I asked as I looked back to the water washing past us.

"We're on the Ortagaad Sea," Carden replied quietly and gravely as he studied the waters surrounding us. "We left the Port of Travarna a few hours ago from the coast of Gorvenna."

"You're almost out of High-Realm, Princess," Tallinn told me, looking to her right. "That distant coast there is Grotojan, the ancestral home of the Orcs. Somewhere ahead of us in the far distance is Valloran, domain of the Vampire Lords. And, of course, to the east are the Black Peaks and Gorth'lak itself."

"That can mean that this passage has only one destination for us," Carden sounded darkly worried.

"Castle Ortagaad," I nodded, gazing towards the Black Peaks and the red flashes of Dread Mountain far away in the distance.

"How do you know that?" he looked to me with a frown as I turned my gaze to him.

"When I woke up after the ritual," I explained, sure to keep as much secret as possible, "the Shadow Lord was there. He said that he was sending me to Castle Ortagaad so that Grishk'kinnar didn't corrupt me. He... He said he wants me to stay as I am... That he wants me to stay *"pure"*."

I decided that it was best not to tell them about his uncomfortable proximity or his dire attraction towards me. I felt terrible enough as it was already and didn't want to relive the horrors that Grishk'kinnar had presented me with.

"He came and told us the same," Tallinn murmured thoughtfully. "He said that since he had given you his word to safeguard us from harm that leaving us in his dungeons would only break that oath."

"A Shadow Lord's word is his law," I recalled Morod's words when I had made my deal with him.

"Was that supposed to be mercy?" Carden snorted and rolled his eyes, looking to me harshly. "Castle Ortagaad is a cruel and sinister place where the cold penetrates the stone and chills you near to death. Then there are the stories..."

"Stories?" I was uneasy. "What stories, exactly?"

He looked pale as he spoke slowly and tensely: "Prisoners - whether guilty or not - often go there only to be tortured for the pleasures of the jailers. There are no liberties, no kindnesses, no true mercies but the mercy of fiends within those walls. I've even heard rumours of victims being used in bizarre experiments..."

"Experiments?" I was breathing deeply, but slowly, feeling more and more worried.

"No one escapes Castle Ortagaad," Carden grumbled and looked down at his feet. "No one ever has. It is set on a lone island atoll surrounded by jagged rocks and frozen ice sheets, the very waters themselves alive with death."

"You're scaring her, Carden," Tallinn warned him sternly, narrowing her gaze at him.

"I am sorry, Leander," he said with all honesty, his face softer. "It's just... I've always feared that place. Only two ways exist to escape those dark, damp, frosty cells: Pardon by King Thoralf or... or death."

"Do you think...?" I didn't get to finish my question as a hard hand slapped over my mouth, stopping me from speaking.

I wriggled as I felt a rope being pulled around my waist, binding me to the wooden rack I sat against, then a second hand crushed around my throat. Carden and Tallinn moved to react, both tensing immediately at my attacker's actions.

"Stay your tongues," Ulric whispered into my ear, eyeing off my friends coldly. "Do you want to bring them down upon us?"

I glanced up at him awkwardly, struggling to see past my shoulder and my wild strands of hair. He was leaning over my left shoulder, his expression severe, but not cruel, fear in his eyes. He lifted his fingers from my mouth, but kept his palm pressed to my cheek so that he could easily silence me with a reverse of that movement.

"Bring... bring what down upon us?" I whispered in a trembling voice.

"Out there," he nodded to my right and I followed his gaze.

I saw a sweeping black fin emerge from the water with a smaller one right up behind it, the top of a tail fin swishing slowly farther back. Whatever this thing was it was large, nearly twice the size of the boat.

"W-w-what is that?" I stammered, shaking in his grasp.

"Culler Sharks," Ulric answered lowly with dread. "They're nocturnal daemon-fish that are drawn to the vibrations made from sounds on the water. They've been circling us for the better part of an hour."

"That's impossible," Tallinn remarked as quietly as she could manage. "Sharks don't like the cold."

"*These* sharks are different," Ulric explained softly, watching as another set of fins swept past the boat. "Their hides are as black as coal and they have warm blood to combat the ice. They sun themselves on the waters' surface during the day to gather heat, then hunt at night. One alone can sink one of these small boats."

At that moment there came a loud, terrible splintering and cracking of wooden beams from starboard. I looked up and stared in horror as we saw a great black monster shark with its teeth around the side of the distant boat. It was pulling it over to its port side, the wood shattering as if made of glass and the people on board screaming in panic. It became a feeding frenzy as several more great sharks swept up from the icy gloom below and started to feast.

I closed my eyes and looked away as Ulric released his hold on me.

"What happened?" he asked one of the other guards in a hushed voice.

"Someone sneezed on that boat, Knight-Commander," was the chilling response. "The Cullers didn't hesitate. What are your orders?"

"There is nothing to be done," he replied, turning his gaze back to me. "The Mistresses are awaiting these prisoners, and we *must* make the castle safely before the night thickens. Coax what speed you can from the sails but do so in silence."

He passed us by and that was when I noticed that Tristan was onboard with us, hidden beneath his brown hood, watching the sinking boat and the sharks massacring their victims in the dark waters beside us. He saw me and gave me a softened expression, but I turned away from him and back to Carden and Tallinn, ignoring him.

We remained silent the rest of the way, all of us fearing to bring down the Culler Sharks' terrible onslaught. But there was no sign of them again, not even a shimmering black fin breaking the waters' surface.

For another hour the boat sailed beside its companion vessel in complete silence, only the washing of the tides against the hull and the flapping of the sails sounding in the stillness. Then, out of the icy fogs and black night, there came a great shape rising from the sea.

An enormous castle of dark grey stone rose up on a snow locked atoll island, standing at least twenty feet from the sea's waves. A gigantic tower stood highest on the western slopes of the island flanked by tremendously ancient stone walls, ramparts and battlements, a pointed top at its peak. Smaller towers surrounded the compounds within, these mostly the battlement topped watchtowers. Other buildings branched out from the keep, which was a monolithic marvel, set there with easy access to the western-most tower. Hanging over the ocean walls from chains on wide wooden beams were narrow gibbets just big enough to fit a fully-grown man inside. Some were empty, but others had bodies, whether alive or dead I couldn't tell.

The boats rounded to the eastern side of the castle, passing the south-eastern end where the keep's walls were set above the sea and the cliffs below. A huge cavernous mouth was open beneath the eastern walls in the rocks, a kind of covered cove lying within. This opening was flanked by two watchtowers that controlled an enormous portcullis gate between them.

The boats entered the cavern and the portcullis closed behind us with a resounding boom following the initial breaking of the water. We were brought to a stone dock built at the water's edge, both boats mooring there with ease. I noticed a large ship with three masts docked not too far away, its hull bearing the crest of the Gorvennan Royal Family.

What's that doing here?

Ulric moved to me and untied the rope around my waist, grabbing my arm and hauling me to my feet as Carden and Tallinn were taken by other guards. He shoved me onto the dock, my legs wobbling from the swaying of the tides. I nearly fell into the water, but he caught me and pushed me into Carden, who awkwardly steadied me with his shoulder, then glared at him.

We made our way in silence up the high stairs that reached the entrance to the castle's main courtyard, following our captors without resistance, then through a second courtyard and into the keep. We were led up a grand staircase, this part of the castle well-lit and very warm against the chill outside. Black and golden tapestries hung from the walls and the grey stone pillars, two statues of golden carved gryphons flanking the stairs that led to the throne room.

I looked to Carden, not knowing what to say, but wanting to feel the safety he always brought with him. He tried to look reassuring, but it was a thin veil, his own worry all too clear to me.

We entered the throne room, a long golden carpet leading from the doors between more great pillars to where two oaken thrones sat on a dais before an enormous stained-glass window. As with the stairs, two great golden gryphon statues guarded the dais, set in permanent snarls with their heads raised majestically.

I nearly gasped, staggering the sound as I faced the figures sitting in the thrones.

The man I knew well; King Thoralf Kenrick, long-time friend of Uncle Aric and my father. He was a proud man with jet black hair, only a little silver in its long strands, his beard short and kept neat. His eyes were purest emerald and he had always held a kind presence, his face having aged though since the last time I saw him in Arvon when I was fourteen.

He wore his golden crown with its seven points and was dressed in robes of gold and silver, a black velvet coat held around his shoulders. But he didn't look right. His once vibrant eyes were pale, and his face drawn as if he were ill. He was staring with a blank expression, all the light of life he possessed now in darkness.

Beside him sat Keilantra, dressed in a black velvet gown and a golden silk under dress, golden detailing on her dress' high collar, around her hips and on the cuffs and shoulders of her sleeves. Her black hair was tied up at the nape of her neck in a heavy bunching, the Gorvennan Queen's Crown set delicately on her head. But what really drew my gaze was the pendant that hung from her neck, gleaming gold with a topaz gem set as its heart-stone. The gold dragon suddenly made sense to me.

Oh my Gods! She's a Pendant Holder! Like me! How?! How could someone so wicked gain control of one of the Pendants?!

"My King, my Queen," Ulric strode forward with one hand on his sword's hilt at his side, bowing his head lightly. "I have come with the prisoners sent from our ally."

King Thoralf said nothing, still staring blankly as Keilantra sat back with a hard glare, tapping her heavily jewel adorned fingers impatiently on the arms of her throne.

The guards brought the three of us closer to the thrones as I noticed Tristan moving off to the side nearest Keilantra. He stopped by the dais and pushed back his hood; his eyes locked on her as if he were making an extra effort to avoiding looking at us.

Carden cried out in pain and Tallinn followed, the guards hitting them both in the back of the knee with the base of their halberds. Ulric pushed my shoulder and I dropped to both knees quietly between the two Guardians, my eyes focused on the King and Queen.

"He sent *all* three?" Keilantra sounded bored as she eyed us with indifference. "I thought it was only the girl he wanted us to care for."

Care for?! I thought with an indignant mental snort. *Why do I doubt that?!*

"It is the Master's wish," Manth appeared from the shadows behind her sister's throne. "He gave his word, and Grishk'kinnar corrupts humans who linger in its prisons. That is how we build our armies, after all."

Keilantra sighed: "Ah... yes. Of course."

"Who... who are they, my love?" Thoralf sounded old and distant as he spoke, looking so sick in his mind. It broke my heart to see him like that.

"They are prisoners, Thoralf, darling," Keilantra told him gently. "They have committed such *terrible* crimes."

"That's a lie!" Carden shouted angrily. "We have committed no crimes, either in Gorvenna or anywhere else in High-Realm!"

"We are Guardians!" Tallinn added earnestly. "We have sworn an oath to protect the innocent from evil! Evil like those two *foul* women before you, Sire!"

"What?" Thoralf looked to Keilantra and Manth, then to Carden and Tallinn. "Evil? Guardians?"

"Lies spoken to confound you, dear husband," Keilantra mewed into his ear. "They are the worst kind of criminals."

"I see..." he nodded, settling back like an old man too tired to make any further efforts.

"King Thoralf!" I called to him, drawing his gaze. "Please... we are not criminals! You know me!"

He stared at me as if he were trying to capture a long-forgotten memory. "Do I?"

I nodded fervently: "Yes. You were friends with my father, Prince Ewan Aldrich of Aldegaad. Your son, Anders... He and I were friends growing up..."

"Anders..." I could see that he knew his own son's name at least. "He's my son..."

"Yes," I nodded more vigorously, my voice gentle and hopeful. "You've known me since the day I was born. Please, King Thoralf. Remember..."

"I know your face..." he stared hard at me.

"I'm Ewan's daughter," I told him, hoping I could remind him. "Leander. My name is Leander. Do you not remember me?"

"Leander..." he tested my name in his mouth, listening to it. "Ewan's youngest daughter... Leander..."

I half smiled. "Yes! Yes, that's right! I'm Leander Aldrich! Please, please, help us!"

"It is a trick, Thoralf," Keilantra manipulated into his ear. "You are tired, and your imaginings grow wild. Perhaps you need rest."

"Yes... Yes, I need rest," he spoke as if hypnotised. "Goodnight, dearest Keilantra..."

"Goodnight, my beloved Thoralf," she permitted, then nodded to a guard who led the King through a side door and out of sight.

All hope I had found then faded and I slouched my shoulders, staring at the floor.

"I did not expect that," Keilantra admitted, turning her eyes to meet mine. "Seeing you nearly undid everything."

"What have you done to him?" I demanded coldly, fixing my eyes on hers.

"She's bewitched him," Tallinn hissed with fiery eyes pointed at Keilantra and Manth. "They are the sisters of Raven's Rest in the far north, the Witches of the Mountains..."

"Very good, young ranger," Keilantra nodded as she regarded Tallinn evenly. "Manth and I are indeed the sister witches of Raven's Rest."

"You've poisoned my King's mind!" Carden snarled, tensing his wrists against his restraints, determined to break free. "You've used terrible magic to sap away his wits and memories!"

"If I remember correctly, boy," Keilantra turned her gaze to him harshly, "you were a criminal in Nargilith and condemned by the man you so ardently defend as your King."

I looked at Carden in shock, but he said nothing.

"Bring him closer," the Queen commanded in a soft tone.

Two guards dragged Carden forward as two more held Tallinn and I back. Keilantra stepped from her throne and moved to stand over him. She placed her hand to his chest just over his heart and glared into his eyes without ever blinking.

I noticed then that Tristan looked uneasy, pressing himself farther back into the nearest pillar and clutching at his own chest. I frowned at him curiously, then turned back to Carden and Keilantra.

To my horror, Carden started to grunt in agony. He was sweating, his neck and shoulders straining and his hands clenching into fists behind his back, twisting against the ropes binding them. He moaned and closed his eyes, gritting his teeth hard.

What is she doing to him?! I feared silently, watching on with wide eyes.

"Your heart is strong," she assessed, digging her fingernails into his skin and the cloth of his shirt. "It knows the touch of true love. How powerful it would be..."

"Stop it! Please!" I screamed in panic as he started to shake violently. "Please! Just stop! You're hurting him!"

"Sister, dearest," Manth spoke quietly from the throne, little more than a black figure in the shadows, "remember the Master's promise."

Keilantra ripped her hand away abruptly and Carden slumped to the floor, breathing hard and suffering the residual pain from her magical attack. At the pillar he stood near, Tristan relaxed and took a breath, his face pale and green as if he had expected to see the most horrific sight.

"Take the boy to the lower prisons," the Queen commanded. "The ranger shall be secured in the West Tower for now. Leave the Princess. I have need to speak with her alone."

"What have you done to him?!" Tallinn screamed as Carden was carried out by two guards, squirming as she was dragged kicking behind him. "You unholy daemon bitch! What have you done to him?!"

I cringed and trembled as the doors were closed behind me and I was left alone with the Witches, helpless on my knees before them. I tried to suppress my tears, my chest heaving and my heart racing as I feared for Carden. I could only hope that he would be alright.

Keilantra turned her green-eyed gaze to me, smirking coldly as she considered my face.

"So, it is *you* who holds sway over his heart," she perceived, pressing her hands together before her. "And he holds the same over yours..."

I cringed and recoiled as she drew nearer to me, looking up at her fearfully, my lips shut tight and my jaw clenching. I twisted my wrists against my restraints, but all that did was give my skin friction burns from the tight wrappings.

"Your Ladyship," Tristan stepped up to us quickly as Ulric moved closer behind me, drawing the woman's sharp gaze. "I was wondering about our deal. I did all that you asked of me. I would like to get what's mine and depart for the mainland."

"Very well," she sighed with annoyance. "Go to the Sanctum and I will give you what you seek once I am done with the girl."

"Many thanks," he nodded then swept after a guard who was to escort him, but paused and looked to me with an apologetic stare: "Listen, lass, I'm sorry..."

"Just go," I hissed and glared at him.

He nodded glumly and turned from me, leaving the room through the same side door Thoralf had.

"It's hard, is it not?" Keilantra sounded like she was mocking me as she spoke. "Trust is such a rare thing to come by."

I just stared at the floor before her feet, my lip trembling and my eyes hurting against tears, but I wasn't going to allow myself to cry before this wicked woman.

"Now," she said, moving closer to stand over me, "you may be wondering why *I* am so interested in *you*."

"Not really," I replied, deciding to play this differently to how she was probably expecting me to. "You serve Lord Morod. I'm here because he wants you to keep me prisoner for him."

"True enough," she agreed. "However, you and I share much more in common than you think."

"Like what?" I met her eyes again, my face feeling hard from my fear, grief and anger.

"For now, let us focus on that which you and I both possess," she said, holding something silver and gleaming in her left hand.

I stared at it longingly. "My pendant..."

"Yes," she nodded, smiling coldly at me. "As you've said, Lord Morod has entrusted you to my keeping. It is good to know that you cannot do anything without this."

I couldn't take my eyes off the silver pendant and its purple stone. I wanted to snatch it from her and run as fast as I could, but with my hands bound behind me and so many guards surrounding me there was no hope of that succeeding, even if she wasn't a witch.

"You have seen that I too have command over the heart of a dragon," she stated, dangling my pendant in front of me, teasing me with it. "Tell me, how did you come by yours? And be truthful."

"My... uh... my uncle, King Aric, gave it to me," I replied, meeting her eyes now.

"Not your father then?"

I shrugged. "He... he was there and told me that they had discussed it, but it was my uncle who gave it to me."

"I see," she nodded thoughtfully. "I received mine from my grandmother."

"It is as we suspected, sister," Manth said, moving to stand to my left, her black eyes dark beneath her raven hair. "The Pendants pass through blood and their own choice, not through chance."

"And... do *you* have a dragon?" Keilantra continued to question me.

I nodded uneasily. "Yes. She... she's not with me right now."

"Of course not," she said, folding my necklace into her palm. "A Holder must have their Pendant on them at *all* times for their Dragon to be able to come to them. Somehow, they sense us and come at our call."

"I... I didn't know that," I felt like a stupid child before her knowledge.

"You've had it but a short time, girl," Keilantra stated, moving towards me and holding it before my face. "I would have you call your dragon here now."

I stared at her in disbelief. *Gods, has she got a death wish? Does she even know what calling Amethyst here would mean for her?*

"What?" I asked in confusion, frowning. "Why?"

"Why do you think? I want to ensure that you cannot escape us," she stated.

I could only guess at what she meant and immediately shook my head as my heart fell sick in my chest.

"No... No, I... I won't do that to her," I refused, recoiling from her and shaking my head. "Besides... I don't know how..."

"It is *very* simple," she explained. "You must grasp the Pendant in your receiving hand and call both in words and in your heart, and she will hear you. Do it."

"No..." I shook my head, trembling.

"I will not ask nicely again, girl," she spoke through her teeth. "Call. Your. Dragon. Now."

"No," I refused again, more firmly this time.

Pain suddenly shot through my body and I screamed shrilly. I fell to my side and squirmed involuntarily, realising that Keilantra was hurting me with some terrible unseen magic. Her right hand was held over me, her fingers curling like vicious talons. It was like my nerves were on fire, the pain beyond all of my imagining. It was even worse than what I had suffered in Aneuran's dungeons. I could only whimper and scream, the ropes binding my arms only adding to my suffering as my limbs wrenched violently.

Then, just as suddenly as the convulsions had started, they ceased, and she glared at me as my screams fell silent. I lay there, breathing hard, tears bleeding from my eyes.

"I can make the pain *go* or I can make it *worse*," she hissed at me with quiet anger. "I do not care if you suffer in order to get that which I seek. Now, call your dragon."

"No! I won't!" I shrieked and screamed in agony as she struck me with her spell again for my refusal, releasing me only a moment later.

I whimpered as she grabbed my hair and jolted me closer to her, painfully bending my neck and spine backwards as she glared down into my eyes. She held the Pendant near to my face and made sure I could see it.

"You *will* do as I ask, girl," she told me in a cold, cruel, loud voice. "Call your dragon to this castle, then give me control of your Pendant."

"What?" I stared at her incredulously, my voice weak and shaking with pain. "You want my Pendant?"

"Control of it," she confirmed.

"But... but you already have a Pendant that you can control," I pointed out. "You don't need mine."

"It is not about *need*, but *want*," she said slowly. "Now, call her and give me control."

"I don't know how!" I said honestly, shaking hard and feeling sick, but I had conviction. "And even if I knew, I wouldn't *ever* help you!"

She threw me to the floor and kicked me in the ribs. I cried out in pain, looking up then as she snarled down at me with the ferocity of a savage beast.

"If you insist on continuing this," she murmured icily, holding her right hand towards me with dark energy rippling through her fingers, "then, I shall be all too happy to oblige you with the pain you so richly deserve, you insolent little bitch!"

I stared at her in horror and waited, bracing my body for the terrible, magical onslaught, then closed my eyes as it came again along with my screams...

Chapter Twenty-Four
Fire and Ice

I don't know how long I had laid there screaming and pleading against the pain. I lost all sense of time once again as I had too many times before. All I knew was that she was relentless, her spells causing me horrific agony unlike anything I had ever imagined could exist.

Lying there with my arms pinned beneath me and my senses wandering away, I tried to listen as the onslaught of her attacks finally ended. Her voice was not more than a murmur in my stressed hearing, my mind unable to determine the words that were being spoken.

I could hear my own sobs of pain clearer than anything else, my body and my spirit separated now to help me recover from this horrible supernatural torture. I opened my eyes, my vision failing as I watched the frustrated gold and black clad woman speaking heatedly to Ulric. She jabbed a finger at me with rage, the muffled sounds telling me that she was yelling, her face red and her eyes blazing.

The Knight bowed his black haired, lightly bearded head and snapped his fingers to two guards as my eyes fell dark.

When my vision returned, and my senses came back from numbness the men were carrying me by my arms between them. My boots scraped against the stone floors, my legs hanging limp and too weak to help me stand. My body burned with pain still, but I couldn't even scream or cry, my voice quieted and my throat raw.

A tower stood before me as they led me through the walkway open to the air, its point high above and its walls ancient and grey. To my right and my left, I saw courtyards below, high walls reaching up to surround us.

Ulric led the way through the archway entrance into the tower, which was hidden on its north side and under the cover of an auxiliary building attached to it. Torches glowed on the walls and there was a heavy door that could only be opened by the jailer keys, which the Knight carried with him.

They took me up a dark stairway that encircled the outer walls of the tower. As we passed each floor, I could see a heavy door with a barred window leading from the stairs, darkened cells waiting beyond, though I couldn't tell if they were occupied.

We came to the top of the stairs and the final door, Ulric opening it with a heavy groan from its worn old hinges. They took me to the farthest cell from the entrance, opening the barred door quickly. Each cell was a space behind a dark stone archway, the vertical and cross bar walls added to block the large gaps with the door set in the centre to create each cage.

Weakly, I tried to steady myself as the two guards held me tightly, Ulric facing me and looking into my half-closed eyes. He placed his hot hand to my cheek, and I tried to pull away, but I didn't have enough strength to effectively do anything.

"This is going to be your new home, Princess," he told me. "So, you'd best get used to it here."

I couldn't even try to speak, my mind still too numb to even bring words to my lips.

"So beautiful," he caressed my face, his want so clear in his eyes and voice, "so young... How much I desire to know your intimate touch."

He nodded to the guards and I felt them untie me, ripping the bindings away from my wrists. Ulric took me by the arm and turned me into the cell as the guards left.

"At least this should keep you out of trouble," he hurled me into the room.

I hit the stone floor hard and cried out with a small whimpering grunt. I lay there on my stomach, weakly lifting my head to look up as he shut me in and locked the door with a heavy groan and a loud bang.

"I look forward to the next time I get to watch you suffer, Princess," he smirked at me through the bars, then turned away.

In only a moment or two, I heard the door to the floor shut and lock, then there was silence.

Exhausted, I slumped my face into my arms and lay there on the floor, my body hurting too much to move. I tried to turn onto my right side, moaning and closing my eyes tightly for a moment at the agony that still cut into me like a cruel dagger.

My eyes fell on the single narrow window in the wall several feet above me with a step up to it. It had bars dug into the stone vertically, the chilled air slipping through its unshielded opening. The pale light of the moons shone into the cell as they had begun their new crescents, just barely visible from where I lay.

A sigh escaped my lips and I lay my head on my right arm, my left to my stomach as I closed my eyes to rest and hopefully recover from the pain.

"Princess?" I heard Tallinn's voice and turned over to the cell across from mine. "Princess Leander, is that you?"

"Tallinn?" I turned onto my left side and crawled to the bars of the cell, leaning against them and looking out towards where her voice came from.

She emerged from the shadows of the cell, her blonde hair straying around her shoulders. Her face was thick with worry in the light of the torch, her clothes bearing new rips and very crumpled.

"Are you alright?" she asked me gently.

I shook my head, a pain in my chest when I breathed: "Not really... Keilantra tortured me."

"Why?" she hissed angrily.

"My Pendant," I answered, fighting to keep my voice level against the pain. "She... she wanted me to call Amethyst here."

"For what purpose?" she frowned.

I shrugged, even that action drawing unrelenting pain to my nerves: "S-S-She... s-s-she said she wanted control of my pendant."

"But that couldn't work," Tallinn recalled one of the many discussions we had had since I got it. "Did Mithras not tell you that the Pendant cannot be used by anyone other than you?"

"He did," I nodded gingerly.

"Then how could that even work?"

"I don't know," I hesitated as I thought of the wicked woman who was so content to hurt me. "But she has a pendant too."

"What?" Tallinn had an incredulous expression on her fair face. "Are you saying she's a Holder? Like you?"

"Yes," I closed my eyes as pain shot through my sternum again. "It's a golden one with... ugh... with a topaz heart-stone. That gold dragon that attacked me in Gorth'lak was her Dragon Protector... like Amethyst is mine."

"And she thinks she can also command yours?" there was doubt in her voice.

I shook my head uncertainly. "I don't know. But she wasn't kind when I refused to help her."

Tallinn fell quiet for a moment, then softly asked: "What did she do to you?"

"She used some kind of pain inflicting magic on me," I replied, the memory and the remaining affects so much that tears started down my cheeks again.

She didn't speak and I saw her sit gingerly down on the bed that rested against the wall in her cell, the faint light of the moons visible through the window behind her.

"Did... did they... hurt you?" I asked her softly, every word a painful effort.

She nodded grimly. "Yes."

"What did they do?" I asked in a meek voice.

She shook her head grimly, remaining stoic, though I could see the pain in her eyes. "I think it is better that I do not utter a word of what was done. Needless to say, they shall pay for all of this. *Every last one* of them."

I could only guess at her meaning, my mind racing with all the terrible torments that could have been forced onto her. After all, they were torments that I feared as much as anyone else and had just narrowly avoided so far. I chose to think that it had been more basic and blunter than what it most likely was.

My head was swimming and I closed my eyes for a moment, trying to push away the pain as it hit me like the swells against the base of the castle we found ourselves in. Then, I turned my eyes back to her.

"Where's Carden?" my voice was so small and lost as I spoke.

"They separated us," Tallinn answered quietly. "He was taken to the lower prisons. At least, that's where they said they were taking him."

"I remember," I nodded, staring at the floor before me. "Then, is this the West Tower?"

She nodded; her eyes soft as she looked to me. "It's the highest and most secure section of the prisons. I do not know where Carden is from here."

I started to cry, covering my forehead with my hand and leaning my elbow on my knee, my other arm coiled around my stomach tightly.

"This is all my fault," I sobbed quietly. "I never should have trusted Tristan..."

"No it isn't. How could you have known what he was planning to do?" Tallinn sounded sympathetic as she watched me from what felt like so far away.

"I had a bad feeling when I first met him," I confessed. "I wasn't sure why he was so willing to help me..."

"He is a snake and a liar!" Tallinn hissed with quiet anger. "If I ever see him again, he better be ready for a fight!"

"We should have never followed him to that warehouse. Amethyst tried to warn me... and I just sent her away," that made me cry harder. "If I had only listened to her, returned to Fawkner's home and heeded her warning, then we wouldn't be here now. Gods, you warned me, Tallinn, and I ignored you as well."

"Please, do not wear the blame of this," she said softly. "I did warn you, yes, and while you were right to take the chance to get the information we sought, I did not press my misgivings as ardently to you as I should have. I should have simply refused to give you an option rather than accepting your decision," she seethed at herself and looked up at the ceiling. "Curse my unwavering unwillingness to question a royal! I should have taken charge like a Guardian is supposed to!"

"Then... then I guess we're both to blame," I rested my head against the bars, my hands on top of my knees. "But... I suppose we did find out what the Shadow Lord wanted with me at least."

She just nodded, the two of us falling silent for a few moments then. I let my eyes fall shut again as I tried to rest my body, the pain from the Witch's torture still coursing through my nerve endings. I just wanted to feel relief, but it seemed as if I was just going to suffer endlessly. I tried to at least ease my heavy breathing so that I could find a little comfort, if nothing else.

"The others would have returned from the Citadel by now," Tallinn said, trying to sound comforting. "Dolin and Holger will surely have told them what happened, and Aldwyn will be making a plan as we speak."

"They won't find us, Tallinn," I sounded a little harsh as I looked to her, but I was losing all hope. "High-Realm is too big a place to search. *Only* Amethyst can rescue us and *only* if I call her."

"Do you know how?" she asked softly after a moment of silence.

I nodded, breathing back my sadness and stopping my tears. "Keilantra told me how... but I would need my pendant to do it."

"It will be alright," she promised with gentle kindness. "We *will* find a way out of this place and get it back. Then, Carden and I will get you to safety, and we'll find the others so that we can decide what to do now that the Shadow Lord is restored to physical form."

"I should never have agreed," I closed my eyes, crying into my hands. "I let my love for Carden and my friendship for you get in the way... and I might have just doomed all of High-Realm..."

"Leander!" her calling out my name instead of my title surprised me and broke me from my despair. "You are *not* to blame for any of this! The fault lies with Morod and his followers, *not* you!"

I just nodded sadly, then whispered: "I think Carden blames me."

"He doesn't," she assured me. "He's worried for you, as am I. You have taken more punishment and pain in one year than any of us have in all our current years combined. Honestly, I am amazed at how strong you are to have survived all of this. Believe me, Leander, we *will* get through this. I know it," and she truly did believe it.

"You're right, Tallinn," I nodded, wiping away my tears. "Thank you for grounding me. I don't know what I would do without you."

"Think nothing of it," she said, then urged me: "Try to rest. You need to recover your strength."

I nodded and lifted myself onto the cot that rested against the wall. Curling up under the blankets, I fell asleep almost immediately despite my horrible pain.

* * * * *

The clattering of keys and the releasing of locks woke me from my peaceful sleep seemingly only moments after closing my eyes. I sat up and set my feet to the floor, bleary eyed and drowsy. Sunlight shone through the window to my right and I couldn't help but wonder how long I had slept this time, though I could feel that my pain had gone.

Leaning forward, I managed to get a glimpse through the left side of my cell to see Ulric and two guards dragging a black-haired girl onto the floor. She had her head down, her clothes in shades of grey and brown, clearly those of a commoner. They threw her into the cell nearest the door beside Tallinn's, the Guardian watching them with the fierceness that I had come to see in her eyes at such actions.

"Does your cruelty know no bounds?!" she demanded, drawing Ulric's heavy glare. "How many innocent women do you covert in this place?!"

He slammed his fist against the bars of her cell, making her step back, but her hard stare didn't falter.

"Watch your tongue, Guardian," he hissed at her viciously. "*Only* the Princess is protected by my Mistresses' and his Lordship's will. *You* I would be all too happy to school in the ways of obeying a man."

She said nothing as he turned away, glaring at him as he faced me. He smiled at my dishevelled appearance and leaned against the bars of my cell casually.

"Well, look who finally woke up," he chuckled, staring straight towards my chest and mentally undressing me to my disgust. "Feeling hungry, Princess? I bet you are," he snatched a bowl of food from a guard who was handing them out.

I didn't speak as he put it through the bars and set it on the floor, just glaring out of the corner of my eye at him. He set a water jug and cup down, then continued to watch me with a deep-seated perversion in his green eyes.

"You've made the Queen rather angry," he said with cruel amusement. "Refusing her is never wise. You might want to consider that before you next meet her. After all, we do have quite the collection of torture tools and implements in the lower prisons. You won't want to refuse her again."

He laughed softly to himself, satisfied that he had frightened me with his threats. While that was true, I only felt a numb anger as I watched him leave, the door shutting and sealing us back into the silence of the tower.

"At last your eyes open," Tallinn looked to me, relief on her face. "I've been worried, Leander. You've been asleep for nearly two days."

"It seems that I keep losing so many days to weakened sleep," I murmured thoughtfully as I studied my surroundings in the light of day.

"Are you still in pain?" Tallinn asked me as I slowly got to my feet.

"Not really," I replied gratefully. "I still have some aches, but not the agony that I had."

"You should eat," she urged me.

I nodded then took the bowl from the floor and sat on the bed as she stood with hers. There wasn't really much there, just a little hardening cheese with some old brown bread. It couldn't be called a meal, but I was so hungry that I didn't care about its condition or scant portion.

"Such treatment of prisoners should be a crime," Tallinn commented, more in musing than anything else. "This food is barely suited for a rodent, let alone a human being."

"I'm just grateful to have food," I responded, surprised by my hunger. "I haven't eaten since before we were in Gorth'lak."

"Oh. I forgot," she sounded apologetic. "I am sorry, Princess."

"It's fine," I replied and looked to her. "And you can keep using my name."

"You're right," she nodded, despising the food she was struggling to eat. "There is no longer any need to stand down ceremony in your presence, Leander."

"Thank you," I swallowed some of the bread mixed with cheese awkwardly, looking around at our prison surroundings. "Have you got any thoughts on how we can escape?"

"If I could get the keys and weapons from a guard, perhaps," she thought aloud, "but from there I do not know what to do. We know nothing of the layout of this castle."

"Then there's an entire icy and frozen sea between us and the mainland," I reminded her. "We couldn't swim. We'd freeze in minutes."

"I know all about this place," a soft voice called and we both moved to the bars of our cells to look for the source.

The girl the guards had just brought in stood at the door of her cell, shivering and holding her arms around her for warmth. She was about my age, very beautiful, with fair olive skin and black hair, her green eyes strangely old for such a young face.

"I've been here for a few years now and I know where most parts of the castle are," she expressed quietly, looking between us nervously.

"Why do you tell us this?" Tallinn asked with suspicion.

"I overheard the guards saying that you're a Guardian," she confessed and looked to me. "And you're a noble?"

"I am," I nodded. "My name's Leander."

She gasped: "The Aldegaadian Princess? You are the Great Heroine's descendant..."

I chose not to say anything to that, knowing that such a distinction had brought me nothing but trouble in the last twelve months.

"What is your name?" I asked her softly.

"I am Helena, your Highness," she replied with a slight curtsey.

"Why did they bring you here, Helena?" I wondered, feeling so sorry for her already.

"The Queen and her sister are witches," she explained with a fearful breath. "They cast spells and practice such terrible tortures on young women like us. We are brought here not because we have committed a crime, but because they seek to use us for their dread amusements."

"Disgusting and cruel," Tallinn growled and drew Helena's gaze. "If you can help us escape, we will take you with us. Do you know of a way?"

She nodded. "The guards are lustful and arrogant. If one of us could seduce one and steal his keys, we could escape the tower. But we'll have to knock him out."

"I'll handle that," Tallinn looked to me. "Leander, can you seduce him and somehow get him near my cell?"

"Why me?" I felt a little annoyed that she should suggest I be the seductress.

"You're the Princess," she replied with convincing reasoning. "Who would be more attractive and forbidden to them than you?"

I sighed and nodded. "Alright. I'll do what I can," I moved to the edge of my cell and called loudly: "Guard! Guard!"

The door unlocked and the guard who was standing in the corridor beyond entered. He came to my cell and looked me up and down curiously as I pulled my arms around me and shivered, trying to look as vulnerable as possible.

"What is it?" he demanded, though he was studying my female form with desire.

"It's so cold in here," I told him in a small voice, fluttering my eyelashes at him. "Could you... could you get me another blanket? Please?"

He smirked lustfully and nodded. "Alright."

He disappeared for a few seconds, then returned and unlocked my cell. He moved to hand it to me, and I shrugged, giving him an appealing look.

"My fingers are so numb," I murmured to him, allowing him to see my cleavage under my dress. "Could you... put it around me?"

Smirking lustfully, he reached out his arms to swing the blanket around me and I took my chance. I kicked him hard in the groin and he cried out as I shoved him backwards out of the cell. He staggered, still holding the blanket, dropping his keys as he slammed into Tallinn's cell.

She didn't hesitate, grabbing him around the neck and applying a stranglehold. He choked and gagged, grabbing at her frantically, and I jumped forward, trying to pin him to the cell bars to keep him steady. There was a sickening crack as Tallinn turned his head and he slumped to the ground.

"You... you killed him?" I stepped away in shock.

"He was no innocent, Leander," she reminded me and pointed to the floor. "Get the keys."

I quickly found the keys and unlocked her cell. I then freed Helena as Tallinn took the sword the dead guard had sheathed on his belt. My adrenaline was working at over its normal response and I felt both flustered and afraid.

"We need to find Carden," I said as she joined Helena and I near the door from the cells.

"Do you know how to get to the lower prison?" Tallinn asked the other girl.

Helena nodded: "Go back to the entry into this tower and enter the prison building over the bridge next to the keep. Go down three flights of stairs and that's where the lower prisons start."

"We'll need an escape," Tallinn said and looked to me.

"I need my pendant," I turned to Helena. "It's as small as a locket, silver with a purple stone, hanging on a chain. The Queen wears a gold one very similar."

"It'll be in her study," the girl was incredibly knowledgeable, to my surprise. "I'll get it. But why do you need it?"

"It's one of the Dragon Pendants," I told her. "I can call my dragon with it. I think she could fly us out of here."

"It is as good a plan as any," Tallinn agreed. "But where should we call her?"

"How about the main courtyard below this tower?" Helena suggested. "It's right on the seawalls."

"It sounds plausible," Tallinn agreed. "Alright, let's go."

I handed Tallinn the keys and we started to make our way down the tower. In minutes, the three of us were pushing through the tower's door and out into the snowy air. Tallinn led the way with her sword ready, Helena and I staying close behind as we moved quickly.

We rushed down a set of stairs to the level below us and entered the next building as Helena sneaked off towards the keep. The two of us followed her directions and made our way to the lower sections of the castle, entering a long corridor lined with cells. The prisoners ignored us at first, but some of them started to call out and reach for us once they noticed our presence, enticed by the sight of two young women walking free before them.

"Leander, hide!" Tallinn whispered urgently and we ducked into the cover of a dark alcove as two guards went to investigate the noise of the prisoners.

They passed and I felt myself relax a little, though not much.

She glowered after them. "We could spend ages searching for him in this place."

"What should we do?" I asked uncertainly, staying hidden in the shadows.

"Ask someone," Tallinn replied and waited for the two men to return.

She immediately struck one dead, then kicked the legs out from under the other, pointing the sword at his throat threateningly. I was shocked by her ruthless and deadly efficiency, staying back so I didn't get in the way.

"Right," she snarled at him viciously. "You *are* going to help us find our friend, the other Guardian that came with us. Understand?"

He nodded feverishly, staggering as she dragged him to his feet and forced him to lead the way.

The guard helped us find the corridor that we needed in the maze that was the lower prisons very quickly, Carden resting in the fifth cell from the entrance.

"Tallinn? Leander?" he was stunned, standing up from where he lay on the bedroll on the floor.

"We're getting out of here, Carden," Tallinn told him and made the guard unlock the door.

He sprung out and pulled me into his arms as she pushed the guard in and knocked him out. With the passion of a man whose life was renewed, Carden kissed me deeply on the lips. I held him tight, joy building in me to the point of eruption as I wrapped my arms around his shoulders, holding onto him for dear life.

We both took deep breaths as we unlocked our lips, and I smiled at him as he grinned at me.

"I was so afraid I would never hold you in my arms again, Leander," he breathed a warm smile.

"I am so glad that you're alright," I confessed.

"This isn't the time," Tallinn said urgently and hurried past us. "We have to move."

Carden took me by the hand and we hurried at a near jog back towards the way we had come. There was so little resistance facing us that I was beginning to grow suspicious of it just as I was over Helena's intimate knowledge of Keilantra's fortress.

This is all so strange. It's almost too easy...

As we sought our exit, we came across a guard post and armoury, Tallinn easily unlocking it with the stolen keys. She took a bow and a quiver full of arrows as Carden selected a sword from the racks, my eyes darting to the corridors as they searched the room. I kept expecting to see guards coming down the corridors at any moment, but there was nothing. I was left with an even deeper feeling of unease, but I ignored it. I was just too desperate to escape.

Tallinn handed me a sword: "Are you very skilled with a blade?"

"I've trained ever since I was eight years old," I replied, taking the sword. "I can't say I'm the greatest fighter, but I can hold my own."

"That's all you need to do," she replied, then led us from the guard post.

We exited the prison and hurried down the stairs as the late afternoon sun struggled to pierce the clouds. The two Guardians were very careful to watch for guards as we came across Helena where she waited uneasily under a covered arch.

"You're here!" she was so relieved, turning to me quickly. "Here, I got it while no one was around."

She gave me my pendant and I felt myself relax at the sensation of its cool touch.

"Thank you, Helena," I fastened the chain at my neck, taking my sword up again from Carden.

"So, what's the plan?" Carden asked as we turned our eyes towards the courtyard full of guards before us.

I grimaced at the sight of so many men arrayed against us as I hid behind a wall under the arch. *Okay... so, it isn't too easy...*

"Leander will call Amethyst to come and get us from the castle walls," Tallinn explained.

Carden looked to me with surprise. "You can do that?"

"I can now," I said softly.

"Be ready," Tallinn urged as we edged into cover. "We need to be able to..."

"Prisoners escape!" came a terrible shout from somewhere above us. "It's the Guardians!"

"Move!" Tallinn leaped from the archway with the bow in hand and started firing at the guards trying to block us.

She shot arrow after arrow without any sign of slowing as Carden began engaging guards with his sword and dropping them hard. They ran with me between them, the three of us fighting fiercely to reach the walls. I kept my sword at the ready, determined to protect myself.

"I want the girl alive!" Keilantra's shriek from a high above walkway startled me, and I looked up to see her rushing with Ulric and several guards at her heels down a set of stairs, making their way towards the courtyard.

"Where's Helena?!" Tallinn realised as she downed a guard from the wall and threw another into Carden's attack.

I swung my sword to block an attacking guard's strike, parrying and dodging him. I kicked him hard in the stomach and he fell backwards as I looked for the other girl. She was nowhere to be seen.

"We can't stop now!" Carden shouted. "Push for the walls!"

I felt guilty, but he was right. This was our one shot at escaping this terrible place and we couldn't waste it.

We kept fighting, Carden and Tallinn killing anyone who came near us while I found myself hesitant to do the same, unable to slay even one man at all. My only focus had to be surviving this sudden explosion of enemies and escaping the fortress, yet I couldn't bring myself to kill in order to do it.

Tallinn downed the last couple of guards on the wall near the stairs up to the walkway that could possibly interfere, clearing our path.

"Princess, this is your chance!" she shouted, out of arrows now and taking up her sword.

"We'll keep them busy!" Carden assured me as I gave them an uneasy look. "Just go! Now!"

I nodded and, with my skirt hems in my left hand and the sword in my right, I ran as fast as I could towards the stairs. I staggered up them, knocking back a guard and throwing him from the stairs into the courtyard with a few blocks of my sword.

As I reached the wall, I closed my eyes, grasped my pendant in my left hand and with all my heart called softly: "Amethyst... I need you..."

As if in answer, there came a great roar and I opened my eyes. A shimmer of purple scales caught in the sunlight as it brightened the sky, great magenta wings beating against the wind. With a calling roar, Amethyst swept up from below the wall I stood on, bellowing loudly as if she had been waiting there for my call.

I felt my heart leap with joy, and I smiled as I watched her sweep up over the castle.

Her roars distracted all our enemies and drew their gazes as she started turning down towards the courtyard. She tore stones from the battlements and cast them into the scores of enemies surrounding us, the men screaming and trying to avoid being crushed by the Dragon's strikes.

It worked! I was overjoyed, my heart and soul soaring like the Dragon was. *She came! She really came when I called!*

Amethyst turned her gaze to me as my pendant's heart glowed brightly, her roars echoing as if she were calling to me.

Then, another roar broke the air and Kuldar's monstrous golden shape appeared. I saw Keilantra standing on a walkway with her hand gripping her pendant, it's stone glowing bright gold as she glared at Amethyst.

"Amethyst! Watch out!" I cried in panic.

The two dragons started to fight, Amethyst so much slighter than Kuldar and lacking the one attack he possessed. He breathed bright orange and red flames towards her, but Amethyst struck back by slashing snow from the castle's top right at him. As fire and ice mixed in sprays of fizzling flames and rainwater the two dragons continued to fight, crashing against each other with ferocious roars.

I gripped my pendant and urged with all my will that Amethyst should win. She kept striking, so much faster than he was and able to escape his attacks with ease.

"Amethyst, please, be careful," I murmured hopefully, my heart pounding with anxiety as I kept my eyes locked on her.

"You should be more concerned about yourself, Princess," Morod's voice came from behind me, shredding a slither of cold dread down my spine.

I could see the shadows forming out of the corner of my eye and looked over my shoulder as he materialised. I panicked and tried to pull away, but he grabbed me by arms so suddenly and firmly that I couldn't, wrestling me against his chest.

"AMETHYST!" I screamed in panic.

Amethyst turned and roared, rage in her orange eyes at the sight of him holding me and she dived towards us as I fought against Morod. He twisted my wrist, making me scream in pain as he forced the sword out of my hand, leaving me only able to fight him by digging my nails into his wrists as I struggled against his reach for my pendant.

"Bring her down, Cathal!" Morod roared.

"No!" I shrieked as the great black dragon appeared and slammed into Amethyst in mid-flight.

I kept my left fingers tightly curled around the Pendant, refusing to let go even as he snatched and groped at it.

He won't win! Not again! Never again!

Amethyst somehow managed to keep slipping between the two larger dragons, but I wasn't sure how long she could keep it up. She was determined to reach me, desperate to save me from the Shadow Lord's struggling grasp.

Morod suddenly crushed my hand between his fingers and made me cry out in pain, his other hand grasping my throat and finally tearing the chain from my neck. In response, the Pendant's stone went suddenly dark as he wrenched it from my hand and held the necklace up away from me. He grabbed me around my mouth and tightened his hold on me as he snarled into my ear, making sure that I had no choice but to watch what happened next.

I cried out in horror as my dragon was suddenly struck by both evil ones at once. They fell from the air and slammed into the courtyard just out of our sight, dust and debris raining up behind one of the buildings as the structure shook all around us...

Epilogue
Condemned

I couldn't take my eyes from the dust cloud that marked where Cathal and Kuldar had crashed Amethyst into the castle, my heart screaming and thrashing as much as I was. Morod tightened his grip around my mouth and cheeks to stop me squirming, my body instantly complying under such heavy threat.

"A brave attempt at escape, girl," he hissed into my ear. "But you have only condemned yourself, your friends and your dragon by these actions."

I whimpered against his clammy palm, tears burning my eyes.

"Come," he dragged me forcefully down the stairs and back into the courtyard, bracing his other arm across my midriff tightly as I tried to claw at him with my nails.

The scene before us was like an enormous disaster had struck. Broken stone littered the ground, the armoured bodies of Gorvennan guards strewn all around us, but there were still more to keep us prisoner.

The guards parted as Morod carried me forward and I saw Carden and Tallinn on their knees, the Revenant standing behind them with one clawed gauntlet around each of their throats. The Revenant had somehow incapacitated my friends with his sudden arrival and had forced them into submission, their hands at their sides, their weapons on the ground.

Helena stood beside him with a sinister smile on her face, her cold gaze turning to me as Morod brought me to stand before them, Keilantra joining us with a cruel smirk.

"You really *do* need to learn to watch who you trust, Princess," Helena smiled as her eyes turned black.

She held up her hand and her body and clothes changed; her dress becoming black and violet with a black cloak, her skin paling as her hairstyle reorganised into longer, neatly tied bunches around her shoulders.

Manth smirked as she saw the shock on my face from revealing her spell, now replacing Helena: "After all, they may not be what they seem to be."

Keilantra sneered at me victoriously. "I knew if the girl was desperate enough and thought she had the chance to escape that she would call her dragon here, right into our waiting trap. How predictable she is."

I struggled in Morod's grasp as he handed her my pendant again. He freed my mouth from his palm and pinned my arms tightly to my chest, his hands curling firmly around my slender wrists.

"What shall be done with the Guardian filth, Master?" the Revenant asked in his deep, metallic sounding voice.

"Secure them in the lower prisons for now," the Shadow Lord decreed, glaring through my hair at my face. "We will make the appropriate preparations and they shall be sent to Arnath, into your keeping, Revenant."

"What?!" I looked up at him as Carden and Tallinn reacted fearfully at the news. "But you promised me you wouldn't hurt them!"

"And I will not," Morod confirmed with a nod under his hood. "However, their proximity to you is dangerous for my plans. I would have you isolated and alone, so they shall be sent to Arnath, *far* from you."

I didn't know what to do. My chest heaved and I tried to fight the panic at knowing that they were to be taken from me.

"As for the Dragon," he decided, "she will remain here, chained and locked so that she cannot fly or move."

"I shall see to it at once, Lord Morod," Keilantra nodded and started issuing orders, her men rushing to do as she commanded.

"Take the Guardians away," Morod ordered sternly.

"Wait! Wait, please!" I pleaded, looking over my shoulder and through my hair at him. "Please... can I... at least say goodbye to Carden? Can I just have a moment with him? Please?"

He considered this, then nodded softly. "Very well. But be swift."

He shoved me forward and I ran straight to my lover's arms, dropping to my knees as Carden held me tight. I felt hot tears on my ice-cold cheeks, my eyes squeezed shut and my fingers crushing the fabric of his shirt so hard that my hands shook.

"I'm sorry," I sobbed into his shoulder. "I'm so, so sorry..."

"Shh... It's alright, sweetheart," Carden had tears falling as well as he lifted my chin to meet his gaze. "It's not your fault, Leander. Okay? It's going to be alright."

"I love you," I whispered with all my heart. "I love you so much, Carden..."

"I love you too," he swore to me and we kissed.

It was the most grief filled kiss I had ever known, my tears tainting it with so much sadness as my heart tried to bind with his desperately. I couldn't stand the thought that I might never see him again, that pain worse than any other I had ever known.

Ulric abruptly pulled me away and I reached out desperately, grabbing Carden's hand as I cried: "No! No, please!"

The guards took Carden by his arms as others lifted Tallinn to her feet, trying to separate us. Carden was stubborn, refusing to let go of me, squeezing his large fingers around my slender wrist.

"Be brave, my love!" he urged me. "Be brave!

"Carden!" I sobbed as they finally pulled us apart, my tears blinding me as Ulric held me tight by both arms. "Carden, no! No!"

"It *will* be alright, Leander!" Carden shouted as they dragged him away, struggling to stay with me by planting his feet and thrashing against their holds. "I *will* come back and free you! I promise! I PROMISE!"

He was taken away and I knelt on the ground, crying in Ulric's grasp, my hands on my knees and my head down as tears flooded my cheeks.

"How sentimental," Keilantra mocked and gestured as I looked up through my tears. "Take her back to the top of the West Tower. Manacle her so that she cannot attempt escape again."

I closed my eyes against the burning tears and bitter winds as my heart shattered inside my chest, her words only deepening my pain.

Ulric pulled me to my feet and dragged me from the courtyard, half carrying me as I just slumped in his arms. I lost all sense of my surroundings, and before I knew it, I was being forced back through the tower door on the top floor.

The two guards who had followed us pushed me to the far wall, turning me to face them as they took up the chains that were bolted to the corner. The chains were long, a shackle set into the end of each so that I still had freedom enough to move my arms and walk around the cell. Not that that was a comfort. They slipped my wrists into the cuffs and locked them tight, the chill on my skin feeling so vivid and real.

The guards left and Ulric drew my teary eyes as he lifted my chin with one finger, staring down at me.

"I told you things would only get worse for you if you kept trying to resist. Perhaps now you will do as you are told, girl," he smirked, then turned on his heel and left me, locking me into the cell with a heavy clank and a hard snap of the locks before leaving the tower altogether.

I stood there feeling numb, cold from the icy air at my back and the frozen metal of the shackles on my wrists. I had nothing now and chose to wipe the tears from my eyes so as not to feel any deeper chill than that which already invaded my body and heart.

I turned my hands and studied the shackles, wondering if it were possible for me to slip through them, but I knew I couldn't. I turned then to the window and looked through, trying to see if I could catch some glimpse of Amethyst, but my cell didn't face where she had been taken down.

I sighed sadly, my tears still flowing and rolling down my cheeks as I twisted my hands together subconsciously, lost in terrible thoughts and left wondering what would become of my friends and my dragon... and even myself.

"Feeling the bitterness of defeat, Princess?" the Shadow Lord's low voice came from behind me and I felt a new anger rising in my chest. "I would hope now that you have learned that there is no resistance you can offer that will save you from my power," he said, standing just outside the bars of my cell. "You are utterly helpless against me."

I turned around and threw myself at him with a scream of rage, the chains going taut and pulling my arms behind me with a hard jerk. I couldn't even reach more than a foot from the bars, my eyes savage as I glared at his amused expression.

"Why have you done this to me?!" I demanded in a seething tone, glaring through my tears at him. "Locking me away from friends and what's left of my family?!"

He just watched me, unmoved, unchanged, his eyes harsh beneath his hood.

I turned to the window as my rage built, then I spun back, losing it all at him at once: "You've taken *everything* from me! *You* were the one responsible for my parent's deaths! *You* incited the Aldegaadian nobility to turn against my bloodline and murder our King!" I stepped closer, glaring at him, my fists tight at my sides. "*You... You* have hunted me ever since I was a baby to use me for your own ends," I shook my head, my voice quieter, but still angry. "And now... now that you've succeeded... now that you've used me in your dark ritual to regain your powers and stripped me of my ability for change..." I looked around at the cell with disbelief and such powerful anger: "...you've imprisoned me here, in this foreign fortress controlled by a cruel Queen pulling the strings of a puppet King."

I stared straight into his eyes and dared him not to look into mine as I finally asked the question that burned in my soul.

"Why?" the word felt bitter, but needed as I spoke it, my voice trembling and my body tight with rage. "Why not imprison me in your own fortress? Why not set me free if you have no further use for me?"

Then the answer hit me; a sudden knowledge that made me feel so sure and so much stronger than I had before.

"I know why... It's because you, Keilantra, my Uncle Fane and all of your ilk have one thing in common," I said, a small smile appearing on my lips as I stared him down despite his height over me. "*You're* afraid of *me*. You're afraid that I will be like my ancestor for whom I was named; she who defeated the Darkest Shadow and flung you into the hell which you *desperately* clawed your way out of," he was glaring at me now and I felt such a strong sense of satisfaction at seeing that: "How pathetic *you are*, Shadow Lord, frightened of a helpless teenage girl. How *small you truly* are."

"You think that I fear what you might become?" he questioned with cold surprise. "You think that *I* could know terror at the sight of a pathetic little slip of a girl like *you*?"

I just stared at him, determined to be brave.

"You *are* afraid of me," I replied harshly. "You're weak... You're *nothing*!"

As if the bars bent to his will, he stepped through them like he was still a ghost, startling me.

"Foolish girl," he seethed with the first anger he had ever turned towards me. "I *am* a Shadow Lord! Invincible, immortal, omniscient! I have lived fifty times your lifespan and destroyed warriors with *far* greater strength and prowess than *you*!"

Fear gripped me as I staggered away, my back hitting the wall, leaving me with nowhere to go as he put his hand around my throat. I cried out in panic and felt fresh tears begin their run down my cheeks as he plied the slightest bit of pressure to my neck.

"If I so chose," he warned me, "I could extinguish your wretched little existence with not but a flick of my wrist."

"But... but you said you made me immortal," I reminded him, shaking hard with all of my confidence now gone.

"Immortal does not mean you cannot die," he told me, glaring into my steel blue eyes. "I can still take your life... And I plan to..."

I couldn't comprehend what he had just said, my trembling body weakening, and his hold was all that kept me standing: "You're... you're going to kill me?"

"Yes," he nodded, his face deathly calm. "Not yet, however, but you *will* die at *my* hands."

I whimpered, sobbing in terror as he brought his face closer to mine, my hands pressed to the cold stone walls behind me.

"This little game of ours," he said coldly, "will one day come to its final end, and only *I* shall stand as the victor. And as you know your last moments approach, you will look back fondly upon your time in this cold, dank tower cell, and long to return if only to forestall your end a little longer..."

He let go and I somehow managed to stay standing as he walked to the door, though I trembled in petrified terror.

"Savour what time remains to you, Princess Leander," he urged, turning back to me with a smirk appearing on his hideous grey face, "for you do not have much left..."

He evaporated and became a black cloud of shadows that slithered away into all the dark corners of the tower, leaving me alone to contemplate his dark promise.

I dropped to sit on the cold stone floor, pulling my knees together and closer to my hips, holding my arms around me, my hands gripping my shoulders in terror as I cried. My chest was rushing with my breaths and I felt as if my heart could now give out and end me before his return.

I... I don't want to die...

I buried my face into my hands and cried beneath my dark hair, fearing that there was no escape from the fate he had planned for me...

The Story Continues in Book 3...

Pendant of Dragons
The End of All Things

Excerpt from The End of All Things

The Sanctum?! my heart began to race wildly. *That's where they take all the other girls that never return! Why would they want me taken there?!*

Ulric heaved me by my shoulder, lifting my arm hard as he forced me quickly away from the cages and towards the stone archway. I easily lost track of where I was being taken, the close corridors and narrow stairs all looking the same in the barely broken darkness, and I was soon being brought into the keep once again.

Ulric took me up the grand staircase that led to the floors above, not caring that I struggled to keep up with him. He led me down a long corridor with windows on all sides, one view beyond showing me the courtyards below, the other displaying the far distant spread of the sea. It was sunset, the golden orange hues of the sky choked dark by the heavy clouds that cast deep snows over everything surrounding the castle.

We turned right and passed by closed doors on all sides, virtually no guards stationed here. He brought me to the very last door at the end of the hall and opened it.

I was shoved through, losing my footing and hitting the hard floor with a grunt of pain. I turned over with the rattling of the chains on my wrists to face the crude knight and the two guards standing at his back.

"Now, you be a good girl and wait here for the Mistresses," he told me in the mocking way someone would speak to a child. "They shan't be too long."

With a chuckle, he closed the door behind him, the locks sealing with loud booming clicks.

Hesitant and uncertain, I turned my gaze from the door, already knowing it was pointless to even try to fight it open.

I took in the room, ill at ease by its decor and floor plan. It was a cold black stone place with an almost rounded design. To my right and before me were two enormous windows with cruel looking black frames holding the glass in place. To my left was an old desk and a couple of chairs, a collection of shelves set behind the desk. And lastly, in the centre of the room - as I had expected from all the fairy tales I had ever read - there was a large cauldron set over an unlit fire pit built into the floor.

Slowly, grasping my teal velvet and blue linen skirts so as not to trip, I got to my feet and started to carefully explore. There were at least a dozen black bookshelves that stood tall against the walls, many more set behind the desk. They were all stocked with books and various other less friendly things. Set around the room were also display cases, though I was too uneasy to dare to go near them.

This really isn't somewhere I expected to end up, I worried as I looked at all the witchcraft artefacts that surrounded me. *I don't think me being here is a good thing.*

There was a mirror set to the wall between the two windows, a full six feet in height and framed with ebony. *I haven't seen my reflection in so long. I wonder how bad off I am.*

I moved to the mirror and was shocked by my reflection. The girl in the glass looked like me, but she was frailer, though not dangerously underweight. My collarbones were a little more defined and my frame was slimmer, but I could tell by my shoulders that I didn't have bones poking through with a complete loss of my health. My face and much of my skin was smudged with grime and dirt, my hair hanging dark and lifeless over my right shoulder and down to my breast. My hips looked more obvious now beneath the tightened bodice of my dress, the fabric easily sliding from my shoulders as the weight of the over-sleeves dragged them down my arms. But it was my expression that worried me the most. I looked drained of all vitality, like some terrible thing had been drinking all the life from me. I still appeared to be eighteen, but tired and weak, barely the same girl I had been in Arvon however long ago.

I look awful. How can I have remained so youthful and yet become so haggard? Is this what loneliness, starvation, torture and imprisonment can do to a human being?

I pulled my gaze from the mirror and turned my attention back to the room. Falling on my old tendencies, I found myself very quickly studying the books on the shelves. There wasn't a single one I would have considered reading, many - if not all - written on subjects of witchcraft for the use of evil.

Fitting, of course, considering the women whose Sanctum this is.

My eyes travelled then across one of the shelves directly behind the desk and I felt sickened to my stomach. There were dozens of glass jars set there, each one containing a human heart within its transparent confines. Worst of all, the hearts were still beating.

I was horror-struck by the sight. *What of the people these hearts belonged to? They aren't alive, are they? This really is a dark and evil place.*

Turning my gaze from the jarred hearts, I looked to the desk, desperate to find something to take the haunting image from my mind. There were parchments, scrolls and a couple of old books laid out there, most of the scribbling in languages or runes that I couldn't understand. But there was one that drew my gaze, marked with drawings of four black dragons surrounding a creature of black flame and shadow.

I studied the designs, then turned my gaze to the book beside it and began reading the last page left open.

Chief and most atrocious of all ancient evils are the Beasts of Ragnarok, the heralds of the End of All Things. With them the world was plunged into the terrors of the World Ender and plagued with Famine, Pestilence, War and Death on a scale beyond all reckoning...

I frowned. "Ragnarok?"

I read on: *These princely evils were defeated long ago by the Blood of Innocence so that they would never again threaten the world. Yet, should the Seals of Ankorect ever be broken the evil shall spread into the world once more and the World Ender shall rise again with the Lunar Joining and the Dragon's Key...*

My frown only deepened as I read the words scrawled over the page.

What does any of that mean? Blood of Innocence? The Seals of Ankorect? Lunar Joining? Dragon's Key? The ancient scholars were very cryptic in their writings. Why did they never make these things clear?

I turned the page and found myself staring at a drawing of some terrible, sweeping form with great wings of smoke and shadow, blue flames glowing from beneath deepest darkness. The eyes of the hidden monster glared up at me and I felt a terrible chill fill my chest as a new fear crushed around my heart.

I jumped as the door unlocked, quickly backing away from the desk with the clattering of my chains and the rustling of my dress. My breath caught in my chest and my heart skipped a few beats as my eyes set on the opening door and the figures that traversed its threshold.

The Witches stared at me coldly as they entered the room, Manth remaining solemn while Keilantra immediately smirked at me.

"Ah, Princess..." the Witch Queen hissed.

Titles by Isabella Frost

Pendant of Dragons: The Aldrich Legacy (Book 1)
Pendant of Dragons: Custodians of the Past (Book 2)

Visit whitelightshop.com

White light
PUBLISHING